*May, 1536. The Queen is dead. Long live the Queen.*

When Anne Boleyn falls to the executioner's ax on a cold spring morning, yet another Anne vows she will survive in the snake-pit court of Henry VIII. But at what cost?

Lady Anne Seymour knows her family hangs by a thread. If her sister-in-law Jane Seymour cannot give the King a son, she will be executed or set aside, and her family with her. Anne throws herself into the deadly and intoxicating intrigue of the Tudor court, determined at any price to see the new queen's marriage a success and the Seymour family elevated to supreme power. But Anne's machinations will earn her a reputation as a viper, and she must decide if her family's rise is worth the loss of her own soul . . .

Praise for **MY LADY VIPER**...

*"Author E. Knight proves that though there are a plethora of Tudor novels out there a writer can still create a fresh and unique view of one of history's most treacherous courts, that of England's King Henry VIII. Schemes and scandalous trysts abound in 'My Lady Viper', making for a very captivating read. Racy and deliciously sensual, once started I was hard pressed to put the book down. I eagerly await the next installment in E. Knight's stand-out Tales of the Tudor Courts series!"* ~ Amy Bruno, Passages to the Past

*"E. Knight breathes new life and new scandal into the Tudors. This is an engrossing historical fiction tale that readers will love!"* ~ Meg Wessel, A Bookish Affair

*"A brilliant illustration of a capricious monarch and the nest of serpents that surrounded him, My Lady Viper is an absolute must. Intricately detailed, cleverly constructed and utterly irresistible."* ~ Erin, Flashlight Commentary

# MY LADY VIPER

## Tales from the Tudor Court

By
E. Knight

Cover Design by The Killion Group, Inc.

Copy-edited by Joyce Lamb

ISBN-10: 0990324508
ISBN-13: 978-0-9903245-0-8

\*\*\*\*\*\*\*\*\*\*\*\*\*\*\*\*\*\*\*\*\*\*\*\*\*\*\*\*

## *Dedication*

To my husband:
who mopped away my blood, sweat and tears as I embarked on the
amazing, heart-wrenching journey through Anne's footsteps.

# *Acknowledgements*

As with any book, a writer cannot do it alone. There are many people I wish to thank for helping bring this creation to life. First, and foremost, is my husband and daughters who have been such a huge support to me over the years, and endured the hours I spend researching, writing and talking endlessly about my characters.

Many thanks to my grandparents, who invited me to visit them in France many times throughout my childhood (and for my mom who brought me!). Without walking through castles, royal gardens, art museums and Monet's house/gardens, at such an impressionable age, I'm not sure I would have developed the passion I have for history.

Much thanks to my father for giving me my first Ken Follett book to read, introducing me to all that is historical fiction, and for indulging me in hours of documentaries and historical movies, as well as for taking me to Ireland where I fell in love with the soil, castles and raw beauty of the Emerald Isle.

My Lady Viper was a true labor of love, and I could not have written and published it without the help of the following people: Stephanie Dray for reading endless chapters and helping me to revise, listening to me vent and talking me down off of ladders. Kate Quinn for knowing how to write excellent copy. Amy Bruno for helping me to find advance readers, setting up my blog tour and the release party. My copy editor, Joyce Lamb, who bled with me over tense issues. My critique partners, Kathleen Bittner-Roth and Tara Kingston, who read the chapters of this book in its beginning stages years ago, and encouraged me to keep going.

How could I not issue my thanks to the wonderful writers who've inspired me? Ken Follett, Alison Weir, Margaret George, and so many more!

And last but never least, my readers. Without your dedication to my books, your support and pure awesomeness, I would not be able to do what I do. Endless gratitude!

# CAST OF CHARACTERS

The court of Henry VIII is vast in occupancy, and for this story, while I've used a number of its inhabitants and key players, I have also for the sake of the reader's sanity and confusion, taken liberty to neglect a few. Even still, the number of characters within this book is staggering, and as such, necessitated an introduction of sorts. Additionally, many people in history had the same names, and so while reading, it can become confusing who is who.

**Main Characters**:

*Anne Seymour Stanhope*–wife of Edward Seymour, sister-by-marriage to Queen Jane Seymour.

*Edward Seymour*–brother to Queen Jane Seymour.

*Jane Seymour*–third wife of Henry VIII.

*Henry VIII*–King of England.

*Sir Anthony Browne*–member of the king's Privy Council and knight of the realm.

*Henry Howard, Earl of Surrey*–son of the Duke of Norfolk, cousin of Anne Boleyn. He wrote a poem to Anne Seymour, verses of which grace the beginning of each chapter. I have made a lot of conjecture on my part in regards to Surrey, which I've noted in the back of the book in my author's note.

**Secondary Characters**:

*Anne Boleyn*–Queen of England.

*Jane Rochford*–widow to George Boleyn (brother of Anne Boleyn).

*Ambassador Chapuys*–Ambassador of Spain. Close to Queen Katharine of Aragon and her daughter Princess (then-Lady) Mary.

*Archbishop Cranmer*–Archbishop of Canterbury, Thomas Cranmer. Instrumental in Henry's "great matter" of annulling his marriage to Katharine of Aragon, as well as in the Dissolution of Monasteries. He was King Henry's "main" man of the cloth.

*Secretary Cromwell (later Sussex)*–king's secretary. Loathed by most because he is from humble origins and yet presumes to have a hold over His Most Royal Majesty.

*Elizabeth "Beth" Seymour*–sister to Jane Seymour and sister-by-marriage to Anne Seymour.

*Thomas Howard, Duke of Norfolk*–noble member of Henry VIII's Privy Council. Uncle to Anne Boleyn. Father of Henry Howard, Earl of Surrey.

*Elizabeth Bourchier, Lady Page*–mother to Anne Seymour, widow of Sir Edward Stanhope, and remarried to Sir Richard Page.

*Elizabeth "Lizzie"*–half-sister to Anne Seymour, the daughter of Elizabeth Bourchier and Sir Richard Page.

*Sir Richard Page*–Anne Seymour's stepfather.

*Michael Stanhope*–Anne Seymour's older half-brother. Born to her father and their father's first wife, Avelina. Michael played several significant roles throughout the Tudor era.

*Richard Stanhope*–Anne Seymour's older half-brother. Born to her father and their father's first wife, Avelina. Cause of death unknown, date questionable.

*Will Somers*–king's fool.

*Sir Francis Bryan*–member of the king's Privy Council and knight of the realm.

*The Lady Mary*–also known as Princess Mary, daughter to King Henry VIII and Katharine of Aragon.

*Anne of Cleves*–Henry VIII's fourth wife of German descent.

*Katheryn Howard*–Henry VIII's fifth wife.

*Catherine Parr*–Henry VIII's sixth wife and a rival to Anne Seymour at court.

*Anne "Annie" "'Nan" Bassett*–maiden in Queen Jane's court. A known lover of the king's.

*Thomas Seymour*–Queen Jane's brother. A second son, who was often seen as jealous of his older brother Edward's position.

*Gertrude, Marchioness of Exeter*–Anne's ally and friend.

*Henry Courtenay, Marquess of Exeter*–ally of the Seymour faction.

*Reginald Pole*–traitor to the king, sides with the pope and is abroad.

*Margaret Pole, Lady Salisbury*–Reginald Pole's mother.

*Henry Pole, Lord Montagu*–part of the Seymour faction and a gentleman of the king's privy chamber. Brother to the traitor, Reginald Pole.

*Charles Brandon, Duke of Suffolk*–Henry VIII's close childhood friend, widower of Henry's sister Princess Mary (Queen of France), a noble member of the king's Privy Council.

*Edward "Eddie" Seymour*–First child of Anne Seymour and Edward Seymour. (I have fabricated his nickname.)

*Edward "Beau" Seymour*–Second child of Anne Seymour and Edward Seymour.(I have fabricated his nickname and history.)

*Francis Newdegate*–Edward and Anne's steward.

*\*\*\*The various Katherine's are spelled differently to differentiate, but also because I found proof of those various spellings for each of them.\*\*\**

*Dear Reader,*

*Not much is known about the Duchess of Somerset's life before she became a duchess. Using what information I could find through extensive research, conjecture based on facts and a liberal use of creative license, I've written My Lady Viper – Tales From the Tudor Court, to illustrate this prior period of her life at court with the famous Tudor players already known to so many readers.*

*Gracing the beginning of each chapter are several lines – in order of appearance – from a poem written by Henry Howard, Earl of Surrey, allegedly about Anne Seymour. The poem was of great influence to me and the inspiration for this book.*

*In the back of the book you will find my author's note, which goes into more detail about my research, the history that I altered and where I used fiction to fill in the blanks. You can feel free to read it now, or wait until the end, since it does contain spoilers.*

*I hope you enjoy reading the story as much as I enjoyed writing it. Anne Seymour was a fascinating woman, and one who I know dealt with a lot of hardship in life. She has been named a vicious viper of a woman, but I like to think that beneath her steely court exterior, she was a woman with heart and soul.*

*Happy Reading!*
*E. Knight*

*MY LADY VIPER*

# IF LOVE NOW REIGNED AS IT HATH BEEN

by
King Henry VIII

*If love now reigned as it hath been*
*And war reward it as it hath sene,*

*Nobel men then would sure enserch*
*All ways wherby they might it reach;*

*But envy reigneth with such disdain,*
*And causeth lovers outwardly to refrain,*

*Which puts them to more and more*
*Inwardly most grievous and sore:*

*The fault in whom I cannot set;*
*But let them tell which love doth get.*

*To lovers I put now sure this case —*
*Which of their lovers doth get them grace?*

*And unto them which doth it know*
*Better than do I, I think it so.*

# CHAPTER ONE

*Each beast can choose his fare according to his mind,*
*And also can show a friendly cheer, like to their beastly kind.*
*A lion saw I late, as white as any snow,*
*Which seemed well to lead the race, his port the same did show.*
*~Henry Howard, Earl of Surrey*

*London, Court of Henry VIII*
*May 19, 1536*

Dead.

The queen would soon be dead. Her head cropped short of her neck for a crowd on Tower Green to watch.

*Poor, poor Anne.*

The king's pardon we'd heard whispers of had not yet come. But surely he must! There was no coffin prepared. Not even a discarded box. Rumors that the king's secretary Cromwell had convinced King Henry VIII against a pardon ran rampant. A lack of coffin had to be evidence that Cromwell had not succeeded.

Even as Anne Boleyn emerged from the Tower, dressed in a gray gown, her red, quilted petticoat showing with each step she took, the genteel fabric swishing back and forth, I looked about frantically for the king's man to say this was all a show, that she would be spared. Her skin was pale, her lips red. Her black as night

17

eyes calmly scanned the crowd, searching for something — perhaps the king himself. My heart went out to her. That she could put on such a façade at the time of her execution only proved she was indeed a queen and of noble birth. Four of her ladies-in-waiting walked with her to the four-foot-tall scaffold. She passed out alms to the poor along the way, her movements slow and deliberate. Her last queenly duty. A shiver stole over my body.

Those who'd shunned her in life now greedily accepted her coin. How backward people were. Even I felt remorse for the events that would take place. For even though not a friend of mine, she did not deserve this.

Queen Anne, now dubbed Lady Anne — her marriage to the king annulled just hours ago — took the rickety steps slowly, regally, perhaps more like a queen now than I had ever seen her before, though she still did not touch the grace of the late Queen Katharine of Aragon — Henry VIII's first wife — whose poise and decorum were unmatched at court. Lady Anne's ladies appeared sullen, but in truth, not one shed a tear. Even *my* eyes stung, but these ladies were not her friends. They were ladies Henry had supplied her with in the Tower — women who would not sympathize with Anne.

"Good Christian people, I am come hither to die." Her voice rang out over the hushed crowd. I swallowed hard, not certain that had I been in the same place I could have summoned the strength and found my voice.

I glanced briefly beside me at my husband, Edward. He stared intently before him and I wondered if he was seeing right through the spectacle, or if he watched every move, every person as keenly as I did.

The crowd leaned in, some with hands covering their mouths, tears in their eyes. Others with brows furrowed, lips thinned in a grimace.

"Good Christian people, I am come hither to die, for according to the law, for by the law I am judged to die, and therefore I will speak nothing against it. I am come hither to accuse no man, nor to speak of that whereof I am accused and condemned to die, but I pray God save the king and send him long to reign over you, for a gentler nor a more merciful prince was there never, and to me he was ever a good, a gentle and sovereign lord." She looked up toward the heavens, her long slim fingers folded gracefully in front of her. "And if any person will meddle of my cause, I require them to judge the best. And thus I take my leave of the world and of you all, and I heartily desire you all to pray for me. Oh, Lord, have mercy on me! To God I commend my soul."

Anne reached up and removed her headdress, replacing it with a white cap one of her ladies handed to her, the same one who helped to tuck in her long raven hair. She was still beautiful, hauntingly so. The four ladies hurried to surround her, removing her white ermine cloak, her necklace.

The executioner stepped forward, begging her pardon for doing his duty to king and realm. She nodded solemnly, told him she willingly gave him her pardon. Still, her eyes searched, and I found myself searching, too. I'd had a hand in this, but... Guilt and panic twisted my stomach. I had never wanted her to die, just to be set aside as was good Queen Katharine. That is what everyone said would happen. He would not truly kill Anne Boleyn. It was all to frighten her, and the rest of us, into obedience, wasn't it?

And yet, no messenger with a pardon.

No one shouting for this debacle to end. Sweat trickled down my spine and yet I was cold all over.

The executioner bade her to kneel and say her prayers. She knelt on wobbly knees, her frame slender and stiff, eyes glazing over, perhaps a moment of fear when she realized her execution was truly eminent. She righted herself, both knees locked together upon the straw that had been laid to catch her blood when the deathblow should be struck. I stifled the urge to run forward, to shout for them to stop. To beg my husband to search for the messenger who was surely on his way with the king's pardon. Another wave of panic seized me. I took deep, gulping breaths and tried to maintain my own noble bearing.

Anne Boleyn straightened her skirts, smoothing them down the front and covering her feet behind her. She turned toward her ladies, asked them to pray for her, then faced the crowd.

"To Jesus Christ I commend my soul. Lord Jesu, receive my soul," she repeated over and over, her lips moving, twitching, her fingers clasped tightly in front of her.

A moment of panic seemed to take control of her. She looked about herself aimlessly, fingered her cap, muttered to the executioner that perhaps she should take off the cap. The man tried to console her that he would strike when she was ready. He went to put the blindfold on her, but she stayed his hand, shaking her head.

I failed to quell the sob that escaped my throat. I could picture myself kneeling there. One moment full of confidence and poise, and the next my mind slipping and utter fear taking over. Within those few seconds of her fumbling, I prayed heartily His Majesty would come to pardon her. The executioner motioned to one of her ladies, who gently tied a linen cloth to her eyes, her piercing gaze having unsettled both the executioner and the crowd, myself included.

*Oh, dear God! Have mercy!*

With her voice shaken but strong, Anne told the man she was ready. She began to pray again, "My God, have pity on my soul. Into thy hands, oh Jesu, have pity on me."

The executioner silently pulled a four-foot, shining, steel blade from within the straw. He held it alight, the sun beaming off its length, drawing my eyes to the macabre sight.

"Bring me the sword," he ordered loudly as he tiptoed behind her from the other direction. The man was tricking her about where he stood!

Anne turned her head, not aware he was no longer there. He lifted the sword high behind her, two-fisted, his hands trembling slightly, and then swung in an arcing motion down, severing her head from her neck in one swipe. I squeezed my eyes shut, my hands coming to my own slender neck.

It was done and could not be undone. This horrible deed was real. Not a dream. Not a lesson in anything except the cruelty of this world and the men in it. The cruelty of our king.

And I wanted to scream. I wanted to scream, but could not, for I was sister-by-marriage to the next queen — Jane Seymour. I could not show that I grieved for this young woman, cut down in the prime of her life. I had to be completely focused now on my husband, his family and moving us upward in the realm. Keeping us alive. Keeping us in power. Personal feelings could not play a factor. The king's desires, Jane's needs, and Edward's love and approval were all I sought to concentrate on.

As heartily as I had prayed for the king to intervene, I was now no longer as shocked as I should have been at there being no pardon. I stood, my face now void of emotion, as the executioner held Anne Boleyn's head for the crowd to see. Although, it was said they held the head for the opposite reason, so the one beheaded could see the crowd and their body, now headless on the platform, blood pouring from the severed neck.

Was her mind still alive? How long would it take for her to pass? Her lifeless black eyes staring out at the crowd indicated she could no longer be with us. Catching sight of the Howards — Anne Boleyn's family, our rivals — I quickly glanced away. I could not look at them. Could not meet their eyes when their beloved was dead and they'd done nothing to save her.

I'd done nothing to save her.

Cannons fired, their loud booms making me jump slightly. The firing of the cannons would let the king and all the realm know the deed was done, the queen was dead.

Cheers resounded in my ears, which shook me. The people were now glad she was dead? All the tears and remorse they'd shown her while she stood there, pleading for God to have mercy on her... I glanced around and was relieved to still see a few with tears in their eyes.

I suspected that most of the cheers were likely from courtiers whose secrets she'd held, along with the power to dispose of their lives. They cheered with relief. No longer would they have to worry that Anne Boleyn would betray them. No, they'd done *that* themselves.

Backstabbers, the lot of them ... and I suppose I was lumped in with them, now. A moment of disgust swirled in my gut but was quickly gone when I thought of my duties to our family, to the realm.

The crowd rushed forward, perhaps trying to cut off a bit of her hair, collect her blood. The vile creatures would keep it, sell it, whatever their whim.

But her ladies quickly jumped from their kneeled positions, tossed a white handkerchief over the queen's prone head, and tried to protect her body from the pressing spectators. Perhaps in death what little compassion they'd had for her in life came forth. No one was there to pick up the queen's remains. No coffin was waiting for her severed parts to be placed inside. The four ladies, speaking in hushed, frantic whispers, gathered her head and body.

I stepped forward, feeling as though I should help. Good God, for as much preparation that had gone into the execution—the building of the scaffold, finding the swordsman—so little had been done for her in the end.

My husband's hand on my arm stayed my movement, and I watched in dismay as the ladies wrapped their queen in white linen, tossed bow staves from an old elm chest and placed her body in its depths. Where would they take her? Burial plans had not been made, either.

I could watch no more. I turned from the gruesome, troubling scene, my gaze catching sight of Jane Rochford. She'd been the one who said the heinous things that condemned Anne Boleyn. Sex between brother and sister—Anne and her brother George. Lies, all of it. But those lies had been to our advantage, so none of the Seymours said anything against it.

Perhaps that was the reason for the disgust I felt for myself, now turned on Jane Rochford. Evil, vile creature. I could scarcely look at her.

But when I did, a smirk turned the corners of her lips. She looked happy.

"Lady Seymour." She nodded toward me.

I nodded back but did not try to hide the disapproval in my gaze. She'd single-handedly seen to the death of her husband and the queen. I supposed she wanted to be in the king's bed.

I tried to keep my thoughts from my face as I turned from the crowd. Did not they all want to be in his bed? But now, Jane would be. Our Jane.

There were rumors that His Majesty was riddled with disease from some previous maid he'd bedded repeatedly only to find out she'd been bedding the entire court.

I shuddered slightly, rubbing my arms to ease away my horror of it all.

I found myself craving the comforting touch of my husband. Edward spoke in hushed tones to two courtiers and the Spanish Ambassador. My mind still reeled and I couldn't concentrate on what they were saying. But I did notice the absence of the courtiers' wives.

More horror clawed at my insides as I reflected upon the plain truth of our situation now.

Life in great King Henry VIII's court was like walking a double-edged sword—one false step, and you were massacred. I had to tread carefully in all things. We would all have to tread carefully. What happened to Anne and her family could happen to us.

If my true objective was to secure our status, a realm of our own making, then we needed to learn from the past but also move forward without another backward glance.

Because the past was filled with transgressions aplenty.

Flashes of angry flesh assaulted my memory and I shook my head to dislodge them. No. I could not think any more about Anne Boleyn, nor could I think of Surrey. The young courtier, son of the Duke of Norfolk, had taken it upon himself to fall in love with me. Written me poems, whispered in my ear, danced with me, begged for my affections, and at each turn I'd pushed him away. He'd sulked, until one night my denials of his affections did not work. He'd caught me alone. Crushed his lips to mine. Yanked my skirts up. Scratched my flash. Pinned me. Slapped me hard on the face. And then he was... Bitter, angry, ugly memories.

He'd taken from me what he had no right to. I bit the inside of my cheek hard, drawing blood. We all had our hidden monsters. I could only thank God that Edward had been walking down that corridor and heard my cries. Edward had saved me. Edward Seymour.

And that is why my allegiance must now be to him and his family. Our family.

A swath of red velvet caught my eye. I watched Jane Rochford slink away. What pain would she cause next? Edward's gaze followed her out and a stab of jealousy took me for a moment. My husband was not always faithful. Would she try to take him to her bed? I thrust my chin up.

That was one woman I would not abide. And I was certain with her recent betrayal of Anne Boleyn, Edward would steer clear of an affair with her. But who would he choose? I supposed, to give the man some credit, he was always deep within his cups when such occurred. And a wife's duty was to care for and obey her husband — and did scripture not state that forgiveness was a virtue? I liked to think of myself as a virtuous woman.

But so did Anne Boleyn. And now she was dead.

I stepped closer to Edward, feeling his warmth, his power. Edward was a powerful and passionate lover. Sometimes brazenly so.

I could not blame Edward for trying to flaunt his authority and masculinity. His previous wife had cuckolded him in the worst way — with his own father — and bore the vile man two children whom she tried to pass off as poor Edward's. Even the king had begun to deny that he was Princess Elizabeth's father, that Anne Boleyn had made a cuckold of him. How many fathers were there whose children weren't really their own? For this very reason, I must be cautious. I could never have done such a thing to Edward. He had been too good to me. There were tricks every woman should know and secrets every intelligent woman took to the grave. If the adulteresses held an ounce of intelligence, they would have kept their own counsel and made certain their partners did the same.

"My lady, come." Edward clutched my arm, startling me, and pulled me through the throngs of people, back to Greenwich Palace to our suite of rooms now permanently housing us at court.

Henry had awarded us the apartments only last month, evicting his secretary Cromwell on our behalf. The man had been more than happy to do so, however, when he'd learned the reason.

Secretary Cromwell was a touchy subject on anyone's lips. Rising from the ranks of the lowborn, he'd somehow managed to land a position with Cardinal Wolsey, also a man of low birth, and was there noticed by King Henry, who'd made the lawyer into his secretary and now elevated him to the peerage. However, the man was becoming increasingly powerful and rich. Cromwell had grown wealthier than half of the court's nobles, and his men were everywhere. A man like that was dangerous.

We all had cause to be suspicious of him with his rather tight hold over the king. The notion of which drew Edward's ire along with most of the court. The man harkened to believe he ruled over the king, and such a mindset was a dangerous thing—especially since the king often listened to him. But since he was willing to aid our cause, I was making an attempt to like the man.

Our rooms were connected through a series of hidden passageways to the king's own rooms. Henry VIII's latest interest for a wife was my sister-by-marriage Jane. With our connected rooms, he'd been able to court her privately, although all of court knew of their romance, and the rumor had even spread like wildfire across to the continent.

He'd already assured us the engagement and their betrothal would be announced imminently. Henry considered that Jane would be his first true and lawful wife. No issue of consanguinity, like with Katharine, and no issue of him not being legally free to marry, as there had been with Anne. Both previous queens were with the Lord now. And there was no one who would naysay the king. I supposed, for Jane, I should have been happy. For my family and the favors that had been bestowed on us, I should have been proud. But witnessing the destruction and pain that all of this had brought left me feeling weak and sick of heart.

We swept into the room, owning it, taking pride in our status at court. Jane was not here but waited for us at Wulfhall, the Seymour family seat in Wiltshire. We would meet with her again soon, but my lord husband had wished to see the deed—Anne's execution—done, and in the flesh so he might further foolproof our elevated status.

Our rooms were large, with a presence chamber and Edward's book room flanked by our respective bedchambers. Rich burgundy drapes adorned the windows, and we were lucky enough to have a view of the beautiful gardens.

Tossing my cloak over a chair, I watched as a maid quickly ran to pick it up. I walked to the windows, opening them to let in the spring breeze. I needed air. My stays felt like they were suffocating me, squeezing my ribs. Perhaps I would retire so that I might remove them, lie in bed and sleep away the misery of the day. A fanciful wish, for now, hard work was truly in store for us if we wished to see this marriage through and our family rise.

I squeezed my eyes shut, again trying to get the image of Anne's lifeless eyes from my mind, reminding myself that her death had been necessary in order to move our own positions forward. No matter how vile such a thought was.

*Jane, what fate will your end be?* For surely if Edward and I did not do everything in our power, Jane would be... what? Pushed aside like the stoic and beautiful Katharine I had served from my youth or butchered on the block like the twenty-nine-year-old vivacious, fierce Anne Boleyn?

"Dear God in heaven." I prayed for a miracle. Jane's end would surely mean ours, and I was not ready to feel the executioner's blade. I had so much to live for!

I waved to the waiting footman for him to bring me some wine, and I dropped into a chair near the hearth. The man rushed toward me and handed me the goblet, the metal cool, the wine soothing.

Edward paced the room, running his hands through his dark chestnut hair, then over his chin, tugging at his tightly trimmed beard. He saw me with my wine and grabbed it from my hands as I went for another sip. He gulped the wine. I rolled my eyes. The footman rushed to hand me another cup. Wine in hand, I drank deeply, letting the rich flavor fill my senses and gentle my frayed nerves. Edward had had the wine brought in from France, and I admitted it was much better than our English wine.

"Why do you pace so? You are making me dizzy." My tone was irritated, perhaps more so than I'd intended, but it had the desired effect. Edward ceased tramping the presence chamber.

He took a long sip of wine, his gaze roving my form.

"I was thinking of my sister."

I nodded, having surmised as much. His thoughts were most likely along the same lines as my own. I finished my wine and waved for the footman to refill our cups. After this morning, and what was ahead, Edward and I could use an added boost to our courage and something to smooth our nerves. He started pacing again.

Always plotting, always planning. The man never sat still. Although, I could not blame him. Our position within the court was treacherous, and I found myself pacing more than only occasionally. One wrong thing said or done, and everything could end. My throat tightened just thinking about it. Even on a rumor, as had happened with poor Anne Boleyn, we could be extinguished.

It would not have mattered that Edward was brother to the future Queen of England and, God willing, uncle to the future king. The king executed anyone he pleased. Now more than ever, we must tread lightly but with heavy feet, inserting our thoughts here and there, seeing our wills be done. We must love the king as we should and seek to remain in power — at any cost.

Well, almost any… Some secrets were better kept hidden deep within a buried treasure chest, the key long since rusted to dust. Our heads must remain intact.

At times I found myself disgusted by all this. Life would have been easier if I had been the wife of a simple squire, as Mary Boleyn had made certain to do after being tossed aside by the king, betrayed by her sister, and widowed by her courtier husband. I shook my head slightly. *Do not wish such things, for those things which one wishes for can often come into being.*

But I could not help it. Courtiers were almost as ravenous as a pack of hyenas. We hovered on the outskirts of the field, pacing, pawing, growling, waiting for whatever scraps our lion king left — and we would fight for the best pieces, the most succulent, the most sought after. And the Seymours had those pieces now.

We must beware of the hyenas on the outskirts waiting, biding their time to snatch our prizes.

Edward stopped his pacing and sprawled in the chair beside me. Slamming his cup on the side table, his long slender fingers came to tap at his temples.

"She must bear him a son and soon." His brows were furrowed, his lips pursed.

"The wedding date has yet to be set." I placed my cup gently on a side table, took a deep breath—as deep as my cutting stays would allow. Taking a nap had become more and more enticing.

"Soon. I have no doubt, they shall be married within a month." He nodded his head as if confirming this information to himself. "Bishop Cranmer has issued a dispensation for their marriage just this morning."

"And I have no doubt, she will soon conceive a child, God willing, a prince for the realm."

Edward's frown decreased as he took comfort in my words. As wives went, Edward had often told me, I was far above the rest. He sought me out for conversation, political and the like, heeding my advice. Such was rare for a man to see and believe the things his spouse said. The gentler sex was often tossed aside, our opinions and ideas thought to be witless and naïve. I often wondered if the richness of my blood made me different than others, for I was descended of kings. Whatever the reason, I was much comforted and took pride in Edward's opinion of me.

"Our entire future—our very lives—depend on her bringing forth a son."

His words echoed my fears. More than one wife gone, having failed in that respect. Not that they hadn't tried. Katharine had delivered of a prince, who sadly had passed before reaching two months of life, and Anne herself had delivered a boy, although he was stillborn.

*Oh, please, God, let Jane deliver a healthy, robust son!*

"Yes," I answered, unclear of what else to say. I had lost energy for a clever answer after perhaps our three-hundredth conversation on the topic. My prayers were now my only answer to his statement.

"You must see to it," he demanded.

My brows furrowed, and I opened my mouth to respond but quickly shut it again. I sat forward, catching my Lord Seymour's deep brown gaze. "And how am I to do that? I lack...certain equipment."

The conversation was getting dangerous. What was he implying I should do?

Edward grunted and stretched his legs out before him. "Always one for words, my lady." He drummed his fingers on his thighs, drawing my gaze to his lap.

He was well formed, athletic. I licked my lips, hungering for this conversation to end and for Edward to take me to bed. After this morning, I needed to be whisked away.

"You will teach her. You are certainly knowledgeable enough in the art of seduction."

For a moment I feared he thought me an adulteress, and I let his words sink in, not knowing how to respond. But then his eyes met mine. Desire emanated from their depths. He meant only for how I had succeeded in pleasing him. I stood and went to stand between his legs, my hands resting on his broad shoulders. I leaned down, my lips brushing his.

"Teach her, I shall."

# CHAPTER TWO

*Upon the gentle beast to gaze it pleased me,*
*For still methought he seemed well of noble blood to be.*
*~Henry Howard, Earl of Surrey*

*May 20, 1536*

Whereas yesterday barely a sound could be heard throughout the long halls and the evening meal had been quite somber — echoes of Anne's jovial and vibrant laughter had almost seemed deafening in the silence — today was anything but. This morning, Henry had announced his betrothal to Jane to his Privy Council at Hampton Court, and we Seymours and more than half the court had sighed with relief.

Laughter, music, talking could be heard in all directions as I headed toward the king's chambers with Edward, the most important courtiers and ladies having transferred here from Greenwich. Excitement raced through my blood, as the second piece on the chess board was moved and showed in our favor. The muscles of my face felt strained from having to keep a stoic countenance rather than smiling widely as I wanted to.

I had heard from Edward that Sir Francis Bryan had delivered the news to Jane about Anne Boleyn's death, while she'd waited on the Strand last eventide. He'd also said that Henry, dressed in white mourning clothes, had hopped onto his barge and rowed quickly to Jane's side, where he had had dinner with her before retiring to Hampton Court. I'd spent the remainder of yesterday in bed with a headache—although I suspected it had more to do with my sick conscience over Anne Boleyn.

*Plain Jane.* My sister-by-marriage was perhaps the opposite of everything the king's previous wife had embodied. Where Anne had been bold and vibrant, Jane was meek and quiet. Where Anne had questioned religion—even persuading the king to reform!—Jane was pious and humble. Where Anne had been dark and beautiful, Jane was pale and plain. Dark versus light. Anne had been outspoken; Jane was docile. Anne had ridiculed Katharine of Aragon's existence and had had the Princess Mary stripped of her title and declared a bastard, Jane was sympathetic toward them, held great respect for Katharine and compassion for Mary.

Anne had been accused of witchcraft, but already people said that Jane was full of goodness. It was an opinion held by many, except for the ambassador to Spain, Chapuys, who had been saying there was no way Jane could still be a virgin. The man had been spreading heresy that at age five and twenty, having spent so much time at the English court, which was rife with immorality, her maidenhead had certainly been in jeopardy.

Chapuys needed to be silenced. Perhaps I would have to be the one to see it done.

"My lady, have you heard?" I turned to face Jane Rochford, shaking her grasp from my arm. I felt as though her devil's touch burned right through the fabric of my gown.

Although I could barely tolerate the woman, whenever she had a rumor on her lips I felt it my personal duty to listen, if only to stifle the words from her mouth.

"Go on."

"The Princess Elizabeth has been taken to Hatfield, the king having ordered her from Greenwich and away from his sight."

I nodded and kept moving forward, Jane Rochford on my left, Edward on my right. We skirted our way around painters and workers. Jane Seymour had arrived after the sunrise, early enough to not be noticed by those at court, and now, at nearly nine o'clock in the morning, we would soon have her formally betrothed to the king. It sickened me that Lady Rochford, a woman full of venom and deceit, would be allowed to attend Jane.

Already, servants at Henry's various palaces had begun replacing Anne's falcon badge with Jane's own emblem, a phoenix rising from a castle amid flames and red and white Tudor roses. Initials that had been painted throughout the halls and monogrammed on linens with A and H were now being hurriedly covered to present J and H. Jane's motto was modest and most appealed to the king: "Bound to obey and serve."

She was wise enough to take my advice on this motto, and I was glad for it.

We arrived and greeted the king and future queen very formally. The betrothal ceremony was over within minutes, and Henry urged us to take Jane back to Wulfhall, which we agreed to most readily as the wedding ceremony was set for ten days' time.

Ten days until the Seymour name would be forever linked with Tudor.

*Monday, May 29, 1536*

We returned to Whitehall Palace, all the wedding preparations complete. Jane's apartments, although slightly altered, still shouted Anne Boleyn. Jane fingered some of the bright purple and maroon upholstered chairs.

"We must have these changed to more muted colors. I am thinking sage and gold might do." She turned in a circle, her blonde hair delicately swishing against her back, her eyes filled with the same emotions I felt—fear, guilt, sadness.

I nodded my agreement. The toned-down fabrics would suit Jane immensely and change the effect of the room to a more modest state. Anne Boleyn had been outlandish. Jane needed to embody humility.

I waved away the attendants so that it was only Jane and I in the room. She looked at me, confusion in her eyes, and I motioned for her to sit with me by the banked fire.

"Jane, we must speak about an urgent matter." I paused, taking in the pure countenance of the future queen. No one could be that pure, especially having gained the attention of King Henry, a man known for his amorous appetite. Was there any credit to the words Chapuys had so brazenly spoken? My eyes were drawn to her breasts, pushed to the limits of her gold and ivory bodice embroidered with pearls. If she took too harsh a breath, her nipples would surely burst out. They were quite plush, her breasts... She could not have been so naïve to display her décolletage in such an enticing way. Perhaps little pure Jane was a bit more knowledgeable than we'd all given her credit for.

"You were saying?" She had a way of looking at me as if she knew all my darkest secrets and still forgave me. I felt almost dirty for what I was about to say.

"It is a matter of some delicacy."

Jane pursed her lips and turned her head, interested, curious. Her hands were folded demurely in her lap. Jane Rochford took that moment to enter, but my glare in her direction sent her scurrying away. Even still, I leaned closer to whisper. No need for the viper's tongue to spread more rumors.

"I am certes you know that tomorrow, after the wedding, you will be expected to perform certain duties."

Jane nodded. I noted the whiteness of her knuckles. She was nervous. Perhaps my thoughts did not have any credence? I must forge ahead as Edward had bid me, as uncomfortable as I was with this conversation. I had a duty to Jane, a duty to Edward and a duty to myself. If I neglected that duty, did not put my fullest efforts into it, then we were all dead. A vision of my own lifeless blue eyes startled me. I quickly composed myself, licked my lips.

"Are you well aware of what happens in the marriage bed?"

At this, Jane laughed. "Surely, Anne, you cannot think I am that innocent. I've been at court long enough to witness the act!"

"Have you..." I let my question hang in the air.

She gasped, her hand fluttering to her neck, her blue eyes widening. Could it be she already feared the executioner's blade? For the glint of sun off his blade was never far from my own mind.

"Dear God, no!" she exhaled.

I took a deep sigh. Virgin blood on the sheets tomorrow night would certainly save this queen. I wouldn't be surprised if the king waved the bloody stain before all of London. Thank the Lord, my dear Edward had known my own plight and not blinked an eye when our marriage bed had not yielded bloody sheets. "There have been rumors," I murmured.

Jane sighed. "I've heard. Chapuys, I believe. But no matter, I will soon be back in his good graces. He seeks only to reinstate Lady Mary into the king's good graces, a goal I also have."

Sweet Jane. It was moments like this, when I saw the goodness in her, that I wished she had been married off sooner to a nice man, a man who would treat her well, love her, cherish her. Were it not for the good of the family, I would not wish King Henry on anyone... well, except Lady Rochford, perhaps. A woman whose devious machinations reminded me of my own, and everything I hated and feared in myself.

I would have been a different woman were it not for Surrey. The moment he attacked me, he robbed me of more than my maidenhood. He hardened me. Transformed me. Embittered me such that I could never give my husband — or any man — the purest, softest part of myself. But to Edward, I *could* give my loyalty and hard determination. My machinations and deviousness.

And I hoped it would be counted as love, in the end.

So I was not entirely like Lady Rochford.

Certainly, Lady Rochford did not calculate in the same way as I did. I was a woman who planned for how each act I took would cause a reaction, and on top of that another reaction, until a chain of events fell into place like dominoes. But Lady Rochford, she acted out of vengeance and was never more than half a step ahead or several feet behind. She was dangerous for everyone.

"You will be expected to perform your wifely duty often, until you are with child, and most likely soon after you've delivered, you will be expected to resume your duties. The king will need at least one prince and will surely wish to have a spare," I said.

"This I know." Jane's face went pale at the reminder of the one thing the king's previous wives had been unable to deliver.

She was under a mountain of pressure to perform a deed she had no control over. A deed that two previous women before her had not—but there were two sons at least born to the king, though not of his wives, but from his mistresses.

What was it about being Henry VIII's *wife* that made conceiving a male so difficult?

Jane worried her bottom lip with her teeth, her fingers tightening in her skirts. My heart going out to her, I reached forward and clasped her hand—small, cold and trembling slightly—giving her a gentle squeeze. "You will persevere, Jane. You will make the king happy."

I hoped that at least a small measure of my confidence ebbed through her.

Jane flicked her gaze to me. She didn't speak, only nodded.

I, too, feared having a child and was blessed with a husband who agreed it was not the right time to start a family. Edward wanted there to be no doubt in whether our first child was his—and not the creation of Surrey's attack. But then, he'd also not wanted to ask so much of me, knowing I'd been in a fragile state upon marrying. Despite what we'd been taught by the church, I took precautions, albeit rudimentary—and penance for doing so—to prevent our conceiving. But Jane did not have that luxury. She'd be expected to quicken with child within the first year of marriage.

"Jane, we are sisters now. I am here to help you."

Her eyes, still wide, gazed into mine. She was petrified.

"Anne, should I have a girl..." She swallowed.

"Nonsense. A boy it will be. We shall ensure it."

Her eyes widened, and I could see the pulse in her throat jump. "How?"

"I have spoken to several midwives, and they have all told me that a woman can track her monthly to figure out when she is most fertile. During your fertile time, intercourse should happen on that day, but not a few days after and not a few days before."

"How is it possible for them to know this? How can I keep the king from me?"

"If you cannot keep him, there is a remedy. Vinegar. You will use it as a wash."

Jane fingered her gown, listening to my words. I was not much for potions or planning a pregnancy, and the words the midwives told me seemed true enough. I only prayed they worked…

"You should eat a lot of fruits and vegetables, not so much meat." I continued to list the advice given me, until Jane looked ready to faint. I myself was starting to feel light-headed. "Why do you not rest? Remember, I am always here for you, and I will guide you, sweet Jane."

She grasped my hand as I stood. "Would you sit here, read with me for a while?"

It was the least I could do, help this poor soul to settle her nerves. I poured Jane a cup of wine and pulled her Bible from a trunk. We started at the beginning and read for over two hours. Exhaustion seeped into us both, and soon I tucked Jane into bed for a nap, before crawling in beside her to seek my own slumber. Jane had been taken by night terrors as of late and begged me to stay with her should she need comfort.

I did not tell her that I had night terrors of my own, and we might both wake up screaming.

*Tuesday, May 30, 1536*

The day had arrived. Jane would marry King Henry VIII of England and soon would be pronounced Queen Jane of England.

My heart constricted with trepidation. Literally *everything* hinged on this marriage.

The ceremony, held in the Queen's Closet at Whitehall, was small and private, only those pertinent people, messengers and ambassadors attended. Archbishop Cranmer presided over the ceremony. I was overcome with emotions, and they all tangled up inside, threatening to make me go mad. I was happy, excited, terrified, nervous, and my emotions replayed again and again. My hands were clammy, and nausea ruled my belly. My only solace was the virginals played so sweetly, the voices of the choir like angels. Jane, too, looked like an angel, her smile sweet and genuine.

I was struck then, as I watched her gaze on the king with kindness and he in return, that perhaps they were actually in love.

Was it possible? I did not believe Henry capable of the emotion, but I supposed I wanted to believe it, for Jane's sake. Relief was added to the mix of emotions jumbled within me.

Edward squeezed my fingers. "Remember our wedding?"

"Yes," I whispered. We'd had a small ceremony. And we'd gazed much on each other as Jane and Henry did. It was a happy time. Edward, my savior.

"Everything is falling into place." He kissed my knuckles and then released me as we listened to the couple exchange their vows.

From across the nave, my attention was caught by a tall, handsome courtier, new to court. His features were reminiscent of Roman statues and beneath his feathered cap, his brown hair curled in a charming way. I swallowed around the sudden lump in my throat. Unwanted sensation wove its way around my ribs. He was beautiful. Stirred something foreign inside me. Disturbed me. His dark gaze connected with mine, holding me captive. There was something vaguely familiar about him, but I could not connect where I would have known him from. Fire flashed in his eyes, causing my stomach to clench. Who was this man? Why did he stare so?

More importantly, why did I stare back?

The virginals sounded loudly, ringing in my ears, and bringing my attention back to the event at hand. When I glanced back across the nave, he was gone. A rush of apprehension and fear filled me. Sweat pooled against the dip in the small of my back, and I sucked in a breath, in desperate need for air. Why had I stirred so with this stranger?

No good could come from this.

With the ceremony ended, I forced the incident from my mind, and we followed the royal couple to the great hall, where Jane sat for the first time in the queen's chair beneath the canopy of royal estate. Henry sat beside her, lifted her hand in the air, and shouted, "My wife! My Queen. Sweet, beautiful, Jane!"

The crowd of courtiers cheered. My heart lurched in my chest, and I did allow one small smile to escape. Servants passed around wine, sweetmeats, cheese, bread, fruits and other delicacies, of which I could only nibble as my stomach still revolted against food. Tension ruled me.

Henry presented Jane with over one hundred manors, forests and an income to support her household. But on a more personal note, he presented her with a wedding gift, a gold cup designed by the reputable Hans Holbein himself. Jane's motto was inscribed numerous times on the design, and the letters J and H were intertwined with a love knot. Jane thanked Henry with a kiss and then had a footman pour wine into her new goblet and drank from it merrily.

I caught myself looking for the mysterious courtier, praying he was not near, but each time I redirected myself to Jane, the king and my husband, until my mind no longer wandered. And by what could only be considered sheer luck—or divine intervention—he had disappeared. I started to relax. Another move had been made on the chess board, and it was in the direction of our own victory. I should have been pleased, ecstatic that things were going our way. But I couldn't help but think of those who had come before us, and they too must have looked on with triumph in their eyes, only to find some time later that death graced their doorsteps.

My gaze caught on Secretary Cromwell as he strolled the perimeter of the great hall, looking smug, though he must feel the tension of the king's displeasure, surely. The man had been shocked when his chambers were taken so swiftly and given over to the king's new favorites—us—though he hid it well.

I refused to be caught off guard as Cromwell was. I would know beforehand if the king sought to strip us of our entails.

From the court's lively appearance, it seemed most were pleased with the situation, but I could not help spying the Duke of Norfolk as he glowered in a corner. Wherever the duke was, his son, Surrey, my bitter enemy, was not far behind. A cursory glance did not show him to be present at the moment, but that did not mean he would not arrive. The duke spoke to another courtier, hands moving wildly, most likely displeased with his fall from grace. He'd been seen lamenting about the palace of his love for the king, how he'd been wickedly used by his niece—Anne Boleyn. A ploy, for I am certain he had a hand in the rise and fall of his beloved niece, but the king fell for it all the same. After all, Norfolk was on the committee delegated to investigating her numerous sexual affairs.

I touched Edward's hand and smiled. "Will you excuse me, my lord?"

He looked toward where I nodded my head and smiled. "With pleasure."

Since I was merely a woman, men did not think twice to continue their conversations. Spying on courtiers was easy, especially when I jumped into the dancing crowd near Norfolk.

His whispers were hushed, but nevertheless I caught the words he spoke.

"She is a Catholic. We must be wary. The possibility is entirely there that she will convince Henry not to continue with reform."

"What of Elizabeth? Will our own princess be thrust aside like Mary? Will Mary be put back into the succession and Elizabeth left in the cold?"

"Those are my fears as well."

No plans were hatched, but their very fears only said more than words. A plot would be put into place soon. Another Howard girl would be thrust under the king's nose. I was more aware now of what schemes our enemies might seek to play.

When we returned to Greenwich for Jane to set up her household, I was heartily disappointed when Jane Rochford was chosen as Lady of the Bedchamber. I had had hopes for that position to be mine.

I was Jane's sister-by-marriage after all. But I comforted myself in knowing the queen did not choose her own blood sister, either. I conceded that it was smart of Queen Jane to give the scorpion such a position. Lady Rochford was a major player in Anne's downfall. Giving her the position knocked out two birds with one stone: a thank you, for now Jane was queen, and a closer eye could now be held on the vicious woman—a duty that was then relegated to me.

# CHAPTER THREE

*And as he pranced before, still seeking for a make,*
*As who would say, 'There is none here, I believe, will me forsake.'*
*~Henry Howard, Earl of Surrey*

*Whitsunday, June 4, 1536*

"Ambassador."

Candlelight filtered throughout the great hall, casting shadows in the corners. Musicians played a merry tune. Courtiers and ladies crowded the room in celebration of Jane being proclaimed Queen of England. Glasses clinked, laughter resounded. Jane was at the height of her happiness. The king appeared completely smitten. A new realm was upon us. Energy fairly burst from the seams of the room.

By the king, I saw his bastard son, The Duke of Richmond, had been invited to court. The man, young and sprite, just coming into his own. A vibrant, first-rate image of his father. Nice turn of leg, broad strong chest, firm jaw, thick reddish hair, and a small beard on his chin. He was a handsome boy. Beside him was his wife, Lady Mary Richmond—formerly Mary Howard, cousin to Anne Boleyn.

Chapuys turned toward me, his brow cocked, perhaps surprised I would seek him out and address him.

"My lady." He bowed, his features schooled into a mask of non-emotion. A perfect courtier.

"Would you be so kind as to have a word with me?"

"Certainly, my lady." He offered me his arm, and we strolled about the great hall, other eyes following each step we took.

I did not want to waste any time in getting to my point with the man, and I also did not want to chance an interruption before I had said my piece. "I have heard certain things about our new queen." I glanced at Chapuys out of the corner of my eye. Had his skin suddenly paled a shade? His brows knitted together in concentration, although no other outward signs of concern showed. "Rumor has it you've made comments about Her Majesty's virtue."

At my forwardness, the ambassador stopped his promenade and turned toward me. My hand, which had rested on his arm, now lay limp against my side. Several people surrounding us stopped their chattering, hoping to catch a whisper of our conversation. No doubt on the morrow rumors would escalate as to the subject of our tête-à-tête. I glared fiercely at those who so openly eavesdropped, and several returned to their own business. Others, including Lady Rochford, were not so receptive.

"Do you deny it?" I asked, my voice hushed, my face blank of feeling—for which I prided myself on. It took great practice to keep emotions from one's face.

A glint came into his eye, and his mouth twitched into a slight smile.

"I see Queen Jane has a champion in you. Your relationship as her sister-by-marriage no doubt excuses your boldness. However, in future please, my lady, know that Her Majesty has my full support, and I would never wish ill fortune upon her. I have heard from her own lips she supports my Lady Mary."

He cleverly avoided answering my question and instead sought to quell my ire at his past transgressions. His words could have been taken as an apology for having offended Jane and our family. I decided that was the stance I would take, and in so doing could possibly count the ambassador as an ally—which we could use more of in droves, being the new faction in court and the Howards even now plotting to regain their status. Even still, he was now warned that we would be watching him and that further sullying of her name would not be tolerated.

"As do I." I lifted my chin, showing him his rebuke of my speech would not have me cowed, and with my words also imparted an alliance of sorts.

"Good to know. Friends at court, and in such impressionable positions as yourself, are always beneficial."

*So, he understood.* I offered him a smile. "Indeed, sir."

"I bid you good evening, my lady."

He bowed, and I curtsied in turn, trying to brush off the sting of dismissal. To replace the sting, I soothed myself with the thought that now it would be known about court that I hadn't the timidity of most courtly ladies and I would indeed fight for me and mine.

"Lady Anne." The voice of King Henry behind me surprised me so greatly I jolted, nearly bumping into the couples dancing close to where Chapuys and I had been speaking.

I turned slowly, my head bowed, and curtsied, ready for him to call the guards, fearful he'd overheard my conversation with the ambassador. Whatever Jane's plans and support may have been, offering my own so openly for Mary was a dangerous business. Henry was extremely angry with his daughter, wanting her imprisoned for her insolence in denying that his marriage to her mother was null and void, although Edward had convinced him otherwise. Word had it that Henry had even sent the Duke of Norfolk out to threaten her, and threaten her he had, telling her he'd have smashed his daughter's head against the wall until it was as soft as baked apples had she treated him thusly. But how could a father force a daughter to conclude he'd never been married to her mother when, in fact, he had? Not that I could voice such, as it went entirely against the Seymour family's allegiance.

Would my own head be crushed into a quivering, bloody mass if King Henry — or my husband — found out I held affection for his daughter Mary?

"I see you've acquainted yourself with Ambassador Chapuys." He leaned in toward me, his eyes searching mine.

Inside I shook, and I desperately wanted to search out the crowd for Edward, for the comfort of his strong body beside me gave me courage. But instead I forced myself to meet his crystal-blue gaze.

"Yes, Majesty."

"An interesting conversation you had?" His eyes sparkled, and a smile touched his lips.

Was I mistaken? Had he not heard? Or had he, and he approved?

"Rather droll, actually." I chanced a smile and was rewarded when his grew.

"I often find the man a bit stiff with conversing myself. Would you care to dance?"

I slowly and silently blew out a deep breath, relieved at not having to explain my words with Chapuys and not being a crushed baked apple beneath his boot.

"With pleasure, Your Majesty." Although pleasure was not exactly how I felt in his arms, more like a sense of dread and unease.

*June 5, 1536*

Court had been making merry, and I was now a viscountess! Just this morning, His Majesty had bestowed the title Viscount Beauchamp on Edward. Jane not married a week and already we had been elevated. I had to keep my practiced cool, even though I'd wished to clap and sing and spin in circles.

"My lady." A footman bowed in my direction.

I set down my sewing and glanced at the other ladies, who tittered and laughed as we completed our embroidery in the queen's chambers. Although I myself was not Lady of the Queen's Bedchamber, Jane insisted I sit beside her daily. Our conversations about her wifely duties to the king continued, and she'd even asked my advice on pleasuring a man. An apt pupil she appeared to be.

"Yes?"

"Lord Beauchamp requests your presence in his library."

I turned to Jane. "Would you excuse me, Your Majesty?"

Jane inclined her head and smiled. I was so proud of her regal bearing. She had the makings of a great queen.

I walked swiftly to our apartments, wondering what had happened to cause Edward to summon me. He was seated behind his desk, sifting through letters and other various documents. He looked up as I entered.

"My lady wife."

His smile broadened as he stood from his desk and came toward me, waving the footman from the room, who quietly backed out and shut the door behind him. When he reached me he did not stop but pulled me into his arms, his warm lips pressing to mine. It was not a chaste kiss, but one meant to garner a reaction. I sighed into his arms, tasting some sort of sweet fruit on his lips.

He pulled his mouth away but kept his arms around me. "Are you enjoying your time with the queen?" His fingers danced circles up my spine.

"I am, indeed, my Lord *Beauchamp*." I smiled winningly, knowing how much he enjoyed hearing his new title upon my lips.

"I have just come from a meeting with the Privy Council. There will be a new Act of Succession placing Jane's children as first in line for the throne. And in just a few days' time, Jane will enter London in state. Her coronation is planned for this October."

"Oh, Edward, this is marvelous news." It was hard to tamp down my excitement with all that was going so well for us.

He kissed me again, this time deeper, and warmed me all the way to my core. I was becoming dizzy with excitement, even in broad daylight. Would he take me to bed? Had he changed his mind and decided we should now start a family? I quelled my fear of such a request. As we were becoming elevated, we would have need of an heir.

"There is more good news," he said, his lips moving toward my neck, and then up to the shell of my ear.

I murmured something, I do not know what, as I was completely melting in his embrace.

"The king has hinted to me that once Jane has been through her coronation, I will be awarded with an earldom." At this, the backs of his fingertips danced along my chest, teasing the tops of my breasts.

"An earldom?" I gasped, half in shocked surprise and half with desire seeping through my pores.

"Yes. You will be a countess." He tugged the front of my bodice down, exposing one nipple. "We'll amass a fortune, lands, homes, and titles for our children that, God willing, you deliver safely."

"The thought brings me pleasure." He'd mentioned children, and how cleverly, too, knowing I would do whatever it took to see that my children advanced in the realm. My children would have all that and more. They would be powerful, left with a legacy that Edward and I had built of our own two hands.

"As it does to me." He teased my nipple with his teeth and tongue until I writhed against him, my hands clutching the hair on the back of his head.

His lips sought mine again, and then he lifted me in the air, settling me on his desk. Our mouths were frantic, kissing lips, cheeks, necks, ears. His hands were everywhere at once, on my breasts, lifting my skirts. My hands were on him, pulling his shirt from his breeches, reaching toward the thing I sought most.

When we joined, it was rapid, it was furious, filled with pent-up desire, our bodies rocking the desk back and forth, our moans filling the air.

So filled with pleasure was I, I hardly noticed how unseemly our behavior was—coupling in the middle of the day on his office desk, my bottom crinkling whatever documents were placed there. I took what he gave and gave back in return. We joined for pleasure, for celebration at our elevated status, for the fact that he'd saved me from ruin, and I was forever grateful to the fact.

When it was over, I lay back on his desk, sated and still mildly delirious. He kissed my nose and pulled my skirts back down over my legs before righting himself.

"You please me much, my lady."

I smiled lazily. "As is my duty, and I do it with pleasure."

He circled back around his desk and took a seat. I stood and fixed my honey-hued hair and headdress in the mirror that hung over the hearth.

"How goes things with Jane?" he asked.

"Very well. She has employed the tricks I taught her, and the king seems like a very pleased man. I suspect she will be with child soon."

"The court seems taken with her."

"Yes, I think just about everyone is. She is so regal, so *good.*"

Edward smiled. "Keep an eye on her. You will be her conscience and my ears."

"My lord." I curtsied to my husband and left the room, nearly bumping into a tall, muscled form.

"Pardon me, my lady." His voice was smooth, sensual, sending a thrill of unexpected excitement along my skin.

I looked into the eyes of a courtier whose name I was not familiar with, but whose dark gaze had haunted my dreams since I first saw him on Jane's wedding day. *Him.* His dark hair was pulled back in a queue. A devilish dimple appeared in one cheek when he smiled, and smoldering eyes gazed into mine. Again, that sense we'd met before, but where, I could not dredge up from memory.

My gaze was riveted to his mouth, wondering briefly what it would be like to kiss those full lips. Shame filled me. Had I not just been within Edward's embrace? But when I was with Edward it was because he'd saved me. Because it was my duty. Not because I felt… I refused to succumb to these forbidden feelings. Feelings that would force me to betray everything I knew to be holy and good. From the way the courtier lustily gazed at me, my blood already pumped a wanton dance through my limbs. My fingernails bit angrily into my palms. *For shame, Anne! You've just made love to your husband!*

The chastisement of my conscience served as a good reprimand, and my blood ran cold. This courtier stood against everything I valued in myself.

He turned a well-muscled leg and bowed. "Sir Anthony Browne, at your service."

I gulped, feeling panic well in my belly. I had to escape this room, before I melted into the floor or hurled myself through the window.

# CHAPTER FOUR

*I might perceive a Wolf as white as whales bone,*
*A fairer beast of fresher hue, beheld I never none*
*Save that her looks were coy, and froward was her grace:*
*Unto the which this gentle beast did him advance apace.*
*~Henry Howard, Earl of Surrey*

*June 6, 1536*

"I never thanked you." Elizabeth Seymour, my sister-by-marriage, sauntered toward me. She was beautiful, with gorgeous bouncing curls and eyes that were wild in a way the sea was on the scallop of its waves. Men desired her.

"Thanked me for what, Beth?"

She sidled up next to me in my dark corner, her eyes sweeping down in a way to take in my gown and bejeweled fingers.

"If you had not thrust our Jane under King Henry's nose, we would not be standing here, would we?"

"Ah," I muttered, observing the court in all its glory, marveling that I had a part in the way things were. From the top of the vaulted ceiling to every hidden nook and the great space between, laughter bubbled over. Cheers, boisterous voices and the occasional shout mingled with the musicians, who provided the evening's enchanting sounds. Above all, the booming voice of King Henry VIII, or his roaring laughter, dominated the room. This was *his* court, *his* England. And every single person within the realm knew this. "I suppose. But he would have noticed her somehow or other."

"Not likely. The Howards were hard-pressed to replace the queen with one of her cousins." Beth smirked in her haughty way. She was blunt as a knife in the gut.

"We may have planted the bait, but your sister is and was exactly what the king desired."

Beth laughed. "Indeed, my lady. But let us pray his eyes do not soon stray to another luscious Howard. Our king's appetite may not be so well pleased with my modest sister. I must away." She curtsied. "This last dance is for a lucky gentleman, your brother, and then it is back to the country for me."

"It is most assuredly Michael's good fortune to have you grace his arm. *Bon voyage!*" Despite my attempts to be jovial, her words haunted me.

"*Oui, ma soeur.*" Beth dipped low in a curtsy and then vanished in the crowd to locate my brother. Besides Edward, the one male I could count on at court. My eldest brother, Richard, was still as volatile as ever, and I walked on the cracked shells of eggs when he was near. He was another reason I feared for my life—for more often than not, when the king was angry at one, he thrashed his punishment on the whole family unit. And should Richard entreat the king's ire...

I took a slow sip of cider and suppressed a shudder, wishing for something a little stronger to take the edge off the fear that Beth had summoned, for she had a valid point—one I'd been avoiding pondering. Richard would be back soon. I would have to be cautious and seek out information from one of our spies about what he'd been up to. The tang of ale and apples washed over my tongue, and I let it settle a moment, taking in the full flavor.

The Tudor court perpetually exhibited only the finest of food, drink and entertainment. Only the best for the king. Even his candles were made from premium wax. Those in the great hall and the king's other chambers were infused with special herbs and flowers.

"Are not thou a pretty king with emeralds and rubies surrounding thy neck like the grande dame of all thy court!" The king's fool, Will Somers, pulled me from my dire thoughts as he frolicked about, making jests of the clothing styles, Henry's jewels and choice of councilors. The fool gestured to Henry's councilors. "And your ladies in tow with you!"

Henry laughed and kicked out his foot, but Somers quickly rolled away.

I could not help but snicker, for the men spent just as much time preening as the women of court. What a shame it would have been if all had not looked their best. My gaze shifted to the spot next to Henry. Jane sat pretty as a summer rose on her throne, a peaceful smile upon her lips. At last, a smile that was not hardened with strain around the edges.

Yes, I had had a hand in the way things were tonight. And judging by the new diamond and jade ring upon my finger, my kindness was being repaid. But it was not really a kindness, was it? I was only taking what was duly mine. I had set the plans in motion, so to speak, for it was I who put a young piece in front of Henry while Anne observed, and watched the sparks fly.

Oh, and fly they had.

"My lady." Chapuys interrupted my reverie. He nodded his head and bent a leg in front of me. His eyes were hard and cold, belying the friendly smile upon his lips.

"Excellency." I nodded and curtsied.

"I pray that all is well within your family?"

"We are fortunate to report only good things."

Chapuys chuckled, perhaps at the shortness of my answer, or at some internal jest of his own.

"And you, Ambassador?"

"Very well." He turned and gestured at the court. "The people are so very taken with our new queen. My own master, His Imperial Majesty, has it in his mind to set up an alliance between England and Spain again, given that Queen Jane is of such an... admirable disposition."

I inclined my head. "That is indeed good news. I am confident His Majesty will be most pleased to hear your proposal." I had my doubts Henry would be pleased at all. His moods shifted with the tides, and he might form an alliance on impulse but change his mind come breakfast. Henry's previous wives were a perfect example of his changing moods.

"That is my hope."

With nothing further to say, he moved on to the Duke of Norfolk. Our conversation had been a little tense, but I was pleased to see that Chapuys and I were at least still on biddable terms.

"Sister." Michael came up beside me, and I gifted him with a true smile. "You were deep in thought. Might I trouble you for a glimpse into the mind of such a genius woman?"

"You have a way with words for ladies, Brother."

"I've been trained well." At this he handed me a fresh cup of wine and waved a groom over to take my empty cider mug.

"Do tell, Annie."

I smiled at his reference to my childhood name. "I was recalling the night of Henry's public explosion."

"Which one?" Michael chuckled, and both of us looked around to make certain we were not overheard.

A slight pang of guilt whittled its way into my heart. Michael was closer to me than either my mother or brother Richard, and yet I still did not feel I could confide completely in him. One's own internal thoughts were best left there, for if they were to slip delicately past your tongue, the ax might be just as swift to cut it off.

"The night Henry loudly rebuked Anne for her temper when she lashed out at the young lady, Claudia, and the king himself for dancing and making merry."

"Ah, I recall the night. The moon hardly shown and rain pelted the roof, the *ting ting* of its droplets echoing in the great hall. The music had stopped. The crowd was silent. Thunder boomed and lightning flashed, only emphasizing the king's ire, like the heavens backed up his very words."

"You've always had a flare for drama, Brother. You make it sound like the prologue to a play."

"Most events at this court have proven to appear the stuff of make-believe."

"Yes, well, that is the way of the court."

Michael nodded. "What made you think of that evening in particular?"

"No reason. You know what made that night all the worse? Claudia bid my instructions not to pay respects to Anne as she was expected to do. Seeing as how the king was already enamored of Claudia and only hours away from gaining his great reward, Anne's outburst only made him most angry!"

"Ah, yes. He hotly told his queen where she ought to take her thoughts and loudly complained to all the court of Anne's importunity. It was only a matter of time before he set Anne aside, and by then you and Edward had already put your playing pieces on the table."

"I played a part in that night." But the words sounded full of dread even to myself.

"And I thank you for doing so. I would not have garnered a position among his groomsmen if not for you."

"You are the second person to thank me this eve."

"And who was the first?"

"Elizabeth Seymour."

"A delightful young woman."

I eyed my brother suspiciously. "And not for you."

Michael bowed. "I will always accede to your great desires, my lady. What think you of Jane Rochford?"

At this, I nearly snarled. "Do not even think about it, Brother. It still disgusts me that Jane Rochford took it upon herself to have revenge against her philandering — and most probably buggering — husband, and in so doing took out a queen in the process. I swear by all that is holy, one day she will see her foul ways put to the test, and, I daresay, she will not be the champion." At once I realized what I had said and was at least fortunate enough to have spoken the words to my brother — despite my strict rule of keeping my own counsel. Had I not also seen to Anne Boleyn's downfall? Played people as though they were chess pieces? I brushed the guild aside.

Being the older brother that he was, Michael saw fit to goad me further. "Pray, tell me what you think of the lady."

"Oh, posh!" I swatted his arm.

51

"Mayhap I shall see if the vixen is in need of a dance with a man who does not covet male flesh."

I gasped and was rewarded with raucous laughter from Michael as he swaggered off.

I had barely enough time to recover from Michael's teasing before his spot beside me was filled by another figure. Apparently, the dark corner of a room was a most popular place.

"Good evening, my lady." The smooth, sensual whisper of sweet breath tickled along the shell of my ear.

*Sir Anthony.* He'd sought me out in my private spot in an alcove of the great hall. Out of sight from others, his hand brushed the small of my back, sending shivers racing up my spine, partly from fear and partly from desire. Fear, for the sensations his light touch gave me were forbidden. Desire, for a man as beautiful as he was, to taste something I had never had. Freedom. Choice.

Edward loved me, yes. But he'd married me to protect me after Surrey's violation, and I'd felt after being compromised that I had no choice. Over the past year, we'd both decided it was a good match. We worked well together, and had the same goals. But Anthony... He touched a part of me that had not been allowed to speak.

"Sir," I responded, a slight quiver in my voice.

"Why are you all alone? No husband on your arm?"

I thought a moment at his choice of words, no husband on *my* arm, as if I wore Edward and not the other way around.

"What makes you think I was not awaiting Lord Beauchamp?" I asked haughtily.

"No particular reason, other than he is... otherwise engaged."

I sought a glimpse in the crowd of chestnut hair topped with the dark-green velvet cap, ostrich feathers jauntily stuck from the side, which I had given him on his birthday. There it was, and with it my husband, ogling the décolletage of a young court lady. Miss Elizabeth Darrell, I thought. My lips pursed into a frown.

"Hmm," I said, irritated that I had not seen him with her before and that Sir Anthony was the one to point it out to me. "Do you make a point to show me my husband prefers the company of some other gown than mine own? Hardly a gesture expected of a gentleman."

He bowed, his dark eyes catching mine. For a moment I thought to drown myself in their depths, wishing for him to take me somewhere private, stroke my own ego, which had been sorely bruised with the sight of Edward so outwardly flirting with another.

Until now, I'd never indulged in the baser attitudes that seemed to encumber most at court. Philandering, adultery. They disgusted me. And yet... Even Edward sneaked away when he thought I was not looking to taste the nectar of another. Why had not I? Why should I not indulge my desires? *Because I am stronger than that. Because I love and respect my husband. Because to do so could jeopardize our future.*

"The man ought to know he's already obtained the prize." Anthony's lips curled at one corner, giving him a devilish sort of look, and his gaze roved up and down my form. The expression in his eyes was one that made a girl dream of romantic poems and a midnight rendezvous. With that one smile, my senses were sent into a whirl. I felt breathy, my heart racing. Almost like I was standing before him, already nude. But I remembered who I was, and I recovered by turning up my nose and glancing away. How dare he make me think such things?

He chuckled gaily in my ear. "Your reputation precedes you, my lady. Though you were rather serious as a child, if I recall."

"My reputation?" I looked back at him sharply. "We've met before?"

"So you do not remember me?" He pursed his lips and glanced away. "Well, you were a petite thing when you first came to court to serve Katharine of Aragon. But look at you now. Grown, and fierce. And ever so lovely." The man had the audacity to wink at me. "They say you are a viper in a den of rabbits." His lips crooked in a teasing, sinful smile, and I wanted to slap him and kiss him all at once.

I sucked in a breath. Should I be offended by his nature and words? Or by my own thoughts? I vaguely remembered him dipping low and kissing my outstretched fingers. Of asking me to dance, and whirling me around. Of giving me ribbons and sweets. Pulling me on his team to play boules. But he was a man then, and I a child. Now we were both grown, and his fondness for me did not seem to have waned.

"But I do not agree," he said. His fingers tickled against my own. The room suddenly felt warmer, and it was not from the heat of summer, since the evening had finally brought sweet relief from the humid air. "Your cunning and intelligence, I quite admire, as I do your spirit."

I was relieved he did not think me a viper, but I did not know why. Did people really think me so cold? For certes, I did not smile, nor offer words of comfort often, but I wasn't cruel without purpose.

Had he said these things merely to see me riled? Was it because of what I'd done to secure Jane Seymour's success — that I'd forsaken the queen, flaunted women before the king to see her enraged?

"To me, you are a plush... red... apple." Each word he spoke slowly against my ear, his finger trailing up my spine, plucking the buttons at the back of my gown. "An apple I wish to sink my teeth into and feel the sweet juices as they run over my tongue."

"Sir!" My head snapped toward his, mouth open in outrage as I said it, perhaps too loudly, as a few eyes gathered toward our spot.

"I think we can help each other, *sweet* Anne."

He used my Christian name without my permission. Such insolence! But I liked it. The man was daring, and I found myself intrigued despite the impropriety of it all.

"I do not see how." I stepped away and eyed the crowd for Edward. He was now trailing discreetly behind Miss Darrell, who'd rounded a corner at the far end of the great hall. My feet itched to run after him. How dare he make a mockery of me!

Anthony took a step back, lest our closeness have tongues flapping about court. "Surely, you do. I am a member of the king's privy chamber."

I narrowed my eyes at him, rewarded only with a merry smile and sparkling eyes.

"As is my husband."

"This is true, but your husband is brother to the queen. Some secrets are kept from his ears."

What he said could have been true, but why would he offer to share those same secrets with me?

"It would also be my pleasure to introduce you to a few of my friends, who might I say, would be advantageous to you?"

This last favor would indeed have been of great importance to me. Because of Edward's position at court, I was often avoided, unless someone wanted something whispered into the ear of the king.

"And what do you want?" For I knew what I could get out of him. Information. And see to it that he could carry out any plans I'd put in place. But, what exactly, he wanted from me was a mystery.

Sir Anthony's eyebrow crooked upward, and he licked his lower lip deliciously. "Friendship..." His voice trailed off as his eyes swept the whole of my form, lingering on my sensitive spots. "Special friends we could be."

Heat flooded my face, and I was certain my cheeks showed flaming red. Had the man gone daft? Propositioning a married woman of noble blood, the king's own sister-by-marriage, in the middle of courtly festivities? And, what's more, I did not believe him for a minute. What more did he seek from me? I was aware that some may have called me easy on the eyes, and some may even have raved at my soft, honeyed beauty, but I was not naïve enough to believe Sir Anthony wanted only sexual gratification. There was some other means he hoped to gain.

"Sir! I am a married woman," I hissed, furiously checking the crowd, all too aware of the curious gazes that were intent on reading our lips.

Anthony laughed and chucked my chin with a finger. "I often want what I cannot have, my lady."

"Never." I dipped a curtsy. Already too many eyes on us. Time to part company.

My heart pumped so fast I thought it might burst from my chest as I made my way to my seat at one of the long trestle tables. I was too fidgety to take my seat and instead stood, grabbing a few grapes and popping them into my mouth. I glanced toward the dais where King Henry and Jane sat idly chatting. Jane motioned me near.

"Your Majesties." I curtsied low and bowed my head.

Jane inclined her head to me as did Henry, and then he stood, regal in cloth of gold and a collar of black diamonds and rubies.

Despite his thickening waist and injured leg, King Henry could still rival even the most handsome courtiers. He always had been a truly beautiful prince. Ambassadors raved to their respective foreign courts of Henry's tall stature—for he was a head taller than half the court—his broad chest, well-muscled physique, red-gold locks, piercing blue eyes and charming and intelligent mind. He was the whole package. Except for his moods, which changed with the coming of the tides and the whispers of the wind.

"Lady Anne, will you dance?" The king smiled solicitously and gestured toward the other dancers.

I was a bit surprised by his request but quickly nodded my head in acquiescence. He stood from his chair and descended from the dais, taking my hand and wrapping it around his arm.

"Do you recall the first time I asked you about dancing?" His blue eyes twinkled, and with a wave of his hand, the musicians began a lively *pavane*. Henry twirled me, and we both clapped, falling easily into the rhythm of the dance.

"I do." It was the first time I had met King Henry. I had been but a young girl of twelve when Queen Katharine had invited me to court to serve as a maid of honor along with my mother. I had been enamored of the glittering gowns, capes, doublets, caps, headdresses and jewels. But nothing had prepared me for my first introduction to Katharine, who had sat so stoically upon her throne. She had been gracious and kind and had bid me to read her a passage from the Bible. After the reading, she had dismissed me, and later that evening I had been faced with the tall and muscular frame of Henry VIII of England. "You called me Little Anne, and I recall my mother's mortification at my exuberance."

I frowned slightly as I remembered just how my mother had pinched the back of my arm discreetly, after I had gushed to the king. I hadn't meant to overstep my bounds, but I had been truly enamored of the steps of the dance and that I had been invited to court with a chance to practice those steps. And what had been even more thrilling had been the chance to dance with the handsome and congenial king. But the king had only laughed at my girlish antics, a sound that had tickled the ears, for it was pure delight in what he had found humorous.

Mother's voice as she'd rushed to apologize still rang in my ears. *"My apologies for my daughter's forthrightness. She is just come to court and is new to what is expected and proper."* My mother's voice had sounded so whiny to me, and it had irritated me that even with the king's humor, she had felt the need to make excuses for me. Before I had been able to open my mouth to voice my opinions, I had received an even harder pinch to silence me.

King Henry's eyes had exuded mirth, just as they did now, and I still found myself eager to please him as I had in my youth.

Henry's head fell back with his renewed laughter. "You frown so! It was all in good sport. Lady Page's strings are so easily twisted. But what a pleasure it was. You succeeded very well in acting just as regal as the other ladies at court and your dancing was—is divine."

I smiled and tossed my gaze in Jane's direction. She was engaged in a rather lively conversation with a few other court ladies. All of them were dressed to the highest fashion, with slashed sleeves and vibrant ribbons of colored silk pulled through. The king was in such high spirits this evening, and despite being a court lady for half my life, I found it difficult to know just what to say.

"You are too gracious, Majesty."

"As the second hand of God, it is my duty to be gracious to those who are loyal to me." His heavy words were accompanied by a jovial smile. "I hear your mother is soon to return to court and bringing her daughter, too."

Just the mention of my mother's name had my chin lifting, shoulders squaring. Phantom stings tingled the backs of my arms as if my skin remembered her pinches.

"My stepfather is to return to your service?"

Henry chuckled, but his eyes held warning. I would not forget that Sir Richard Page, the man who'd married my mother and gotten another daughter on her, had been a close confidante of Anne Boleyn's and even Wolsey's before her. The man had tread on dangerous ground, and Henry had banished him from court. I shuddered to think of my mother coming so close to the scaffold at her husband's own hand.

"Indeed, he is. I have a mind to make him Sheriff of Surrey under the Earl of Surrey. What think you of that? And your little sister Elizabeth shall serve England's new queen as a maid of honor."

"I'd rather hoped to get away from my family, Your Majesty," I gave the king a conspiratorial smirk, though my insides burned with anger that my family would be that much closer to my enemy. "And here you are seeing that I'm once again surrounded. Are you trying to send me away?"

King Henry laughed. "Would you have me toss them in the Tower?"

I knew he was jesting. But the words, *yes, please,* teetered on the tip of my tongue. He teased me with his power. "I thank you for the offer, Your Majesty, but I must decline. I'd not want to put *that* much distance between us."

The king laughed all the more. But my limbs were going numb from fear. Was this the king's way of keeping me further on edge? I was hardly a consequential person... Had someone else put the notion in his ear to punish me? To make mine own stepfather answer to the one man I abhorred almost as much as Lucifer... It was insufferable. If invited to stay for a visit at my mother's castle, it would be entirely plausible that Surrey could come unannounced, only putting me further into his path. And then he might possibly try to—I swallowed hard—violate my person once more.

Furthermore, I hardly knew the girl, my half-sister, but would surely become acquainted with her soon. Would my mother thrust her daughter into my care, seek my patronage to advance herself?

The music for the *pavane* began to die down, and with the fading music I forced my worries away. I could not think about it now. I needed to concentrate on getting through this evening, keeping my attention on the king. He was known to get cranky when not the full center of one's consideration.

"What was the dance you'd learned just before coming to court all those years ago?" he asked.

"The *galliard.*"

"You shall dance the *galliard* again this evening. I have the desire to reminisce in younger days."

I sighed inside, heavy-hearted. I had no interest in reminiscing in earlier days. The past was best kept there. The future was where I wanted to be — titles added to my name, power and riches for my family. Edward and I at the right hand of the king and queen. Aunt to the future king. Nobles, most established and respected.

He snapped his fingers and instructed the musicians to change the music. All eyes were on me as I began the steps, swaying my hips and taking the king's arm. Some gazes were outright jealous, some angry, some blank, but most were calculating. Better he dance safely with me where I could keep his vision in line with Queen Jane. The Earl of Surrey, Norfolk's son, and the very man I despise most, watched me most intently, as if sensing keenly my distress. I somehow managed to keep my surprise at his appearance at bay. He snickered. I wanted desperately to wipe the image of his face, the stain of his past violation of me, from my mind. Why had he come to court? Sometimes I felt it was only to torment me.

Why all the sudden did it appear that nearly all my past would be coming back to haunt me? Now all we needed was for my brother Richard to return, and the court would be a merry hell indeed.

I ignored the begrudging scrutiny of the courtiers and court ladies and gave King Henry my full attention. Perhaps remembering earlier days would not be so bad, returning to youth before I had been soiled by the wantonness of court and viciousness of human nature. I wished for those happier, naïve days sometimes, and since the king had asked for it, and I was willing to give it, I did, letting myself fall completely for the music, the instruments leading my limbs in a swaying decadence.

When the dance ended, he led me back to the dais and to Jane.

"Your sister-by-marriage is a superlative dancer, my love." He kissed Jane on the forehead, and I was pleased his affection was so public.

The Duke of Suffolk approached. "Your Majesty, if you'll allow me to interrupt."

Henry's face split into a wide smile, just as it always did when Charles Brandon came around. The two were the best of friends, despite Suffolk marrying Henry's sister in secret... Poor Mary Tudor, may she rest in peace.

The king perfected a courtly turn of his leg. "If you'll excuse me, Madam, Lady Anne." He bowed first to his wife and then to me before disappearing with Suffolk into the crowd.

Jane patted the seat next to her. I moved to take it.

"Are you enjoying this evening?" she asked.

"I am. His Majesty's fool is at the top of his game tonight." As if on cue, the man jumped upon a table that housed a group intently playing cards. He switched around a few hands, which earned him a hard kick in the rear.

Jane laughed, the pure tinkling sound almost magical. I smiled in turn. She had that effect on people. One wished to be happy with her.

"Anne." She motioned me closer, and we leaned our heads together in confidence. She smelled of pears and honeysuckle and all manner of sweet things.

"I am nervous about tomorrow." She bit her lip, and I noticed the white in her knuckles as she entwined her fingers with mine. "How will the people accept me? I am their king's third wife and his last wife they despised. They all want so much from me. What if I fail to deliver it?"

Tomorrow she would enter London in state, taking a barge along the river. Rumor had it her entrance would be much more lavish than even that of Anne Boleyn's, at which Henry had spared no coin to see his new bride presented to the people.

"Oh, Jane, do not let your nerves work the better of you. You have a loving husband, the support of the people. Just look around." I motioned to the crowd of several scores of courtiers and court ladies. "Everyone here supports you. The people of London and indeed all of England are behind you."

She nodded, her eyes downcast. "Yes, but I have heard that there are those who secretly are not supportive. They believe I will put a stop to the Reformation, encourage Henry to make amends with the Pope."

Indeed, I knew there were those, especially the Howards, who had fears of such — nearly the entire last decade of Reformation had begun with their doing, or rather Anne Boleyn's, but was she so much an independent? With an uncle like Norfolk pulling the strings, it was more likely the puppet had followed the rule of her master.

And, secretly, I did hope that Jane would push the king to return to the old ways, the way of the true and right religion. I worried for the sake of our country and its people. A break from Rome and some of the most powerful European nations left us vulnerable. At any given moment we were enemies with one or the other of the Holy Roman Empire, Spain, or the French. God save us all if we were enemies with them all at one time.

But there was no arguing with the king and his desire to be Supreme Head of the Church. Breaking from Rome and the Pope made Henry richer and more powerful than any English king before him. But I dared not utter a word for or against anything and have advised Edward to remain a friend to all. For one whisper of our true beliefs could leave us with air above our shoulders and our heads tossed out like the rubbish in a chamber pot.

"Do not pay credence to rumors. Remember, the king wishes you to be his true and obedient wife. When the time is right, you might whisper to him of your opinions, but now is not that time and to do so only puts you at risk. Tongues will wag at will. Make nothing of the words spilling forth." I patted her hand and sat back. Already, wolves were hunkering closer to hear our words.

"You are my tower, Anne. Without you to lean against, I might succumb to my fears." She smiled for the sake of the onlookers, but her eyes betrayed her true feelings. If I were the queen and married to Henry, my eyes would show just as much fret and fear as hers. There had been a time in my girlish naïveté that I had held such hopes—to be a queen. But they had been only girlish fancies, and I had had such respect for Queen Katharine that I never would have gone to the lengths that Anne Boleyn had. And even *she*—God rest her soul—had garnered my respect.

"Nonsense, you are a strong woman Jane. And the king loves you. The people will, too."

"Yes, but there is still one thing I have not done, and I fear *he* might grow angry soon."

"My queen, you have only been married a week. These things take time. Edward and I have been married almost two years, and I have yet to conceive." I failed to tell her we had done so on purpose. She needed only to hear encouraging news. "Give it time, woo him to your bed often, be certain he is pleased and sated, and soon your belly will swell with growth."

A vibrant light came into her eyes, and she stood, offering me her hand. "Shall we dance, then?"

"Yes!" I stood, and we jumped enthusiastically into the dancing throng.

I swirled, twirled and hopped with each string of music, following the dance as I had been taught to do. But it was even more than just following the ritual steps. I truly loved to dance. My hips swayed, and my arms waved gracefully in the air before I clapped my hands. The freedom dancing brought, if only for a moment, took me away to a dream land.

My hand, up in the air as I clapped, was brought to the lips of Henry Howard—Surrey— sending a violent jolt of revulsion careening through me.

"At last we dance, *ma cherie*." He lifted me in turn, his hands gentle, his breath thick with wine.

As he was a Howard, I was already predisposed to despise him. And on top of that, every time I saw him, I felt pain.

I remembered his angry fists on me... tearing at my clothing, splitting my lip. But it had been gentle at first. Reading poems, holding hands, and making love to me with his words. Dancing with me at court, playing boules with me in the garden. It was innocent love, and love is what I had felt despite the cautious glances from my mother. For the first time I'd allowed myself to succumb to courtly love instead of being cautious. And I'd lost.

"*Kiss me, Anne. Show me what those sweet lips taste like.*" He had pulled me into an empty storeroom. But kissing had not been something I'd been ready for. I had spent nights awake dreaming of what his full lips would have felt like on mine, but when it had come down to the doing, I just had not been ready. I had resisted, tried to excuse myself, but his words had stilled me. "*Wherefore I would you wist, that for your coyed looks, I am no man that will be trapped, nor tangled with such hooks.*"

Anger, fierce and vicious, had flashed in his young eyes and I had been trapped by his wooing and then trapped by his unwanted ardor. He'd mistaken my innocent flirtations for being coy and wicked. I had tried to explain, but he had not understood. A true hothead if there ever was one. He had wanted only one thing and that had been satisfaction—gratification for the time he had spent wooing me.

His hands had been strong as he'd gripped my arms and brought his lips down hard on mine. I had tried to turn my head, but he'd held me there, blood dripping into my mouth, either from having bitten my own tongue or from him as he'd bitten my lips in an attempt to open my mouth to his invading tongue.

I had tried to scream, but his hard mouth had silenced me, and then the crack of his hand across my face had left me dizzy. Even still, I had pushed his hands away, tried to kick out, as he had yanked my skirts up and tore at the bodice of my dress. His fists had left bruises, his teeth had left marks.

Images of his rough body thrusting upon me sent bile rising to my throat. The only reason he could have been seeking me out was to rut around for information. Or worse still, he was on some sort of priggish progress to stroke his own ego. He so enjoyed to rub in my face that he had once held power over me. Our past was best kept buried deep in the very cesspits of purgatory.

"I am *not* your darling. We may dance, but do not think I will warm your bed this night or any other," I sneered, trying as hard as I could to put up a strong front, even though I only wanted to cower. My arm laced through his as we took the steps forward and back. I searched the crowd for Edward, hoping he might give me reprieve of my current suitor. I was pleased to see he'd returned to the great hall and that there was no woman on his arm, but my ire was pricked when he only smiled and gave me a wave of his hand. My heart pulsed rapidly. I was left to my own defenses, and it was about time I took charge.

"Who said anything about a bed, my lady? The cold stone floor will do for me." Surrey's face was close to mine, menace in his voice, wickedness in his eyes.

"Loathsome boar," I hissed. Just like Surrey to try to torment me. His perversion knew no bounds. I lifted my chin and squared my shoulders. I would not be a coward. He'd forever changed me, and never again would I bow to a man. Unless, of course, he was the King of England or my husband.

"Maddening wench," he retorted.

Our dance became vicious as he tossed me and turned me, and I stomped on his toe and pinched his arm. I wished to cause him harm. Tried to extricate myself from his grip. But it was all to no avail, and as I did not want to cause a scene, I continued to dance with the raping bastard.

"You consort often with the queen, *Lady* Beauchamp." His words were whispered on a breath and meant for my ears alone.

"Of course I do. She is my sister-by-marriage, our queen, and I most humbly serve her."

He snickered and twirled me around. "Aye, those things are true. But I say you prod too high above your origins."

I might have been the daughter of a knight and he the son of a duke, but it was my family relation who was the current queen, and his tie to the throne was dead and buried, so I snatched my hand away from his and stopped dancing. I now cared little for causing a disturbance. I only wanted to distance myself from the man who conjured up painful memories. "It is not I who gropes for more than what gifts and honors I receive from our most gracious sovereign. Your grandiose beliefs in your own importance are exactly that, grand flights of fancy, *my lord*. You'd drink the blood of any noble should it raise your status."

Surrey dipped in close to me. "You wound me with your tongue."

"I will do nothing with my tongue when it comes to you." I turned in a huff, needing the comfort of Edward's arms, his kind words. But before I could search him out in the crowd, Surrey gripped my hips tightly from behind, stopping me from walking. His fingers dug through the fabric of my gown and underskirts and bit into my flesh.

"Do not insult me, woman." He bit the shell of my ear gently. At once I was filled with repulsion and anger. Flashes of memories best left buried tormented my mind.

"Unhand me," I hissed, digging my nails into the backs of his hands.

He did so with a laugh and sauntered away, plucking a wine goblet from the hands of a courtier and downing it. He tossed the empty cup to the floor and twirled another lady around. The crowd laughed and clapped at his jubilant nature. But Surrey was anything but jubilant. He was a dangerous man. We Seymours would need to be wary of him, and me especially, for with tonight's encounter, I had an extreme sense of foreboding. The man may have wanted to see to the downfall of the Seymours, but worse, I felt he wanted to see me fall—and fall beneath him in a depraved and utterly horrific manner.

I walked from the court, my hips stinging where he'd likely bruised me. The evening entertainments no longer held their fancy for me, leaving a bitter taste to sweep over my tongue.

"How dare you make a mockery of me in front of the whole of court!" I shouted when Edward entered my bedchamber later that evening. The goblet of wine in my hand flew out as if by its own accord, smashing into the hearth. I stood to confront him, dressed only in my nightrail. Edward's indiscretions becoming more frequent and public.

I had no right to take notice of them; I knew I had no right. But after what I had endured...having to dance with Surrey. Having to pretend that every moment of it did not make my flesh crawl. I wanted more than Edward as a husband. I wanted love. I wanted more. Too much to ask, I knew, but I wanted it!

He stalked toward me, his brows drawn together, clothes in disarray, as if he'd only just left his lover's bed. I could smell her, the sweet, tangy scent of Mistress Darrell, *a whore*. How dare he? I could not stomach it, and my gut twisted, threatening to toss up my accounts.

He gripped my upper arms tightly, fingertips and nails biting into my flesh through the thin linen cloth of my attire. "Do you spew your scorn at me, *wife?*" His breath washed over me, strong with liquor, lips contorted in anger, spittle landing on my cheeks.

I wriggled free and stumbled away. I myself had had more than my fair share of wine this eve, and part of me intimated that I should go to bed, forget this confrontation, but it had already begun, and I was no longer in control of it.

"You are my wife, my property. I saved you from the vile hands of Surrey, and this is how you repay me?" He walked toward me, but this time did not lay his hands on my person. His angry breaths came quick, his chest visibly rising and falling. Arms waving out to take in all of our possessions. "Rose you up from the depths of a knight's daughter to be the sister to a queen, and yet you tell me who I can fuck? I give you my name, money, a title, a home, indeed your very life, madam." His face came within inches of mine. "I shall conduct myself however I deem fit, and you will suffer it," he growled.

"You speak to me of never making a cuckold of you like Catherine did, yet look what you do to me! You hypocrite," I said lowly.

Edward's eyes lit with rage, with the mention of his previous wife's name, and for the first time, I thought he might strike me. "Do not speak her name to me. You know never to speak her name!" He took a step back, hands curled into fists at his sides. "Never say her name again," he whispered.

He stumbled backward, head down, shaking it from side to side. I realized then just why he felt the need to flaunt his masculinity. Catherine had taken an ax to his bollocks, and he needed more than anything to have them reattached. When he looked up and his eyes met mine, they shone with regret, disgust. But for what I did not know. Did he regret marrying me? Was he disgusted with me? Or did he regret our argument? Was he disgusted with himself?

Whatever his reasons, I was made to swallow his words, although they hurt. For they were true enough, despite my mother's family background linked to royals. Who was I to suppose a say in anything he did? Was not it the way of women? We were brought up to obey our husbands, indeed made to say it when we vowed to honor and cherish them as well.

But no matter what the church, my mother, father, all of society said, I refused to bow to it. I was worth something. I was worthy of his respect. He may have saved me from Surrey's violent hands and certain ruin. He may have helped me to rise over the past year, but I helped him rise now. I stood tall, shoulders back, chin lifted as I faced him.

"My gratitude, your lordship, for giving a woman of such humble origins all she might need to thrive at court."

"Don't mock me, wife. I know your true heart." His gaze slid over me, filled at once with desire and something else, close to disdain.

"What do you know?" I asked, voice shaky.

"That you're as stubborn as you are cunning. You cannot fool me. Do not even try. Despite what you think of yourself, I still own you. You are mine and you will obey me."

My voice grew deeper with my anger, hurt, cracked on every few syllables. "Hear me now when I say, if this is how you conducted marriage with *her*, then you shall expect the same fate from me." Edward's eyes widened as he took in my words. "I am not your property, a cask of wine to be devoured and then pissed out. And you owe just as much to me for our current position in life as I owe to you."

Edward's lip curled into a sardonic smile, as he studied me, nodding as though coming to terms with what I'd said. He bowed. "I am humbled." He stood tall and gazed at me, taking me in. His face showed not a shadow of his feelings, but his eyes were dark, swirling pits of emotion. His soul was out on display, torn and tattered and lost. I'd cut him to the core with my words—and he knew I meant them. He came forward slowly, cautiously, until he was only inches away. His voice was soft, yet still bit hard. "One of the many reasons I married you. A serpent's tongue you have."

When he turned to leave, I didn't stop him. Hadn't the energy. Tonight's battle would forever change us, but perhaps for the better. Maybe now Edward would know that I refused to be trampled on. Perhaps tonight, I truly had become that viper.

# CHAPTER FIVE

*And with a beck full low he bowed at her feet,*
*In humble wise, as who would say, 'I am too far unmeet.'*
*~Henry Howard, Earl of Surrey*

*June 7, 1536*

"Disgusting fly!"

"Pardon me, my lady?" Edward asked, his eyes watching me curiously as I batted away a fly and a horde of gnats.

We sat on the king's barge, surrounded by courtiers, and not even the gentle breeze flowing off the Thames could break the thickness of the humid air. With each waft of summer wind, I either caught the scent of fish, garbage, sweet honeysuckle or lavender flowers, baker's bread, or smoke from cook fires along the shore. The menagerie of scents was overwhelming and turned my stomach, even with the meager contents of my light breakfast.

Today was unusually hot, and it seemed every bug in London had decided *I* would be a nice sweet to partake in. Even the lighter satin fabric of my gown did little to alleviate the heat. Would that I was a Grecian goddess who had men employed to fan away the heat—and only a thin swath of linen to wear.

"Nothing, my lord, just taking in the splendor that is the Thames on a summer morning." Sarcasm seeped into my voice, and I had to check myself. Luckily, Edward was the only one paying attention or some gossiping courtier might have taken it to mean I did not want to be at this joyous occasion. Because of our status, we were allowed on the barge that held King Henry and Queen Jane, along with Norfolk, Surrey, Edward's brother Tom, the Lady Mary, Suffolk and his wife, Catherine, and of course Henry's gentlemen of the privy chamber and Jane's ladies-in-waiting. All were dressed in their finest. Cloth of gold, satins in shimmery blues, silvers and greens. Jewels around their throats, and stacked on their fingers. An event at court was always the best time to show off your riches, wealth and status.

I looked down at my own fingers, bedecked with rubies, diamonds and sapphires. I supposed I was not any different. I turned to Edward, taking in his jeweled and feathered cap and diamond-studded doublet. Nor was he.

Edward smiled warily. Perhaps he was still conflicted about how to react around me after our argument from the previous evening. It was my fervent prayer that he would never flirt so openly and lecherously in my presence again. I did not know how much more of it I could take. He loved me well, our coming together was always passionate and pleasurable, but still I could not shake the thoughts of who else he was pleasuring. I bit my lip against whispering a plea for him to stay true to me. Eventually he would come back to me alone, as it had been right after we married. When court had forgotten of what a cuckold his father had made of him... But I wanted them to forget now. I wanted Edward for myself.

But it was not only Edward's infidelity that had my nerves on edge... My encounter with Surrey had left me even more incensed than I would have been if I had only just observed Edward with the light skirt. But seeing as how he had left me to my own defenses with the one person on earth he knew had stolen my innocence, using me without regard for my person—I was all the angrier with him.

Until now we'd been drifting at a leisurely pace along the Thames, but suddenly the barge shifted forward with a surge of power, letting us know the procession was now in progress. I gripped the rail to steady myself and placed comfort in the strong and steady grip of Edward on my elbow. Edward and I took our places among the elite who were privileged to ride with King Henry and Queen Jane on their procession from Greenwich to Whitehall. This was Jane's entering London in state, and for a girl who'd never been raised to take her place as a royal, Queen Jane stood up to her new title with all the stoicism a queen could gather. She waved with regal poise to the gathering crowds along the shores, her back straight, head held high. Her hair was impeccably curled and styled, her ivory silk and lace gown with gold embroidery, pearls and emeralds was in perfect order, and a delicate gold crown sat upon her head.

Several of the barges in front of us held musicians seated in neat little rows. I watched their mouths and fingers working.

"Jane, my wife, my love. Hear you the music?" King Henry asked.

Jane smiled and nodded. "'Tis beautiful."

"Written just for you," he answered in a low voice that was only heard by a few surrounding them, "by me."

Jane gasped and tilted up on tiptoes to place a kiss on Henry's lips. Many years had passed since the king had sought to compose his own music. He was an excellent weaver of notes and verse. Many of his compositions were played at court often. But what an honor for Jane, that he'd come back to music just for her.

I turned back to the barges holding those special players, the song a delight to the senses. Never before had I been privileged enough to see them play from such a vantage point. My position was usually upon the shore or at a window. But even still, I had never seen a procession quite as bold and magnificent.

Music filled the air with a sense of mysticism. I took a moment to look at the blue sky, a few clouds floating with an innocence that made me remember my days as a girl. How I wished to lie upon their fluffy softness. The music was joyous and filled the bubbling courtiers and court ladies with smiles. King Henry's teeth shone white around a proud smile, and even England's new queen had a modest curl to her lip.

The sounds of sackbuts, shawms and drumslades floated over the river. The mixture of woodwind instruments, booming drums and regal trumpets was astonishing. Even the instruments held new and powerful beauty. Upon the river they were clearer, ringing out in all their glory to the new queen.

Soon, the flies and gnats were forgotten, and I found myself swaying to the music and all it represented. Jane was queen. The Seymours had risen. We would prevail.

I squeezed Edward's hand and was rewarded with his own flex of fingers. He was forgiven for the moment in my mind, and in that silent treaty, we once again forged an alliance with each other to spread our wealth, build our name, and grow our status within the realm.

As we passed the Tower of London, the beginning of a four-hundred-gun salute startled me, but soon my blood pumped in tune. Cannons answered the Tower's call on barges with booming salutes of their own. What great pomp and squalor! And all for Jane! Magnificent, and yet, unassuming, Jane!

But a sudden thought squelched my joy for a moment. *Did anyone remember that just a fortnight ago those same guns cracked in the air to signal the death of Anne Boleyn?*

I took a moment to look around, my mouth suddenly dry. Courtiers smiled, waved, cheered. Merchants, nobles and peasants alike waved and ran up and down the shores, trying to catch a glimpse of us as we passed. Even some arms and heads dangled from the barred windows of the Tower.

The king was his charming self in that moment as well, loudly proclaiming his pleasure.

Then it struck me. The people mirrored the moods of the king. If he was in mourning—they mourned. If he was angry—they rallied for justice on his part. If he was filled with merriment—they laughed and danced. We were all little puppets, and the world, the king's stage. We cheered today, but what would we do tomorrow? Or even tonight?

"Are you not well?" Edward leaned down, his forehead touching mine for less than a second.

I sighed at the irony. "I was only recalling the last time we heard the loud booms of cannons."

Edward hissed a breath. "Do not even think it."

I only nodded, washing my mind of thoughts of Anne Boleyn. Edward was right. I could not even *think* it. "My mother and Sir Richard shall come to court soon." The excitement was noticeably absent from my voice.

Edward inclined his head. "I have heard he shall be made High Sheriff of Surrey."

"Mmm hmm."

"How very fortunate they have returned to favor with the king, being your kin. This is good news, is it not?"

"'Tis indeed good for them."

"But not for you?" Edward leaned a little closer to make our conversation more private despite the loud goings-on of the procession, which would hardly let anyone overhear us.

"Sheriff of Surrey, Edward. Do you not understand?"

"Ah." Edward stroked my arm reassuringly. "But Sir Richard shall answer to the king and not Henry Howard."

I wanted to ask why he'd not rescued me from the loathsome Henry Howard, Earl of Surrey, the night before, but I held my tongue, not wanting to start another fight, especially on this monumental occasion.

"'Tis a fact, but they shall still have contact with me, more than enough contact. I worry overmuch for my family."

"And for yourself?"

"Yes." I chose to confess Henry Howard's threats from the night before. "Surrey says he wants to see me fall. 'Tis a perfect opportunity to try to bring me to heel."

"But you forget one thing, love."

"What is that?"

"You are married to *me*. I shall see that no harm comes to you."

I nodded, fearing that the only response I could give would be to ask where he was the night before when I needed him. I gazed up at the Tower as we passed. Great streamers and banners hung from its walls depicting the king's and queen's initials, their arms, and Jane's motto, the phoenix rising, a representation of renewal through

73

Jane's own self-sacrifice. She promised to renew the Tudor dynasty, to have it hold steadfast through the birth of a prince. A grave and somber day it would be if Jane could not uphold her promise. So many promises uttered from lips, but how could one really have guaranteed their validity? Even Edward's promises to keep us safe from the Howards... Edward was smart, formidable even, but the Howards were strong, too, maybe stronger. I crossed myself quickly and said a prayer.

*Sweet child of God, Jesus, bring us a prince. Keep us safe!*

Our barge slowed its pace and gently rocked back and forth. I tightened my arm on Edward's to steady myself. I was not used to riding in the barge quite yet—this only my second time. My legs were made for walking or riding a horse. The rocking, no matter how benign, still seemed to throw my balance off.

Jane turned around and caught my eye. I was taken aback by the joyful sparkle in her gaze. Why did it feel like ages since I had seen her so truly pleased?

We passed beneath London Bridge. White and yellow posy petals floated through the air, landing in Jane's hair like snowflakes in the winter. Children and women stood atop the bridge, tossing flowers and wreaths down on us.

The king plucked a few petals from Jane's hair. "She loves me, she loves me not. She loves me, she loves me not. She loves me!"

The people cheered in reaction, and Henry grasped Jane to him for a kiss. This only caused further shouts from the people, and even we courtiers joined in.

When finally he let her go, Jane waved while Henry tossed gold coins to the people, some of the gold falling recklessly and forever into the water, the ripples in its murky depths the only proof they were once there.

After High Mass, we returned to Whitehall, where a hunt had been arranged, followed by a picnic, dancing, and tonight there would be fireworks. The heat started to get to me, though, and when we disembarked from the barge, I declined to attend the afternoon festivities and retired to my room. I was sweating, lightheaded and touched by a bit of nausea. I swayed on my feet. I would not have been able to stand much longer—even on solid ground.

I did not know whether it was the infernal heat and my wretched gown or the rocking of the barge that had done me in. Either way, I barreled into my room and slammed the door shut, beckoning Jenny to me.

"Help me, girl." I tore at my gown, my movements rushed, frantic, only seeking the relief of being free from it. Jenny's fingers flew over the ties of my gown and corset, stripping me down to my chemise.

"My lady, this might help." My maid handed me a great fan with an ivory handle.

I greedily snatched it from her fingers and fanned myself, waving for her to hand me the mug in her hand as well. I tipped the mug to my lips, the pleasure of cool liquid against my tongue enough to elicit an appreciative moan. Liquid dribbled over my chin onto my chest, but I did not care. I drank the entirety with great gulps, until finally I felt somewhat myself.

Jenny rushed to open the shutters at my window. But even with the window thrown open, the air was still stifling. It was only mid-June, and already the heat was so unbearable.

I flopped onto the bed and continued to fan myself, wishing I could stay in my room the rest of the evening.

"Anne, are you feeling better?"

What little reprieve I'd had was over. Alas, Edward had come to fetch me. My solitude at an end, I curled my lip with disappointment.

"As best I can be with this infernal heat."

Edward chuckled. "Perhaps we ought to make a progress north, where it is a little cooler?"

I sat up, excited with the idea, especially knowing that soon it would be even hotter. "I would enjoy that immensely."

He nodded. "For now, as the new reigning family in court, we must show our faces, thwart rumors, uncover any plots."

"Impeccable judgment, my lord."

I tossed my feet over the side of the bed and stood, sauntering toward Edward. His heated gaze raked over my frame, almost as if until now, he had no idea I was in only my thin-as-air chemise. I hungrily soaked up his admiration. His ardor reinforced my

75

conclusion regarding his adultery—he was seeking to replace his manhood. But it was my place as his wife to make him feel that way, was it not? I could make him feel like more of a man in more ways than one. I could bed him well, and I could keep him informed of court secrets, help him gain more power.

Edward reached out and with one finger, trailed a path from my collarbone to the ribbons tying my chemise in place over my breasts. With one gentle tug he could have the fabric gaping open and my breasts exposed for his viewing. He fingered the silky ties for a moment before turning away. "You could tempt an angel, Anne."

"Want to be my angel?" I teased.

He laughed and turned back, pulling me in for a kiss. I melted against him, living fully in this moment of abandon, a moment where conspiracies, risks, and ascension were not in the forefront of our minds. Only the two of us, our bodies, our desires. But it ended all too quickly.

"Dress for now. Later, we will... abide our baser appetites?"

I nodded, my lips still tingling and my mind not ready to take on the machinations of court.

By the time I was ready for Edward to escort me to the great feast Henry had planned in Jane's honor, my undergarments were already soaked through with sweat. The sun had yet to set, and my only hope was that once the dark of night fell, a cool breeze would waft in from the windows to ease my suffering.

We walked together down the corridor of our joint chambers, through the many winding passageways, down spiral staircases, until we reached the great hall already swelling with courtiers. The scents of bread, succulent meats and sweets reached my nose. Music pulsed in the air. Hands were clapping, mouths were singing, cheering.

King Henry's court in celebration was one to be rivaled. Never would a courtier say they were not entertained when imbibing on the king's good hospitality and talent for merrymaking.

Again the image of puppets came to mind. I prayed the king was still in such a convivial mood on the morrow.

And I prayed that I could keep Edward satisfied and in my bed tonight.

*June 8, 1536*

Edward had been sent on an errand by the king. He would be gone nearly a fortnight, and in the meantime I was responsible for retaining the Seymour status at court. Luckily for us, Edward now had the power to appoint his allies in key posts within the royal household, even as lowly as a mere groom. Our own spies were everywhere, keeping us well informed as to the goings-on with both courtiers and the royal couple.

I finished writing a few letters of correspondence, sealed them in wax, stamped them with my crest and was handing them to a waiting groom when Jenny rushed in. "My lady, Sir Anthony Browne has come to address you."

*Anthony?* My lips thinned, and I drummed my fingertips on the desk. We hadn't spoken directly since that evening exactly the week before.

"Send him in please." I rubbed my hands against the length of my gown, half to smooth the wrinkles out and half to wipe the nervous sweat from my palms.

I stood by the hearth as he came in, sweeping a low bow to me in such a way that I was able to peruse his form with female appreciation. Such broad shoulders, a narrow waist and long, lithe legs. A little flutter of butterflies danced in my belly. I squared my shoulders and prepared to fend off any and all physical reactions to the handsome, charming man of the privy chamber.

"I trust your morning is going well, Sir Anthony? What news do you bring?"

He stood, his eyes flashing with humor. "My lady, might I come only to inquire on your health and happiness?"

"You might, but both you and I know there must be some other reason for ambling down the hall from His Majesty's chambers and to my own. Especially when you are aware my lord husband is away."

He chuckled at that, turned to a footman. "Some wine."

The footman rushed to fill two goblets and handed them to us each. I nodded to the servants, who quickly left the room, the door closing quietly behind them. Sir Anthony sat in a high-backed chair, the cushion I had embroidered myself of a wolf howling at the moon.

"You are a very astute woman. A formidable woman."

I smiled and took a sip of my wine, letting it mull on my tongue a moment before swallowing. I did not see myself as thus. I was merely a woman who had opinions, an education and a mind to use it for my own good. "Formidable? Am I really so terrifying?" I perfected a coquettish turn of my head and slight curtsy, my hips moving gently, arms delicately at my sides. The move had the desired effect, and Anthony smiled, laughed and patted his knee.

"Come sit, right here."

If I had drunk several casks of wine, I *might* have indulged him, but instead I took the seat opposite him, as was proper, and set down my wine on the table beside me, afraid he'd see how it shook in my hands. As much as the man would persuade me to form a more intimate companionship with him, I would hold my ground in my refusal. Edward was my priority, and as I had promised him, I would not do anything to jeopardize that. Despite how many wells he'd dipped his wick into.

"Suit yourself, my lady. My lap will be barren without you."

I waved away his flirtations and narrowed my eyes, now truly curious about his visit, and trying to subdue my heightened interest in the man's appealing lap. What draw did this man hold for me? I couldn't figure it out to be anything other than him pursuing me, desiring me, and me being able to push him away or pull him closer.

"To what do I owe the pleasure of your company?"

"Ah, I see, no idle chitchat with Lady Beauchamp. Very well, I have come to inform you that a new Act of Succession has been passed in parliament. It states that when King Henry passes on to heaven," at this, he crossed himself, as did I, "the crown will be passed on to Queen Jane's children, a right noble, virtuous and excellent lady."

Keeping my face void of emotion, I said, "I am aware of this already, sir, as it was passed several days ago."

"Yes, but the part which continues to decree his previous daughters, the Ladies Mary and Elizabeth, as illegitimate and without rights to the throne is what I thought might interest you."

"How would that interest me?"

"Are you not a supporter of Mary?" He leaned forward, his fingers gently caressing my hands, which lay folded in my lap. I bit the inside of my cheek to keep from sighing at the pleasant sensation that made my skin tingle and pushed his hands away.

I dare not tell this man that Mary and I had been close friends as children—even though she was six years my junior. My caring for her was personal and nothing more, and I'd never let it influence the Seymour goals in any direction. Jane's children would always come before any of King Henry's other offspring.

"I have been a friend of Mary's for some time. I served her mother."

"And?"

"And that does not mean I wish *her* to come before the children of our own current, right and true queen." For I had to always support Jane and the Seymours if I was to see myself rise in position. I could very well be a duchess one day. "What is the meaning of this, sir?"

The conversation was bordering on treasonous, and I was not interested in taking part.

"My lady, please, no need to get your pluck up. I am your friend, your most humble servant." He got down on his knees before me, sucking the breath from my lungs. What in all of London was he doing? He pressed his lips to my hands, my knees, his hands gripping mine.

"My lord!" I hissed, trying to pull my hands from his, clamping my knees firmly together. I searched frantically around the room, feeling relief and disappointment that there was not another soul in the room. If there had been, he would have ceased this foolishness!

"Do not deny me, Anne." More kisses were pressed to my fingertips. "I am but here to make a pact with you."

He stood abruptly, as if his own passion had startled even himself. I was stunned speechless. Never had a man, not even Edward, groveled at my feet. Anthony began to pace. 'Twas a

79

completely new experience, one that was frightening yet liberating at the same time. As much as I was tempted, I could never indulge him, but all the same it was a flattering concept. Was it possible that this man, Anthony, held more than a passing fancy for me? Or was it simply my body he wished to conquer? I narrowed my eyes, suddenly suspicious that perhaps he had a bone to pick with Edward and sought to gain his revenge by taking me to bed.

I opened my mouth to say just that, but he interrupted me.

"The whole of court, London and England, might be fooled, but you have not let your ruse go by on me!"

"What?" I whispered, shocked and confused.

"Edward is at once owned by one and all. He is friend to everyone, enemy of no one, and each body and soul believes he is on their side. I know you are the one who leads the strings. You are the one who makes the decisions. I've seen him look at you for approval before acting, and I know how much Queen Jane seeks your council."

"Sir Anthony, if you will, relay your purpose." I pinched my lips closed tightly, disgusted with his antics. To try to fool me into thinking he had feelings... the cad!

"See!" He thrust his finger out, pointing at me, a broad smile on his lips. "Lady Anne is the one behind the wheel, captain of the ship and most forthright." He stopped abruptly in front of me. "I want to be first mate. To walk beside you."

"You cannot, *Sir* Anthony. We cannot. 'Tis not appropriate given I am married." My heart constricted in my chest, and I could not help but gaze at his alluring, yet completely forbidden, mouth. I almost snorted with self-disgust.

"Then let me be the sails, let me propel you forward, let me whisper to you of the wind."

"Enough with poetical innuendos. Out with it! Are you proposing to be my eyes and ears?"

A small dimple appeared in the crest of his cheek as his smile broadened. "At last, the lady has seen the light."

"Why?"

"We all have a part to play and wishes to see granted. I do believe we want the same things. What better way than to work together to ensure the future of the realm? Of ourselves?"

"I do not think we want the same things at all, Sir Anthony." I glanced toward his lap where he'd begged me to sit not long ago, a shadow of doubt regarding my statement creeping into my mind.

"'Haps that is the case, but I do know we both want the Seymour faction to persevere, and that we are both enemies of the Howards."

I eyed Anthony critically. Perhaps this friendship had merit. I desperately wanted Edward to gain power—be elevated from viscount to duke. Mayhap any information I gained from Anthony would help. Then Edward would be true to me, and only me. He would see how I had elevated him, loved him, been loyal to him alone. I was a hundred times the woman Catherine Filiol was. But the question remained: What did Sir Anthony desire? "How can I trust you, sir? Perhaps you seek my friendship only to taunt my husband?"

Anthony laughed at this. "Taunt Lord Beauchamp? Never, my lady. You may hold the strings when you are with him, but the man is formidable in his own right as well."

"What do you seek to gain in return?"

"A title, holdings."

I nodded. He wanted what everyone desired. "And trust?"

He held out his hands, imploringly. "How can I prove my loyalty?"

"You mentioned friends at court."

"Ah, that I did." His wicked grin returned.

My nipples tightened, and I stood abruptly and walked to the window to hide the reaction of my body to his smile. I felt him before I even heard him, the heat of his body behind mine as he came up to the window. He was too close. I would have done better to stay in my seat.

I turned, only to find him inches away.

"Set up a meeting, Sir Anthony." I ducked away from him and went again to the hearth. I could not seem to get far enough from the man, and from the growing attraction taking over my being.

81

"You seem out of breath, my lady? Are you not well?" But the devilish twinkle in his eyes told me he knew exactly why I was having trouble breathing. *Rogue.*

"'Tis the infernal heat." I rushed to pick up my fan Jenny had left on a side table for me, and then I sat back down, still too stunned by how Anthony's presence provoked me, made me insane. 'Haps it was that Edward and I were not getting on so well, and Anthony was offering me attention. Regardless his plans for an alliance, real desire emanated in his eyes and despite how it went against my morals—I liked it.

Anthony narrowed his gaze, watching me for what seemed like an hour, when only seconds passed. He came closer, knelt before me again and laid his head in my lap. Unable to stop myself, I reached out and stroked his hair before I realized what I had done. It was thick and soft and soothing. I gasped and yanked my hand away.

"Sir Anthony, please. You must remove yourself from my person." I was completely undone. Edward was the only other man to illicit a response from me.

The only other man to touch me had been Surrey. I'd given those little sparks a chance to burst. Wondered at his flirtations and taken a leap. And he'd wickedly taken advantage of my naïveté, however many years older I was than he. Flirting with me outrageously and leading me on until the moment he'd taken it too far. Men were not to be trusted. I had avoided all intimate contact with men up until the present, keeping my distance, remaining impartial, aloof, never giving all of myself. How could I after watching my beloved Katharine of Aragon sob every time her husband took a lover, and then when she died of heartache when he set her aside. Why was it, that now, with Anthony, things were changing? I pushed at him to get off of me. Why was my body, my mind, betraying me?

"My apologies, my lady." He lifted his head, and for a moment I could no longer breathe. He looked as if he might kiss me. But I turned away and placed the fan between our lips, flicking it furiously. He stayed on his knees.

"A secret for you, my lady."

I waited with bated breath.

82

"If Jane does not have a son, King Henry will see to it that his bastard son, the Duke of Richmond, succeeds to the throne. He has already drawn the papers up, and bribes have been accrued to sway parliament in his direction."

My eyes widened. "Thank you." I did not share my opinion on his words, but merely gave him my appreciation for such news. When Edward returned, there was much work to be done to make certain that Henry's bastard by Elizabeth Blount, did not make it to the throne. Jane must bear us a prince!

"Will two days work for you?" His gaze caught mine, eyes heavily lidded, his lips partially opened I wanted to run my fingers over them, see if they felt as soft as they looked.

"Two days?"

"The king and queen are hosting a garden party. I will see to it that you are introduced to several connections at court that will be beneficial to you and our cause."

"Cause?" I hated asking questions like this, like some sort of dull-witted lump, but I had been so distracted I lost track of our conversation. This man was dangerous for me. I prided myself on my quick wits.

"The Lady Mary—if, for some reason," Anthony paused and crossed himself, "Jane doesn't bear a son, shouldn't Lady Mary be next in line and not the bastard?"

I narrowed my gaze. "I did make myself clear that I will not be party to any machinations that endanger Queen Jane, did I not?"

"With respect, my lady, we also want only what is best for Queen Jane and her issue. We also seek to see the Lady Mary restored to her rightful position at court."

I nodded. "And what of the Duke of Richmond? Where do these friends of yours stand with him?"

"They are in agreement with myself, that only those *legitimate* heirs should have rights to the throne—Lady Mary and Jane's children."

"What of Princess Elizabeth?" Anne Boleyn's child was also a legitimate child once.

"She is not our concern. The girl will most likely take after her mother's rash and radical behavior and beliefs. What good could come of having her on the throne?"

I nodded. Anne Boleyn had changed the face of a country, and ravaged everyone in her path—though not always her fault. Nevertheless, having her child on the throne sent fear barreling through my blood, for wouldn't she seek vengeance on those who'd been disloyal to her murdered mother?

I stood, dismissing Sir Anthony. "Two days then."

He raised to his full height, bowed to me and grasped my hand. His lips brushed my knuckles, and he whispered, "Nothing brings me greater pleasure than doing as you command."

"I do not care who she's meeting with..." came the voice of Edward's brother Thomas beyond the door, and then he burst through.

My hand was still held in Anthony's, fingers nearly touching his lips. We instantly looked guilty, as Thomas' eyes went from me to Anthony. Thomas' brows furrowed, and a spark of anger filled his dark gaze. My cheeks flamed, and I forced my eyes, which had been wide, to close slightly.

"Sir Anthony. What are you doing here?" His voice was cold and hard, not at all curious about the visit, but accusing.

"He came to see Edward about a matter of state," I interjected.

My brother-by-marriage's chest was puffed out, and he grunted. I willed the heat away from my face. Edward's first wife had ruined any chances I might ever have of being thought of as innocent. I could see Thomas had already judged me and found me guilty.

"Edward is not here, Sir Anthony. You should well know that."

Anthony was quick to recover, dropping my hand and standing again at full height. He stepped forward, an easy smile on his face. "I know it well, Sir Thomas. 'Tis simply that I needed to know where to send my missive, and I figured Lady Beauchamp would be the quickest way to gain access to it."

"You could have asked me."

"Indeed, I searched for you but could not find you. Where were you?"

Thomas clamped his jaw tight, and a vein popped out in his neck. "None of your affair."

Where had my brother-by-marriage been? Now I was judging someone who looked more guilty than innocent.

"My apologies, sir," Anthony said with a bow.

"Never mind." He gave Anthony one last glare before turning suspicious eyes on me. "Anne, I came to see if you might need escort to the queen's chambers for the evening meal?"

"Yes, thank you."

We all exited my chambers in silence. I was relieved for the moment to have disaster averted and thanked God in heaven that Thomas hadn't barged in while Anthony's head had been on my lap.

Sir Anthony might have been helping me inadvertently to regain my husband's full attention, but he was a danger. A liability. One I was not certain I could trust altogether, and now I would have Thomas' eyes on me, too.

*June 10, 1536*

The gods had blessed us. Somehow they'd provided for a beautiful summer day, without the sweltering heat. Even a light breeze blew. Fountains churned and flowed water into the gorgeous ponds dotted with swans and lily pads. The crunch of gravel under feet on the various walkways served as a background hum to the chatter of courtiers and ladies and lightly played strings of the musicians.

Garden parties at Hampton Court could only be rivaled by those at Versailles in France—or so Anne Boleyn had lamented about to her ladies in her presence chamber—but I would never say such a thing to King Henry, who already felt the competition flowing harshly between himself and King Francis.

A game of boules was being played on the green, the king himself in the lead. I watched as he bent a leg forward, another behind and then with the smooth black ball in his hand, he swung back and flung it forward, knocking several others out of the way.

Those observing the game clapped at his superior skills, to which Henry bowed.

Next up was Sir Anthony Browne. I averted my eyes, our meeting from two days prior still fresh in my mind. We hadn't spoken alone since that time. The sun was beginning to paint an orange and purple rainbow on the horizon. Nightfall would arrive soon, and I had yet to be introduced to anyone like he'd promised.

I turned at the rustle of skirts behind me. A maid I did not recognize stood, hands clutched together, the only outward sign she was nervous.

"My lady, come with me, please."

"Pardon?" I frowned that a servant.

"I was sent to fetch you," she said, eyes darting. "My lady said you would forget but to remind you of your arrangement to meet."

Light dawned with her words. The promised connection. "Ah, yes. Lead the way."

I followed as she led me quickly through a maze of shrubs so tall they towered easily two feet above me. When she stopped, I was confronted by a cloaked and shadowed figure. The sun found it hard to reach all the way inside the maze.

The maid curtsied, collected coins from the figure, and then disappeared.

I stood still, shoulders squared, waiting for the person to reveal her identity to me. Finally, after what seemed like several minutes, two pale, delicate hands slipped from the folds of the dark fabric and pulled back the hood, revealing a jeweled hood atop silky chestnut locks. The lady's piercing emerald eyes took me in.

I gasped, my shock evident at seeing the Marchioness of Exeter. Standing before me was a powerful woman. One who'd had no qualms about remaining in contact with Queen Katharine after she was set aside. One who'd approached Chapuys about placing Lady Mary on the throne—even though she denied it and no proof was ever found.

"My lady," I muttered, unable to say more. She had been banished from court and in hiding ever since. The king and his council suspected her of treason and had even ravaged her houses looking for incriminating correspondence. But to no avail.

"Lady Anne." She walked forward, her gait slow and purposeful. A small smile curved her pink lips, and little wrinkles appeared at the sides of her eyes. "I've been told by a mutual friend you were looking for more... acquaintances."

I blocked out the sudden sense of foreboding that rippled along my flesh. Joining forces with a woman suspected of treason could only end in a blade against my neck. I swallowed hard. There was still time for me to turn around and leave, pretend I hadn't seen her. Yell for the guard to come and arrest her.

There was Edward, too. How would he feel about me linking our name to that of Exeter?

I took a step back for a moment, fully prepared to leave. But I thought better of it. I could use a woman like Lady Exeter to gain support from those who felt Mary should have been on the throne. Her supporters were vast, the majority of England, which upset the king most. But if they were on our side, on Edward's side... then perhaps Edward could persuade the king to embrace his daughter once more. Bring the king once again in full command of his country, which was now so divided. Avoid civil war. In the end, protecting Jane.

A relationship with someone like the marchioness could lead to power—or my undoing. Without thought, I rubbed my wrist, feeling the strong heartbeat beneath my skin. It was dangerous, that was for certain. If things were to go wrong, that strong beat beneath my fingertips would cease.

*Without risk, there is no gain.*

"You'll excuse my surprise, my lady, I was not aware that I would be gaining an acquaintance of your reputation," I remarked, chin thrust forward.

Lady Exeter chuckled, deep and throaty, her little white teeth showing between her lips. "Lady Anne, you are one to speak on reputations. I am surprised we have not become friends before now."

At this, I smiled. Lady Exeter was a smart and daring woman. I instantly liked her. "Fair enough."

"Might I enlighten you on how we can find a relationship to be mutually beneficial?"

I took a moment before answering, wanting her to think I was truly at odds with how to respond—even though I had already decided to correspond with her. "If it pleases you."

"Ever the female courtier, Lady Anne." She walked a few feet to a white, marble bench and sat down, arranging her cape over the mossy-green brocade fabric of her skirts. "I am on very good terms with the Lady Mary and with Ambassador Chapuys."

I nodded. "This I know."

"Did you also know that I am close friends with the Duchess of Suffolk? That I dine frequently with the Countess of Salisbury?"

I pursed my lips, knowing that these women would certainly be able to provide me with the means to gain information regarding the Howards and the state of the political current. Lady Exeter could tell us who was plotting what, should I require it.

"The duchess and her husband invite me to dinner often. Suffolk himself is like a brother to the king. But, alas, while he shares information with the marquess and I, he is reluctant to sing our praises to the king."

"I would not doubt it given their past volatile relationship," I said. "The king has already banished him from court once for marrying his sister, imagine what he'd do for consorting with the king's enemies?"

"He seems to think we only need bide our time before he can whisper our names before the king."

"And Lady Salisbury? Your relationship with her alone is dangerous. Her son Reginald Pole has sided with the pope, openly berating King Henry's break with Rome—and laying his own claim to the throne. He is being sought after for offenses against the king as we speak." I swallowed hard. Never would the king know my own true Catholic heart.

The marchioness chuckled again. "But do not you see? Lady Salisbury and her eldest son, Lord Montague, would do anything to prove to our king that they have no ties to Reginald Pole. They would not see their own heads on pikes gracing London Bridge."

I narrowed my gaze and took a step forward. "And what exactly are you saying?"

"They will give Reginald up... They will tell where he hides in return for favor within court—favor you can restore to them. They'll give him up for their very lives. But they won't tell just anyone. They will only tell me."

"And you will give up the man to the king's guard?"

"Not I, but my lord husband. Once we have returned to court." She stood and walked over to me, her hand fluttering out to tuck a stray hair back into my headpiece. "I am also *not* a Cromwell supporter."

Now this made me smile, for who really was besides the king? Lowly Cromwell's sway over the king would soon come to an end, I was certain of it. "I see we shall be very good friends indeed."

"My husband is also *not* a Cromwell supporter. Help to put our name back to rights. Gain us entrance back at court, and together we shall see Cromwell, the puppet master of the king, fall. The lowborn son of a drunkard should never be allowed to plan the fates of those born of royal and noble blood."

I dipped a curtsy. "I could not agree more."

Now I just needed to convince Edward of the same. We needed friends, the more the better in order for us to gain leverage and for me to become a duchess.

# CHAPTER SIX

*But such a scornful cheer, wherewith she him rewarded!*
*Was never seen, I believe, the like, to such as well deserved.*
*~Henry Howard, Earl of Surrey*

*June 11, 1536*

"But you have influence, my dear." My mother's calculating eyes flashed with anger as she stalked across my presence chamber to grasp a cup of wine from the sideboard.

Sir Richard Page, my stepfather, shouted, "For Christ's sake, Anne, your sister-by-marriage is the queen!"

I bit back a retort and instead mustered enough willpower to give them their due respect as my mother and her husband, as I had been taught, despite my instincts raising arms about it... "Yes, she is. However, if the king does not wish to give you apartments at court, who am I to gainsay him? Is it not pleasing enough that he should make you Sheriff of Surrey?"

Mother rolled her eyes heavenward, arms tossed up in the air with disgust. "What good came of bringing you to court, immersing you in this life, and seeing you elevated, if you will not offer help to your own mother and father?"

I refrained from reminding her that Page was not my father, and thank God for that. His ambition and willingness to put his family at risk reminded me all too much of my own brother Richard.

"A sheriffdom? Really, Anne, do you think I have no ambition? I want a title! I want more land. The only way I can ensure that happens is if I am housed at court," Sir Richard Page railed.

"I shall inquire, if it pleases you," I responded, although I had no plans to do so. The fact that the king had seen fit not to give them apartments meant they had to rent a home in London, and, quite frankly, I much preferred that. More to the point, they'd only recently been banished from court. One must accept the meager crumbs offered before gobbling the meal.

"Well, Lizzie shall stay with you until you make it so." Page pursed his lips and furrowed his brows, challenging me to say otherwise, regarding my eleven-year-old half-sister.

"I will see about placing her in a room with some other girls her age." Lizzie sat on a nearby bench, her lip curled sardonically. The illusion was disturbing. She was the image of her father, and I could almost see her meddling in other people's affairs or, at the very least, spying for her father.

"We should like it better if she were to be in yours and Lord Beauchamp's apartments," my mother stated, her jaw set.

Their insistence made it clear the only reason they wanted Lizzie with me was for their own personal information, making me more determined to have her placed elsewhere.

I took a deep breath and centered my gaze on first my mother and then Sir Richard. "I understand your desires. However, it will be beneficial for Lizzie's training if she is housed with other girls. This will allow her to make friendships and keep their same hours." I glanced at my mother. "You recall when you brought me to court that I was also housed with other girls and not yourself?" My mother nodded, her lips pinched so tightly together they were only a thin white line. "And, as you well know, Lord Beauchamp and I are extremely busy with court matters. I have not the time currently to take Lizzie under my wing."

A loud knock at the door interrupted their replies, and I was grateful for it. The conversation had become dull, and I no longer wished to argue the merits of why I would not bend to their will. I'd surely ruined any respect my mother had had for me as a dutiful daughter, but I could not forget the past. They'd both been there and done nothing about Surrey's flirtations. They'd seen him drag me from the hall, both intent, from what I'd learned later, on trapping him into marriage, no matter the pain it caused me.

Sir Richard Stanhope, my eldest brother, sauntered into the room. *Oh, dear God in heaven!*

When it rained it poured! Why was God punishing me so? I glanced toward the sideboard, where wine goblets, pre-poured, sat out. I needed the extra courage even a few sips of wine could provide.

Richard was tall, as Michael was, his dark hair unruly and skin tan from serving the king as a knight and spending much of his time outdoors. He wore a fancy embroidered doublet of black and green, a codpiece that was grossly overstated, and soft leather boots.

He entered the room with a sneer on his face. "Lady Page." He bowed. "Sir Richard, Lizzie. Dear Anne." His voice belied the endearment. He came forward and kissed my cheek, the bristles of his short beard scratching against my skin.

When he straightened, he looked about the room, taking in the contents and apparently finding them lacking. "Well, I see the whole family is nearly here to beg favors from the one member who has been so elevated in courtly status."

Disgust radiated through me. I may have been elevated, but I deserved it, and if anything, I had suffered more than most of them. And how like Richard to have been so blunt and honest. Here I was, in a room filled with those I either detested or resented — except for Lizzie, whom I barely knew.

I put on my lady-of-the-court's face and tamped down my feelings. Delving into the past would do nothing now. "Richard, I am so glad to see you have returned. I take it your progress went well?"

He snorted in disgust and stalked to a nearby table, plucking an apple from a bowl. He bit into the fruit, and juices spilled over his chin. "I was successful, and still the king keeps my own great reward from me. I seek marriage. And I've an eye for a sweet wife of high birth."

My stepfather let out a burst of taunting laughter. "And you think your sister can help you there, boy?"

Richard flamed at the derogatory remark—for he was over thirty winters—making a sucking sound on his teeth with his tongue. I prepared for the barrage of violence that would surely ensue, especially since he and Page were of similar age. But, instead, Richard said with a deadly calm, "She damn well better."

My jaw went into a spasm, as I had clamped down so hard to keep from screaming at the lot of them. Mayhap, I could just leave the room and hope they tore each other to shreds instead of me. When had my mother become so conniving? I had known her for more than a humble woman when we had first come to court, but now she reached beyond what she was given. The king owed them nothing and what he gave wasn't good enough in her eyes. I could not ask for too much without jeopardizing my own future. It was dangerous—for me.

"She cannot even gain us court apartments—a bed! And you want a wife? You must seek your fortune elsewhere. Lady Beauchamp has no influence at court." My stepfather came close to me, his scent that of horses, sweat and stink.

I longed for Edward, but his trip north had been extended. I longed for his support against intruders and power-hungry people. People like my relatives, indeed my own mother. As much as I wanted to, I was nearly incapable of outright refusing her. I was normally strong, but in this... there was only so much I could bear. I stiffened my back and managed to look my stepfather in the eye.

"You and Edward have managed to keep your secrets well hidden," Page whispered. "Surrey has equally kept his mouth shut, but I suspect the payment your mother sent him was bribe enough. Do as we ask, or I will expose you."

I stifled a gasp, and my fingernails dug deep into my palms. I inclined my head as I did not think I could speak. Our gazes locked and I let all the hatred I felt for them spear his eyes. Damn him. Damn them both.

At last, my stepfather broke my gaze and motioned for Mother and Lizzie to follow him. "We shall see you this evening. I must attend to our lodgings in town. Do see that Lizzie has a bed for tonight." They retreated through a door held open by groomsman.

But I still could not relax. My brother, Richard, stood in the room still, arms crossed and brows furrowed at their retreating figures.

On the sound of the door clicking closed, he spoke. "If ever I saw a man in need of flogging, I am certain that man would be a likely candidate. I am glad to not be forced into their company often."

I had an overwhelming urge to shout at Richard that I wished he would be flogged as well.

"I find myself growing tired. What is it you need, Brother?"

"Did I not make myself clear? I want to marry."

"Whom did you have in mind?" I feigned boredom when all I wanted to do was run screaming.

He chuckled, and some of his usual orneriness disappeared. "I had no one particularly in mind. I thought perhaps you would mention to the king I sought a wife."

"I shall. Now if you will excuse me?"

"My lady." He bowed low and plucked another apple from our bowl before taking his leave.

As soon as the door shut, I crumpled into the window seat, forehead against the glass. What was I to do? If they revealed my secrets about Surrey—indeed if Surrey himself revealed our past—I would be ruined! Edward would be ruined. Damn them!

Angry tears filled my eyes, stinging the rims and lids. I could arrange for another bribe out of my own income, but how long would the extortion last? I could not allow our past to become known. Surrey had to be dealt with.

I needed to escape this place. My breathing tightened, my chest burning from lack of air. I was suffocating here.

I pushed away from the glass and stood. How I hated being at the mercy of those around me. As much as I knew it was not in my nature, sometimes I did long for the life of a simple country wife. No court, no kings, no queens, no blackmail.

"Edward, where are you?" I knew my plea for Edward would go unanswered. He was out on campaign, securing our future, and building his own self-confidence.

How I longed to go northward, even just for a short time. I went to my writing desk to pen a note to my husband.

*Dearest Edward,*

*News arrived today that your trip north had been extended for another fortnight. I humbly beseech you to let me join you, for I still remember your promise to allow me to accompany you north on progress. I eagerly await your response as I have news to share with you for which I think you will be most intrigued, and I seek your advice on other matters.*

*With love and affection,*
*Anne, Lady Beauchamp*

*June 13, 1536*

Two days had passed and still no word from Edward. Angry tears stung the backs of my eyes, threatening to spill over, but I forced the salty liquid to remain in place. I would shed no tears for Edward. He'd left me with a task and I had no need to complain, save for the fact I wanted to go northward. I wanted to be away from this place. From its people, from the constant prying eyes and hatched rumors and plots. Acid burned in my stomach from tension and lack of food. My neck ached from being in a constant state of uplifted chin. My head pounded. Even my ears buzzed from having to spend so much time eavesdropping.

But who was I to complain? I was Lady Beauchamp, sister-by-marriage to the king and queen. My apartments were attached to the royal rooms. My every whim would be satisfied if I only deigned to ask. And, hence, there was my answer. I had only to ask. Jane had seen to it that Elizabeth Page was housed at court with the other young girls, and Jane would for certes understand that a mother and father wished to be close to their only young daughter.

Before he'd left, Edward advised seeking his brother, Thomas, out for council, but I refused. The man was still angry at me for having seen me with Anthony, although he had made it clear he would say nothing to Edward, and would for now take my word for what it was. I let out a long sigh, my temples aching.

Night was already upon us, the sky black, hardly a star in sight. But the blackness still twinkled with the lights of candles in windows and torches set on the stone walls surrounding the castle and city. London. Night would not stop the city dwellers and residents of the castle from living their lives.

Taking a deep breath, I walked back to my writing desk and sat down on the scarlet, embroidered cushion. My arms rested against the ornately carved oak, so delicate and feminine with its swirls and roses. The chair and desk were a gift from Edward on Christmas last year.

I dipped my quill into the ink pot set neatly at the corner and began to scratch my words onto crisp new parchment, and attempted to appease my husband in hopes of a reply. Edward needed to be reassured in my ability to maintain our household while he was away. It was my duty, and he had more important things to worry about. He need not be concerned that his woman was at home floundering. Or philandering.

*Dearest Edward,*

*I am as always your most humble and obedient wife. I will do my duty with pleasure. My patience will persevere, and I eagerly await your return. If there is anything you need whilst away, you only need but ask. All is well at court, and what needs be whispered in your ear can await your return.*

*With love and affection,*
*Anne, Lady Beauchamp*

After signing my letter to Edward, I sprinkled sand over the ink so it would not smudge, folded the parchment, and stamped my crest into the red pool of melted wax I dribbled onto the loose ends to seal it shut. I kissed the seal and set the letter aside.

I pressed my hand against the rosary embedded in my sleeve and rubbed the smooth round stones. 'Twould not be good for anyone to see me with a Catholic relic. I stood abruptly from the writing desk and approached the *prie dieu* in my bedchamber to pray. I needed strength to endure, strength to face my enemies and friends alike. For it felt like I was surrounded on all sides by people who haunted my past, my present and my future. I shuddered and knelt on the cushioned kneeling pad, eyes closed, fingers clutched together in prayer. When I finished, there was a silence about the castle, night fully upon us.

A renewed fortification filled me. I was strengthened and resilient once more—at least for the time being.

But my letter writing was not done, and this time I did not need ink.

I pulled from my writing desk a clean quill and a jar of lemon and orange juice. A smile curled my lips. Who had ever been such a genius as to create invisible ink should be commended. All the reader would need to do was hold the paper to candlelight for the words to appear. I dipped my quill in the juice and penned a letter to the Marchioness of Exeter, as she'd instructed me to do, explaining the delay in Edward's trip and that I would be in contact with her as soon as I had the chance to pave her way back to court. I still had a few ideas of how I could place her name upon the king's ear.

I took a jeweled hairpin from my jewelry chest and tucked it against the letter, folded the parchment around the pin, sealed it with wax and ribbons, and called Jenny forth. The marchioness had informed me she would be staying at a house in London until they heard from me. Giving Jenny a gold coin for her silence, I sent her on her way with my gift of the pin and unbeknownst to Jenny, my secret letter. Thank the Lord in heaven for loyal servants.

Even with the time nearing ten o'clock, I was restless. Sleep would not come to me tonight. I paced my bedchamber, awaiting word back from the marchioness, and contemplated my brother Richard's situation.

I would keep my eye out for anyone who would make a good match for him. There were several of the queen's ladies who were maidens in need of a match. But my brother, as volatile as he was, was less of a threat now than my stepfather. Richard might lash out, get into fights and spout nonsensical things that could be construed as treason, or spew words meant to hurt and crush and damage, but he was still my brother, and he would not whisper of my secrets.

I did not have to wait long for Jenny to return with another blank parchment sealed in wax around a jeweled sewing thimble. I waved her from the room and opened the letter, holding it close to a lit candle. Slowly, the citrus juices darkened and burned into the paper from the heat of the wick. Brown letters appeared, and I read them eagerly with a smile.

*Dear Lady Beauchamp,*

*We were pleased to receive your correspondence and understand the delay. If 'tis any help at all, Lady Salisbury has revealed to me that her son, Reginald Pole, has written her a letter recently with some very intriguing information. Perhaps you might take it upon yourself to speak with your dear sister, and she could lend a hand in having us reinstated at court.*

*Eager to serve and please His Majesty,*

*Lady Gertrude, Marchioness of Exeter*

Yes, mayhap she was right, although Jane was hardly in a place to whisper desires for reinstating those banished. Perhaps a talk with Sir Anthony was in order. He, having the king's ear, might have known just how to proceed. Becoming friends with the man may now serve its purpose.

*June 14, 1536*

The *click clack* of my slippers on the stone floor echoed off the walls of the gilded antechamber in the king's chapel as I paced the room, hands fisted together, fingers numb from their wringing.

Everyone had gone from Mass nearly half an hour ago and would be now breaking their fast. I should have been with the queen and would no doubt be questioned for my lateness, but this was the only time I could safely break away to meet with Sir Anthony.

Soon, the clicking of my heels was joined by the click of another, more steady, heavier foot. *Anthony.*

I turned just as he stepped into the shadowed antechamber.

"My lady." He bowed and then came forward to place a kiss on my wrist, his lips lingering too long. I suppressed a wicked shudder and yanked my hand from his grasp, forcing myself to be disgusted. Edward had been gone too long, and I longed for intimate touch. *Edward, come home!*

"Sir Anthony, please, if you've the will, rein in your flirtations for this day. Our meeting here must be quick as we are both in need of returning to our respective sovereigns."

"As you wish, my lady." He swept his cap from his head and bowed to me again in an exaggerated motion.

I rolled my eyes, which gained me a lusty chuckle from his throat. I could not help but smile. For as flirtatious as he was, and as repulsed as I wanted to be, he still elicited some emotion from me.

"I've met with Lady Exeter and had correspondence with her. She and the marquess have need to return to court and be granted an audience with the king. The information they contain is of great importance, and I am certain once His Majesty hears of it, he will agree it is vital to the functioning of his realm. Suffolk is reluctant to aide their cause, but if someone else were to champion them, he might step up to voice his pleasure at such an occasion. And you know very well Cromwell prefers to keep everyone from court who might influence the king."

Anthony nodded, tapping his chin. Why must he do that? It only brought attention to the firmness of his facial musculature, to the squareness of his jaw. I had a moment that I pictured myself nipping his strong jaw with my teeth, but quickly shut that thought away and willed the blush starting to rise on my chest from such wanton thoughts to cool. How quick I was to judge Catherine Filiol, and even Edward himself, who no doubt had his cock in many a camp whore while out on campaign, yet here I was dreaming of my lips on another man.

"What news do they wish to impart on His Majesty?" Anthony finally asked.

Our whispered voices were muffled, not echoing as loudly as my steps had.

"The whereabouts and future plans of Reginald Pole. Even now he works for the pope, upsetting the Catholics against our king."

Though my heart was Catholic, my head was thoroughly loyal to the king and the Seymours. I briefly touched the rosary sowed within the fabric of my wrist, asking God's forgiveness for betraying my soul in order to keep my head.

Anthony's eyebrows shot up. "How did they come by this news?" Together, we walked to a nearby altar and lit candles, so to anyone walking by, we might have seemed like two courtiers intent on prayers.

"Lady Exeter is a close confidante of Lady Salisbury, who informed her that she's been in recent contact with her son. Lady Salisbury and her eldest son, Montague, would do anything to disassociate with the young Pole, even giving away his whereabouts."

Together, we knelt on the altar stair, my skirts cushioning my knees from the stone. Filtering down from the high-arched ceilings, we could hear the virginals and the sweet voices of choir boys as they practiced for Evensong in the nearby cloister.

"Sad how the thought of your head being severed can make a mother turn on her own son, is it not?" Anthony whispered, his head cocked as he pondered his own question.

The thought alone made me shudder. And I swore the candle light flickered. To think I was willing to play a part in the downfall of yet another—that would most probably result in their death—turned my stomach. But for the sake of keeping the Howards away from the throne—to save Jane and my family, I would. If it were my child, I would never dream of betraying our bond. His comment reminded me of my own mother. She had thrown me to the wolves where Surrey was concerned, and would continue to do so if I let her. She'd stood by and done nothing, and still did nothing as her husband threatened me. What made a mother so harsh?

And how could I encourage such cruelty and betrayal in another mother?

But I could not allow such doubts to take hold inside me and root out the end result, which was for mine and Edward's family to move forward, for this reign to continue and succeed. My goal was to seek out those who would see it put to an end and make certain they disappeared, because if not for them, it would be me fading from this place.

"Tragic," I mumbled, and began to recite the Lord's Prayer in my mind.

"I will speak with Suffolk. Naturally, when Beauchamp returns, we shall have his support, and whilst he is away, his brother will support us as well. I do believe I might be able to convince His Majesty's Groom of the Stool to insinuate a rumor to pique the king's interest."

"Rumor?"

"Mmm… Mayhap he heard talk of Lady Salisbury having a letter recently."

"That should do." I could only imagine the king's eyes widening, his lip curling up, but the smile not anything pleasant as he saw the coming of his revenge in sight. "Are there any others we can count on our side?"

"I already know for certes Sir Nicholas Carew, the king's Master of the Horse, and Sir John Russell will aid us. If I can get perhaps one more lord of great standing, Suffolk will indeed assist us."

"What of Shrewsbury? He's got power and wealth enough to entice Suffolk."

"Yes, I will see if I can enlist him on the morrow. Sir Francis Bryan and Sir Thomas Wyatt come to mind as well."

Ah, Sir Francis — the renowned lover of women — and a loyal servant of the crown. And Wyatt… Anne Boleyn's first love, long before she was married to King Henry. The voices of the choir and virginals ceased, leaving the antechamber in an eerie silence. We stood from our prayer positions.

"I will keep you informed on their decisions to aid us in returning Lord and Lady Exeter as well as Montague to court."

I nodded and began to walk toward the main cloister of the king's chapel. Anthony grasped my arm, and the renewed enchanting voices of the choir hushed the gasp that escaped from me.

"There is something else you should know."

"And what is that?" I wrested my arm from his grasp, the press of where his fingers had been still warm through my gown.

"The Howards are conscripting girls." Anthony ignored the shake of my arm and took my hand in his. I could not help but notice how warm and firm his grip was. How I secretly wished he might rub those strong fingers up the length of my arm and down my spine as he had in the great hall. But it was shameful for me to think that way. Indeed, being close to him was becoming dangerous. Perhaps our further correspondence should be through secret codes and letters.

"Conscripting girls?"

He nodded. "When Jane becomes with child, Henry will need a distraction, and with his reputation, his distractions soon become queen. They plan to wave a pretty piece around Jane's retinue."

I sighed. I would have to put a plan in place to make certain our own harridan was within Henry's sights and perhaps rumors of a pox on whomever the Howards brought into play. My own lip curled much as I had imagined the king's would at hearing such rumors.

"The king is also starting to suspect that his councilors and privy chamber men may be more sympathetic toward Mary than even Jane's own children. He's started to question us at length. I do believe I am out of his line of sight now, but we must tread lightly in any talks of Lady Mary."

My stomach tightened. Were there men within the king's household conspiring to elevate Lady Mary over Jane's issue? Such would have to be avoided at all costs. A vision of the king, face almost purple with rage, shouting, spittle flying from his mouth, as he ordered his guards to arrest each and every member of his council and privy.

"Do be careful, Anthony. If he catches wind of even the slightest rumor, be it truth or not, he will retaliate."

"Yes, my lady. But now you know we stack allies on our side. We may even be able to count Cromwell on our side some days. Others, he is so flustered—but he's created enemies with so many, he cannot be trusted."

"Cromwell!" I hissed. "Do not dare propose that jackanapes is on our side!"

102

Anthony made a motion with his hands for me to keep my voice down. "Calm yourself, my lady. All of us are treading lightly now, until Jane is able to place Mary back within the good graces of His Majesty, which will only make her look more virtuous to the king and the people. Pulling Mary back into King Henry's fold will show that Jane is confident in her ability to issue him a child—and that she is the rightful successor of Queen Katherine—not Anne Boleyn. 'Twill also appease those who hanker to raise Mary above Jane. There is no reason for it. Jane is the rightful Queen."

I nodded, taking in the information he provided but not wanting to make any verbalizations of my own for fear of my voice rising once more. The shuffling of feet indicated that people were beginning to come into the chapel for confession and prayer.

"We must away, Sir Anthony."

"I will send word to you."

I nodded and hurried from the antechamber, lifting my skirts away from my ankles so I might make a quicker escape—before anyone noticed that we'd been together.

Today, I would make a list of all the girls that would be witty and intelligent, and somehow would still come off as naïve, to dangle before the king. The Howards would not usurp our position, not when we'd finally wrested if from their cold, vicious fingers.

*June 20, 1536*

Darkness of the night enveloped us—fitting since I was looking for a whore for my king. My cloak was pulled tight around me, the hood shielding my hair and face from view. We'd long since passed through the gates of Hampton Court and now rode our horses gingerly up the main city streets of London. We'd taken a small boat from the castle up the Thames to a dockside where three rag horses awaited us. From there, we'd crossed into the city.

Despite the hour, the streets were busier than I had imagined. Light-skirts, merchants, knights, peasants, peddlers, drunkards, all walking up and down the streets, lingering in shadows or already passed out in their own excrement. The scents of the city rivaled that of the Thames the morning of Jane's coronation. Fish, bread, ale, vomit, urine, feces, roasted meat, unwashed bodies, all of it assaulted the senses.

I looked up at the sky to judge the hour by the moon, but all I saw was rooftops and smoke from chimneys. The air was thick with stench and smoke. How did the people live here? When I was a girl, I had met a woman once who told me she'd never left the city except for the one time she'd gone to Anglesey Abbey in Cambridgeshire to pray for a cure for her mother's illness. To be born, live and die in the suffocating atmosphere was something I would not wish on anyone. This business could not be done soon enough so that I might return to the comforts of my own chambers within the castle walls.

"We're headed to an inn in Cheapside," Sir Nicholas Carew said, his voice muffled from the hood of his own cloak. No one would be able to tell that the three riders were none other than Lady Beauchamp and two knights armed to the teeth.

"And she will be there?" I asked.

"On my honor, my lady," Sir Anthony answered.

I nodded, even though neither of them would have seen me.

At long last we arrived at the Wattle and Daub Tavern, where Sir Nicholas and Anthony dismounted. I sat in stunned silence. Did they really expect to get a drink of ale prior to me conducting my business?

"What are you about? Whoring and drinking were not part of the plan," I snapped. With each passing day that I was without Edward, and threats surrounded me, bitterness took over. I longed for some bit of happiness, but such dreams were purely fantasy for me. Happiness looked like rain in a hot summer drought, and I felt delusional for even imagining it would someday be upon me.

They both looked at me, their faces startled in the moonlight. "My lady, you are mistaken," Sir Nicholas answered.

"Am I not?" I waved to the hanging sign and pinched the bridge of my nose to keep from exploding at their ignorance. "Is this not a tavern?"

Anthony had the nerve to chuckle. "My lady, 'tis a tavern, you are correct. *But* the inn is upstairs."

My hands tightened on the reins of my horse, biting into my flesh through the leather of my gloves. I was grateful for the darkness of night to hide the blush on my cheeks.

"My apologies," I grumbled, unwilling to admit more than that.

"You are a true lady." Anthony came to my side and held out his hand to help me dismount. His voice was filled with mirth. "Else you would have known the inn was above stairs."

"Humph." I was more than a little irritated they were having a laugh at my expense.

"Come then, we must hurry." Sir Nicholas opened the front door of the inn and immediately we were awash in noise — really the only way to describe it. Shouts, instruments being played out of tune, laughter, chatter, the clang of mugs and loud belches. With the noise came another stench I would be happy to never smell again.

Briskly, we entered and climbed the stairs, where Anthony knocked once on a wooden door that had seen better days.

A matronly woman answered the door and bid us enter. There, standing in the center of the room, was the person I had come to see.

"My lady, sirs," she mumbled and then dipped a curtsy.

The matronly woman bounced beside her charge. "Annie and I were so pleased you wished to see us."

I nodded and removed my cloak so I might get comfortable, then came to stand before the young girl.

"Mayhap you want to see my other daughter as well?"

"No, there is room for only one." I gave my attention back to the girl. "Turn around."

Anne Bassett turned a perfect, graceful circle. The girl, nearly eighteen, would be perfect. Her gown swished around her. She was slim yet curvy, her chestnut curls enough to entice even myself to touch their silky threads. Her eyes were a bright blue, innocent-looking but lit with mischief when she smiled. Her mother had been trying for years to get her a position at court, and whereas Anne Boleyn would not accept her for the girl's flirtatious and beautiful countenance, I would see to it she was put in place.

"If you are to be a lady in Queen Jane's retinue, you must appear to be modest and chaste. Her Majesty does not tolerate idolatry or unvirtuous behavior." I walked around Annie, examining her from head to toe as I ticked off each item. "Her ladies are all required to dress well. The queen herself will want to tell you how you should appear. Have no fears for the costs. I will absorb them myself. Attending Mass is a must. We read Her Majesty passages from the Bible daily, and you must pledge allegiance to her in all things."

Annie nodded. "Yes, my lady."

"Can you dance or sing?"

"Both, my lady."

"Oh, she is so very talented!" the older woman gushed. I silenced her with a glare.

"Let me hear you," I instructed, coming to a stop in front of the girl, my hands folded at my hips. I felt bitterness at her excitement, for coming to court would melt her sweetness into a puddle of disappointment and regret.

Annie opened her mouth, and the most breathtaking song issued forth. I was impressed and lifted my brow with an appreciative nod.

"And a dance?"

She began to dance to her own song, her arms arching delicately, hips swaying, feet moving in perfect formation. I was reminded of a younger version of myself, and instantly I resented her for her youth and innocence.

"Well done. I think Her Majesty will be pleased to add you to her household. Come sit with me a moment."

Annie followed me to the chairs by the hearth and sat prettily.

"Are you aware of why I sent for you?" I had not made the express desire for her company clear in my letter, only alluding to my wishes for her to meet with me about the possibility of her coming to court.

"You wish to please the queen and king and for me to experience all that life at court has to offer."

A very diplomatic answer. "Yes, both of those reasons are quite true. But you will have one other duty. When Queen Jane begets a child, you will keep the king's eyes on you and you alone—unless, of course, he has eyes for Her Majesty. Do you understand my meaning?"

"You wish me to become his mistress?" Her eyes lit with fear and flicked to the matron. Perhaps she would not be the right choice.

My gaze shifted to the older woman, who stoically kept her face void of any emotion. Well played.

"If he so wishes, I do expect that. But do not fear. He will not take you to wife and I will make certain you know how to abstain from conceiving a bastard. We simply wish to keep any Howard girls out of his bed."

Relief flooded the girl's features. "I understand."

But did she really?

"Do you think you can accomplish what I ask? It is of the utmost importance. The Howards will seek to place a girl within Jane's court who not only entices the king but pulls him from his wife completely, which will not end well for anyone involved. We simply want a young lady who keeps him sated until it is time for him to return to his true and rightful wife."

Annie sat forward. "I can do as you ask. I swear it."

I smiled and patted her hand. "Good girl. Shall I introduce you to Her Majesty on the morrow?"

"I would be honored." She paused, worrying her lower lip. "May I ask one question?"

"You may ask as many questions as you like. You and I will be confidantes for a long time."

"What of a match for myself when my duty is complete?"

From the corner of my eye, I watched her mother nod. I could almost believe Mistress Annie Bassett was a Seymour. She would not go unpaid for her generous offer, and most generous it was. A woman's virtue was the only thing she had to bargain with in a marriage deal—that and a large dowry—and I was stealing the former.

"I will supply the dowry myself. Any man would be lucky to have you. I will see to it he is generous and wealthy."

"Thank you, my lady." Annie stood and embraced me.

"No, thank *you*." I stepped away from her, nodded to her mother and pulled my cloak back on.

The two women curtsied and bowed their heads as I, Sir Nicholas and Sir Anthony exited the room.

Let the merrymaking begin.

# CHAPTER SEVEN

*With that she start aside well near a foot or twain,*
*And unto him thus did she say, with spite and great disdain*
*'Lion,' she said, 'if thou hadst known my mind before,*
*Thou hadst not spent thy travail thus, nor all thy pain for-lore.'*
*~Henry Howard, Earl of Surrey*

*June 21, 1536*

Jane's eyes gleamed with interest as she caught sight of Annie Bassett beside me, but she quickly composed herself and was once more the regal Jane we all knew well. "Anne! Come! I've the most splendid idea for a tapestry. I can envision it hanging in the great hall." Jane's hands raised in the air as she smoothed an imaginary tapestry onto a fictitious wall.

The queen's chambers were abuzz with excitement. Ladies tittered here and there. Brightly colored threads of yarn and silk floated in the air, skirts spread out on the floor as ladies sat on pillows surrounding the queen.

I smiled and walked toward her with Annie following. Once again, Jane's eyes roved over the newcomer.

"Majesty, might I present Mistress Annie Bassett. She has been eagerly hoping to come to court and serve you most humbly."

Annie curtsied. "Your Majesty, I hope only to learn by your gracious example."

"Can you sew, Annie?" Jane asked, her brow furrowing slightly as she fingered a length of fabric. "Everyone is required to work on this tapestry."

Annie nodded. Her face was the utter mask of naïveté and trust. I could not have done a better job myself.

Jane flicked her gaze to mine, her eyes saying what her lips would not—that she knew exactly why Annie was there. Pain etched for a small moment around the corners of her eyes, and my heart went out to her, for I knew how well it hurt to see a husband stray. But Jane also knew how important it was to have a woman we chose ourselves grace His Majesty's bedchamber. A woman who would not aspire to be queen, nor hatch plots against Jane.

"Welcome to court. I am pleased to have you as a maid of honor. Has Lady Beauchamp informed you of all that is required and expected of you?"

Annie shot me a quick glance, and I nodded imperceptibly.

"Yes, Your Majesty."

"And do you swear, as God is your witness, to live a chaste, virtuous life, seeking only to serve your sovereign and God?" Was there a warning to the girl in her words?

"I do, madam."

"Hmm..." Jane tapped her lip as her eyes roved over Annie's form. "You will need to request funds from your family for a new trousseau. Your French hood will not do. The women of my court must conform with the English style. Your bodice must be lined with pearls." Jane scrutinized Annie's dress, which did have some pearls on it but not nearly enough. I hid my smile as this was exactly how I had wanted things to play out. Jane would reign supreme in Annie's life. "I am guessing there are no more than one hundred and twenty pearls on your bodice. If you want to attend Mass within my entourage, you will need to double that. No other jewels on your gowns. Pearls signify chastity and yet at the same time show a level of richness that cannot be acquired by those of low birth." Spoken like a true descendent of Edward III, and meant to put Annie in her place. Now I was certain Jane knew exactly what I'd done.

Annie nodded, lowered her gaze. "Yes, Your Grace."

"Get some thread and take a seat. The king's birthday is in seven days. We have no time to waste. I want to make him a large embroidered tapestry for him to use at his pleasure. I imagine it hanging in this very castle for another hundred years or more." She stood and spread out a large piece of royal-blue silk fabric, the edges embroidered with silver and gold thread. "I want the finished product to be a great garden, resembling pleasure gardens, but above it all, I want a phoenix rising, soaring."

My eyes widened at the project Jane had planned. Normally, something of this magnitude would take months and months, yet Jane had given us only a sennight. I took a seat on the floor, crimson thread in hand to begin embroidering a rose.

"We shall take shifts. Not one moment will pass until the king's birthday that there is not someone working on the tapestry."

I would sew until my fingers bled, as would all her ladies. We loved her that much, but above all, we knew such a gift would please His Majesty greatly. And in the court of Henry VIII, pleasing the king was the key to keeping your head.

*June 28, 1536*

"Higher! Lift your lance, you dolt!" the king shouted out to one of the men on the field. A tournament had been planned for the king's birthday. Jousting this morning, followed by a hunt and then a great feast with a play in the gardens. Jane would present her tapestry to the king at the end of the play. "Does anyone here know how to attend their lance?" He looked around the tent, seeking agreement, irritation marring his face. Several courtiers muttered and nodded.

I suspected that the king's irritation was more from not being able to seat the horse and participate himself. The king had once been the best jouster in England. Fierce and royal he was on his charger mount, lance couched under his arm, body covered in rich armor. I still remembered the exhilaration I'd felt the first time I'd seen him barreling down the list field. My breath had caught, heart had stopped. A sensation I would never forget. But at the request of his physician, Henry chose to sit out today's joust. Which meant the hunt following would be fierce and mayhap reckless.

King Henry turned back to the field, engrossed in the tournament. When Suffolk, the king's dearest friend, rode out onto the field, the king cheered loudly. Pleasure covered his features. Henry tapped Jane on the arm, pointing toward the field, showing her what excited him.

I stood behind the seated king and queen, using an ornate fan to wave at Jane and myself. We had been again blessed with a mild day, but with the number of people stuffed into the tent, the heat from all of our bodies, coupled with the summer temperatures, did make it somewhat stifling.

Edward had sent word he would return to court early to partake in the celebration of His Majesty's birthday, having concluded his business abroad. I could not wait for him to return and keenly felt the angry heated stares of Sir Richard Page and my mother from across the tent. I had requested of Jane to ask His Majesty for court rooms for them. She had sympathized with them as doting parents wanting to be nearer their daughter, but the king had still denied the appeal. To make matters worse, he had denied Page's last request for an audience.

But Jane had whispered to me that the king was only doing it to put them in their place and that he would soon grant their requests.

Despite my assurances to Page that such was the case, he still threatened to expose my secrets.

Edward could not return soon enough! He was only a day later than he'd told me, and part of me worried that some accident had befallen him. Edward was a stickler for a schedule and very rarely was he late.

A great rumbling in the crowd drew my attention. Courtiers bowed and court ladies curtsied, parting to allow someone to pass. I strained my neck to see who should garner such attention. When I was finally able to catch sight of who had them enthralled, my breath hitched. Edward had finally returned. I smiled and blinked back stinging tears. My heart skipped a beat. We'd been apart before, but this time had seemed so much harder than any other. I suppressed the urge to run to him, to jump into his arms and press kisses to the flesh of his cheeks, forehead and lips.

He still wore his riding clothes, which despite their functional appointment were richly embroidered and of the finest quality of deep green, brown and beige brocade, black-threaded embroidery and crusted jewels. He made for an impressive figure.

Our eyes connected, and for a moment time stood still. Even from a distance I could feel the spark of our attraction renewed, my love for him vigorous and alive. This was why I stayed true to him, because of how he made me feel and how gazing deeply into his eyes, I could see my feelings mirrored there. Longing, desire, passion. I forgave him in that moment for his neglect, for he'd returned to me—and truly, what choice did I have? I could live in misery, or rise above it.

He approached the king and bowed. Only a few feet from me, and my body was like a spring ready to coil and burst. He and Henry exchanged a few words, which seemed to take hours. I wanted to shout, *Enough already, let me have him!* But, of course, I had to control myself. My foot, however, had a mind of its own, and I tapped it relentlessly, without notice, until Jane looked down at my slippers and then smiled up at me indulgently.

"Majesty, let my brother greet his wife. I do believe she is eager to have him returned to her," Jane said.

Henry glanced over his shoulder at me with a smile. He patted Edward on the shoulder and then dismissed him, returning his attention to the field.

I walked forward and curtsied to Edward as was appropriate amongst the people. He bowed in turn and then took my hand in his. It was warm and rough, and my stomach clenched in response. He squeezed it as he brought it to his mouth, his eyes sparkling with delight.

"My lady, it has been entirely too long that your presence has not graced mine." Ever the gentleman and courtier.

"I am pleased you have returned safely. I trust your journey was successful?" My voice sounded squeaky, and I felt ready to burst.

"Very."

He offered me his arm, and I linked mine through his, taking pleasure in the muscles beneath my fingertips. I absently stroked him. "Come and sit with us. The tournament is quite lively."

He leaned in and whispered in my ear, "I wish to seek comfort in our chambers."

I laughed a little and squeezed his arm. My core clenched, and my nipples tightened at the thought. It had been so long, and I had been so tempted by another, I needed the reassurance of Edward's hands on me, his lips and tongue tantalizing me, and his cock thrust to the hilt. Somehow I managed to answer, "All in good time, my lord."

My gaze darted around the crowd of courtiers within the tent and fell on Sir Anthony near the rear of the tent, talking animatedly with a few other men of the privy chamber and several of Jane's maids of honor. He glanced up when he saw us, his eyes flashing with some unrecognized emotion. Was it jealousy? Anger? I could not tell and dared not stare too long. He quickly recovered and excused himself from his party, sauntering toward us.

For a moment, panic infused me. Would he disclose that he'd been intent on rutting with me the entire time Edward was away? Dear Lord, I hoped not. And even after the fear passed through my mind, I knew it was something that I had no need to set credence with. I did not blink as he walked forward, coming closer and closer. I said a silent prayer that all would be well.

"Lord Beauchamp! At last!" he said, arriving to shake Edward's hand.

"Sir Anthony." I did not miss the tone of irritation in Edward's words. Had Thomas told him? "I have missed court. You shall have to fill me in on all the goings-on since I have been away."

"Indeed, sir, I will." He turned toward me, his lids lowering a moment as I lifted my hand. "My lady."

He pressed his lips to my knuckles briefly, and it was all I could do to keep a flush of embarrassment and shame from covering my breasts, throat and cheeks. All I could remember was our heated conversations and how those lips had lingered on my wrist, how his fingers trailed delicately up my back as he tried to entice me. Beside me, Edward went rigid.

114

"Sir Anthony, do tell us what had you and your company in a height of excitement?" Trying to speak normally of things of little importance came to me easier than I thought it would.

"Ah, yes." He chuckled. "We were taking bets on who would win the tournament."

"And who do you think will win?" Edward asked, turning to face the lists, where another set of competitors raced toward each other.

"My money is on His Grace, Suffolk, as is Sir Nicholas's, but the rest of the group believes Surrey will be the champion. Who would you stake your claim on?" Anthony's question could have been taken in so many ways. I knew he was outwardly referring to the joust, but internally, I could not help but wonder what he referred to. Did he wonder if I would choose him over Edward? Or some other courtier instead of himself? And why would he even believe that I would make a choice? Or did he know about Surrey, and this was an insult aimed to hurt?

My gaze returned to the list field, where Surrey sat atop his horse, his faceplate lifted as he pointed and shouted at his opponent. It took me back to another time and place, where I could hear his voice echoing in my mind.

*"You are a spitfire, Lady Anne... Come let us go into the garden where I might read you one of my poems. I want to make love to you...with words..."*

*"Let me kiss you, Anne. Let me feel your supple body pressed against mine."*

Bits and phrases from a past best forgotten invaded my mind. Almost as if Surrey had heard the words himself, his head popped up, gaze searching the crowd until he found me, then he smiled. But his smile was not one that would melt a lady's heart. His smile sent chills of dread racing along my flesh. Panic started at the edges of my mind, and I squeezed closer to Edward, seeking his strength and warmth. But even still, the nightmares of the past forced their way into my mind.

*Surrey's forceful hands as they yanked at my skirts, thrust into my innocent passage, the pain as his nails scraped over the sensitive flesh. Me, pushing him away. Him, slapping me hard, telling me to hush and let him love me. Then the pain of his male appendage as it thrust inside me, nearly ripping me in two...*

Edward's voice pulled me back to the present, and I was extremely grateful for the disruption of my thoughts.

"I do believe you are right, Sir Anthony. Suffolk has a fine form on a horse, and his handle with the lance is near perfection. Although he is less likely to take a risk, and we all know Surrey has no qualms," his gaze flicked to mine, "and mostly acts before thinking. A very interesting sight it will be. What does the king say?"

"Or course, his money is on Suffolk. The two go back to boyhood days, and no matter how angry he's ever been at the man, their bond is stronger than blood itself."

Edward's gaze roved over the crowded tent and landed on Annie Bassett. "Who is that young lady?"

"She is our savior."

"Savior?" Edward turned sharply toward me.

Anthony leaned in close and lowered his voice. "The Howards have begun to make inquiries to place a girl within the court to entice the king. When I heard this, I notified Lady Beauchamp."

Edward's gaze narrowed as he scrutinized Anthony, and in my mind I could only picture his thoughts. He was wondering whether I had slept with the man. "My wife?" he growled.

Again, my stomach fluttered with nerves. The anger radiating from Edward was nearly palpable.

"Aye, my lord. I hope you do not think it was too forward of me?" Sir Anthony said.

Edward shook his head and turned to me for some measure of comfort. His eyes filled with question.

"Your brother was unavailable, my lord, else I am certain Sir Anthony would have sought his counsel instead."

At this, Edward's features cleared of doubt, and I hoped he had no more thoughts of me making him a cuckold, and if he did, he was not going to ponder them any longer.

Anthony's gaze connected with mine, and I tried with all my might to keep a straight face. "In fact, Sir Anthony has been most helpful with keeping me well-informed of the goings-on at court, so I might apprise you upon your return."

"I thank you, sir." Edward nodded in Anthony's direction, but he seemed anything but thankful. He still looked suspicious, and I spied Anthony give a self-satisfied smirk. What had happened in the past between these two men? Why did I feel as though I was missing something?

Again, Edward pulled me from my thoughts. "Where is my brother?"

"The king sent him north with some correspondence for the border lords."

All of them ceased their talking as the Lord Privy Seal, Cromwell, entered the area and immediately sought out the king with some news.

"If you'll excuse me." Edward left quickly and made his way toward the king, throwing a cursory glance over his shoulder, his hard eyes meeting those of Sir Anthony's.

He was going to listen in on what Cromwell had to say. Increasingly over the last few weeks, I'd noticed how the high council members were becoming irritated with the man. They were mostly angry that a man of such low birth not only felt he could usurp them all with his power, but that the king allowed it.

A simmer was beginning in the bottom of the pot, a few bubbles reaching the surface, but in just a few months' time, the water would pop and burp and slosh over the edge — Cromwell would end up floating in that angry boiling pot, the council members stirring him into stew.

My gaze connected with Anthony's for a moment of exaggerated intensity. For that brief interlude, I felt he could see into my soul, felt myself being swept into the depths of his charms. Willpower won out over shocked curiosity at how much this man affected me, and I pulled my gaze from his. There was more to the man than met the eye, and I could not let his handsome looks and charming ways blind me to the truth — he must only be using me.

"My lady." Sir Anthony bowed and headed discreetly away.

I made my way back toward Jane, biding the time until Edward returned to me with news. I fanned myself furiously, more from my interaction with Sir Anthony than from the heat. Like wolves going in for the kill, Edward, Norfolk and several other council members surrounded His Majesty as Cromwell relayed whatever news it was he had.

Greedy men. All of them, even Edward. Albeit, who was I to judge? If I could have, I would have stood right there with them.

The rest of the tournament went by in a flash. Suffolk won, just as those who knew him best thought he would. Surrey's risky behavior only deterred him in the joust, and calculating Suffolk took the advantage. After being knocked senseless by Suffolk's lance, Surrey stood on the outside of the list, cursing and sputtering. Several of his grooms took a hit to the face, and I shuddered. His violence gave me a jolt, sending me back to that awful day I'd rather forget.

I bit my lip hard, tears coming to my eyes as the world of the past took over.

"My lady?" Edward's voice broke into my terror.

Always Edward. Thank God for Edward. And if that hadn't been a sign from the Lord above, then what was? No matter what, I had to remain with Edward and I could not break his trust. He had saved me from an awful fate, and that alone was worth the rest of my life.

"Can I entreat you to accompany me on the hunt?"

I looked around the great tent, and all those who'd been in attendance had filed out toward grooms with waiting horses. Dogs on leashes barked rambunctiously — eager for the run and the fight.

I nodded.

"You were far away just now. Where were you?"

"Hell," I muttered.

Edward gazed at the list field, understanding dawning on his face. "We could return to our chambers, if you wish it?"

"No, let us enjoy good company, a good ride, followed by wine. Lots of wine."

Edward laughed. "Ever the resilient woman, my lady wife is."

"Only because of you." And I truly meant it. For as strong as I was, without Edward, could I survive? Not with the demons chasing me in my mind and now in person.

Edward led me to the horses, and we mounted. I did not carry a weapon, preferring to go along for the ride and exertion of it. Edward had bows and arrows strapped to his back and a sword at his side. I truly enjoyed the excitement of racing after a stag or boar.

Courtiers were all mounted and ready, almost champing at the bit as the horses were. The excitement was palpable, and we all waited on King Henry. Queen Jane was already seated, and well seated she was! No one would have ever guessed from her delicate frame and docile manner that Jane was a fierce horsewoman. Finally, the king was assisted onto his horse by several grooms—as it had become increasingly difficult for him to mount by himself—and then outfitted with his weaponry. He turned to the crowd of a score or more courtiers, all ready to ride, and raised his sword in the air.

"To the hunt we go!" he shouted.

We all responded with a shout in return. The dogs were let go, their masters racing after them, and then Henry jabbed his sword forward, kicking his horse into a gallop, clumps of grass and earth flinging out behind his horse's hooves. Exhilaration bubbled in my blood as I urged the horse into a faster gait and felt the muscles in the mare's flank compress as she shot forward.

A good hunt was exactly what I needed to forget my anguished thoughts from earlier. Edward smiled over at me as we raced over the hills and fields and to the woods beyond. Henry's hunting park was stocked full of deer, and all the dogs had to do was find at least one massive stag for His Majesty to bring down. We did not have to wait long.

"There!" the king shouted, his voice feverish with his thirst to bring down the animal. His form was rigid, tall, and for a moment one might almost have seen the prince he'd been, filled with youth and zest for life.

As one unit, the horses and dogs turned in a race to catch the stag. The animal sensed us before he saw us, his ears pricking, and then he took off at a pace that rivaled the strides of our mounts. Bounding into the air, he ran for his very life.

But our horses and dogs had more stamina. The masters of the dogs whistled, calling the animals back as Henry arched his bow and took a shot. The animal fell straightaway, a piercing scream on his slick black lips, an arrow through his ribcage, most probably puncturing his heart.

"For the people of London!" the king shouted, showing his generous side. The stag would be butchered and served to the people.

For a moment, the thought of the stag being so like us courtiers fell to the forefront of my mind. We resembled this helpless animal. Bounding through the forest of the castle as we sought to stay alive, only to be brought down by the king and the dogs who served him. If we weren't careful, he'd shoot an arrow into our hearts and slice our throats, serving our remains to the whole of England.

I turned my back with a shudder as the king dismounted and sliced the neck of the deer to end its life, since it still breathed. The huntsmen then gutted the animal, and everyone prepared to return to the castle to clean themselves up. Soon, games would begin in the gardens before the feast, play and fireworks.

After brushing my hair and pinning it back beneath my hood, Jenny left me for a few moments of rest. I sat at my dressing table, gazing into the metal looking plate at my face. Were those wrinkles appearing at the sides of my eyes?

I pressed the lines and stretched the skin to make them disappear.

Hands came over my shoulders, and strong fingers kneaded the muscles that had pinched. "My mother used to finger her eyes just the same." Edward's voice was smooth and comforting. "She used a special herbal cream. I do not remember if the lines went away, but I do remember her mood being lifted."

"I shall have to seek out the remedy." I leaned back, reveling in Edward's presence. I wished he never had to go anywhere, or that I could go with him. At the same time, I hated that vulnerability, how much power he had over me.

"My sister Elizabeth has the recipe, I do believe." He leaned down and kissed the skin just behind my ear, sending a shiver of anticipation racing over my flesh. His eyes met mine in the mirror. Desire and promise filled their depths. "Are you ready to return to the festivities?"

I slipped my hands onto Edward's on my shoulders and leaned back, giving him an honest answer with a smile of intent. "No."

He chuckled. "'Tis the truth I am not either." He bent to kiss my neck again. Desire careened from the spot his lips touched to my very core. "I missed the taste of your flesh, sweet Anne."

I bent my head to the side to allow him greater access to my flesh, and he took full advantage, kissing the length of my neck to my ear. My eyes closed in ecstasy.

"Will we be sorely missed?" I asked.

"Aye."

"Is it worth it?"

Edward did not answer, only sighed. I knew the sound, heard his thoughts in that one breath. I felt the same way. I so wanted to climb between the sheets and lay my head on the feather tick, wrapped in Edward's arms as our bodies came together in rhythm. But, at the same time, if we were to never return this evening, the grief we'd suffer would make those few moments of bliss seem utterly miserable.

"We must attend to our duties," Edward whispered, and the moment the words left his mouth, I wished he'd never uttered them.

"Take me north, Edward. Take me on progress."

"We shall shortly. Come August, the king will wish to travel northward where the heat is less. For the moment, we must remain at court, show our faces... but I promise tonight..." He pressed his lips to mine, his tongue skimming the crease in a tease of promise before he pulled away. "Now, tell me what urgent news you have that caused you to write me so often?"

I frowned recalling how little he'd replied, but shoved it away. He'd returned! I stood from my dressing table and hooked my arm through his. At last I was able to tell him of our new allies. "'Tis in regards to the Marquess and Marchioness of Exeter."

"They have been banned from court." Edward eyed me warily.

"'Tis the truth, but they support Jane as queen—they support us. We will be stronger with them here at court."

Edward's eyebrows raised at this. "How does Lord Exeter presume to gain King Henry's agreement to their return to court? He has banned them for treasonous thoughts. Never proven, but he is not likely to recall them to court."

"You know the stir Reginald Pole is causing across Europe. 'Tis said he is even in league with the Pope himself."

Edward nodded. "I've heard."

"Lady Exeter is on close terms with Lady Salisbury."

"That will not support her cause."

"But, indeed, it will. She is willing to tell the king the whereabouts of Reginald Pole."

At this, Edward's countenance brightened. "Indeed, the king would be most interested in such information."

"Yes. Do you think you might be able to arrange an audience with His Majesty?"

"'Tis possible. I will need the support of other council members."

I smiled and walked my fingers up the front of Edward's charcoal doublet. "Sir Anthony and I have been hard at work garnering you just such support. Shrewsbury and Suffolk will aid you."

"Then I shall see it done." He paused a moment and took my hands in his. "I do not like you working so closely with Sir Anthony. The man is... dangerous."

"I shall be careful, Edward."

"More than careful, Anne. Do not be alone with him. The man and I... Let us leave it that we do not get on well."

I nodded solemnly. "I shall heed your words."

"Now what of Page and your mother?"

"You are aware they've been returned to court, and Page will soon be offered the sheriffdom of Surrey."

Edward's face clouded, and he frowned. "The news was relayed to me. It is most unfortunate that he should be working so closely to your enemy."

"Yes." I did not want to relay to him how Page was blackmailing me. Edward had enough worries. He did not need to fret over my family and my past, which already was a black mark upon his conscience.

Instead, I kissed him tenderly. We gave a longing look toward my bedchamber before leaving our apartments to return to the gardens. By the time we arrived, we'd missed the presentation of the tapestry to the king, but from what Queen Jane's maids of honors informed me, King Henry was driven nearly to tears by his thoughtful, generous, kind and loving wife.

My fingers still stung from the hundreds of holes pricked into their flesh. After the feast and dancing, Jane asked to be excused, feigning light-headedness. I knew the real reason. Fireworks scared Jane. She feared a fire that would ravage the city of London, a recurring dream she'd had.

We tucked her into bed, and I returned to my apartments. The fireworks echoed off the walls in my bedchamber. I sat before the fireplace and waited. My lord husband would be returning to our rooms soon and hopefully would have more news on our alliance with the Marquess and Marchioness of Exeter as well as the other members of the Privy Council.

But more than the sharing of news, I waited up for the sharing of our bodies.

# CHAPTER EIGHT

*Do way! I let thee know, thou shalt not play with me:*
*Go range about, where thou mayst find some meatier fare for thee.*
*~Henry Howard, Earl of Surrey*

*Night of June 28, 1536*

"You are not asleep," Edward stated the obvious as he entered our suite well into the night. He'd crept in quietly, shutting the door with care. When he'd turned around, the only light in the presence chamber, from the crackling hearth, played shadows across his face. Seeing me perched and curled in the window seat obviously startled him, as he raised his brows and gave just the merest of jumps.

"I could not sleep."

"Meddlesome minds cease to rest." He sauntered forward, tall, lithe, powerful. A teasing smile played at the corners of his mouth.

I chuckled. To some it might have been an insult, but Edward prided me on my ability to meddle. I supposed this was partially why we got along so well, and even more so the reason he trusted me to take care of our fortunes while he was away.

"Something of the sort. Come sit, have some wine."

Edward came to sit beside me, his warm thigh pressed to mine. I handed him a cup of wine. He took a long sip, his shadowed eyes taking me in. I gazed into their depths, watching the flickering firelight play along his irises. He seemed to be thinking of where to start the conversation, and I let him. Sometimes it was better to let the man think he was in charge. He was much easier to mold when he thought he was in control. The thought struck a chord inside — perhaps I should give this same advice to Jane. A soft smile covered his lips, and I returned the gesture, filing away my intent to inform the queen of yet another way to meddle with the king.

"Come now, so quiet. Are you not wondering where I was tonight and what I was doing all this time I have been away from London? My meeting this evening with the king?"

I turned a coquettish smile and a saucy pop of my shoulder in his direction. "Dear husband, it is the duty of this wife of yours to wait until you are ready and listen to all you wish to tell me."

He laughed and patted his knee, his arms coming around me as he settled me onto his warm and familiar lap. The intimacy of the gesture startled me for a moment. It was almost jarring. For all the outward indiscretions he'd indulged in, and the ones I had played in my mind, the two of us were a match. I sank into his lap, letting the warmth and strength of his body melt into mine.

*Edward.* My husband, my savior. I reached up and touched my lips, my fingers wiping away nothing... just following the motions of Edward's fingers as they'd wiped blood from my swollen and torn mouth some years before.

"Since you are being so patient, I suppose I will start from the beginning." His voice startled me, but I had enough composure to play down my jump for only a jerk of rearranging my skirts. He took another sip of his wine and then set it on the side table. He pulled my head down to rest on his shoulder, his fingers threading through the ends of my hair, and I let out the breath I had been holding. "The king sent me to look in on several monasteries he will be dissolving. I was calculating goods, land, taxes, and gauging the hearts of the tenants, the clergy within."

"And what did you find?"

The fire crackled and popped in the background. I toyed with Edward's beard, and he caressed my back. A moment of guilt passed over me. He was such a good man, had done so much for me, and I was relieved I'd not fallen prey to Sir Anthony's advancements, no matter how he stirred me. Despite all I owed Edward, my very life in fact, I could not seem to control the pounding desire Anthony's presence elicited. Nay! The very thought of the man brought my heart to crescendo, moistened my palms. I cringed inwardly. Edward's first wife had betrayed him thusly… and with his own father—who sired two children on her, whom they tried to pass off as Edward's. My stomach churned. I could not. Would not.

"Half the monasteries are robbing the king blind." Again, Edward's voice jarred me from my thoughts, and I pushed the sinful recollection of Anthony's strong fingers from my mind. I must concentrate on Edward! What he had to say was important, and all information must be stored and filed away in the great vast canyon that was my memory, only to be recalled when needed.

Edward continued as I parted the way and paved a path in my mind for what he had to say. "A percentage of their tithes are supposed to go to King Henry, but there is a lot more gold in coffers than records in the books. It also appears they are harboring many jeweled relics. We had to repossess many a wagon full. His Majesty was made a rich man while I was on progress."

He laid his head back against the shutters that I had secured tightly and closed his eyes. I moved to straddle his waist so I could better massage his shoulders. His hands came to cup my behind, kneading the flesh there.

"And what of the people? Did you get a sense of their support of the king? For Jane?" I asked, worried over what I'd heard of people fearing the changes to our faith the king had mandated—those same people that were supporting Lady Mary. His breathing was even, and he did not move, did not answer. He looked ready to fall asleep, and we had so much left to discuss. I kissed the side of his neck to awaken him. His fingers gripped my hips, rubbing sensually as he rocked me back and forth. Far from asleep he was.

"I feel trouble is coming down the road," he whispered. "The monks were angry. They argued at first, but then they acquiesced, saying they wished to please His Majesty." Edward nibbled a path from my ear to my collarbone. "As they stood by silently watching, I could see the anger seething in their eyes. Peasants, merchants, even some noblemen gathered, expressing their displeasure, but none moved against us. The silent ones, fury bubbling under their calm exteriors, are the ones I worry about."

"When the time comes, you will be prepared. You've the fortune of seeing the smoke before the fire truly breaks into heavy flames."

With change there was always opposition. Even here at court, when new families rose, there were those who tried to suppress them. I did believe Edward was right. Trouble would come soon for the king. Whether it was in the way of the people, the clergy, the Pope in Rome, other monarchs, someone would not sit silent as King Henry took down their relics, changed the rules of the sacrament, harbored new thoughts on religion, gave power and credit to heretics and men of low birth—like Cromwell.

"What of Cromwell?" I moved my hands from his shoulders and began to massage his temple. Edward's head fell forward to lie against my breasts. I sucked in a breath, having missed the sensuality experienced between a man and a woman. Once again, Sir Anthony invaded my thoughts. How was I to get rid of him? Perhaps I should tell Edward the man was making untoward advances. Edward would have him gone in a moment, attending some task abroad, or thrown in the stocks for a crime he'd not committed but plenty of people bore witness to. No, I must be the one to strike him from my mind. And I must do it soon, for I truly loved my husband, would not want to hurt him.

"They whisper it is all his doing. The king can easily blame an uprising on *Secretary* Cromwell." Although his voice was muffled, the sneer in his tone was evident.

"Well, perhaps you might make mention of the whispers to His Majesty." I gasped as Edward pulled the ribbons from my chemise open, baring one breast for his examination. He palmed it, weighing it, massaging it, and then brought his lips to the turgid peak. My gasps for air turned to a murmur of appreciation.

"Indeed." He paused a moment, indulging in my flesh, but I sensed he had more to say. "They also voiced their ire at the Lady Mary being forced to renounce her parents' marriage and her title as princess." Here again, he paused, paying homage to my breasts. By the time he was through, I panted heavily, no longer able to focus as well as I should. "I think now might be the time to have Jane express her interest in the lady's status."

"And what of our new friends?"

"They will return to court shortly. The king is most interested in the whereabouts of the traitor Pole. He is a Plantagenet and gaining support quickly across Europe to take the throne. There are even those in England who believe he is the rightful heir, and that Henry VII—the king's father—was only a usurper and our own king a pretender. Pole is a threat the king will want to be rid of most expeditiously."

I nodded, and there ended our speech. I stood and led Edward to my private chamber and the bed in which I had spent the last fortnight dreaming—albeit regrettably—of Sir Anthony. But shame had no place in our marriage, and I reminded myself that while he was away, Edward had surely indulged himself between any number of women's thighs. My fantasies of another man could hardly have been criticized when they'd only happened in the darkened night of my room when I was all alone.

Edward lay down atop of me. "Promise me you will take care of Mary with Jane?"

"As it is your wish, my lord." I lifted my legs around his hips, eager for him to slip inside me. My fingers slid a path down his back. Edward kissed my lips gently, lovingly. He was in no hurry. I lay back and let him make love to me, pleasure radiating throughout my limbs.

I would see to it that Jane made mention of Mary, and Edward would stir the beginnings of suspicion on Cromwell. If all worked out in our favor, Cromwell would fall, and there would lie an opening to more elevation, for the king would need a new secretary and Lord Privy Seal, and my lord husband would be a perfect match. With Edward as secretary, our way in England would be paved.

*July 1, 1536*

"Are you happy, Jane?" King Henry asked.

A select number of ladies of the queen's bedchamber and the king's Privy Council stood quietly in the room, breath held at this last question, as the royal couple indulged in a private meal. As a collection, our torsos moved forward to better hear the answer. Jane opened her mouth and closed it—a fish out of water. My chest grew tight from not breathing. I glanced around at the others in the room.

The women were seated behind the queen, and the men stood behind the king. A visible show of who was stronger. Men vs. women. The king vs. his queen. Should either sovereign have need of something, we were here to serve. But at the moment, the only thing we were truly interested in serving was our ears. *Answer, Jane!* The shout inside my mind did little to make the words come out of Jane's mouth. Seconds felt like an eternity. The clock on the mantle ticked thirty-three times.

A musician played the lute quietly. Candles were lit in the wall sconces and on the table. The room was bright, and although the king and queen sought privacy away from court, the dozen or so of us courtiers negated such a true happening. We all pretended interest in our own thoughts, but every person's ears were trained on the conversation at hand.

I ducked my head and grimaced. My stomach turned in knots, and bile rose in my throat. Edward and I had partaken in a light supper before attending our sovereigns, but once again I had not been able to eat much. The scent of grease and meat had made me queasy these past few days.

Finally, Jane took a deep breath and smiled, her eyes sparkling clear and blue. "Yes, Your Majesty. You have seen to my every comfort, and I am much obliged for your love and grace." She picked at some seasoned vegetables on her plate with her fork, pushing them around as a small child would but not bringing the food to pass her lips.

King Henry broke out in a wide grin, seeming either not to notice Jane's nerves or seeking to soothe them. "I have a gift for you."

At this exchange, the group of men stood taller, the women sat straighter, all of us visibly relieved at the queen's answer and the king's respective response, a testament to the king's volatile moods and how much the court was attuned to them, indeed in sync.

He waved over a groom, who presented him with a small package wrapped in purple velvet. The king held onto the gift and seemed to watch his wife, who eyed the package.

"What do you think it is?" he asked, his voice filled with mirth.

Jane folded her hands in her lap. "I could not guess, Majesty, but I am confident with your most excellent taste it is a gift I will cherish for all seasons."

"I do adore you, Jane," Henry breathed with a passion that I hadn't heard in some time. I was struck then with how much he truly cared for her.

Henry handed the gift to Jane, who took it with slim white fingers. He was forever bestowing gifts on her, and she accepted them with grace.

I strained forward just a bit as to go unnoticed, while Jane unwrapped her gift. A glittering brooch of pearls, rubies and diamonds inlaid in gold emerged.

"It is beautiful," she breathed, clutching it to her chest. "You spoil me."

"No, Jane." Henry leaned over the table and took one of Jane's hands in his. He kissed her gently on the knuckles, his lips lingering perhaps a moment longer than was proper. "It is you who spoil me. A husband could not ask for a better wife, and a king could not ask for a more humble queen." The way he said "queen" was drawn out on his lips, as if he wished to impart on her the import of what he had said. The king always seemed to have a never-ending wealth of well-thought-out speech. His words were gracious but meant to mold. He thanked her, loved her, but at the same time told her he expected her to remain humble.

"Thank you." She inclined her head in her usual fashion, which only made her look more virtuous, and Henry's smile widened. She handled the king well. Very well.

"Is there anything you require?" he asked, taking a large chunk of bread into his mouth.

Now was Jane's chance. Would she do it? I silently prayed that she had the nerve to do the Lady Mary justice. I had had a long conversation about the matter with the queen, and she had even admitted to me it was a subject she felt very close to her heart and had in fact been planning to approach His Majesty on the topic very shortly.

She met his eyes, her mouth opened and shut again. She must have been thinking about it. *Dear God, do not let her back down now!*

"What is it, Jane?" the king urged. He set down a chunk of meat he'd picked up, sat back and folded his arms over his chest. His expression was open, as if he hung on to the air for the syllables of her speech, but his countenance was reserved, closed off. I would have hated to have been on the receiving end of such a conundrum. Was the king open to her request or not?

"There is one thing." She put her utensils down, the clink echoing in the silent room. Each courtier once again held their breath, and the musician even played at a quieter tone. I chewed the inside of my cheek, indeed biting into the flesh enough to draw a drop of blood.

"Yes?" Henry raised his brow. His countenance remained unchanged. He waited, almost like a lion waited on the sides for his prey to make itself an easy target. He expected her to make a mistake. He was a pessimist, thinking that each person he loved would soon toss him and his values in the wind. And, indeed, if one wasn't with him, one was against him.

Slim fingers folded in her lap, Jane sat up straighter, chin lifted slightly as she faced the lion head-on. Her words were hurried, as if she feared she would not finish if she spoke too slowly. "I would request that the Lady Mary might come back to court. I am lonely and in need of someone close to my rank to make merry with."

A dark cloud consumed the king's eyes at first, and we all thought he might become angry. I twisted my fingers together, knuckles whitening, as I sat on the very edge of my chair. But then he laughed—a jubilant sound. Even still, with the king you never knew if that laugh would end with you in a prison cell or with gold in your hands.

"Then we shall have her here, for I would only wish to see you merry."

131

Jane smiled innocently and thanked His Majesty. I breathed a sigh of relief and unclenched my fists, which I had not realized left my fingernails digging into my palms. I was not the only one, as the ladies surrounding me sat a little less stiffly in their seats, and those men who'd locked knees relaxed their stance. In fact, the very walls seemed to expand and contract with a breath of relief at His Majesty's giving mood. With Mary back at court, it should appease many in the land who sought to move against His Majesty and Jane.

"Is there anything else, My Queen?" He sat forward, his expression challenging.

I wholly expected Jane to decline and continue to eat her pheasant with ginger sauce, but instead she perked up, leaned her head closer. And I fought hard to hide the incredulous look on my face. The queen was tempting fate to be so bold.

"I heartily beg you to leave the monasteries as they are." Jane's voice was filled with emotion as she choked out the words, the last few said in a whisper as she lost her nerve.

At this, Henry slammed down his napkin and rose. I jumped a little in my seat, suppressed a gasp, my nails once again digging into my tender palms. My brocade and jewel-encrusted gown felt suddenly heavy. My headpiece squeezed the sides of my head. My emerald and gold necklace choked me.

*No, Jane!* The king had already agreed to have the Lady Mary to court, and with this one last request, pure and sweet, Queen Jane could devastate all of our well-laid plans!

Bracing his hands on the small table, King Henry leaned toward his wife. The air was thick, and I, along with several courtiers, visibly cringed, if only for a second. Would he strike her? The air in the room was sucked out, as every lady and gentleman took quick and shallow breaths, expecting the worst.

"Kindly do not meddle in my affairs." His voice was whisper quiet, alarming. A shiver passed over my spine. "You are queen, bound to *obey* and *serve* me. Do not presume to offer *me* advice. Bear me a son and make merry with my daughters. That is *all* I require of you."

His words must have stung Jane, for she envisioned herself in love with the king, and his ire, and reminder that she was only a womb to bring forth a child, would dampen her spirit.

She bowed her head, her hands in her lap. "I am most humbly sorry, Your Grace. If it pleases you, I will never bring up such a topic again."

"It pleases me." Henry slumped back into his chair and popped an almond into his mouth. "Shall we continue to make merry, Jane?"

His countenance changed to one of joy, and one would not have thought he had just been so menacing, towering over his petite wife. I looked from one to the other, not certain I fully understood that he'd forgiven her so easily, that he hadn't changed his mind and told her she could no longer have Mary at court. But 'twas true. Verily, he sat there, happy as a clam, gazing at his wife.

"Yes," she whispered.

"To you, then!" He raised his goblet, and she to his. They clinked glasses, and he downed his in one large gulp, while Jane sipped prettily.

I took the chance of glancing toward Edward, who stood stoically to the right behind Henry, but his gaze never left the king. I wanted to gauge his reaction. There was no light in my husband's eyes, not a curve of his lip to show he was pleased or displeased. No doubt his pleasure at Mary coming to court was outweighed by his fear for Jane and anger at her request about the monasteries. He would have words with her later, of that I was certain.

My gaze moved to Anthony, who stood beside Edward. He was staring at me with an intensity that made me want to squirm. Could he see my discomfort growing? As soon as our gazes connected, he looked away. Was he angry with me? He could not be, for there was no reason, other than I hadn't indulged in his request for intimacy.

One of the ladies in waiting opened her fan and began to wave herself, and I quickly followed suit. The room was becoming hotter by the moment.

And then suddenly the room heated another degree, as once again I caught Anthony gazing at me. He wet his lips, hungrily, like if there had been no one else in the room, he would gave stripped me bare and pounced on me. At one time, such a thought would have had me shaking and running from London, but for him... my blood heated.

I longed for Anthony—for the freedom he represented—as much as I wished he would disappear. Confusion warred within me. Duty, loyalty, love for my husband clashed with pure desire, curiosity and, if I was honest, the unadulterated passion Anthony promised.

But I could not come undone. If I was going to be successful at this court, rise to the ranks we strived for, I could not let an affair of the heart—or the loins—take over my whole state of mind. I was not a young maid. I was a woman grown, age six and twenty. Only one time had my feelings for a man nearly ruined me, broken me. And that same man still affected me, sending the blood rushing like the icy Thames through my veins. I could not let a little thing like infatuation ruin all of our carefully laid plans.

Even as I thought it, my subconscious struggled. Infatuation was not what I felt for Anthony. I did not know how it happened, but in only a few weeks, his heated stares, his promises of pleasure had begun to strike some forbidden chord buried deep inside me. That chord had trilled its way to the surface, and now, I sat while a bitter battle crashed within, tempting me to rush behind the curtains and drag Anthony with me. Steal a kiss, feel his beautiful lips on mine. I looked down at the skirts of my gown and my jeweled hands folded there.

*Silly chit!*

Just as Jane was descended from Edward III, I was as well. Royal blood flowed through these veins. Indulgence, flights of fancy, were beneath me. Demeaned my bloodline. My legacy.

When I looked up again, I caught the gaze of Surrey. He smirked, and I narrowed my eyes at him, wondering what he thought he might know about me beyond the disgrace in which he played such a part. The man was so volatile, a firework ready to explode. He was dangerous to have around court. He would surely be the ruin of someone else, and I prayed he did not get his talons buried beneath my flesh again.

He silently pursed his lips as if to kiss me, I wanted to jump up, shout and strike him. Instead, I sniffed and turned my head. The last thing I needed was another loaded match with the man. I needed all my armor for the days and years ahead, and he would only drain me of my wits in one conversation.

"Ladies, gentlemen, we bid you goodnight," King Henry said. Engrossed in my thoughts, I had not seen King Henry rise. He waved his hand, dismissing us from his presence.

Courtiers began to file out, but I took notice that Jane stayed behind. I skirted my way around to her chair, curtsied. "Your Grace, will you require assistance?"

Jane grasped my hand and squeezed. It was not she who answered, but Henry himself.

"Lady Anne, she will not require anyone this evening, save myself." His voice was calm, solicitous. He offered me his hand, and I kissed his ring before rising.

Jane blushed at the king's very obvious desire for her.

I nodded and quit the room, only to run headlong into the object of my own desire.

# CHAPTER NINE

*With that he beat his tail, his eyes began to flame;*
*I might perceive his noble heart much moved by the same.*
*~Henry Howard, Earl of Surrey*

*Night of July 1, 1536*

"My lady, I must have a word with you." Anthony stood close, his frenzied words whispered.

"Sir, this is entirely inappropriate, should Edward—"

His hand came up quickly, his finger pressed to my lips. "Not another word." With that, he gripped my arm and steered me down the opposite direction from the other courtiers. I looked about frantically, hoping someone would call out to us, praying for Edward to turn and yell for Anthony to take his hands off my person, but before all that could happen, we melted into the shadows as if we'd never existed. Calling out now would only draw attention and I had no desire to bring shame to my family.

Anthony opened a door and ushered me inside. The room was dark, black and smelled musty. A storeroom of some type, and it only brought back a flood of memories. Surrey. Pain. Shame. I closed my eyes and took a deep breath, willing the tremors to subside. This was not Surrey, but Anthony. A man who, for the most part, I trusted.

"Pray forgive me, Anne."

I opened my eyes and could barely see the outline of his form. His fingers slid up the length of my arms and gripped me at the elbows. His breaths were shallow, hitched, and then even.

"This is unseemly. Let go of me."

He let go of my arms and walked away. "'Twas not my desire to put you in this position. I know how dangerous it is to sneak about, but it was imperative I get word to you."

My skin burned where he'd touched me. My chest ached from holding my breath.

I breathed deeply of the musty air and tried not to cough from the staleness. "On with it then, sir. What is it you need to relay to me?" I tried to sound as if our relationship was purely business, as if I never thought of him in intimate ways. Did he believe me?

Anthony's soft chuckle was the only answer I needed. He did not.

He came forward again, only inches away. "I admire your spirit, Anne. But someday both of us will lose this game of desire. Don't fight it. We're on the same team."

I ignored his comments, knowing deep inside the validity they held. Part of me *wanted* to lose. To lie in his arms. But to do so would have been to risk too much.

At his resigned sigh, I knew he understood I would not give his desires credence.

"I've just had word from the north. They are planning something. With the king's dissolution of the monasteries, the people are bursting with anger, pain. They feel as if the king is shunning God himself."

"That is preposterous. The king seeks only to take the rule of the church from a man in Rome. He himself is ordained by God to rule his people. Why not be the second-in-command of the Lord's word?" It felt preposterous even coming from my own lips.

"You need not preach to me, madam. I am well aware of the truths our king so humbly lays before his people. I am but a messenger. And it is far worse than we may think."

"How so?"

"The people are rallying behind Lady Mary. They want to put her on the throne and oust her own father. What's more, my own brother came to me in a flurry this morning to tell me he'd heard rumors of a plot to murder the Duke Richmond."

I gasped. "'Tis impossible! The king's own son? Who would do such a thing?" Yet, inside my mind, I knew any number of people who would.

"My guess is Cromwell. He is a jealous man and is afraid that Richmond, now grown older, stronger, popular with the people, may demand a place in the succession, perhaps raise his own army."

I jolted. Cromwell, again? The man would see everyone close to Henry dead if he could.

"Does the king know?"

"Not yet," he whispered and came closer. In the dark, I could see his head move to examine the door, perhaps checking for shadows underneath the frame. At court, there was never a lack for spies, and it was possible at least one of them skulking about had seen us enter the room.

My eyes finally adjusted to the dark, lightening the shadows. When he turned back to face me, his lips were only an inch away from mine. My heart thudded, felt like it flipped, constricted. Suddenly, my mouth was dry, my lips chapped. I licked them in an effort for relief.

I backed away, but his arms reached out around my waist and pulled me back. "Do not," he murmured, his lips pressed to my forehead. "Do not pull away this time."

A sense of panic seized me. I could not move, could not breathe. My heart beat so rapidly, at any moment it might burst, killing me instantly. And I almost hoped for such a sweet death.

I tried to suck in a breath, but my swollen throat rebelled. With Anthony, though we were mired in politics loving him gained neither of us anything more than a small piece of joy. And I wanted that joy, wanted something only for myself that I could clutch to my chest forever. Not share. Anthony knew nothing of my past. Of my ruination and Edward's saving me. I was not tainted in Anthony's eyes. Not beholden to him for anything.

Meanwhile, he pleaded with me, his lips murmuring whispers over the bridge of my nose, to my cheeks, my chin. I was unable to move, limbs locked, and could only let his lips traveling over my flesh continue. *No! Anne, no! Stop him!* my mind shouted at me. But there was nothing I could do. I let him, almost going limp as I succumbed to his kisses, and then his mouth hovered over mine. The torment of waiting was almost too much. I had to taste him, despite the angel on my shoulder yelling *no*. Despite the husband who waited for me in my chambers. The desire was too much, the need to feel his lips on mine too strong.

I pressed forward, connecting my lips to his. My stomach twisted and turned as I did so, and I knew how wrong and utterly forbidden this was. We stayed that way for a breath, not kissing, just mouths pressed together. And then passion took over. Our heads slanted this way and that, mouths pressed, lips opened, tongues thrusting. It was a heated, hungry kiss, one that had been waiting in the foreground for weeks to come. A starving man come to a feast. We tasted of each other, he of sweet wine mixed with the pears of my dinner. I wrapped my arms around his neck, and he grasped my hips, pulling me against him. Wantonly, I rubbed my body against his. I wanted to be one with him, to be so close that one could not tell where one began and the other started.

The click of boot heels outside the door shocked us both back to reality, else I know we'd have lain on the floor and let desire take its course. I swiftly yanked back. What in God's name was I thinking? Never before had I allowed such passion to take over. The loyalty I prided in having for my husband abandoned me. I pulled away and smoothed my skirts, grateful he hadn't had the need to run his hands through my hair and ruined my coiffure. We waited until the sound of footsteps passed, both of us breathing heavily.

"I cannot live without you," Anthony murmured, coming close once more. "I've never met a woman like you, Anne. You're so passionate about everything. Even your kiss makes me feel as though I've died and gone to heaven. You're everything a man could desire. Strength, beauty, intelligence, and so desirable. Don't push me away, Anne. Be my lover."

I stepped back, hands out to ward him off. I shook my head. "No, Anthony. No. This was a mistake." But even as I said the words, I doubted them. He made me feel like I was soaring. So forbidden and yet so enticing. Not even Edward made me feel the way Anthony did. But he didn't know the real me. Didn't know the past I kept hidden. I could not let my base desires rule, trump over my plans to rise in the realm.

"Can you not see we were meant for each other?"

"It was one kiss, sir. And not something we shall repeat." How had I let this get so out of control?

His breath came out in a whoosh. "Pray forgive me, my lady. I let my desires get away from me."

But it was not only him. I let him, wanted him, too. "As did I," I admitted softly.

"I know you better than you think, my lady. But you are also a woman in need of someone to stroke her feminine side. Someone to desire your company not for what you can bring them, or what they did for you, but because they desire to be by your side." He paused, sucked in a breath. "I'd set aside my wife if it were possible to put you in her place."

His words struck deep. For companionship not weighed down with debts was the one thing I did desire. A true and free love. But wanting something as frivolous as that was naïve and ridiculous. And he was talking about setting aside a wife, just as our king had done. Just as I feared Edward might one day do with me. I shook my head. Unwilling to continue speaking on it further.

Love was for peasants, and even they could not always put food on the table. What I had for Edward was real enough. We respected each other, and while we did not while away our days singing and reading poems, I did believe we had a high level of love for one another.

Anthony came closer. "Let me love you, Anne. Without fear of being beholden to me, or I to you. Just two people partaking in the joys of each other."

His words dripped like honey, sweet and tantalizing, and while I let his enticement wash over me, somehow he pulled me into his

140

embrace again, his breath against my neck. I shivered, my flesh rippling with errant yearning.

"No," I nearly shouted. "I must go." Edward was waiting for me, and if I supplicated to my desire and Anthony tonight, my husband would know.

Anthony nodded. "I will come to you tomorrow, while Edward meets with the king."

I hadn't known of their meeting, but I did not doubt it would happen. I did not acknowledge Anthony's promise to come to me, for doing so would have been to ask for it. If he came, I would be there, and if he wanted to kiss me again, I wasn't certain I could deny him.

The shadows danced particularly overmuch tonight as I passed through one corridor after another on my way to my chambers. I encountered no one outside the door to the storage room Sir Anthony had pulled me into, but that did not mean that no one saw us. We exited one at a time, myself first, as I was eager to get back to my own private apartments.

As if proving my point, long slim fingers thrust from the darkness of the corridor and gripped my arm, tugging me into an empty alcove.

"What in heaven's name are you doing?" My mother's shrill hiss resounded in my ear.

I disengaged her fingers from my arm, my flesh tender and bruised where she'd gripped me, and thrust my chin upward. "Pardon me?"

Her eyes narrowed and darted about, searching for something or someone. "I saw you. I waited after the king dismissed everyone to find you. I saw you with *him*."

What could I say? My spine straightened to the point I thought it might snap. I could not deny it. "And what exactly do you *think* you saw?" I kept my voice civil, despite wanting to explode. Why did she and Page have to return to court?

"I saw a lover's tryst," she spat.

I made something of a disgusted snort, my hands folding in front of my pelvis in a way that made me appear overly relaxed. "You must be jesting, Mother."

"I make no jests about it. You sully your already tarnished reputation. Lucky for you, Beauchamp would have you when no other man would. I do not know why I bribed that bastard Surrey to keep quiet about your wantonness. You cannot keep your legs closed. Perhaps I should approach him and tell him his discretion is no longer needed, then all of court will know of your wickedness. They will know you are not the proud Lady Anne you portray, but another court whore. It shall bring you down to your knees where you belong, praying for your sins." She sucked in her breath and straightened taller, as if trying to tower over me as she had when I was a child. Her eyes narrowed. "Tell me what you were doing with that man."

I bit the inside of my cheek, drawing blood to keep from shouting at her. How much I despised the very air she breathed. Made fists to keep from wiping the scowl from her face with my nails, clawing away at the cruel words that spilled from her lips like venom from a snake. "The man I just spoke to is working for Lord Beauchamp, Mother. He had news to relay to me that was not suitable for... lesser ears." My point was made, that his words were not for her but for me alone, and that she was not as powerful as I was at court. Despite her threats. I would not, could not, let her see how her vile words affected me.

She stepped back as if I had physically slapped her. "Be careful, Daughter. There are many ears and eyes that dance along King Henry's walls. Your stepfather has yet to be called before the king again. The travel back and forth from our lodgings to court is hindering our cause. Do you not recall what is at stake?" She flicked her gaze about, her paranoia clear. "You, too, might find yourself ousted from court. No matter who your sister-by-marriage is. I have glossed over your indiscretions in the past, and I shan't do it again."

Her words may have been a threat, but the woman wouldn't dare ruin her own chances at climbing higher within court. Before I could respond, she slinked away and disappeared into the shadows.

Then her last words struck home. *Indiscretions.* Fury bubbled to the surface, and I stifled a scream. My fingernails dug deep into my palms. *Indiscretions!* Forsooth, she would never view Surrey's rape and abuse of my body as anything other than my own fault on account of my dirty and whorish disposition! In her mind, and that of Sir Richard Page, I was the one to blame. And with Sir Anthony, I was. But not with Surrey.

My hands came up, and I slapped at the stone wall, my teeth grinding. "Bitch!" I slapped again harder, and harder, until my palms stung and my hair hung loose around my shoulders. My breathing was heavy, and my heart pounded against my ribs.

Slowly I came back to myself and realized where I was. A passing groomsman scurried away. Stoically, I smoothed my skirts and hair, taking deep, cleansing breaths.

I had lost my temper, and in a corridor! I crossed myself and walked quietly away, praying no one had born witness to it.

"My lady, I have been waiting for you," Edward stated upon my return to our chambers.

"My apologies, husband, I had need of privacy." Hopefully, he would take my statement for what it was and not ask what type of privacy I'd needed, or else I was prepared to tell him I'd run into Sir Anthony and tell him what he'd said. But I'd take our kiss to the grave.

"Do not apologize. I have not been waiting long. Come have a glass of wine. I have news for which I seek your counsel."

I strode to the empty hearth where Edward poured us each a healthy goblet of wine. We clinked glasses, took a sip and then I sat in one of our low-back mahogany chairs. Despite the embroidered cushion, I still could not seem to get comfortable.

"The Marquess and Marchioness of Exeter are due back to court imminently. They had speech with His Majesty earlier today, and promised to inform the king of all news regarding Pole's uprising."

"Did they reveal Pole's whereabouts?"

"Indeed, they did." Edward sat down and stretched his long legs out before him. "Our place is even more secure."

"This is most excellent news." My voice was even, surprising me, for inside I still shook. I took a healthy sip of potent wine.

"I thought you'd agree." Edward gave me a lopsided grin.

I sat up straighter. Why did he have to be charming when I felt so guilty? "And what of Lady Salisbury and Lord Montague?" How must they feel for betraying their own relation's location to Lady Exeter?

"Lady Salisbury will be employed as a governess to the king's youngest daughter, Lady Elizabeth. Lord Montague has the good fortune to return to court and serve His Majesty in the privy chamber."

"The closer to court the better for His Majesty to keep his eye on them?"

"Exactly." Edward smiled at me knowingly. He leaned forward and brushed a stray lock from my face. "I adore how your mind works."

My insides burned with shame. I could not allow him to treat me so lovingly when I had kissed another man so brazenly an hour before. "What is it you seek my counsel on?"

"The king has charged me — *not* Cromwell — with sending two men out to find Pole and disperse of him." Edward's face filled with pride.

"I assumed he would need to exact punishment on Pole."

"You are well acquainted with the men at court. What think you of Sir Nicholas Carew and Sir John Russell?" Edward asked.

I felt like squirming. I could not help but wonder at his meaning to my being acquainted with the men at court, but instead I thought on his query. "Sir John was once a formidable man, and undoubtedly he still is, but I think you might take a man more sprite of foot. Sir Francis Bryan comes to mind."

"Ah, yes, the pirate!" He clapped his hands once with excitement. "I should have thought of him outright. 'Tis why I seek counsel from my clever wife."

Guilt riddled me, nausea flooding me. I would not allow Sir Anthony entrance on the morrow. I forced laughter at Edward's enthusiasm, even though on the inside I wanted to put on a cilice as punishment for my sins. "Happy to oblige you, husband."

*July 2, 1536*

Why did pacing seem to calm a person's nerves?

I did not know the answer, only that wearing a path in the hard oak floor of my presence chamber did in fact make me feel somewhat better.

Edward had left for a council meeting with the king not ten minutes earlier. With him, a plea to find my mother and stepfather rooms at court. I prayed that this time the king would show mercy. The threats stacking against me were becoming more than I could bear.

The sun shone high in the sky, and I had flung open the windows in an effort to breathe fresh air, but the only air seeping through the open portal was humid and hot.

Would Sir Anthony arrive soon? I hoped he'd had a change of heart. Upon leaving, Edward said he'd be meeting with the council and then had business to attend to, and he would see me that evening for a private dinner in our chambers.

I dismissed the servants, with instructions not to return until just before dinner, just in case...

A knock at the door had me jumping slightly as I spun around. Sir Anthony. No! I took a deep breath in an effort to calm myself and walked toward the door, stopping to angle a vase of red and white roses just so, in an effort to still my trembling fingers.

When I opened the door, a groomsman stood in the hallway.

"My lady, I've been asked to deliver this to you." He handed me a parchment, bowed and then disappeared down the hall.

I closed the door and tore open the non-descript wax-sealed note.

*My lady,*
*Should it please you, I wish to impart on you that which was promised. I am able to receive you at your leisure in my office.*
*Ever your humble servant,*
*Sir Anthony Browne*

My fingers trembled, the paper crinkling. I curled it up into a ball and tossed it into the hearth, lighting it with flint to burn the evidence of my indiscretion. What did it mean? I couldn't go. Had to remain behind. I spent the next hour pacing another mile into the wooden floor.

Once the letter had turned to ashes, I left my room. My destination… Sir Anthony's office. My steps were quick, then slow, then quick, and I constantly turned to see who was watching, which darkened alcoves held roving eyes. Luckily, I passed through the castle without incident. I had to reiterate to him there was nothing between us. That our kiss was a mistake I regretted. And this was not something I could do in a letter, God forbid it be intercepted.

His office was inside his suite of rooms within the castle, and after only one knock, the door opened an inch. His hand grasped my wrist, and he propelled me inside, slamming the door behind us.

Gripped in his arms, he dipped me low in a playful manner and kissed me soundly on the lips. But I did not feel playful. I nearly choked on my breath. This was not why I had come! Was I only lying to myself? I could have simply sent him a missive that said, *No.*

"I had doubts about whether you'd arrive," he said.

I stood, wholly enthralled yet confused at the same time. I could not allow him to think I came to tryst. I straightened up and pulled from his arms.

"I was not entirely set on the matter, sir."

I stepped away, taking in the simple décor of his room. A few paintings adorned the walls, a large iron cross on one oak-paneled wall, and a marble statue of a man embracing a woman.

"And, yet, here you are." He followed behind me, plucking pins from my hair and attempting to disarm me of my headdress.

I whirled around, stopping him from undressing me further. "I came for the information you promised. Not to kiss. That was a mistake. One we won't be repeating."

Anthony frowned, and huffed a breath. "The uprising shall be diffused. The Duke of Richmond shall be protected."

"How can you be certain?" I asked.

"I told Lord Beauchamp of the news myself this morning. The Privy Council will meet on the matter, and your lord husband will go north to quell the anger of England's people. He will tell them the Lady Mary is coming back to court."

I pursed my lips, irritated that he'd taken the information to my husband himself. If he told Edward, why did he need to tell me? Was that his plan? To push Edward away, so he could have me to himself? Nay, I would not allow it. I would go north with Edward this time. "And Richmond?" If he were murdered, the Seymours would be blamed for we were the only ones with anything to gain from his death.

"I sent word to the young duke of what I heard. He is intelligent, strong, and has his own guard. He will protect himself."

I nodded, glad to have us safe from that scandal.

"Now… A kiss?" Anthony came up beside me, his fingers trailing up my back.

I shook my head, determined not to give in this time. Last night had been a moment's lapse in sanity, and now I knew better. I shouldn't have come. My husband was a formidable man, and I did not wish to ere on the wrong side of his liking. As much as I wanted to be free, if only for an afternoon, I wanted to remain in my position more, to garner a place among royalty for my own children, whenever God saw fit to bless me with them.

"Only a kiss, my lady. I wish to taste the sweetness of your lips once more. To be whisked away to paradise again by the softness of your mouth and the passion of your kiss."

When he put it so romantically, I could only think that one kiss would not hurt. He made it sound like a poem, a story and not true life. And despite my resignation to stay true to Edward, after last night's indulgence I so wanted to feel his lips on mine, taste the sweetness of his mouth, let him run his fingers through my hair. To surrender to the madness of it.

"Yes." The words were out of my mouth before I realized it, and my hand came up to my lips, shocked that I had uttered them. *No!*

Anthony's lids lowered, and a slow sensual smile spread on his lips. He was as pleased with my answer as I was shocked. But before he could reach for me, I turned and rushed toward a chair, sitting straight-backed, my gaze on the floor.

"I do not know why I said that. I cannot kiss you, sir. I love my husband."

Anthony came forward. "But you love me, too."

It was a bold statement, one as a lady I was inclined to take offense to.

"And my darling, vicious little Anne, I love thee." His words were soft and quickly spoken. We barely knew each other. How was it that in only a few weeks, one kiss, and little whispered conversations, feelings of such magnitude could take hold? Apprehension gripped me.

Anthony got down on his knees before me; my eyes widened at his boldness. He leaned up, hands braced on the arms of the chair, his chest pressed to my knees, and brushed his lips against mine. I pushed against his chest.

"No," I whispered half-heartedly. But he pushed gently back.

At first, it was a gentle kiss, the testing of our two wills, but then the kiss consumed me. I spread my knees so his chest fell between them, and his hands came up to cup my face, his tongue swift and fast as it darted against my parted lips.

More delicious than our kiss of last night, which had been hungry, full of desire, passion, this kiss was of surrender. We let go of our two worlds, and it was only the two of us, doing something that could land us in our graves, and yet the taste was so sweet both of us were willing to risk it.

Shame sliced through me, but I shoved it aside like an unwanted royal bastard... My entire life thus far had consisted of giving to others. This moment I was taking for myself—just this moment. And no more.

"Oh, Anne..." Anthony murmured.

Oh, vicious and cruel world, how a weak moment could shake up everything. How one kiss could rock me to the core and a fleeting cruel word from Edward could push me into the arms of another. I knew at that moment, one kiss would not do.

A knock at the door interrupted us, and I barely had enough time to smooth down my skirts and attempt to replace my hair pins and Anthony to straighten out his wrinkled doublet, before my brother Richard Stanhope barged through the door.

My heart, which moments ago had raced, now stopped completely. He looked from one of us to the other, a knowing look coming over his countenance as he no doubt took in my disheveled hair and redness of my cheeks and came to his own conclusions.

"Sister..." he drawled. Then his eyes narrowed as his gaze turned to Anthony. "What's this, sir?"

"It is not as it seems, I assure you," I rushed to speak, coming forward to stand between the two men.

Anthony's chest puffed out as did my brother's. For a brief moment, I feared they would duel.

"Appearances are rarely deceiving, I have learned," Richard replied, his lips turned down in a frown. He inclined his head, a calculating glint entering his eyes. "I shall see you at the next Privy Council meeting, Sir Anthony?"

Anthony ran a hand through his hair. "I cannot conceive of how, since you are not a member of the Privy Council, sir."

My stomach dropped, for I knew exactly where this conversation was headed. And, yet, I was not too altogether displeased, for my brother had inadvertently saved me from succumbing to desire, a mistake of the utmost.

"Precisely, my good sir." Richard's hand moved to the sword at his hip. "And I am most confident you shall endeavor to remedy that by eventide." With a nod in Anthony's direction, he turned to me. "Sister, I shall escort you back to Her Majesty, who is most likely in need of your service."

I did not argue but nodded my head and gripped Richard's elbow.

"Richard—"

"Do not speak of it, Anne. I shan't say a word. Anthony will see me on the council, and you shall see me married to a lady of some rank and value."

I bit the inside of my cheek to keep the bile from rising in my throat. My whole world was quickly becoming consumed by those who would see me about their favors.

A world that I was quickly losing control of—with no one to blame but myself.

*July 12, 1536*

I had spent the whole of the previous day in bed, with the exception of those times I had run to the chamber pot to toss up my accounts.

My maids had hovered over me, and Edward had stayed away, fearing I was plagued with some deadly illness he dare not pass on to the king or queen.

This morning was not much better, but at least the dizziness had passed. I attended Mass and then took to my rooms for a respite before I was to join the other ladies in attendance to the queen.

"My lady." My maid entered the room.

"Yes?" I sat on a chair, looking out the window. It was cloudy, the dark gray sky threatening a thunderstorm. More than anything, I wished to walk outside. Fresh air would do me a bit of good. As much as my room had been aired out and linens cleaned, I could still smell the remnants of sickness.

"Might I speak freely?" Jenny mumbled quietly.

I did not bother to look at her as I swatted a fly away from me. "Have out with it, then." I had no time for idle chatter and really did not see the need to indulge the woman, but if I did not, she would surely continue to pester me.

"As I am aware of your most private dealings, my lady—"

I cut Jenny off there, not wanting to hear another word. Would she begin to counsel me on my own affairs? "Then you best keep them to yourself, if you want to remain in my employment."

She bowed her head and rushed forward. "Begging your pardon, my lady, please, I must say I do not think you are ill. You are with child."

I gasped, my hand coming to my mouth and with it another wave of nausea. With child? "What makes you think so?"

She poured me a cup of watered ale and handed it to me. "I see your bed sheets when I change them... I am in charge of *all* your linens and clothing."

What was she trying to say? My head was light, stars dancing before my eyes. "And?"

"You've not had your courses for nigh on two or three months."

My eyes widened. Was it possible? I gulped the drink and suppressed the urge to run to the chamber pot. Edward and I had been married for little over a year, and not once had I been off course. We'd done our best to see that we did not conceive a child too early, as Edward wanted to concentrate on our position, on Jane. Perhaps with all the goings-on at court and within my mind, I had forgotten to keep track, forgotten to protect myself. I bit my lip. Oh, what would Edward think? Surely he would be angry, for Jane was not yet with child, and the wait for her pregnancy had put a strain on everyone at court. For the king to see that I had become with child would only cause a further rift.

"Are you certain?" I asked.

"Yes, my lady." She broke out into a wide smile. But I was not in the mood to indulge her.

I waved her away. "Keep this news to yourself," I muttered.

When she'd left, I stood and took the rosary I kept hidden in the chest next to my bed. The black pearls felt cold to my fingertips. I knelt below the window and prayed, pressing each bead fiercely with my fingertips as I recited *Ave Maria*.

"*Ave Maria, gratia plena, Dominus tecum, benedicta tu in mulieribus, et benedictus fructus ventris tui Iesus. Sancta Maria mater Dei, ora pro nobis peccatoribus, nunc, et in hora mortis nostrae. Amen.*

Dear God, let this child be a blessing. I pray thee, give Jane a child soon."

I prayed for so long my knees hurt and stomach growled for having missed both my breakfast and the nooning. Those at court must have simply thought I was still ill, and so no one bothered me.

I laid my hand on the lower part of my belly. A small knot had formed there, a tiny swelling, perhaps not noticeable to anyone, even Edward, who was more than familiar with my body. But I could feel it. I was normally thin, some said too thin, and never had I had a bump in my abdomen. I took a deep breath, the entirety of my situation filling me. My heart fluttered. There was life inside me. A small human form growing. My child.

I crossed myself and stood. If Edward ever had any suspicions I was having an affair, he would have confronted me. Even without any outward suspicions because of his first wife's infidelity, he would no doubt question whether this child was his. Just as his first wife had fooled him into believing the two children she bore him were his when they were not, I despaired at Edward believing the same about me.

My head fell back, and I stared blankly at the ceiling, examining the cracks and contours of the plaster, the flies that had made their homes there. Outside, thunder rumbled and lightning cracked. Fierce, white light filled the room.

I was struck with the realization that I must make Edward understand this could only be his child. He would accept that fact. He must.

I sent a messenger immediately to locate Edward, who was just on his way to his library after supping in the great hall. An hour later, Edward sauntered into our rooms.

"Anne?" he asked, his eyes roving over me, concern etched in the corners, for I rarely summoned him.

I straightened my shoulders, nodded to the servants to clear the room and waited until we were alone. Edward watched our staff leave, then turned eyes on me that spilled with fear.

"What is it?" he asked in a near whisper. He came forward, gripped my hands in his. "Has Surrey threatened you?"

I shook my head, letting a small smile touch my lips to calm him. "Nay, husband." Then I chewed my lip, before garnering the energy to burst out with, "I'm with child. We're to have a babe."

Edward's face paled, eyes widened. He stood stunned for several heartbeats before his eyes glistened, and he blinked back the sudden tears. Dropping to his knees, he pressed his hands to my abdomen.

"A babe?"

I nodded. "The first of many," I whispered.

Though he tried to hide his face, I watched as so many different emotions flickered over his countenance. "Oh, Anne. Thank you." He pressed his lips to my belly, and I let out a long held breath. There was no accusations of wrong doing on my part, but complete and utter adoration for the life growing within me.

I pressed my hand to the top of his head. "No, Edward, thank you."

He stood slowly, cupped my face and drew me in for a light, loving kissing. When he pulled away, concern once more clouded his eyes. "We must hide your condition until the queen conceives."

I nodded.

"When the time comes that you can no longer hide the swell of your belly, we'll remove you to Wulfhall."

The thought of leaving court filled me with fear and trepidation, but Edward was right.

"Let us pray that Jane quickens with child soon." For there was every possibility the king would see our child as an insult.

# CHAPTER TEN

*Yet saw I him refrain, and also his wrath assuage,*
*And unto her thus did he say, when he was past his rage...*
*'Cruel! You do me wrong, to set me thus so light;*
*Without desert for my good will to show me such despite.'*
*~Henry Howard, Earl of Surrey*

"How goes it with the king? Do you think you might be with child yet?" I asked Jane, my hand nervously coming to rest on my belly until I realized what I was doing and removed it. Thankfully, Jane was so engrossed in her own thoughts she did not notice.

"He comes to my bed but only twice a week." She walked to sit on one of her chairs, her head down. "I cannot seem to entice him more than that. My courses came a week ago." Her voice was far-off, disappointed.

"Twice a week could still work, but perhaps you might try persuading him more often?"

Jane nodded. "I have yet to ask him myself. I am trying to live up to his ideal of me. Pure, virginal."

"It is good of you, Jane. Let him feel like he is in control. A man is always best to mold when he thinks he's in the lead."

She smiled up at me and laughed lightly. "Anne, you are so dear to me. I do not know how I would survive all this without you." She swept her hand out, and then fingered the sapphire and diamond necklace she wore. Another gift from the king.

"May I inquire of something of a personal nature?"

"At your leisure." Jane stroked the brocade fabric of her gown, her fingers tracing the floral patterns.

"Does he...finish?"

At this, Jane's head popped up. "Truthfully, Anne, there are times I do not think he does, for there does not seem to be much...moisture afterward."

*Dear God, save us if the man is unable to father a child.* "Does he appear angry or frustrated?"

"No." Jane shook her head adamantly. "He is always most kind and solicitous. He caresses my hair, tells me how much he loves me. He stays the night, and sometimes in the morning, he will..." she twirled her hand in the air and blushed, "...again."

How unlike a man to remain so jovial and gratuitous if he was not enjoying himself, and especially for the king. Henry VIII was known for violent fits of temper, and yet to be so kind to his wife... There must have been another explanation. I was no doctor, nor even very versed in medicine, but common sense pointed to perhaps he was able to climax without spending.

"Do you think I shall ever conceive?" Her eyes pooled with tears, and I rushed forward to hand her one of my own embroidered handkerchiefs.

"Oh, Majesty. I do wholeheartedly. You have only been married a short while. Give it time. The king was able to get Katharine with child at least six times, the witch Anne at least two or three times, and you know his mistresses are likely to get pregnant just by breathing in his air. It will happen, I am certain of it."

"I pray it is soon, Anne. I fear with the pressure I am under, I am hindering the process. And, honestly, I know it is a sin to say, but sometimes I am thankful that he does not come to me more often. His leg...festers, and a stench emanates from it." Her head fell into her hands.

I came forward and sat beside her. "You are very courageous and strong, Jane. I have no doubt you will succeed in your duty to king, country and family."

Jane looked up, pressed her lips together, but said nothing, no doubt perturbed at my subtle mention of her familial obligations. It was time for me to change the subject matter of our conversation.

"Well, Jane, this is what we must do to help the king with his own conjugal duties. Order special food and spices to be used with all meals. Artichokes, asparagus, truffles, turtle's eggs, oysters, honey, figs. Tell Cook to use pepper, cloves, ginger, saffron and thyme liberally. These things will boost both of Your Majesties' fertility and raise his desire, so he might visit you almost every night of the week."

"I will see that it is done." Jane stood and clasped her arm through mine as we started to head back into her main presence chamber, where a few of her ladies awaited us to depart for the great hall. The rest had already gone ahead as Jane had instructed. But then she stopped and whispered, "Is Edward terribly angry with me for the other night?"

"The other night, Majesty?" I asked, not wanting her to know Edward had in fact raved nigh on an hour about her rash behavior a fortnight ago.

"You are too kind to me, Anne. You know of what I speak. My requests of the king."

I patted her hand and shook my head, and watched the tension visibly recede from her eyes, her shoulders relaxed. At the root of it all, I had to remember that Jane had much riding on her position. She was the third wife to a king who had no qualms about setting his spouses aside, or even having them executed. And there were plenty of people at court who would do his bidding, and not one who would naysay him. She deserved my empathy, and I would make certain in the future she got it.

When we walked into court, a large crowd had gathered in a corner, laughing. Queen Jane and I, being curious, walked closer to hear their words.

Jane Rochford stood in the middle, in her hand a crumpled parchment from which she read, her free hand moving violently in the air. Her face was flushed, eyes wild and bright blue.

Her gaze connected with mine, and she sneered. "*Sith that a Lion's heart is for a Wolf no prey. With bloody mouth go slake your thirst on simple sheep, I say."* At this she grasped a great cup of wine and gulped it down, wine dribbling onto her chin. The crowd grew more enthusiastic as she continued. *"With more despite and ire than I can now express, which to my pain, though I refrain, the cause you may well guess. As for because myself was author of the game, it boots me not that for my wrath I should disturb the same."*

The Earl of Surrey came to stand behind Lady Rochford. His lip curled in male satisfaction, and his eyes locked with mine. What was I missing? Why had they both looked at me?

"Lady Rochford, where did you get such a piece?" a courtier in the crowd shouted.

"It's mine," Surrey answered with a cocky tilt of his head, his eyes not leaving my own.

When I heard that, I knew exactly what had transpired. The man had written a poem defaming me. Would anyone realize it? Anger raked its nails along my flesh. If I'd had a sword, I would have tried with all my might to sever his head from his neck.

"Well done! Who is the dame?" the same courtier asked.

His lip curled even further, and I had to use great control not to swipe the parchment and burn it.

"No one of consequence," he replied, eyes fastened on mine.

At his last insult, I'd had enough. Luckily, I spotted Edward starting a game of cards. I needed his strength and nearness to calm the tidal waves roiling inside me. Unfortunately, Sir Anthony was at his side. He had not spoken to me in days. Anger filled his eyes whenever he saw me. No doubt, he felt I had cuckolded him with my own husband.

I looked around for another alternative to sitting with Edward *and* Anthony. My brother Michael was nowhere in sight. Elizabeth, Edward's sister, was engaged in a rather flamboyant conversation with the queen and king. My mother and Sir Richard Page scowled at me from across the room. They started forward. The last thing I wanted was a confrontation with them in the middle of the great hall. The humiliation of Surrey's poem was enough. Their descent on me pushed my decision. My only choice was Edward and Anthony.

I approached to a winning smile from Edward and a scowl from Anthony.

"Will you play with men, my lady?" Sir Anthony asked as I slipped into an empty seat at the table.

"My lady wife is quite adept at cards," Edward answered before I had the chance, which worked perfectly fine for me as I was still unsure of the strength of my own voice with my near-lover and husband sitting so closely and amiably to one another.

"Fascinating," Sir Anthony said, his voice lighthearted, but when I looked at him, his eyes gave away his true feelings. Jealousy, anger, desire. "Shall you play then?"

As it turned out, I was quite in the mood to gamble.

*July 13, 1536*

Jane Rochford was going to see the rough side of my tongue this morning.

I swept into Queen Jane's presence chamber, my head held high, shoulders back, chin up, skirts in hand, perfected a curtsy to my mistress, and then turned my eyes on the vile Lady of the Bedchamber.

Lady Rochford openly winced and turned away to avoid my gaze, but she would not get away with eluding me.

"Majesty, if it pleases you, might I have a private word with Lady Rochford?"

Queen Jane lowered her embroidery and eyed me warily. I smiled indulgently, and she nodded.

Lady Rochford literally shook in her satin slippers. Her hands trembled as she curled them in her gown. I inclined my head toward the door and walked into the corridor. Lady Rochford followed. She had grounds to be nervous. Edward and I were both closer to the royal couple than she was, and our power at court was only growing, while she was an unmarried widow of a traitor. Most people of the court despised her, and the rest endured her.

The corridor was empty, save for a few guards posted, who effectively kept their gazes straightforward, their eyes almost glazed over from staring at some certain spot on the walls for the entirety of their watch. Sconces with torches were lit up and down the corridor. Even though it was morning, no natural light lit the way. The door gently clicked closed as I shut it. I took a few moments to analyze Jane's appearance, my agenda twofold: one, to make her more nervous, and secondly, I was looking for something — a mark of Surrey. From experience I knew the man could not have a woman without branding her in some way. Her light hair was in a perfect coiffure, covered by a delicate silk and pearl-encrusted gable hood. Her gown was a light yellow silk, with embroidered pearls on the bodice. Jade earrings bobbed at her lobes. And there it was, a purplish bruise of a lover's kiss hidden, but not well enough, beneath a pearl and jade collar necklace.

I smiled cruelly, having ammunition now to mortify her. Jane Rochford was rollicking herself in an affair. Queen Jane would not be pleased, because she required her ladies to maintain an air of decorum and chastity. "Might you explain the spectacle you made yesterday?"

Lady Rochford's icy blue eyes connected with mine in challenge. "Spectacle, my lady?"

My smile widened when I saw how much I disturbed her. She shifted on her feet. Trying valiantly not to spit at me, I speculated.

"Do not play coy with me. Unless you imbibed a quart of strong French wine, I am certain you will recall your recitation of Surrey's poem last eve."

Jane lifted her chin and pursed her lips. "A lovely poem," she bit out.

"Did you help your *lover* to write it?"

Jane's hand went immediately to her throat, shifting the collar around.

"No need, I already saw it."

Jane's throat bobbed as she swallowed. Her pupils dilated, and her skin paled a shade.

"You might think you know the games courtiers play, the wickedness behind closed doors, secrets whispered." I stepped closer to her, invading her personal space. "You might even believe yourself clever enough to behold such dealings and wield the perpetrators to your liking." I leaned in, my face only inches from hers. Jane held her breath, her eyes only slightly widened as she tried valiantly not to show a trace of reaction. "But I warn you now, *Lady* Rochford, I shall beat you at your own occupation. I shall hang you out to dry, and see to it you never step foot in this court or any other again, if you dare to cross me. Watch your steps."

Jane stepped back and bowed her head, but not before a flash of hatred marred her features.

"My lady." She curtsied, and although she returned to the queen without my permission, I allowed her that much. With luck, I would not have to deal with her again, at least not for a while. For certes, the woman was spiteful, abhorrent, and would seek recourse for my threats.

*July 15, 1536*

Fallen leaves and sticks crunched under the heavy hooves of the horses as we raced through the forest out onto fields and back again in search of the stag the hunting dogs had alerted us to.

Jane kept her seat well beside the king, and I held back a little, my purpose to capture something besides a deer. As the minutes continued to pass, I slowed my horse more and more until no one seemed to notice I was well behind. No one except, Sir Anthony, the object of my diversion.

"My lady, is all well with you?" He pulled up next to my horse, his sweet eyes roving over my form and that of my horse. But I must stop this! I could not think of his eyes as sweet, especially when anger and hurt still filled their depths. The way he'd looked at me over the card table… Our near-tryst had been short-lived and could never happen again. I would only get myself into trouble, and I'd only started on this sordid affair to glean information, not attain another man to flap his jaws at my backside.

"Come," I said hastily, and turned my horse in the opposite direction of the other riders.

At a discreet pace, Anthony followed until the sounds of the other riders could no longer be heard.

"What is it, Anne?" he asked, his voice filled with concern and irritation.

"Oh, posh, Anthony. 'Tis nothing all that bad. I just needed a moment to speak with you alone, and now that my Lord Beauchamp has returned, private speech has been impossible. And, I daresay, you've been avoiding me, at any rate."

"Well, get on with it then."

Anthony had never been so curt with me before. I pursed my lips and gave him a reproving look. "I wanted to make it clear that what happened between us two weeks ago was a mistake. I think we should no longer be seen together."

"Seen together? Why? All of court has seen us together. What difference does it make?"

"You understand my meaning. Do not act as though you do not. 'Tis important we no longer indulge ourselves. If we kept on, Edward would suspect. My brother could have easily been any other courtier."

Anthony looked away, his lips pressed thinly together. I could tell he was angry. I reached out to touch his arm, the muscles of his forearm thick and hard beneath my fingertips. He pulled his arm from my grasp, and cold, hard eyes fastened on mine. Our horses pranced with irritation at our own raised emotions.

"Do you think me a green boy? Some stable whelp? I am not stupid, Anne. I serve a fiercely smart and volatile master. Think you that I do not know how to keep my indiscretions a secret? Think I might burst into your apartments and ravage you on the dining room table as Lord Beauchamp sups? *Fuck* you while he watches?" His voice was raised, and he looked down his nose at me like I was an imbecile.

I was taken aback by his speech, his anger. My reaction was just as violent as his words. I was at once swiftly angry, and I leaned forward and slapped him hard on the cheek. The resounding crack was audible throughout the trees.

What was I to do? I could not turn my husband away, and that was the truth of it. I was married. Edward was my husband, and not Anthony. He had no claim on me the way Edward did, and despite having slipped up with Anthony, I was still loyal to my husband and would not risk our marriage. Nor the damning of my soul.

Birds scattered, branches rustled, and in the distance, cheers and shouting could be heard. The stag had been downed just as I struck Sir Anthony. If the shouts could be heard that closely, the beast must have turned around, the crowd heading back our way. I needed to leave soon before someone was upon us, if they weren't already. King Henry had his spies everywhere, just as my husband, Norfolk and Cromwell did, and any other nobleman high up enough for it to matter.

"How dare you speak to me that way?" I asked. "I came here to warn you, so you would not feel that I backed out of our alliance, or that my affections for you were so shallow as to change overnight. But perhaps you are right. *I* am the one who's been naïve. To think I actually harbored some attachment to you, and thought maybe you might have felt something for me in—"

Sir Anthony cut off my tirade with his hands thrust around the back of my head, hauling me forward, his mouth claiming mine in a fierce, almost violent kiss. I struggled against his kiss, memories of Surrey attacking me rushing to the surface. I pulled back and slapped him again. I felt eyes on me. Although a cursory glance showed me there was no one visible, someone's eyes bored into the back of my head. Without another word, I turned and galloped back to the castle.

The corridor to my rooms seemed longer and darker than I'd ever remembered. A chill swept through the narrow passage despite the warm temperatures outside. The air felt damp, stirred, alive. And yet, I was alone. Or was I? I hurried along, knowing all the people I would have been interested in running into were outside with the king. Anyone lurking in the shadows did so only for some nefarious purpose.

"Anne." My name was spoken in a low, condescending tone, too low for me to distinguish whose voice it was. "Tsk, tsk, tsk." Out of the shadows walked Thomas Seymour, Edward's brother. He shook his head back and forth and wagged his finger. The air left my lungs, and my stomach lurched.

"You've been a naughty lady."

*Oh, God! What does he know?*

My knees grew weak, and despite the sickness I felt in my belly, I squared my shoulders and lifted my chin. "What do you want, Thomas?"

He came closer, his face within an inch of mine. "What do I want? I want a great deal. I want to know why my brother, who is made a cuckold by one wife and made a dog by the other, continues to gain succor from the king. I want to know why I, a real man, remain a groom of the privy chamber, while my brother is made a viscount. I work hard for my king. My sister is a queen. I want my title, too."

I rolled my eyes and crossed my arms over my chest, tapped my foot. "Thomas, you are a younger son. You've done little to bring Jane up in the king's eyes. You also are a fool."

He bared his teeth at me. "A fool? A fool, you say? I would not stand by and let a second wife make a cuckold of me."

"Are you accusing me?" I stepped forward, my fists now at my sides, ready to do battle with the jealous whelp.

"I saw you in the forest with Sir Anthony." His eyes were accusing, and he did not back down.

"Did you? How wonderful for you. Perhaps you heard me tell the man I was ill and to relay this message to Edward?"

"I heard no such thing. I saw him kiss you. I've caught you two before. I warned you then, but you have not heeded my warning."

"He was overcome by the heat, and if you saw him kiss me, surely you saw me slap him."

"If Edward knew, he would make Sir Anthony call seconds."

"A duel would settle nothing and only ruin Edward's chances at a future within this court. Edward is levelheaded, cool, calculating. He thinks before he acts. He is not brash. Perhaps, Sir Thomas, that is why he has risen so high above you."

Thomas clicked his teeth at me. His hand reached up to cup my breast, pinching my nipple hard. I slammed the heel of my slipper down on his foot and was satisfied with his pained grunt.

"Thomas," I whispered in his ear. "If I wish a man to touch me, he'll know it. Do not presume to lay hands on me again. Ever."

"Your ladyship." He bowed lightly, pain still registering in his features. I swept past him, toward my rooms.

I now had yet another enemy at court, and this one hung more scandal over my head than I held over his.

*July 20, 1536*

"Please deliver this message to Sir Thomas Seymour," I said, confidently handing the note to a groom.

My note to my brother-by-marriage was simple. After spending nearly a pound silver, I had been able to dig up quite a few intriguing rumors regarding dear Thomas. Seemed the man had a penchant close to that of Lord Surrey, yet his forceful ways with the ladies had yet to become knowledge to Edward. Indeed, once his affinity for a certain married and noble woman — Catherine Parr — was made public knowledge, Thomas would be ruined. In my letter, I threatened to expose him should he bother me again.

Additionally, the young Seymour had a bit of a debauched side, gambling away his fortune in local taverns while indulging in sexual congress with whores and blacking out from too much drink in horses' stalls.

I smirked. All in a few days' good work, and money well spent. My secrets would stay just that. Yet, it had not solved the problem of having an enemy. That would continue until one of us met our maker, or else we made friends.

There was nothing more abhorrent to me on a hot July day than when I was served a bowl of steaming squash stew for the nooning. It was already dreadfully hot, and to ingest a hot meal only served to make me more miserable. Luckily, a loud knock on our door interrupted the chore of sloshing soup in my bowl.

"I am not expecting anyone. You?" Edward asked.

I shook my head slowly and darted my gaze to the door, my gut clenching in fear.

Edward waved one of the grooms to answer, and we both stood from our table.

My mother, Page and my half-sister, Elizabeth, entered the room.

"A surprise, we weren't expecting you," I said, a subtle hint of hostility in my voice.

"My lady, my lord," my mother and Page murmured, ducking into curtsies and bows. Lizzie pouted as she curtsied but said nothing.

"Shall I have a groom fetch you something to eat? You are more than welcome to join us at our table." Edward held out his hand, indicating they should sit.

Mother and Page both hungrily eyed the table but ultimately declined, much to my relief.

"No, we have not the time for a lingering social call, my lord. In fact, we only wanted to come by and express our thanks for finding us lodgings at court. Our room is adequate, if small." Page sneered and eyed our rooms, which were larger and no doubt much more opulently decorated.

My breath caught in my throat. So their pleas had finally been heeded. Did this mean they would leave me alone? That their threats would be no longer? I fervently prayed it would be so.

Edward nodded. "Very well. Good day to you, then."

Mother and Page looked a little taken aback at being dismissed but said nothing as they dipped again in reverence and left the room.

I returned to my soup, which had cooled considerably. "Thank you, Edward."

"Do not thank me, my lady wife. The king would like to keep an eye on Page. He's apt to bring trouble to the foreground." He wiped at his mouth with a napkin. "Did I mention to you that your brother Richard has somehow managed to become a groom to the king?"

My eyes widened in surprise. For even though I'd had an idea something of the sort would occur, that Anthony would make sure of it, to keep my brother's silence about our near-tryst, I was not confident it would happen so quickly. "How fortuitous for him."

"Yes..." Edward squinted his eyes at me, my guess trying to read my thoughts. Eventually, he looked away and continued to eat his soggy, now cold, squash stew.

*July 25, 1536*

The Duke of Richmond was dead. Several days now.

He'd died suddenly, unexpectedly, and some say, unnaturally. There was no injury from an accident. There was no long, drawn-out illness. Healthy one day and on death's door the next. Fear raced through every Seymour in the kingdom.

We now had no more fear of him taking the throne over one of Jane's own children—but, instead, a fear of who murdered him— and if we'd be blamed for it.

People were suspicious, as was I. Walking up and down the corridors, from the great hall to the queen's rooms, to the gardens and beyond, everyone stared at one another, their eyes casting doubts.

Poor Mary Howard. She had my sympathy in being a widow, especially when it was well known about court that she and Richmond had never been allowed to live truly as husband and wife. But as the Howards were my enemies, I wouldn't allow myself to mourn with her long. The girl would bounce back, and her family would suck her back into their ring and thrust her back out. A pawn she'd be once more.

Rumors rippled across the court. How had Richmond died? Who was to blame?

Because no Howard would end their affiliation with the king, courtiers turned their eyes to us Seymours. We stood to gain from the young duke's death.

Richmond had been healthy but a few weeks ago. Now dead, and interred in secret, too. Supposedly, he'd died of consumption, coughing and spitting up blood. The sickness had come on quickly and abruptly ended his life. They said he had been poisoned, but by who? And why, from the rumors, it sounded as though he had indeed died of consumption.

Rumor had it, the king ordered Norfolk to make the funeral arrangements. The body of Henry Fitzroy was to be wrapped in lead and taken in a covered wagon for burial. But whispers abounded that Norfolk's lazy servants had tossed the body into an open wagon and covered the poor boy with straw. Only two servants had attended his burial.

Bastard or no, a king's son deserved more than that. And we Seymours had had nothing to do with his death.

The queen's chambers were subdued, the older women sewing and mending shirts and the younger maidens making flower arrangements. I was sitting quietly with Queen Jane. She was mending the king's shirts, and I was embroidering a new linen shift for her.

A sudden commotion at the door made us jump, and I pricked myself with the needle.

"Ouch!" Thrusting my finger into my mouth, I looked up to see two of the king's grooms approaching.

"Majesty." They bowed in unison, their expressions grave as they faced their queen.

"Gentlemen." Queen Jane inclined her head, her voice not quavering at all, the only telltale sign of her nervousness the subtle shake of her fingers.

"We have a message for Lady Beauchamp."

My eyes widened, and I clamped my jaw tight.

"Proceed," the queen instructed.

I let the linen and needle fall to my lap as they handed me a rolled parchment. They bowed and backed out of the room, not waiting for my reply. All eyes were on me as I unrolled the parchment to see Edward's long, scrolling hand in black ink, his letters quivering slightly at some parts. I had to read the note four times before I fully understood. The fourth time, I could barely make out the letters as tears pooled in my eyes. My brother, Richard. Treason. Arrested. My hands shook, and I dropped the paper.

I opened my mouth to ask Jane to be excused, but only a small croak came out.

"Go and tend to yourself," Jane whispered. I nodded, now completely blinded by tears. I stood and nearly forgot the letter as it fell to the floor. One of the other ladies picked it up and handed it to me, careful not to look at its contents.

I marched from the room as best I could, head held high, and tearful eyes straight forward. Somehow, I made it to our apartments before collapsing in a heap on the floor, my body shaking uncontrollably, my throat constricting as if the hangman's noose were wrapped tightly around it. I reached up as if to yank at the tethers, but only my necklace was around my neck. I tore at it, ripping it away from me, and flung it as gurgling sounds issued from my throat, my breaths uneven and halting.

One hand at my throat, and another at my heart. I would surely die this minute. The letter must have been poisoned. But in reality I knew that it was not poison of any tangible kind, but the poison of thoughts and fear.

My brother Richard, as much as I detested him, had not deserved the fate the king had given him.

Arrested for treason. Charged in suspicion with Richmond's death.

If the allegations were founded, he would die a miserable and painful death, his body mutilated and no one to answer the calls of his suffering but God. I would see his head on London Bridge every time I passed. 'Twas a lie! Richard would not do something so loathsome.

I knew he was innocent. My brother, my blood, could die as a scapegoat. For someone must be blamed for the king's son's death. Richard was accused of poisoning the king's child. Blackmail or nay, he was my brother. There was no word on who had told the king of this news, but supposedly there was a witness to his treachery.

There was nothing we could do but pray. And pray that someone did not wish a similar fate on me.

Without warning, I retched onto the waxed wooden floor, painful, gut-twisting, throat-burning, until not a drop was left in my body.

News came swiftly, before Richard's trial was to begin, he was found dead in his cell within the Tower. His death a mystery. Some suspected poison, but they would give us no other news than that. His body had been buried before we were notified.

I couldn't summon the gumption to speak. The effort to even rise from bed was too much. How easily any of us could be accused of wrong-doing, and then be whisked from life. None of us were safe.

The following morning, Edward moved my household to the north for a much-needed respite. But truly, I should have said, for escape, at least until fall had returned and the whispers of my brother's treasonous charge were no longer the hot topic amongst courtiers.

I could not be witness to my brother's death, and Edward was fearful my presence would irritate the king.

My mother tried to come to me, but I would not see her. She sent a note, which I burned without reading. I did not wish for her sympathies. She had always hated Richard and me. Any words she said would only be fabrications and falsehoods to put herself within my good graces so she might extract yet another favor from me.

Michael, my other brother, Richard's true blood, had been sent overseas to gather information for the king from Brussels, and had yet to learn of Richard's fate. I did not wish to be the one to tell him, but I knew coming from my lips, the hurt would be lessened. He would be the only Stanhope heir left.

I swallowed hard, my tears dried, but the choking feeling in my throat remained. I looked to the heavens and offered a prayer up for both of my brothers. Let God have mercy on their souls!

# CHAPTER ELEVEN

*How can ye thus entreat a Lion of the race,*
*That with his paws a crowned king devoured in the place.*
*~Henry Howard, Earl of Surrey*

*September 21, 1536*

I recalled once that some grand courtier said returning to court after a long absence was like visiting the only privy in the castle on a hot summer's feast day — a body would be inundated with the shit of nearly everyone in attendance.

How right he had been. If I could recall who it had been, or could return to that time, I would have offered up a toast for words so rightly said, for I had been bombarded with person after person. Gossip, letters, and curious, hateful and pitying glances.

I was still in mourning for my brother, Richard, no matter how much our minds had crossed swords. Although I dressed in elegant courtly fashion, around my neck was a delicate black velvet and lace collar. Black diamonds and pearls were sewn in an intricate pattern, and neatly tucked unseen inside the seam was a small portrait of my brother when he had been a boy. The choker was tight, restricting. Reminding me that death was only a breath away.

Life at court went on. Politics, factions, religious reformation and lies wouldn't cease to exist when a body left. Nay, you must run to catch up or suffer being left behind.

I pressed a hand to my rounding belly. Edward had promised me that the king holds no ill will toward me and that he had all but forgotten Richard was my brother. That the king had even pardoned my brother in death, when substantial proof was laid before him that his bastard son had actually been ill. That the witness was mistaken. I breathed a tense sigh, not confident I could believe the king's words but needing to take them for what they were.

Time to leap back into the pit.

Fruitless and futile.

The king and queen had been married five months, and still their marriage remained empty of the promise of a prince. Jane had had a few late menses, but I'd warned her never to tell the king she was with child, or even that she thought she might be, until it was absolutely certain.

With the strain of her position, her menses had been thrown off course, and she was thinner now than she had been in the spring. I encouraged her daily to eat healthfully, partake in walks in the garden, and to use me as a confidante. It could only help her. I worried. One of her ladies had told me that she wakes every other night screaming, drenched in sweat. Night terrors they call them. But Jane refused to talk about her nightly visions.

I thought I knew what they were…

*Jane imagines herself climbing a crudely made ladder, rotten vegetables, eggs, dung thrown at her back by a group of marauding peasants. Nobles stare on, their faces void of emotion, just waiting, waiting.*

*She reaches the top of the ladder, steps onto the scaffold, faces the executioner whose face is covered in a thick black hood. The man who is too ashamed, or too scared, to show the public who he is, yet every night clinks glasses with them in the taverns — everyone unsuspecting that he might be the one to take their life.*

I knew this must have been the source of her night terrors, for I had had the same ones. Our futures were integrally linked. Whether we shared the executioner's ax or the same midwife, there was nothing that could happen to one that would not ultimately affect the other.

Jane would become so overwrought throughout the day that sometimes she would rush to the chamber pot to toss up her accounts. Her practice of serving special foods and spices, and subtle invitations to the king, had improved his number of nightly visits. From what she'd said, it appeared he was actually completing the task. I was hoping she would soon truly be with child.

My belly had swelled a little more since the summer had turned into early fall, but the fashion of the court these days was a tight, high bodice with flowing skirts, and my growing belly was well concealed. No one had suspected my condition. I'd been drinking a concoction of ginger spiced tea and cinnamon each morning, and it had helped to ease my nausea.

Jane was glad that I'd returned. And I was happy the heat had abated somewhat. While gone from court, Edward and I had traveled over England to visit our properties and to get away from the heat. While it had been best for us to stay out of sight, absence appeared to have made the king's heart grow fonder. For he'd given us each presents, myself a new mantle for the coming winter of thick green velvet and lined with black ermine fur, and Edward another manor.

Just after we'd arrived back at court, I learned Lady Mary was to join the court in residence. Her father would be filled with joy at her presence, as would Jane. There would be at least a month of merrymaking and feasts in Mary's honor.

Alas, we had returned. The freedom over the last two months had been a heavenly journey, and I was shocked at the mixture of disappointment and excitement I felt at returning to Greenwich. The Marquis and Marchioness of Exeter had been fully granted credence at court, their suite of rooms returned to them, in our absence. Pleasure washed over me at having another ally, a friend to confide in.

At night, Edward laid with me in bed, his hands stroking over my stomach. He kissed my navel.

Prayed this baby was a girl… That we did not bear a son at least until the Jane and the king had a prince.

I joined him in fervent prayer, for how dare we, the closest of Jane's family at court, conceive a child before the king and queen? It was unthinkable, but God had somehow chosen for this course. Despite the inconvenience of it, a small secret part of me was thrilled to bring a child into the world. To be someone's mother.

I remembered growing up in Rampton, Nottinghamshire. The manor house had been a lavish home—my father seeking beauty and style as well as fortification. I had always been awed at the fact that Normans, who had come to conquer this land, had lived there, built it. And my father had improved on the three-tier step design on the outside, adding brickwork and corbeled outwork with our family coat of arms. I used to dance across the large stone gateway after picking flowers with my nursemaid in the fields—imagining my father, long dead, standing and waving us on.

A small smile crept over my lips as I imagined the small creamy hand of my own daughter held in mine, a bundle of white, pink, blue and yellow flowers filling the basket she held made of her skirts. I would be a good mother. Not like my own mother, who used me and abused me. Who loathed me to her very core.

A knock at the door pulled me from my reverie. I stood from the window seat where I had been staring out at the landscape.

"My lady," Jenny said as she walked into my private presence chamber. "Sir Anthony Browne is here to see you."

A heavy sigh escaped me. Thus far, I had been able to keep our running into each other at a minimum. We'd discussed a few matters pertaining to court, the king and queen, courtiers, politics, but always it had been within full view of others. Not once had we deigned to meet privately. Not after our heated argument in the woods. I'd thought never to share a room alone with the man again. Not with the disdain he felt for me. I could only pray that this meeting now consisted of a business nature only.

I nodded, and Jenny led him in. I could see immediately this visit was solely personal. After nearly two months of separation, he still had feelings for me? How many times would I have to reject him?

Anthony sauntered into the room, his face awash with conflicting emotions — worry, rage, hurt, joy — all at once they whisked over his features, like some tragic play. My insides plummeted. But I squared my shoulders. One of us had to be strong, and that role fell to me.

Jenny left quietly, closing the door behind her. If Edward were to come seeking me out...

"My lady." Anthony swept a perfect bow and took the hand I proffered.

He kissed my knuckles gently, squeezing my fingers. I snatched my hand back, denying the rampant attraction that flared up with his touch. My skin sizzled where his lips had grazed me, but I could not let my baser instincts rule me. Strength. It was in my nature, in the rigid stature of my spine. I pressed my lips together and walked toward the hearth. If anything, the heat of the fire could explain the flush covering my skin.

"Sir Anthony," I started, flinching at the cruel tone of my voice. "I thought I made it clear we were not to meet privately."

He stepped forward, reached his arm out as if he would touch me, but then let it fall to his side. "Anne, please..."

I ignored his plea, but my will was thin, like an unraveling rope. If I did not get him to leave soon, all would be lost. "What is the nature of your visit?"

"So this is how we shall be? Cold, distant? You play a perfect female courtier."

His insult stung, but I could not allow it to rattle me. I lifted my chin and offered him a cup of wine. He declined.

"I have come on two accounts, my lady. One of a more delicate and personal nature and the other, news I've heard from the north."

"The news."

At this, Anthony nearly snarled at me. He came close, his voice low. "Anne, we may have been close to being lovers for only a few brief moments, but I've memorized every line of your body. It has changed."

I gasped. He'd noticed? How many others had as well?

175

His eyes roved over my belly, which was well-concealed beneath flowing skirts. "Whose baby is it?"

"I *beg* your pardon?"

"You know to what I refer. Answer me, damn it!"

I took a step back at his volatile, jealous nature. "The baby belongs to my husband," I hissed with anger, stepping closer. "It certainly would not come from a few ardent kisses with you, sir. And I wouldn't dare take another man to my bed besides Edward."

He laughed cruelly. "I am not in the least worried whether or not the child is mine, Anne. I simply wonder how many men you've allowed entry into your...bed."

My hands fisted at my sides, and more than anything I wanted to throw a vase or scratch at his eyes for what he'd intimated. Was this the rage of a man filled with jealousy? Or that of a man pushed aside, his bruised ego lashing out?

I'd opened myself up to Anthony, allowed him such liberties and such a place in my mind, one that only one other man had ever been allowed to view, and this was how he turned on me? "How dare you! I am no one's whore! Get out!" I pointed to the door, my breathing labored.

"Anne, please, I did not mean..." He came forward, hands out. "The thought of you with another man—"

"I care not for your words or your apology. You have insulted me beyond measure, sir!"

"My love, Anne, please..." I let him take my hands in his, let him caress the palms with his thumbs, but only for a moment before I pulled away. He did not seek to pull me back. Resignation filled his features. "I am a jealous man, Anne. I've wanted you for so long. Adored you. Loved you. I cannot explain my words otherwise, and I most humbly beseech your forgiveness."

"You will not have it today." I sniffed, still seething, still crying on the inside. "Relay to me what news you've brought and then be gone with you."

He nodded, swallowing hard, the masculine knob in his throat bobbing. "I've heard rumor of a band of rebels gathering up north. They are angry, distraught at the dissolution of monasteries. Has Edward mentioned it?"

I turned toward the hearth. If my husband had heard anything new, he had not mentioned it to me. We'd known of the anger up north for a while. Was it really all that different now? Had Edward felt that with my condition I could no longer help him in state affairs? He was going soft on me. How dare he think my condition could not handle such disturbing news! I would have to seek out Lady Exeter soon. Gertrude was always well informed and had a gentle-enough hand to soothe my ire.

"What else?" I asked.

"The council will meet shortly. We have several informants that are due back with news imminently."

I nodded, speaking with little inflection in my voice. "Whatever the news is, His Majesty will surely want to retaliate. But it is imperative that you not let him go north."

Anthony agreed. "His leg is festering much lately. I do not think he will attempt it."

"No matter, he will want to show his authority, his ability to still wield control. But he cannot put himself in the line of danger. Jane has not yet conceived."

"The work of the rebels may be in our favor," Anthony said in a low voice.

"How so?"

"They are sensitive to the Lady Mary. They wish for her to be put back in the succession. It is worse than feared before. We were able to quell their anger during the summer months, but now there is a new leader, and he is garnering much support among the people."

"Hmm..." This could sorely go in the opposite direction. Foolish peasants and reckless nobleman. Did not they realize that by going against the king they would only anger him? He would take it out on Mary. That by wanting her to be in line for the throne, the king might just strip her completely and send her into exile? Maybe even to the scaffold?

"Thank you for bringing me this information. Go now."

Anthony's brows furrowed as he glared at me. "I am not a servant for you to dismiss. As much as you might wish to forget our *affair d'amour* it happened. We happened."

I bit my lip, almost drawing blood. "Do not say such words. The walls have ears. And despite what you think, I hardly believe a few seconds of stupidity count as an affair of the heart."

"One night."

I turned, astonished. "Pardon?"

"Give me one night, Anne. One night to indulge in the passion we both have felt, and I will wash the memory of our love from my mind."

*Our love?* Had he really fallen so hard? But I knew he had. He'd told me, and even though I'd never confessed my feelings, he knew they ran deep. Since then, I'd put it all behind me, forgotten it except for on dark, lonely nights. With suspicions at court rising, there was no place for treachery, and Edward's spies had doubled over the past few months. Any indiscretion would have been brought to his attention immediately. As much as a part of me wanted to go back in time and relive those carefree moments in Anthony's arms, it was not possible. Indeed, it would have meant certain death.

The determined set of Anthony's jaw made me nervous.

"And if I do not?" I asked haughtily.

"You do not want to make me think about that." He ran a hand through his hair.

His threat was not subtle—and I couldn't pinpoint if it was made out for me, or that he himself would go mad with lust-rage. All I could imagine was Edward's fingers wrapping around my throat and that long trek up the crude wooden ladder to a non-descript scaffold. I coughed, my fingers tugging lightly at my mourning choker.

"Don't threaten me. This is not about love, but revenge. Retaliation for my loyalty to Edward. What grievance has he caused you that you would feel compelled to use me so cruelly?"

"Right you are, I am beside myself with envy, Anne. Every night I fall into bed, I imagine you doing the same with Edward. I refused to let my last memory of you naked and moaning be with Edward on top of you, but myself."

My mouth fell open, shocked at his words, and for a moment completely speechless. "You disgust me," I managed to choke out.

"It was not always that way."

178

"Find someone else to plunder. My village is no longer available."

"So witty you are, my lady. But, unfortunately, I happen to know that a certain birthmark graces you... Right. Here." His finger tapped my knee.

"You could have bribed a maid to tell you so."

"Even still, you will not risk my knowledge of its placement."

"You would blackmail me into your bed?"

"If I have to. If I have to get you alone so you can let go of all this." He flung his hands out to the side. "You forget that each time we've kissed, touched, your passion ignites, and it is beautiful. I want you to see what I see, Anne."

"Go away." I thrust my chin up.

"No, Anne." He stepped forward, cupped my face, his lips brushing mine. "Do you not remember?"

Each of our indiscretions tunneled back, flooding my body with the sensations I'd experienced tenfold. I tingled all over, my body desperately wanting to feel what he offered. To escape the madness of courtly intrigue for one night and give into abandon. "One night," I lied. For as much as I wanted to feel Anthony's body overtop of mine, I could never allow it to happen. To do so would be to risk too much. I gazed at the man I'd once loved, and realized I would soon make an enemy of him.

"I will send for you." He left quickly after that.

My throat tightened. I realized then that he'd only come for that — to make our *affaire d'amour* real. The news of the rebels and the meeting of the council were something I would hear about very soon from even the lowliest court mouth.

To my desk I went, hastily penning a note to my confidante.

*My Dearest Lady,*

*I fear our devoted Sir A has come undone. To my attention it has come, threats and rumors are passing his lips. I humbly beseech you, make haste that your lord husband speak to him. For I fear for all our reputations should he truly embark on his intentions, and then to what purpose? So much work we have done, only to have it tossed in the Thames like rubbish.*

*Your most humble and devoted friend,*

*Lady Anne, Viscountess Beauchamp*

I quickly burned the letter as soon as I'd written it. For what more had he threatened than to take me as his lover?

As the last corner caught flame, Edward returned, and I rushed toward him, hoping he'd not ask what I'd just burned.

*October 1, 1536*

It was midnight. And it had begun.

The religious rebellion from the north that we'd feared. They were attempting to bring back Catholicism to the realm. This could only end badly as King Henry had no wish to revert back to the breast of Rome.

The candle on my desk burned low as I read over documents from our many informants. One rushed so quickly to my lord Edward, that the sweat of the messenger's hand still dampened the parchment.

The Pilgrimage of Grace, they called it.

Traitors, all of them.

Tonight, after Evensong at St. James's Church in Louth, a Mr. Robert Aske, peasants, nobleman, clergy, and numerous others by the thousands, began their march toward London. My hands shook as I read the letter. The participants swore they were only defending the suppression of the church and Catholic faith. They upheld their allegiance to the king, His Most Gracious and Noble Majesty. They sought to end the dissolution of monasteries, end the taxes laid on them, purge heretics from the king's council—Cromwell was named.

My breathing was ragged, my heart nearly bursting. This was bad, very bad. I would have bet my life they would never have seen it through. And yet, here was the proof. They had indeed. Who would go against King Henry? Who would sign their own death warrant? For they could not win against the king.

And yet... my fingers trailed to the rosary sewed into my sleeve. In my heart of hearts I'd hoped they would. And to name Cromwell... How fortunate we were.

But, who was this Mr. Aske? What of his family?

I suppose soon enough I may get the chance to find out, for he'd be in the Tower if he was not dead.

The king was angry, enraged. Jane had rushed into our chambers earlier, fearing for His Majesty's anger, that he would leave her to go north and fight the rebels himself. She'd begged Edward to go and talk sense with him. Make him stay.

Edward would do all he could to ensure the king stayed put, even if it meant he had to go up north to quell this rebellion himself, with promises of heads delivered on pikes to His Majesty's presence chamber.

Already, Thomas Howard, Duke of Norfolk, had been charged with taking the king's message to the rebels, and exacting punishment on them all. He'd suited up in his armor and headed out before dawn with an army in tow. Edward would soon join him to make certain this heinous rebellion came to an end quickly. The king grew impatient even when it had barely begun. He could not tolerate when someone went against his wishes. Damn the rebels for betraying their king. His Majesty was in a murderous rage, and I feared nothing would calm him.

The little bump in my belly fluttered. The baby had begun to kick lightly, delicately every so often, reminding me that I would soon be a mother. But my fear for our position, for the king's grace, for Jane, who was not yet with child, sucked the joy from me.

I pressed a hand to my belly, felt a little press of foot or hand as the babe within me tumbled with innocent enthusiasm. My heart skipped with joy, and I sucked in a breath. For a moment I was happy, peaceful. But then my eyes were drawn again to the parchment in my hands.

I must send a letter north. We had allies there. Edward would need a place to stay, to make camp, provisions. We needed someone to infiltrate the rebels to give Edward information about their plans, their hideouts, numbers, their informants, anything that would help us to succeed.

"Jenny! Fetch the messenger."

After dressing for morning Mass, I exited my chambers and nearly jumped through my skin. My mother awaited me in the presence chamber.

"Anne, I thought you'd sleep nearly all day. How in all the realm will you make it to Mass on time to serve your queen?"

"If you were not here, I could leave at present to attend her."

"Humph." She pursed her lips.

My stomach clenched, and before she could say another word, I held up my hands. "I understand your husband sends you to spy on me, or to beg favors of me, whatever the case may be, but at present, I am running late and must be on my way. Perhaps seek me out after Mass is held?"

My mother, surprising me, nodded. I took a breath of relief, but it was too soon.

She straightened her spine and jutted her jaw forward. "I was inclined to accept your proposal, but have changed my mind. I shall walk with you to the queen's chambers."

My teeth ground together, and I suppressed a growl in her direction. "Very well."

"Yes, indeed. Let us away."

We made our way to the door, my mother's hand clasped about my arm. "While you may think I do only my husband's bidding, I do possess my own mind."

"I had thought most do, Mother."

"Your fath—stepfather shall be going to Surrey soon."

"Surrey?" My stomach clenched. Surrey the man or Surrey the holding?

"The king has given him his sheriffdom, and so he must travel there to conduct his duties."

"I see. Shall you and Lizzie accompany him?"

"Unless the queen sees fit to have me about her, then yes I must go. But Lizzie shall remain here, with you as her guardian."

"There you are, my lady." Sir Richard Page rounded the corner near Queen Jane's apartments. He flicked his gaze toward me, his eyes roving over my form. "And with your eldest daughter, I see." He bowed before me as was proper in front of so many courtiers.

"Good morning, sir."

"Has your lady mother told you the news then?" His eyes roved our surroundings as if looking for something. "We shall embark for Surrey within the week. No doubt we will have many more dealings with his lordship, the Earl of Surrey, as well."

I bristled at the mention of Surrey, but straightened my shoulders, playing into their game. I'd no longer allow them to hold me in their clutches. "Indeed she has, and I wish you much luck with your new appointment. A shame you've just received a room here at court, and now shall have to away." Though I was not sad to see them leave at all, quite the opposite.

"I am assured our room will be awaiting us for the Christmas season." Page's eyes lighted with malevolent delight. "Here is the very man now. My lord!" He waved his arms in the air.

I gritted my teeth as Lord Surrey came into view, the hair on the back of my neck rising as it did whenever he was near. Muscles clenched as if awaiting his assault. How dare Page invite the man to my rooms? The bastard bowed to my mother, Page and myself. My mother tugged my sleeve as she curtsied, but I'd never give Surrey the satisfaction of seeing me bow, and I yanked my arm from her grasp.

"Lady Beauchamp, a sight you are this morning. Beautiful as a sunrise," he said with a smirk.

It took every ounce of willpower I possessed not to vomit down the front of his doublet. "How very kind of you to say so."

Why was Page doing this? Did he seek to merely torment me? What motive could he have had for such cruelty?

I turned to my stepfather. I hated to have another female go through the hell Surrey had stacked on me, and my own sister at that, but I could not allow Page and my slithering mother to control me any longer. Lord, I prayed they believed me and held me to be true, for I would have hated for them to see my bluff and force my hand with Lizzie's fate.

"My mother says you shall have to take Lizzie with you. But it has only just occurred to me, that perhaps instead of having her at your manor, she could foster at Lord Surrey's castle with his wife. I am confident you would have a place for her there, would you not, my lord?"

My mother's mouth gaped wide, and Sir Page's face turned nearly purple. I could practically see them both recalling the fate they'd resigned me to, and they'd not want to do the same with Lizzie—especially since Surrey was already married and nothing would come of it but Lizzie's ruination.

They'd not allow Lizzie to go, but let them come up with the reasons why. I was through with them. Let them sputter and spew their venom elsewhere. If they had thought to hold me in their clutches, now let them see I could play their games, too.

"I must away. Queen Jane is in need of me at the moment." I left them all, head held high. Pray let my move work.

*October 31, 1536*

There was a reason they said the devil and his minions came out on All Hallows' Eve, and until tonight, I had thought it all a part of some fantasy made up by the church to quell our evil desires.

Shouts rang out across Whitehall. Angry bellows. I ran toward Jane's apartments to see what the commotion was, only to be pushed back by Edward as I saw King Henry roaring his ire at everyone who dared to cross his path. A chair flew past my vision, the loud crash shaking the wall. A painting was next. And then any object within reach. "Anne, go back to our chambers," Edward ordered.

Servants rushed by, fear filling their faces as they came hither or yon from the king's rooms.

"But Jane," I rushed.

"She is fine. Go. I'll follow you soon."

I hurried back to our rooms, but could not remain calm. The king's bellows shook the entire castle. The clock in our room ticked, but the sound of it was drowned out by the chaos down the hall. My fingers were numb from wringing them, and my feet ached from pacing and turning about the room. There was not a vase, painting or deity out of place as I'd put them all to rights in my effort to keep myself from rushing from our hallowed rooms to make certain in his fit of rage the king had not arrested Edward tried, charged and executed him on some hollow accusation.

"Where is Edward?" I mumbled, wanting to shout it out to the heavens.

A groom stepped from the shadows. "My lady?"

"Nothing." I waved him back to whatever wall he'd hidden himself against and walked to the sideboard to pour a glass of strong wine. I needed the liquid to calm my nerves.

A fervent knock, rapid and continuous, sounded on our door. The groom rushed to answer it, only for it to be thrust open in impatience by Queen Jane herself. She rushed into the room, and my full goblet of wine stayed put on the sideboard as she grabbed my arm and propelled me toward my bedchamber. I was too shocked to respond with anything other than moving where she directed me.

She slammed the door shut behind us and turned in a swish of skirts to face me, eyes red-rimmed, swollen and bloodshot from too many tears shed.

"Jane, what is it?" I came forward and gripped her hands in mine.

"Henry!" she whispered feverishly. "He's gone mad!"

I ushered Jane to a chair by my hearth and settled her in it. I knelt in front of her to listen, fears of my own rushing to the surface. My face, neck and chest felt hot. So hot. I needed air. I stood and opened the window slightly, then came back to kneel before her.

"You must have heard him. Throwing things, breaking things, hitting a groom! He's mad with rage!" Jane's voice was high-pitched. Her fingers shook as they gripped mine.

"What has him so agitated?" I asked, as calm as I could, even though inside I was a tornado of emotions. *Oh, dear God, do not let it be Edward!*

"The rebels in the north, even his own men. He does not think his men wish to support him since they've yet to settle the matter." She wiped tears from her eyes as they began to run anew. "He shouted at me for not being with child."

185

My lips clamped shut, pursed. I wanted to say so much, but anything I uttered would not make Jane feel relief.

"His leg pains him much. He wobbles around his rooms, clutching it. The ulcer has festered something fierce. Puss is oozing through his hose and breeches. He is mad with fever!"

"Is there no one who can calm him?"

"Not a one! Edward tried, and Henry... Oh, Edward!"

My stomach plummeted. My worst fears were about to become a reality. "What? What happened?"

"I've never seen Henry so mad. His eyes bulged from their sockets, his face red and blustery. Spittle flew from his lips." Jane shook her head, almost as if trying to forget the image.

"What of Edward?" I gripped her hands tighter, coming up on my knees so my eyes were level with hers.

"He bade him hold his tongue or he'd be thrown in the oubliette and forgotten about for a century."

I blinked, unable to comprehend exactly what she was saying. The oubliette. A fate I would not have wanted pushed on my husband even when I'd watched him saunter away with some trollop. Men were tossed into the dank, dark, rat-infested holes and left to die. No way in except to be thrown and no way out except for a rope to be tossed into the pit for you to climb.

"No..." I breathed, wondering if my lips moved. My body was going numb, a ringing in my ears. All I could do was imagine my poor Edward curled up in a ball as the rats feasted on his fingertips.

"Edward fell to the floor, put his hands up in prayer." Jane mimicked the movement. "He prayed that the good and mighty king might forgive him. It was unreal, yet I saw it before my own eyes."

"And?" I bit out, becoming impatient. Where was my husband?

"Henry is sending him north to help Norfolk and Suffolk."

Edward did not return to our chambers that night. Instead, a messenger arrived shortly after Queen Jane left with word from him. As Jane had said, he was sent north in a hurry to please His Majesty and hadn't time to return for his things. I was to send a groom with a few items, which the messenger ticked off.

I called Edward's valet into the room, and he worked with the messenger to pack a satchel for him. Then the valet left with the messenger to locate a squire who might catch Edward upon the road.

I was relieved that he was still alive. But who knew how long that would be? He was in the midst of a rebellion, forty thousand strong. The king's men did not nearly rival that number, even if they *were* better trained and equipped. And should things go badly, Edward would have to deal with the king himself.

I shuddered. I did not want to have to sew Edward's picture into my choker. Or mayhap the choker would be handed to my maid as my own throat was slit.

*November 8, 1536*

Shawms and flutes played a haunting melody, following me down the corridor from the great hall. I walked alone, in tune with the music, the click of my heels sounding off the floorboards. I was barely able to see my feet over the ever-expanding waist of my gown. We'd feasted tonight on the return of Edward and Suffolk from the north. They'd been able to halt the march of treasonous English for the moment. Norfolk remained behind to ensure the march went no further.

But I was no longer able to keep up with merrymaking as I once was. I was tired. Mentally and physically. The baby was a heavy burden, both on my mind and my body, and since it was yet a secret, I must endure my suffering privately. Edward understood, and though he wished to come back to our apartments with me, I bade him stay and finish out the night with the revelers who were happy to welcome him home in one piece.

I prayed on this journey back to my room, I did not run afoul with anyone. I had yet to have words with Edward's brother again, but he lurked on the outskirts, waiting for his chance to strike. He looked like a rabid animal, baring his teeth at me. Months had passed since we'd last argued, but in any case, I could sense his ire building to a crescendo. It was only a matter of time before he exploded.

He was angry with me for countering his threats with my own. The jealous whelp watched as Edward and I rose, and he was left all the same. Perhaps I could whisper to Jane of Tom leaving court to see the world, to experience another court would only enhance his abilities and political career. She would agree.

The hair on the back of my neck prickled, and I picked up my pace as quickly as I could. When I turned to look behind me, Anthony's lithe figure dipped back into the great hall. So he watched me. A shiver raced along my spine, and unconsciously I hugged my round belly.

Had he come after me to take what he'd demanded? Relief flooded over me that he'd changed his mind and gone back to the festivities. And yet a sense of emptiness and loss remained.

*November 20, 1536*

I crinkled up the guilt-filled letter my mother so graciously had sent to me. Her precious daughter, Lizzie, who, she felt inclined to remind me, was also my half-sister, was miserable at their manor home and wished to come to court again. I was glad that Page had taken my hidden warning in keeping her at home, instead of allowing her to go to Lord Surrey's house. I had hoped they'd not be so dense where Surrey was concerned, though they had been with me.

My mother lamented that Lizzie was lonely with little people of her station to associate with. Subtle mentions of their correspondence with Surrey and how well their relationship was fostering laced her letter. A dinner here, a judgment at Surrey's court there, a gift of a horse and the collection of taxes. Page was truly enjoying his seat as sheriff, reigning over his own mini-kingdom.

Ever present were her hints at ruination for me if I did not do as she asked.

But I could no longer let her threats rule me as much as she wanted them to. I had a baby growing inside me. Edward and I were creating our own family, our future. Rumors had spread like wildfire before... my own brother, murdered... and yet the accusations of his treasonous heart, which we'd feared would forever taint my reputation, faded eventually.

I would not be able to ignore her for long. Soon they would return to court, and I would have to face them directly.

# CHAPTER TWELVE

*Whose nature is to prey upon no simple food,*
*As long as he may suck the flesh, and drink of noble blood.*
*~Henry Howard, Earl of Surrey*

*December 21, 1536*

Edward's father, Sir John Seymour, died early in the morning while visiting friends in London.

The sweat. Likely, King Henry would remove everyone to Greenwich to be away from the city should more illness break out.

I must tell Jane before I leave. I must away to Wulfhall. Even though my lying in wouldn't begin for another two months, my belly was more than swollen. All of my gowns were too tight, and they'd been let out more times than I could count. I did not think any extra fabric remained. New gowns had been ordered just for this time. I felt like a fat, bloated sow. I'd been keeping to my rooms lately, and when I did walk through court, people had started to stare and whisper, pointing at my increasing waistline. Either they thought me a glutton or they knew the truth.

This morning was no different. Through the throngs of people milling about the corridor, I somehow managed to enter the queen's chambers without losing my temper. More and more, people were lingering outside the queen's rooms. Hoping for this favor or that, wanting to sit in the gracious light of her aura, hoping she would pass along a word or two to the king. Jane had become beloved of the people. And, but of course, she was the kindest, most gracious queen they'd had in the past several years. Some said her disposition even rivaled the great late Queen Katharine of Aragon.

I wondered what Jane's reaction would be to the news of her father's death. Edward had let out a breath of relief upon hearing the news. I thought he'd been secretly scared for the last few years we'd been married that I would take a liking to his father just as his first wife had done. But I would never dream of doing such a thing. Never.

Thomas had not seemed to care much, either. In fact, he was more than perturbed that Wulfhall was now Edward's and not his. He was only a second son, and instead of embracing his birth order, he constantly gnashed his teeth at Edward. His sense of entitlement grated on my nerves, but Edward coddled him, stroking Thomas' ego, and telling him he would gift him with his own manor in the north.

On the heels of the great news of the quelling of the rebellion came a sadness I hoped wouldn't deter Jane from her agendas as queen. The Pilgrimage of Grace had been dissolved earlier this month, but rumors had been floating around that another round of risings would soon begin. The sorry peasants and lowly gentry weren't happy with the king's pardon and grace upon their demands. Ungrateful they were.

The duty had fallen to me to drop both these bits of sour news on Her Majesty.

"Majesty." I curtsied somewhat awkwardly to Jane, who sat rigid in her chair.

She nodded to me. Her face was pale, hair pulled back severely. Purple marred her perfect skin beneath her eyes. She hardly looked like the woman she'd been—before she was queen and married to Henry. Back when she was carefree and happy. I was haunted, as I pictured another queen who looked just as taxed... Anne Boleyn had been carefree before the queenship sucked any ounce of joy from her.

With a graceful movement of her arm, she offered me the seat next to her. I took it, arranging my skirts in a way to hide my pregnancy as best I could. The babe kicked, as if shouting for me to announce its presence.

"Jane." I leaned in, whispered, "There is some news I must make you aware of."

She nodded, not even looking a bit stunned by my statement. News to her must have come in waves, one bad thing after another, and she had no emotion for it any longer.

"Your father, Sir John." I paused, took a breath. "He has passed this morning."

Jane's mouth dropped open, and her hand fluttered to cover it. Tears gathered in her eyes but did not fall on her thin cheeks.

"I am so sorry." I gripped her hand and squeezed. It was cold, small, fragile.

She only nodded.

"There is more." This was the worst part, and I had no desire to keep speaking. I wanted to run from the room, for who was I to be the bearer of such news and orders?

"Tell me," she whispered.

"You are not to attend the funeral."

She whipped her gaze toward mine, squeezed my hand tight. Anger, hurt, desperation, all flashed over her features. "Why?" Her voice cracked on a sob. Pain shredded my heart for her.

"The king says the queen's place is here. He believes it as a bad omen. That if you are with child, it could hurt the baby. Something of evil spirits."

She stood abruptly. "But I am not with child!" she shrieked, her hair falling out of its tight coiffure to dangle around her face. Her once-pale cheeks flushed with color, hands fisted at her sides, then one came rushing to her mouth as she bit her knuckles.

I was startled silent. I'd never seen Jane more than demure, and now she was angry, an emotion I'd never known she possessed. It was shocking. I waved to the others in the room to leave. They filed out slowly, quietly.

"Queens are not allowed to mourn? Was I not a daughter before a wife?" Her voice was soft, and tears did fall this time.

"Your Majesty, I beseech you, come sit." I patted her chair. I wanted to calm her, stroke her hands.

Jane sat down just as abruptly as she'd stood up. Her face fell, defeated. I stood behind her, fixing her hair.

"How?"

"It was the sweat. They say he passed quickly."

Jane nodded. She was silent for a long time. When I finished with her hair, I sat beside her.

"Shall I read you a passage from the Bible?"

But she did not answer my question. Instead she spoke of her father. "He was a good father. He had his faults, as any man does, but in the end he was still my sire."

"And he loved you."

"As any father does a daughter. Let us pray." She gripped my hand in hers and urged me toward the door. "The Queen's Chapel. We must say a prayer for Sir John Seymour."

I followed her, indicating for her other ladies to join us. On our knees we were for hours. The bells chimed at least four times, but I lost count. By the time Jane was ready to leave I was barely able to make it up off the floor. My back ached, my belly strained.

Jane gripped my arm in hers, and we walked briskly back to her chambers. "I need something good, Anne. I need something happy to hear, something to make me smile." She bit her lip, her gaze roving over my belly. She raised her gaze back to mine, her eyes begging. "Tell me something good."

I told her the only thing I knew that would excite Jane, because even if her own womb remained empty, she would be pleased to hear mine grew. She was unselfish in that way. "Edward and I are... expecting."

A smile broke out on Jane's face. "I thought as much! I wish you well."

King Henry burst into our interlude, and we stopped in midstride. "Away we go, my queen." His speech was hurried, and he held out his arm. His guards stood behind him, all grim-faced.

"Where are we to go?" Jane asked.

"Greenwich, away from the city. We shall spend Christmas there, and away from... illness."

Jane bowed her head in acquiescence.

"I am...sorry for your loss. My prayers are with your father's soul." The king sounded almost awkward, as if he were not used to comforting others.

"My thanks, Majesty," Jane whispered.

"Now, we must away."

Moments later, I watched from the window as the king and queen took off with great haste on their horses, their breaths coming out in steaming bursts from the cold. Jane was swathed in black sable furs, as was the king. A majestic pair they made. From my position I watched them journey to the Thames, and instead of climbing upon a barge—I gasped—they rode their horses straight across the frozen river. All the more magical and kingly they appeared, dressed out in finery that would cost a lowly man a lifetime to afford, as they walked on water.

*December 23, 1536*

A cold blustery wind whipped at my black ermine-lined cloak. Small flakes of snow dusted the ground. They landed, and just as quickly melted, on the neck of my saddled mare. Edward had boosted me onto the beast's back, and for a moment I almost lost my balance. My stomach looked like I swallowed a goose, and for as thin as I've always been, having the bubble on my belly had thrown my balance off kilter.

Edward would escort me to Wulfhall, but he must return to court to attend the Christmas and New Year festivities. I would be spending the holidays alone, servants my only company. Why should I have to suffer without his company? Why must a woman bear all the burdens of carrying a child and be ousted from the world? I should be bored to tears, and loneliness would fill my moments. It was unbearable to think on it, let alone know I shall endure it!

Edward shouted orders to one of the servants, and then stepped around the baggage wagon to make certain everything was in order. I peered up at the castle, which had been my home for some time, the people inside my constant company for days on end. Now, I had to leave it all behind for several months.

A shadow crossed over a chamber window, and I squinted my eyes to get a better look.

*Anthony.*

He pulled back a curtain and gazed out at me through the frosted glass. I chewed the inside of my cheek. The king had sent him on many errands since our last encounter. He'd yet to call on me as he'd promised. Was it only a threat to keep me on my toes, or would he wait until I returned? What a game we played. Despite the disgust and anger I had for myself, for him, on most days, I found myself hoping that he would come to me soon. I could not seem to let go or live without him. I missed his arms and the touch of his lips on mine, as brief as our encounters had been. I even missed the fire in his eyes as he shouted at me. Even though I refused to admit it, his love and our limited time together had affected me. It was different than Edward, who I felt more and more alone with. He'd barely touched me since learning I was carrying our babe. Perhaps protecting himself. I don't know.

Anthony inclined his head. I returned the gesture, ignoring the fluttering of my stomach. 'Twas completely dangerous to let his charms overwhelm me again. And his threats had only been those of a spurned lover. I knew in my heart, Anthony was different than Surrey—not violent or hateful but full of hunger and determination.

The baby kicked violently at the change in my body as my heart skittered and my breathing increased. I rubbed a soothing hand over the swell in my gown. Baby Seymour would be with us soon, and I prayed fervently it was a girl. I fingered my arm, where I had sewn my rosary into my gown—this I did each morning. I never left without it. My prayer beads. My salvation.

Without faith, I was not certain I could endure all that I did. Nor trust Edward to remain in contact with all of our allies, see that certain information was gained or passed, for that was a duty I'd not shared with him. I'd been the sounding board, the mastermind. His brother Tom would do all that he could to usurp his brother, of that I was certain. I should remind Jane of her promise to encourage King Henry to send Tom abroad.

"My lady?" Edward called to me.

I turned around in time to see him looking up toward the castle where I had been staring. He flicked his eyes away and beckoned to me. Had he seen Anthony? Were thoughts of the babe in my belly and my almost-lover flitting through his mind?

I hoped not, for as much as I cared about Anthony, I would remain by Edward's side, for we'd married before God and it was my duty. I urged my horse into a slow walk, the clopping of hooves on cobblestone a comforting noise. The creak of the wagons rocking behind me, the occasional crow of a bird and the wind whipping by were the sounds of my journey.

My months of isolation were about to begin.

*January 18, 1537*

Elizabeth Seymour, Edward's sister, arrived today to keep me company for my lying in. Although at five and twenty, she'd been widowed once already, no children had come of her short marriage to a knight. We should see about getting her married again, and once we did, with God's blessing, she would go through the labors of childbirth herself. Already, Edward sought a mate for his sister. The poor girl was as of yet unaware that she too would be made a sacrificial lamb for the Seymour family rising. The groom was my idea altogether, and I was quite proud of my choosing—none other than Gregory Cromwell. Son to *the* Thomas Cromwell—secretary to the king—the very man Edward hoped to replace. A genius plan it was, too, for not only would we infiltrate Cromwell's circle of family and comfort, but strengthen the Seymour name and prosperity by further linking ourselves to the king's Privy Seal. And soon, Edward could have the means to obtain the coveted position of Secretary and keep of the Privy Seal.

I'd been stir crazy with little company. My back ached, and I paced the length of the great hall, my hands rubbing the aching spots around my hips and spine.

"When is the babe due to arrive?" Elizabeth asked. I was so glad of her company and that Queen Jane let her out of service for a few weeks to visit me. Although the trek from court to Wulfhall was not far, I'd had little to no visitors — mainly to keep the news of Edward's own heir a secret.

"Perhaps a few weeks longer. The midwife says the baby's dropped onto my spine, makes me waddle, but I can breathe easier now." I waved my hand in the air. I did not want to talk about the baby anymore. I did not need any more reminders of why I was here, the boredom I was enduring, the isolation. I did not want to think about what Edward was doing, and who was warming his bed.

"Tell me news of court. How is Queen Jane?"

Elizabeth smiled and launched into a litany of comings and goings. Chapuys was solicitous as ever to Queen Jane and His Majesty. He visited with Lady Mary almost every other day.

I waited eagerly to hear if Jane Rochford had been caught in a compromising position with Surrey, but no such words were uttered from Elizabeth's lips.

"His Majesty is having pounds of ginger, peppers, oysters, almonds, artichokes and the likes shipped in. I think he's grown impatient of Jane not producing an heir. Someone must have told him that those items would help to bring forth conception."

I turned my head and snickered. Jane must have told him that herself.

"He is remaining kind to her?" I asked, worried for Jane.

"Well, there was one incident." Elizabeth took a sip of mulled cider as I waited on bated breath for her to continue.

"Do go on." I lost my patience, and Elizabeth looked at me over the rim of her cup, her brows furrowed slightly.

"Ornery when well into your pregnancy, are you not?"

Elizabeth was so much like me that it was sometimes comical. "Yes," I muttered. "Now complete your rendition before I take to my bed and cannot hear the rest of it."

Elizabeth chuckled. "They were at dinner, and Jane commenced her usual barrage of uninteresting but sweet and naïve small talk with His Majesty."

The corner of my lip curled with humor. How much I missed court, and why hadn't I spent more time with my sister-by-marriage? She was quite a character.

"He grew quite bored and even irritated, which is not like him at all when in his wife's company. He tossed down his napkin—" Elizabeth flung her hand just as Henry would have. "Shoved back his chair and stood, hands on his hips. *Jane*, he said in a raised voice, not quite a yell, but definitely startling, *why is it you are not with child? I've spent months laboring over your body, stuffing my face with this delicacy and that, and yet there is no life in your womb!*"

I was struck speechless. My heart raced as I waited to hear how Jane got out of this mess, and without me there to comfort her! A twang pierced the side of my belly, and I took a seat, lest I bring on labor with my worry. Oh, Jane! To have had to endure His Majesty's wrath. Did he suspect she might be barren? She could not be! It was impossible! Yet... married for over seven months now...

"What next?"

Elizabeth tucked a hair behind her ear that had fallen from her hood. "Jane, my stoic, queenly sister, folded her hands in her lap, back rigid, and looked His Majesty in the eye. *Gracious Majesty, a babe will follow soon, I feel it in my bones. It is God's will that the child should not come so soon, so we might come to love one another with so great a passion that nothing could tear us apart, not even those rebels in the north. The Lord, and you, must have wished that the child be born when we can devote so much of our time to growing a healthy babe, and not one steeped in war and rebellion.*"

"And the king?"

"He broke into laughter, threw his arms around her and swung her in the air, lamenting, *God's will be done! God bless Queen Jane!*"

"It worked?" I whispered. Jane was learning so well how to deal with her husband, Henry VIII, the most volatile man alive.

Later that evening I received a letter from Lady Exeter, whom I missed dearly, but did send me almost weekly correspondence. She wrote about Bigod's Rebellion. The rebels had once again taken up arms, as they weren't impressed with the king's keeping of his promises. This time, Norfolk would show no mercy.

*February 5, 1537*

"Hell and damnation!"

Pain seared through my belly before wrapping its way around my back and radiating down my legs. Sweat dripped from my forehead, over my cheeks, down my neck, before seeping into my nightgown.

"My lady, please breathe, deep breaths." The midwife breathed in and out, showing me how she wished for me to emulate her, but the only thing I wanted to do was rip the babe from my belly to stop the pain.

"Stop breathing like that, you wench!" I yelled at the elder woman. My head fell back, and I half moaned, half screamed as another torrent of pain pummeled my body.

My hands fisted into the folds of the blankets on the bed, soaked with blood and clear liquid from my womb. Elizabeth stood to the side of the bed, praying, as did Jenny and several other maids.

"His lordship is arrived," came someone's voice, but I could not begin to think who it was. The black fog of pain was fully encompassing me now. I could no longer talk, no longer hear, no longer scream. I felt like the pain was taking over, yet somehow it was focusing me at the same time. The opening of my birth canal stung with an intensity I never wanted to feel again. Pressure built within me, and I closed my eyes. I pushed hard, bearing down with all the strength I could muster. Some of the pressure released, but the stinging grew far worse, I opened my mouth to whimper, but no noise came out.

Instead I opened my eyes and focused on the door, willing Edward to come into the room and see what he'd put me through. I bore down again, and this time when I was finished, relief, sweet pure relief, filled me. The cry of the babe filled the room, and I fell back against the pillows, spent, exhausted, no longer in pain.

"It's a boy!" the midwife shouted.

I turned to look at the squirming pink child, slick with goo as the midwife swaddled him up. No! Not a boy! It was supposed to be a girl...

"Edward," I murmured.

"A fine name, my lady."

I did not bother trying to correct the woman. I had only been asking after my husband, but I supposed she was right, it was a fitting name for Viscount Beauchamp's son. He was a beautiful baby, and I smiled as a tiny fist came out to wave haphazardly in the air, almost as if the child were triumphantly saluting his own arrival.

At that moment, Edward rushed into the room. He beheld his child, and a look of horror crossed over his face seconds before one of elation took precedence. I knew the feeling, for I, too, had been filled with dread at first. A son and not a daughter. But when one saw one's own child, it was hard to remain filled with anything but joy.

"His name is Edward. We shall call him Eddie," I murmured.

Edward turned to me, the little babe in his arms. I did not think I would ever forget the look on his face. Such love for the wee thing, such love for me. I was more in love with him at that moment than any other, and the little tiny blond-tufted head — gold, like mine — made it all the more spectacular.

"The king and queen are with me."

Fear punched my gut. "They are?"

"Do not worry so, my Anne." Edward came over and sat beside me, kissed me on the forehead and laid Eddie in my arms. "They are both pleased."

Two days later, Eddie was baptized, Jane standing as his godmother and King Henry as his godfather. King Henry titled our little Eddie, Baron Beauchamp.

At the feast following Mass, King Henry stood and gave a speech, which Edward later came up to tell me about, as I was confined to my room until I could be churched. His last words haunted my dreams for weeks to come.

"Boys must run in the Seymour family. My Jane will soon deliver me of a prince. I can feel it." Conviction had filled Henry's voice, his eyes challenging anyone who would naysay him.

*March 24, 1537*

Norfolk had begun executing rebels in the north. Even children.

My babe was nearly seven weeks old, and I had been churched earlier in the week. Free to leave Wulfhall when I pleased. But I was not ready... and now this news. The rebels should suffer the consequences, but the children?

For as much as I had abhorred children before, looking upon my own little Eddie now, I could not imagine his sweet little feet dangling from the end of his body, lifeless from the hangman's noose.

Anthony had written me a cryptic note — the first since I'd left for my confinement. Cromwell would be inviting the leader of the rebels, Robert Aske, to court again in just over a week, under false pretenses. Henry had had enough. He would no longer stroke the egos of men who wished to defame him and his reformation.

I must say that I agreed, and I was surprised that he had let it go on as long as he had. Perhaps Jane had been a sort of peacemaker for the English court. Good for those who wished to rebel, but bad for those who must remain in power.

I crinkled up the letter that Anthony had sent me and tossed it into the fire. No need for anyone to find out that we'd been in communication regarding politics.

Nor for anyone to read his post script.

*I miss you, dearest Anne. My promise of one night has not been forgotten.*

No flowery words, only a reminder of his desire to spread my legs. I huffed an irritated sigh and paced before the warm, crackling fire. I was disappointed. Wished he would have said something more about the heart. But, then again, that might have pushed me over the edge. An edge I knew to cross would mean certain ruin. And yet, if I did not cross it, what would he do? There'd been plenty of spurned lovers and quarrels at court, but to do so would only put shame on our family. Make Edward hate me.

The sooner I was able to return to court and refuted Anthony's insistence on bedding me, the better. I needed to put my relationship with him behind me. Any whispers in my mind of a reconciliation were only the product of an emotional woman. A lonely wife.

Anthony was a distraction. The emotions and sensations he elicited from me would only cause pain — to me, him and any number of other people. I was a mother now. I could not leave my babe, for that was what would happen should Edward find out about my straying heart. He'd send me to a convent or worse. I reached up toward my neck, the familiar choking sensation poignant. I had taken my black choker off since giving birth, but perhaps it was a good reminder of what was at stake, and I should don it once again.

Perhaps the solution to my problem lay with the young and sensual Anne Bassett. So far she'd kept a low profile as I had asked, but having her woo Anthony would be good practice for the time when Jane would be indisposed to His Majesty. It would get him off my case if I could help him become infatuated with someone else... And if he weren't paying attention to me, mayhap some of my own interest in the man would abate.

"My lady, this has just arrived for you." Jenny swept into the great hall, curtsied and handed me a pack of parchment. Jane's royal seal was melted in the wax.

Without hesitation, I cracked the seal and opened her letter, reading it as I walked toward the hearth.

*My dearest sister Anne,*
*I wish for you to return to court and join me by Easter. I hear you have been churched. I have missed your company dearly, and wish to make merry with you, for I have great reason to be happy.*
*Yours in truth,*
*Jane the Queen*

That was in one week's time! I had much packing to do, and I had not thought to leave little Eddie quite so soon. But I supposed he would be in good care. I had taken the time since his birth to arrange his household, as a baron in his own right, son of a viscount, and nephew to the King and Queen of England. He would be well cared for by his team of nursemaids and nearly thirty servants.

I looked away from her letter, my eyes caught by the flames in the hearth. Embers glowed red, and orange licked over the logs. Herbs that had been strewn inside left a sweet earthy scent.

I had grown fond of rocking the little cherub to sleep at night. Becoming a mother had changed me a great deal. I cherished my child as I'd never thought I would. Mayhap Edward would allow Eddie to remain with me at court?

I turned away from the fire. Servants began setting the tables for our next meal. I chewed on my lip. Taking Eddie from palace to palace would have been wholly unfair to the child. Court was no place to raise a babe. Even the princesses never lived at court. A visit now and again would be fine, and Wulfhall was not so very far away that I could not visit often enough. Still, my heart was breaking.

Such feelings had to be banked. Just as I could not let my feelings for Sir Anthony get in the way of the Seymour objective, I could not let my love and infatuation with my son interfere either. Was not all of this for him? The boy was heir to the Seymour family seat. I sucked in my breath, turned back toward the hearth and tossed Jane's letter into the fire with a long sigh. We must pave the way for his future.

# CHAPTER THIRTEEN

*If you be fair and fresh, am I not of your hue?*
*And for my vaunt I dare well say, my blood is not untrue.*
*For you yourself have heard, it is not long ago,*
*Sith that for love one of the race did end his life in woe.*
*~Henry Howard, Earl of Surrey*

*April 1, 1537*

Thunder cracked and lightning made the dark skies white for brief seconds. Inside the great hall, candles lit up the room with an almost magical glow.

Jane Seymour was dressed beautifully in a light cloth of gold gown, jewels sewn along the hems, waistband, wrists and collar, with a matching hood. She danced around and around with one man at court after another until King Henry himself cut in.

As of yet, I hadn't been able to get her alone to hear her good news, but I suspected it was that she thought to be with child.

"So, my lady, you've returned." The voice of Surrey snaked along my ear and agitated every nerve in my body.

I resisted the urge to retch and instead kept my gaze on Jane. "I have." Better to keep our conversation short than entertain him for longer than necessary.

"You were sorely missed."

"By whom?" I asked, hoping my tone conveyed my boredom with his presence.

"By me, of course, and the other courtiers. I suspect Queen Jane was devastated at your long departure, and perhaps even the king himself. There is something draining and mundane about a court that is absent of the famous Anne Stanhope."

"Lady Beauchamp."

"Very formal. I take it we are not friends then?"

"The only reason you acquaint yourself with me, is to pant around the hem of my skirts, hoping I might drop a scrap of some bit of rubbish for you."

"It is not a scrap I hope will drop, but the gown itself."

"Ugh," I harrumphed and turned away from the man in disgust.

"Childbearing has done good things for you." His fingers tickled their way up my arm to my elbow. "Very good." His eyes lingered on my breasts and hips, which were rounder than before.

"You are severely inappropriate, my lord. Kindly refrain from talking to me in so familiar a fashion." My nerves bristled, and the hairs on my arms stood on end.

He bowed low, his eyes holding an evil glint, his lip curled sardonically. "As you wish, my lady."

He turned and left, and I did not waste my breath on a word of farewell. Would I hear a vile and vicious poem about myself on the morrow?

Truly, the man needed to learn a lesson. I gritted my teeth painfully and resisted the urge to toss the goblet of wine I had drained. All these years he'd spent tormenting me. At least now as a woman grown, married and now a mother, I had more gumption to meet him at his level, give him hell right back.

"My lady wife, might I have this dance?"

I turned, eyes widened with surprise and a bit of relief to see Edward standing beside me. He bowed and I curtsied, took his proffered arm and let him lead me to the dance floor, where a new set was beginning.

"I am pleased you have returned. I have not had a chance to talk to you much since Mass this morning. Could we... talk tonight?" he asked as he twirled me.

I knew Edward sought much more than talking, and in truth, I wished to feel his strong reassuring hands on my body. It'd been months since I'd felt desired or passion. But I had also been struggling with the idea of banning him from my bedroom for the time being. I dared not conceive again until Jane did, and even then, I did not want to become with child until after she'd given birth. There were precautions we'd used in the past, but even those hadn't worked—our little Eddie was proof. Queen Jane would need me during her pregnancy. If anything should happen to her, I needed to have all of my wits about me to be strong, and if I were with child myself, I could not guarantee that I would be with her.

"Edward..." I started but was uncertain how to finish.

He swept me in a circle.

"Do not say it, Anne," he whispered in my ear. "I can see in your eyes you mean to set me aside, but do not dare. I need you."

I swallowed hard. The man needed me. And in an odd way, I needed him, too. His strength was what fueled me. And how ironic it was. His strength fueled me to help him be a stronger man. Neither one of us could have survived without the other.

"I shan't say it, but we—mustn't."

Edward nodded emphatically. "We shan't conceive for the time being, but that does not mean we cannot enjoy each other's company."

"Enough. A great many curious ears are straining to hear our words."

Edward remained silent, but twirled me for the next several dances. I was eager to be back at court, even happier than I had imagined I would be, but still I felt the void. I missed my child, and after having born him, the intrigues of court did not hold as much fancy for me.

"My lady, Anne, welcome back to court." King Henry approached me as I left Edward to his own counsel.

"Majesty." I bowed low before him, and when I looked up, I caught his gaze roving over my body.

"I see your time away has kept you well." His smile was solicitous, which I ignored. No doubt, he would promise to keep me very well himself.

"It is good to have returned. I missed the excitement and the company."

"Indeed. Jane has missed you a great deal." He leaned in closer, took my elbow in his firm grip. "I know you are the one to have supplied her with a certain list of exotic eats."

My heart dropped into my stomach. *Oh, Lord!* But when I gazed on his face, I saw him smiling. He was not angry at me, merely amused.

*Dear God in heaven, please send Jane a child! Let her new happiness be for that very reason!*

I nodded and smiled. Swallowing down my nerves, I spoke. "Her Majesty will soon have some news that makes you and her most happy, Majesty."

Henry grunted, bowed in a most royal manner, and then turned to the next object of his fancy — thankfully, the queen herself.

I went to one of the grooms for a cup of wine, which I quickly downed before grasping another. Queen Jane walked up then, her smile radiant and contagious. I smiled in return and curtsied.

"Majesty."

"My lady." She gently grasped my hands. "Will you help me ready for bed this eve?"

"Yes, it would be my pleasure, Majesty." I wrapped my arm through hers and squeezed. She did not feel as frail as she had the last time I was there, which pleased me greatly. She was under less pressure, and if my suspicions were correct, she was also with child.

We entered the queen's bedchamber, and I dismissed the few ladies who waited there. I undressed Jane as she'd requested, pulled a white linen nightshift over her nude body, and then brushed out her long hair.

I found myself examining her belly as I undressed and redressed her. But she was also so thin, and it was hard to tell whether her belly had a slight bump in it or not.

"I cannot hold it inside any longer, Anne!"

207

Jane pressed her fingers to her lips, her excitement nearly bubbling over. She jumped to her feet, and her hands moved to her thin belly.

"I am with child, I know it. I feel it!"

I swallowed hard, my mouth going dry. "How do you know it?"

"My monthly. I have not had it in at least two or three months. And I feel it in my bones, I feel different! I have an amazing craving for quail and quail eggs!"

I rushed forward and hugged Jane. All of our prayers had been answered! A child! I pray, a prince!

"Do not say anything to His Majesty quite yet," I advised with caution, my eyes boring into hers, my countenance serious.

Jane's smile faltered. "Why? His Majesty would be so pleased."

"Yes, I agree. But imagine if you were mistaken? You want to know for certes. Wait until the quickening, when you first feel the baby move. It will be like a fluttering of butterflies in your belly." I clasped her hands in mine, my own excitement taking over. "Oh, Jane! You are almost there!"

After tucking Jane into bed and seeing that one of the maids was settled in a trundle to await her, I headed back to my own chambers. The corridors were quiet, except for the few couples I passed on the way, huffing and panting in alcoves, behind tapestries. For a moment a pang of jealousy hit me. How I wished to frolic and fornicate with such abandon. No worry for the consequence or who might see. But such was not the reality for me. I was Lady Beauchamp. Sister-by-marriage to the queen, aunt to the future prince.

When I arrived at my own apartment it was empty, save for Jenny. Edward had not yet returned from the court festivities.

"My lady," Jenny whispered and handed me a piece of sealed parchment.

I took it from her and opened the plain seal.

*Tomorrow night.*

Those were the only two words. No name, no signature. But there did not need to be. I knew the long scrawling handwriting. My stomach dropped down to my toes, and my vision blurred.

Sir Anthony had summoned me.

*April 2, 1537*

"Do nothing that will allude to your true identity."

Annie Bassett stood in the shadowy corridor outside the darkened music room I had chosen as the location for tonight's tryst. She wore a cloaked mantel over her thin-as-air ivory chemise, and silky slippers. All the items were mine, smelling of my French lavender cologne. I had wound her hair up tightly, coiled beneath a maroon velvet cap. Her hair was so different than mine. Her dark to my blonde. Beneath the cap, hopefully, her identity would be kept for at least a few minutes.

"Are you certain he won't realize?" Mistress Bassett was visibly nervous. Her fingers shook as she clutched the cloak tight to her chest.

"He will not know until it is too late, and by then, you will send him to me."

The man would have worked himself into a lusty lather, waiting for his time to claim me. But what Sir Anthony Browne did not understand was that he did not make the rules.

I did.

Anne Stanhope Seymour. Viscountess Beauchamp. Lady with an iron backbone. My will be done—only that of God and the king before me, and even the latter could be manipulated if needed.

I'd ignored his missive while at Wulfhall and had avoided him since returning. I knew I'd make an enemy of him, but I could not allow myself the temptation. The Seymour faction came first.

I was certain his note to me was a last attempt to regain control—I refused to believe it had anything to do with outright feelings for me. We played a game, he and I. A power game. Who was stronger, who had more allies? Who could outwit the other, and who could play the patient watcher the longest?

My plan for rebuffing his attempt at control was set in place, and I was confident that Anthony would soon realize the error of his ways and forget about a relationship with me, but instead focus on our mutual cause.

Annie Bassett's tear-pooling eyes pulled me back to the present. "Go, and do as I have instructed."

She timidly opened the door. Light from the corridor made a line on the darkened floor inside the room. I stepped out of view, my gut clenching tight. She slipped inside and shut the door. I stood a moment to listen, until I could hear the heavy panting and soft moans from within. He hadn't even bothered to see if it truly was me before pulling her into his arms. I admitted to having a twinge of jealousy, but I wouldn't allow those feelings to rule over me.

Besides, Anthony not noticing right away was half of my plan. I wanted to crush him. To make him forever forget about me. To understand that I made the rules and if he was wanted *I* would summon *him*. Not the other way around.

I would not be a pawn in anyone's games.

I counted off the seconds, waiting for Anthony to burst through the door and demand an explanation. But he did not. I contemplated for a moment whether I should go to the great hall and attend the queen or remain where I was. I felt stuck, uncertain. On the one hand, making my presence known in the great hall, and the lack of Sir Anthony's, would prove to Edward I was a loyal wife. Yet, if I left now, I risked Sir Anthony bursting into the great hall in a fit of rage and making a mockery of us both. In that case, I could end up on the scaffold, tried, found guilty and beheaded for adultery. Adultery was a crime and I was certain Edward would insist I be punished to the full extent of the law.

I pressed my hand around my throat, my breathing constricted. I had no desire to die. None, whatsoever.

I pressed my palms back until they connected with the cool stone of the castle walls, and leaned my head back, hoping that the coolness of the walls would somehow calm my racing pulse and still the sweat that dripped down my spine.

What to do? If I did not leave, Edward could assume I was *in flagrante delicto* and come searching for me, intent on bursting onto the very act itself. He'd had his suspicions of Anthony and me before, and now both of us were absent from the great hall. In that case, he would see me standing guard, burst into the room anyway and find out what had happened.

My stomach tied itself in so many knots it must have been close to representing the ancient Celtic symbols carved on so many a relic. Perhaps it was better to head to the great hall. My presence would quell Edward's suspicions, and if Anthony burst into the crowd shouting accusations, all could be denied. Hadn't Surrey said himself that I had a wolf's tongue?

I pushed away from the wall and took a few steps, my feet suddenly unstable. *Stupid woman*, I chided myself. The Viscountess Beauchamp never walked in shaky slippers. I took a deep breath, let it release slowly. Squared my shoulders, lifted my chin, and walked — one hand pressed to my belly, but only for a moment.

When I turned the corner, music from the great hall, shouts of laughter and loud conversation echoed down the corridor which brimmed with gawking courtiers. They were always looking for some bit of gossip, fodder for their starved minds and mouths. They gazed with bug-eyed glances at one another, at myself, at anyone who walked by and might be worthy of some information or even worthy of a story made up for entertainment. Not surprisingly, Jane Rochford was among the crowd, hissing behind her bony fingers to this lady and that.

I smiled with my court lady's curve of the lips, inclined my head, but my eyes remained cold. Lady Rochford would never receive anything warm from me again.

Heavy velvet draperies hung from walls and pillars. Cloth of gold was swathed from one part of the ceiling to the next. Tapestries adorned the walls. Candles dripping from chandeliers, mounted in sconces and situated in candelabras, lit up every bit of the room. Jongleurs danced and tumbled, musicians strolled and people danced. Bountiful food was everywhere. Great roasted hogs, goose, legs of lamb, seared fruit, roasted vegetables, fresh-baked bread, almonds, olives, dates. Wine and ale flowed. The scents were overwhelming, and I realized at once how hungry I was. This was court at its finest and most merry.

"The Lady Beauchamp," a groomsman loudly proclaimed to the crowd once I entered the grand room. Heads bowed, shouts of "Good eve!" and "Come make merry with us," went up from several passersby, but namely Edward stood out, standing so

211

stoically beside his sister and the king. From outward appearances his features did not change, but I could see when I looked closely that his eyes sparkled with pleasure. So, he had thought I was with a man, and now he was pleased his suspicions had been rendered obsolete.

I walked to the dais and made my curtsy to the king and queen. As always I was impressed with their dress. Jane had such good taste in clothes, as did the king. The chaste queen wore sage velvet, pearls and diamonds around the cuffs of her sleeves, around her collar, down the bodice and the front of her dress, where they wound in pretty swirls to the hem of her gown. Exquisite. His Majesty dressed to match is wife in sage and cloth of gold, with diamonds crusted on his own cuffs and collar. They made an impressive pair.

"Lady Anne, we are so pleased you could join us this evening, for we have a most joyous announcement to make," King Henry stated. I prayed that Jane had kept my counsel and not told the king her news quite yet. He held out his hand to me, and I took it, kissing the onyx ring he wore. "What kept you?"

I was taken aback by his question, as I hadn't expected him to be so forthright. But my training and diligence to remaining elusive paid off.

"Trouble with a servant, Majesty."

"I do hope you were able to deal with the situation?" He inclined his head toward me, and I always got the feeling he could see into my very soul.

"Absolutely." I turned to address Jane, when Edward cut in.

"What was the trouble, my lady?" His eyes challenged me.

Leave it to Edward to see to the very bottom of the pot... he'd learned too much from me already, it was almost endearing. I quirked a brow in his direction. "'Twas simply a new maid I hired. I caught her rummaging through my jewels. Therefore, I had to terminate her employment immediately, and then take an inventory to make certain nothing was missing."

"And were there any pieces missing?" King Henry blustered, his face turning red from anger as he sat forward.

"No, Majesty, I assure you. I concluded that it must have been the first time she'd deigned to undertake the task."

"And you had her removed from court immediately? We abhor the idea of thieves roaming our corridors," the king stated emphatically.

"She was promptly removed."

Jane, who always appeared to grow weary when lengthy conversations about unpleasant things occurred, interjected. "Well, I for one am grateful it is all straightened out and no harm was done."

King Henry patted her hand, gripped it in his own and kissed the back of it. "Lovely, Jane," he murmured.

Jane promptly blushed and bowed her head.

"Onto our good news!" King Henry all but shouted as he stood to address the crowd.

I walked over to Edward and stood beside him, his presence as always a comfort to me, especially with my mind in turmoil as to what could be happening in an empty music room, two bodies nude and panting...

"I am pleased you arrived. I was afraid this evening would sorely be lacking in your presence," Edward bent to murmur.

I nodded and squeezed his hand. I knew what he truly meant to say was, *I am so damned ecstatic you are not fucking that Anthony fellow.*

"I would never wish to be anywhere else."

From the corner of my eye, I witnessed Edward's smile.

"Good lords and ladies!" King Henry started. His hands were raised in the air, a goblet of wine in one.

The music and conversation stopped. His fool, Will Somers, bounded to the dais and then flopped into position at His Majesty's feet, a look of purely concocted adulation on his face. King Henry laughed and gently nudged Will with his foot.

"I have good news. Restorations on Hampton Court are nearly through! We shall be settled and merry there when the time comes to celebrate Christmas."

While the crowd opened into a deafening roar of pleasure, for a grander palace meant more lavish entertainments and fare, I let out my held breath. Jane had kept her secret safe. Hands clapped, pewter mugs clinked, shouts of excitement drowned out the king's voice.

"Pray for us, for I have good cause to believe a son will be born there!"

*And good God, pray for us. Jane is with child. The rising of the Seymour family is almost complete. Please Lord in heaven, bring her a son!*

After much celebrating that night, I allowed Edward to accompany me to bed. Truth was, I missed his arms around me, his lips on my flesh, and the tender way he caressed me, bringing me to heights of pleasure that caused me to forget the turmoil we lived in. My nerves were in such an upheaval from the situation with Anne Bassett and Sir Anthony that I could not bear to be alone. I had yet to hear news of how their evening ended, and this did not bode well for me or our alliance.

And so I lay with Edward. But I still was not going to take a chance of conceiving until Jane delivered a healthy child. I drank a bitter vinegary herb draught after we finished and washed with it for good measure.

Edward left for his own chambers, presumably to work on correspondence and other such paperwork. The man hardly slept anymore. He proclaimed that he never would until our position was solid.

I was nearly half asleep when I jolted awake and sat straight up in bed. Feet slid across the plush carpet. Someone was in my bedchamber.

"Edward?" Had he returned to share the bed yet again? When we'd first married, he'd been known to do so.

"Shh..."

Not Edward. But I could not make out the voice. The shadowy figure loomed closer. Tall, lithe. A man's figure.

At once I knew who the shadow belonged to.

I scrambled from bed, threw on my wrapper, but did not light a candle. I did not want to alert Edward to my consciousness and have him coming in to see why I was not asleep.

"What the devil are you doing in my bedchamber?" I spat in hushed tones.

"Care to explain your little ruse, my lady?" Anthony hissed.

"I do not *care* to explain anything to you, *Sir* Anthony." I hoped to convey my superiority over him, and even in the dark, I could see him flinch.

"We had a deal." He walked forward, but I did not retreat as I wanted to. I stood my ground.

"Now that is exactly where you are wrong. My body, *myself*. I never agreed. I am no bargaining chip for your flights of fancy. Do not presume you can rule over me."

"Shall I call Edward in, and see what he thinks?"

I laughed bitterly at his bluff, for I knew the man well, and death was the last thing etched into his life plan. "Do not play games with me. I've had better teachers, and better seconds than you could ever hope for. Do you forget I served the king's first wife? I've been at court much longer than you," I said with mock bravado, recalling every bit of teaching since I'd been at court as a child. "Want to feel the roughhewn length of rope around your neck? Want to dangle in the air as the breath is choked from your body? While the crowd throws manure, rotten eggs and spits on you?"

He took a step back, and I took a step forward. I had the upper hand now. "I did not think so. You won't mention a word of our transgressions for fear of your own death. You won't so much as breathe of it, for fear all your hard work, the many hours spent on your rise within court, be torn to shreds. You won't jeopardize that."

"It is just as Surrey says," he hissed under his breath. "You, Lady Anne, are a vicious bitch!"

I bit down hard on my cheek, wanting to scream and at the same time wanting to grip my chest, my heart hurt so badly. His words more than stung, they shook me to my core, but I could not let them consume me. I kept my shock, dismay and pain inside. I had to keep up the pretense that he meant nothing to me, for both our sake's.

Feigning that I hadn't heard his comment, I continued, "Furthermore, you will continue to issue to me any pertinent information. If I so much as hear a whisper of your defection, I will see to it you are just another body tossed in a grave at Saint Peter ad Vincula."

"Venomous woman! How does your husband stand it?" But his words weren't meant for me to answer, more to sting. His eyes glittered with anger. His teeth flashed in a near snarl. "You'd not betray me, love, for doing so would unravel all *you* have worked for."

His words... They pained me much. I swallowed back my tears. Steeled my back and pressed forward. This was for the best. This would forever sever us. Save me. Save the Seymours from ruin. "Do not cross me, Anthony. There are plenty of courtiers to replace you."

Anthony drew back, stunned and a myriad of emotions crossed his face. For a moment, I felt guilty. Almost took him into my arms, begged his forgiveness for my harshness. But I shoved my own flights of fancy aside. There could never be anything between us.

"What happened to you, Anne, that makes you so cruel?" He stepped close enough I could feel the heat of his hurt and anger radiating off his body. "I loved you. Would have been good to you. Would not have ever betrayed you."

My fingernails dug deep into my palms and how I hated myself. "You can see yourself out. I believe you know the way?" My voice was sugary sweet, yet underneath tangy and bitter — not much unlike chocolate-covered orange peels.

When my room was empty of the man I'd loved but kept at a distance, I lay back on my bed and stared at the darkened ceiling. I prayed in time he could forgive me. Because, in truth, Anthony may have been the only person who actually loved me for who I was, and not for what I could provide.

*April 5, 1537*

"Where have you been?"

Annie Bassett flinched from the danger in my soft voice, but her eyes remained cast down.

"I have been with *him*."

"Him?" My eyes narrowed. Dare she say it? I turned more fully to face her head-on.

"Sir Anthony, my lady." Fingers clasped together in front of her hips, knuckles white.

"What exactly have you been doing and where?" Jealousy gripped me tightly in the chest, and it took all of my power to keep it out of my tone.

Her feet shifted. "My lady, only as you bid."

"Only as I bid?" I sputtered, my hand came to my chest in mock exasperation. I clenched my other fist at my side, forcing myself not to slap the girl. Betrayal! Full and powerful... I had been betrayed. And yet, there was no one else to blame but myself. I'd pushed Anthony away, and I'd led Annie right to him. Still, I lashed out. "I bid you tease the man for thirty seconds and then relay a message, not spend three days *fucking* him!"

Annie looked up, tears falling from her eyes. "But he said..."

I took a deep breath in an effort to calm myself. Folded my hands in front of me and wiped the anger from my countenance in order to put Anne at ease. "He said what?"

"He said he visited you that night and you told him to do with me as he pleased. That you wished for him to train me in the ways of a lover."

I laughed bitterly at that, pride warring with jealousy. So, he had had his vengeance. He'd known how I would feel, too! Even with my carefully manipulated cold demeanor, he'd seen right through it! The girl's lower lip trembled. *Bastard!* But with that, I knew I would have nothing more to fear from him again. He'd had his revenge. He'd used up my virgin prize, ruined my chances of luring her to the king with a firmly intact maidenhead. On the other hand, at least she would now be skilled enough to keep the king's attention lured until Jane was once again ready to entertain him sexually.

"And did he treat you kindly?"

Now little Annie looked confused. "Yes, my lady."

"You must be tired."

"Indeed I am not, for I spent most of my time in bed..." She trailed off, her face flaming.

"Were precautions used?"

"Yes, my lady. He—"

"I do not care to hear the details. Did he teach you to love a man well?" I suppressed the rage once more rising in my chest. But why? I had a good husband and Edward was a good lover... But there was something different about Anthony. Something carnal and base. And I'd yet to feel it. Perhaps that was where my jealousy sparked. I coveted what Mistress Bassett had experienced. For shame, God would damn me.

"Aye, my lady, he did."

"Then you shall be prepared when the king comes calling for you. It will be soon. Go and clean yourself up and report to the queen's chambers. You will tell her you've been ill."

"Yes, my lady." She turned to leave.

"And Annie?" My eyebrows raised in challenge.

She turned back to face me, her face devoid of emotion. "Yes, my lady?"

"Not a whisper of this to anyone, or it's back to the country with you."

"As it pleases you, my lady."

# CHAPTER FOURTEEN

*In tower both strong and high, for his assured truth,*
*Whereas in tears he spent his breath, alas, the more the ruth (remorse).*
*~Henry Howard, Earl of Surrey*

*April 11, 1537*

"Come, let us tantalize your taste buds." I clapped my hands as a signal for the groomsmen to begin serving the first dishes for our party. A dinner party had seemed the appropriate thing to do in light of all the events surrounding court and my most recent return. A chance to be carefree for one evening.

And to take my mind from Anthony.

The candlelight flickered with the sudden movements of our bodies and the wind we created from flowing skirts as we entered the dining room of our chambers at Whitehall. I took my place at one end of the trestle table, Edward opposite me. A diverse gathering sat between us. A test of those at court. Down the left side sat Henry Courtenay, Lord Exeter and Henry Pole, Lord Montague and his lady wife. Lady Montague was a sickly thing. Pale, thin, and her pallor almost gray. Her once-dark hair lacked luster and was streaked with silver, her eyes red-rimmed and yellow.

The right side of our grand table was filled with Lord Exeter's wife, Gertrude—immaculate as always—the stately looking Ambassador Chapuys and the Lady Mary, dressed in a demure maroon gown with black embroidery, pearls and lace—nearly making my stylish emerald silk gown look inappropriate. Her hair was pulled back so severely, the skin of her face looked stretched at the temples. I imagined beneath her gown a hair shirt scratched her skin. For all her young age, Lady Mary always gave off the impression that she was an old soul. Almost as if her mother, Katharine, sat before me instead of Mary.

I was sad that she and I could no longer be the friends we once had been. Longed for a time when I worried most about what gown to wear and whether or not my mother would disapprove. Lord, it had been so long ago. And now the girl I'd whispered to in the dark stood against Queen Jane's offspring and I had to draw her in.

The groomsmen filled wine goblets and set out dishes of onion soup—a blend of onions, herbs and almond milk—one I happened to know was a favorite of Mary's. Loaves of fresh brown bread were thickly sliced and placed in the center of the table.

A full house we had—for even though our party itself was rather small, the space available for us to entertain at our court apartments was much smaller than our manor home. The king and queen had been invited, but Henry had said he wished to enjoy a private dinner with his wife. I suspected Jane had, in fact, told him she wished to dine with him *sans* their entourage, and that she had great news to tell him.

"So good of you to invite us to dine with you this evening, Lady Anne," Lady Montague said, just before bursting into a coughing fit. Lord Montague patted her back and forced her to sip her wine. "My apologies."

I set down my spoon and wiped my mouth with my napkin. "It is a pleasure to have you all here this evening. I was away from court for some time, and Lord Beauchamp and I thought a small dinner with friends a splendid welcome back."

"Indeed, it is," Gertrude murmured between bites of soup.

"I must also issue my thanks for such an invitation," Chapuys chimed in. "It was a most pleasant surprise and diversion from my usual evenings." He inclined his head to me, Edward and then to Mary. "The company is most diverse and pleasing."

Lady Mary was quiet, only inclining her head and spooning dainty bites of soup into her mouth. I wanted to see inside her mind and know her thoughts, for certainly she must have many.

"My Lady Exeter, I have not had the pleasure yet of welcoming you back at court as well. I spoke with your husband at length earlier this week," Chapuys said.

"Thank you, Ambassador. Court is where our lives are, and indeed all of our friends. We are so pleased His Majesty saw fit for us to return. We are forever his most humble, dutiful and loyal servants."

Chapuys smiled. "*Si*, I have also found the court of Henry VIII to be a home away from home, filled with good friends and allies."

"Tell me, Ambassador. What news from Spain?" I asked.

"Ah, my master has written to me just this morning. They are hard at work filtering out heretics, just as His Majesty, King Henry is. Seems that an ocean between our two countries, and the difference in heads of church, cannot stop the profligates from exhorting their beliefs." Chapuys licked his lips and then attempted to pull some invisible strand of food from his teeth with his tongue.

"Even in the East you will find heretics preaching their gods and virtues. Muslims think Christians are heretics," Lord Montague added.

Edward, whose attention had been intent on the ambassador, now turned in Montague's direction. "Yes..." he drawled. "Any word from Reginald Pole of late?"

My mouth dropped open. I hadn't expected Edward to press poor Henry about his traitorous brother, who still pushed for his claim to the throne. Lady Montague choked on her soup and proceeded to fall into another terrible coughing fit. Henry Pole was so intent on his wife's coughing, he seemed to forget the question.

Lord Exeter chimed in, "Montague has had no word from his traitorous brother. Although, I daresay, we shall not refer to the man as any sort of relation. How goes it with Sir Nicholas and Sir Francis?"

"They have yet to return. Seems they chase a ghost. They get a tip of Pole's whereabouts, his preachings, even a pamphlet he published, but the moment they are upon him, he disappears. The devil's work," Edward said.

"His Imperial Highness is most interested in the capture of this Pole as well," Chapuys said, steepling his fingers, elbows on the table. "He states that two ruling monarchs must look after each other when one is endangered by a usurper. He is willing to help in the search if King Henry will agree to a treaty of sorts."

"A treaty?" Edward asked, his fingers drumming against the gleaming mahogany wood of the table. I was momentarily distracted by his fingers, the way they methodically tapped the wood. Wood that the servants had scrubbed, wiped down with wax and then buffed to a sheen that afternoon. Almost as if he knew how the conversation was going and exactly what he was going to say, only waiting to tick off each and every line of dialogue.

"*Si*, but I have yet to relay the message to His Majesty, King Henry."

Edward nodded, knowing as we all did that Chapuys would not relay the message to us before he'd laid it on the king's ears, only give us a hint. "If it has anything to do with returning to the breast of Rome, you can be certain King Henry will not agree to it."

Chapuys nodded and glanced at Lady Mary. I narrowed my eyes, trying to understand what was *not* said between them. Mary gazed in my direction and then returned her glance to her lap.

What was the sneaking ambassador up to? Was he a secret supporter of the rallies against His Majesty, the people trying to rise up and put Mary in his place?

"My lady, the soup was divine," Mary said, jarring me from my thoughts.

My eyes widened, and I smiled at her. "Thank you. I had heard you preferred it."

Groomsmen melted from the walls and cleared the soup bowls, and placed on the table platters of roasted venison with carrots, garlic and onions in a cream sauce, capon in green sage sauce, and braised salmon with apricots.

Conversation died for a few moments as our guests filled their plates with the tasty dinner dishes.

Amid the clink and clatter of utensils on dishes, Henry Pole's voice rose, sounding hurried, like a sinner at confessional. "The pope is aiding Reginald. My mother wrote me last week to say she'd received a letter from him. The pope pays his way, that he might elude the English authorities seeking him."

"Your mother has heard from him?" I asked, astonished that Lord Montague had not told us before now.

Gertrude and Lord Exeter also looked shocked. Since part of all of them being returned to court was that Lady Salisbury, Pole's mother, would inform them immediately of any contact. Once again, I thought Lady Montague would choke on her food.

He nodded solemnly. "It appears that my dear brother, how I abhor the word," he mumbled, "corresponds with Mother regularly. I've entreated her more often than I can count not to encourage him thusly, but my sentiments have gone unnoticed. She only laments that she is his mother."

"This news does not bode well for your mother," Edward said.

"Certainly not now that she is in the king's employ with one of his children," Exeter said.

Montague spread his hands in question. "What am I to do? I fear if I push her too hard she will not tell me what she knows."

We all mumbled our agreement. "For certes, you cannot allow that to happen. If your sibling happens to relay his whereabouts, that is information most useful to your king. You are obligated to inform him," I said.

"Aye," Montague said, stuffing a large piece of venison into his mouth, the grease dribbling onto his chin before he swiped it away.

Somehow I got the feeling that although he agreed on the outside, internally he was not so resolved. We would have to keep our eyes on Montague, because as anyone knew, blood ran thicker than water, and when you had a mother harping in your ear, you were most likely to do her bidding.

"Ambassador, I am confident you will present His Majesty with the offer from your master of an alliance of sorts," Edward turned the conversation. "But I must also tell you we shall handle the locating of Cardinal Reginald Pole ourselves. It is a decidedly English matter. In fact, upon meeting with the king, we have sent another man to assist in the search, Sir Anthony Browne." Edward leaned back in his chair, hands still laid on the table, but his countenance challenging nonetheless. But he did not challenge Chapuys. Instead, his gaze was steadily directed on mine.

I raised a brow and kept my face clear of concern, for it so happened I was pleased for Anthony to have been sent on the mission. He would take it as something I might have encouraged Edward to do, and even though I had not, I could not have been more pleased for the handsome, arrogant and entirely insufferable charmer to be an ocean away and believing I had gotten my revenge on his tricks.

"I must say I am surprised. I was not aware that Sir Anthony had the skills needed to aid Sir Francis and Sir Nicholas."

I could have hugged Gertrude for voicing her opinion, for the thought had also crossed my mind.

Edward smiled indulgently at her. "It is not widely known, but the king has used Sir Anthony on many occasions for more clandestine purposes."

"Yes, well, we did know he was able to garner information with the ease of slipping a hand into a glove. The man is a genius at his sport," Lord Exeter said.

"A courtier with more talent than that of stroking...egos is always invaluable," Chapuys added, to the merriment of the group.

"Lady Mary, you must tell me, how do you find the newly renovated south gardens?" I changed the subject not only to encourage Mary to speak, but because I was entirely exhausted of politics. I had known going into the dinner party that political speech would play a part, but had had high hopes we might all reconvene our friendships as well. Especially with Lady Mary at the table. I wanted her to know she was a friend of ours — if only on the surface. None other than the queen had welcomed Mary with open arms, in an effort to show the king what a virtuous wife she was.

Lady Mary smiled at me, her expression brightening considerably. "I adore them. The blend of white and red roses amongst the greenery is beautiful."

Conversation turned to the gardens and hunting. Dinner was cleared and replaced with custards, gooseberry tarts, sugared plums and candied almonds. Once everyone was sufficiently filled, we adjourned to our presence chamber.

Musicians arrived shortly, playing lutes and shawms softly in the background. The men gathered in a corner to play their hand at cards, and the ladies sat by the banked hearth, sipping on spiced wine.

Mary fingered the seed pearls on the cuff of her gown. Her dark brown gaze captured mine. Emotion filled their depths—pain the most prevalent. "How is it...being a mother?"

Just from the way she'd said it, the emotion in her voice, the chosen words, the pause in between, I could sense her torment. At one and twenty summers, there were still no prospects for her. Her father was so intent on his own marriages and heirs that he hadn't paid a lick of attention to Mary's future, though I suspected he ignored her on purpose as a child of her own would only strengthen her position. She must have wondered if she would ever get married. There were plenty of women at court, myself included, who hadn't married until later, but it was not generally the case, and especially not for a royal princess. The custom was usual for them to be married early—indeed, most were married before their first bleed.

"Mistress Elizabeth Seymour and Sir Thomas Seymour," a groom announced.

I was taken aback, my words stolen from my throat and completely forgotten. Beth I was pleased to see. Tom, not so much.

Edward rose to greet our newest guests. He turned and frowned in my direction until I was able to recover my shock and stand to greet them as well.

"Beth, darling, come join the ladies. Tom." I inclined my head but did not curtsy to him, nor offer my hand. As a woman in a superior position in society, I did not have to do such things. And it was also an obvious cut to my brother-by-marriage.

Edward frowned at me again, but I dismissed him, pulling Beth with me to sit with the other ladies.

225

From across the room, I could feel the ice of Tom's stare. I gazed at him from the corner of my eyes, not wanting to make eye contact with him. His anger was barely banked. The other men were jovial at times, serious at others, but all through the game, Tom was the same. Barely a nod or grumble, just staring.

The room felt as if it were growing colder, but I knew it was not actually a drop in temperature, but my growing concern for Tom's temper that had me chilled. He was not in his right mind. He looked most unstable. No longer able to stand the chilly glare, I stood up.

"Ladies, what say you to an evening walk in the gardens?" I gestured to the window. "You can see the footmen have lit candles along the pathways."

"Oh, how delightful," Gertrude exclaimed. "Gentleman, would you like to escort us?"

"Indeed, my lady, we'd be much obliged," Edward stated. They laid their cards down and began linking arms with the women.

"My lady," Tom said to me, offering his arm.

I did not want to take his arm, felt that his very touch would freeze me in place forever, but I did anyway.

"I know what your scheme is," he leaned down to whisper.

"What do you mean by that?" I was truly perplexed. Why should he be so angry?

"You control my brother as if he were a puppet and you the master."

"That is not true and entirely inappropriate, Tom."

"All in the eye of the beholder, my lady. I've seen you with Anthony. I know about Surrey as well. Who is next, the king?"

I gasped. "Pardon me?" A chill ran down my spine. What was Tom accusing me of?

"Who will you fuck next? Henry VIII?"

I could no longer stand to hear his mockery and vile words. He spoke them only to make me break. And he won. Rage rushed through me. With a swift turn, I slapped him on his cheek.

"Abominable! How dare you!" I said.

The group in front of us stopped before quite reaching the main door of our apartment and turned to look at the spectacle. My face burned with anger and embarrassment. Why had I let him get the better of me in front of people? I had always been the picture of serenity in front of others, saving my lesser decorum for private moments.

"What's the meaning of this?" Edward snapped. He stomped toward Tom, chest puffed out.

"Vicious, vile bitch!" Thomas came up close, ignoring Edward, his face only inches away, his words echoing those of Anthony. I could smell the alcohol thick on his breath. The man was deep in his cups, and somehow able to fool everyone into thinking he was sober as a daisy. His lips curled into a snarl, but it was not the fear of him biting me that sent chills racing up and down my spine, but the pure and raw rage sparking from his eyes. A man with such anger, hatred and booze running through his veins was a danger to everyone.

"The last thing this court needs is *another* Anne," he hissed.

My gasp was dissolved by the intakes of breath and outraged murmurings of those surrounding me. Just as we never spoke of Catherine Filiol, Edward's first unfaithful, incestuous wife, no one spoke of Anne Boleyn. But Tom just had, and what was worse, he'd compared me to her.

I was stunned speechless. My throat constricted. I felt like I was choking. Thomas Seymour wanted me dead. Thought me no better than Anne Boleyn, deserving a death stroke to the neck. I stumbled back a step. Vacillated on a reaction. Why had he harbored such anger for me? Once, I had thought his petty foolishness to be the jealousy of a younger brother, wishing for things that weren't his, and even later thought him upset with me in order to protect his brother from another failed marriage. But this... this went beyond all that to something deeper that I could not understand. Weightier than him simply being angry with me for blackmailing him to keep his mouth shut.

"Brother, you've gone too far!" Edward bellowed.

Elizabeth Seymour rushed to my side, her fingers entwining with mine. She whispered words of comfort in my ear, but I could not make out what they were, was barely able to understand that she was indeed speaking. Gertrude, too, came up, caressed my arm tenderly, and offered her strong body as support, but I refused to sag. I stood tall, willed my wobbling knees to straighten.

Tom turned from me to look at Edward. "I only tell the truth, and you know it. The woman schemes for power, prestige, money, position, and she'll lift her skirts for anyone willing to offer it. Look how she got you—"

Edward cut his brother off with a hard fist to his jaw. The resounding crack echoed in the silent room. Tom stumbled backward, a trickle of blood spilling from the corner of his lips. Our guests' mouths, which had already dropped open, hung nearly to their chests. Hands were frozen in horror over their gaping mouths. My eyes widened beyond what was natural. They stung, but I could not blink. Could not, *not* see what was happening in front of me.

"Do not *ever* speak of my wife in such a way again, or the next time you shan't live to see morning."

My stomach tightened. My heart flipped. Edward had really just threatened his own brother's life over an insult. For that was all it was, really. Tom was an angry, jealous, drunk little boy—despite his adult age. Right? He could not possibly really want to see me walk across the scaffold, lay down my head and spread my arms for surrender to the ax, could he? And then I knew, fully comprehended as his eyes flicked to mine, disgust and hatred burning holes in my forehead. He *did* want me dead. His gaze turned back to Edward, and it was evident there as well. He wanted Edward dead, too.

"Throw down the gauntlet only if you can raise your sword, brother." Tom wiped the blood from his mouth with his thumb, an evil smile curling his lips. "One day you won't stand so tall. One day you'll have to beg me for favor. One day I will take precedence over you and your *wife*." The way he said the latter word sounded like I was offal to be spit on. "You are not the only male Seymour the king has a tender spot for. You shall see Edward, I will trump thee." He smirked, his laugh rough and scratchy.

"Get out," Edward growled. "Get out before I have you arrested for suspicion of treason."

Tom did not say another word. He did not have to. His threats were loud and clear, and he would not want to be arrested either, else he would not have been able to attempt to make good on his promises.

The sound of the door to our chambers slamming shut was coupled with wood splintering and a crash as one of our paintings fell to the floor. Was it a sign of things to come? The world we lived in ripping apart and smashing at our feet?

Edward whirled on me, anger burning in his gaze. "'Twould be best if you retired for the evening, my lady."

I opened my mouth to speak, but the way his lips curled in a snarl bade me to remain silent. He may have protected me, but I would not go unpunished for this spectacle.

# CHAPTER FIFTEEN

*This gentle beast so died, whom nothing could remove,*
*But willingly to lose his life for loss of his true love.*
*~Henry Howard, Earl of Surrey*

*April 14, 1537*

I kept to my chambers over the next several days, sending Queen Jane my regrets for not serving her. I complained of stomach pains, and she relented for me to rest. Whether she believed me, I know not.

Edward bade me stay in my chambers, which was fine by me. I could not leave anyway, not with the violence with which I had last encountered Tom, the humiliation our guests had witnessed. It was not that I feared for my life, but more that I feared for what Tom could do to Edward, to our position. Families normally rose and fell together, but Tom wanted to be the only Seymour. Wanted to betray us to the king.

Edward had spent the last few days tightening up our defenses. He had paid visits to all those at court we could call friend. Made loans, gave favors. Hired more spies to keep an eye on his brother. Within the confines of my room, I wrote correspondence with Gertrude and, on her suggestion, to the Duchess of Suffolk, the wife of Charles Brandon, the king's dearest friend, both of whom assured me I need not worry about the anger of a man such as Tom.

"We're going to Wulfhall," Edward said that evening. We sat in our presence chamber, he reading over letters and documents, and me working on embroidering initials into a gown for sweet Eddie. How I missed the babe.

"When?" *Wulfhall. Little Eddie.* It felt like an eternity since I had seen him last. Leaving court would be a relief.

"Tomorrow. Jane will accompany us. The king has business in Calais, and he does not wish Jane to travel with him that far—she told him she's expecting."

"Did she? I was hoping she had. I take it the king was pleased?"

"Aye, he was." Edward smiled, his countenance triumphant. "Mentioned something of not eating another artichoke for a decade."

My head fell back as I laughed at this. "Or at least until he wishes to get another babe on her."

"Right, you are! Let us pray the babe is a prince." We bowed our heads, mumbled prayers and then crossed ourselves.

"My sister Beth will also join us, and Jane is bringing the Lady Mary as her companion."

I brightened even more at the added guests. "How long will we stay at Wulfhall?"

"We'll stay until the king returns."

"But I've only just returned to court," I lamented half-heartedly.

Edward turned to smile at me. "That was not your best work," he teased.

"Shall I try again? But Edward," I whined in an exaggerated voice.

He laughed and came to kneel before me. My heart fluttered a bit. "There she is."

"There who is?"

"Do not let us forget who you are, Anne. Do not let court suck the sweetness from you, only to leave a bitter tang."

I nodded, afraid to speak, for whatever sweetness I'd ever possessed had left me the moment Surrey laid his hands on me. My emotions were too raw, too fragile. The vicious words of Tom and

231

Anthony came flooding back. Taunting me. Coupled with Edward's embrace and kind words, it was almost too much. So little time had we spent recently remembering our true friendship and love for each other. Anthony had been a huge distraction for me, and with him gone… I felt that Edward and I had been able to rediscover each other. He kissed me on the forehead and went back to his papers.

The following morning we met Jane in the courtyard. Henry did not want her to ride her horse to Wulfhall, so instead had a gilded litter prepared, replete with a red velvet draped roof and cloth of gold curtains on the sides. Two horses stood stoically, one in front of the other, the litter between them and attached with wooden poles to their bellies by thick leather straps and iron rings.

Fit for a queen. The litter would make our travel longer because the horses would have to walk, but Jane had arranged for servants to ride ahead and set up a picnic in a grove along the way.

"Good morning, Your Majesty." I curtsied to King Henry and kissed his offered ring.

"Lady Anne, Beauchamp." He nodded to Edward, who'd risen from his bow. "Take good care of my Jane. If any harm is to befall on her, you shall suffer for it." He laughed, but the veiled threat was evident behind his jovial attitude.

"We shall take great care of her, Majesty, I assure you. Queen Jane shall want for nothing," I said.

"How lucky she is to have you as a sister-by-marriage. If you have need of anything, Master Cromwell will see that it is provided. I will only be in Calais a short time, but if needs be, I shall return."

I banked the urge to cringe at Cromwell's name. "Majesty, have a safe journey. Upon your return, we invite you to dine at Wulfhall."

"Indeed, it will be my first return stop upon landing at Dover." He turned to focus his attention on Jane, who sat in the litter, peering out at us. "Ah, there you are, Jane."

"Majesty," she inclined her head and lowered her lashes. How she had perfected the look of utter docility, I did not know. Perhaps she could teach me? Although I had never adhered to the saying *you catch more bees with honey than vinegar*. I preferred to swat the bees with my shoe.

King Henry kissed Jane on the lips and murmured to her tenderly. Once their display of familial domesticity was complete, we mounted our horses and were on our way.

*April 21, 1537*

"May I hold your babe?" Mary asked, as I sat rocking the sleeping form of little Eddie in the great hall. The sun shone through a great, stained glass window, which sat below the peaks of the vaulted ceiling over the main door. Little prisms of red, blue, green and gold danced along the polished floorboards.

The last week at Wulfhall had been a rejuvenating retreat. Edward had spent the time visiting our various holdings, while we ladies had spent the days walking in the gardens, reading, embroidering and playing with little Eddie.

"Why, of course, my lady." I handed the gurgling cherub over to her, already feeling the loss of his warm body in my arms. What would I do when the king returned to England and it was time for us to go back to court? My heart seized at the thought. Would that I could be as carefree as some other women, who hadn't the obligation to live life at court away from her children. Would that I could stay here forever, teach him to crawl, walk, talk and write letters to his father. I bit the tip of my tongue to stave off the tears that burned my eyes.

Mary curled her arms around Eddie and held him close. He opened his eyes a moment and burbled at her, his mouth forming a little O. His eyes widened, lashes hitting his eyebrows, and he reached out to bat at her face with a chubby little fist.

"He is a beautiful baby," Mary murmured, and then with longing said, "I hope one day to have a boy just as sweet."

"And you shall." I gazed upon the perfection that was my son. How lucky Edward and I were to have born such a creature.

"I do not share your confidence." Her eyes connected with mine. "I have been promised many times, but never committed."

"Mary, you will. I will see to it. As soon as I am recovered from my lying in with a prince, I will begin making inquiries myself," Jane said. She looked up from her embroidery to gaze on Mary.

I started. Then realized Jane's words—she'd not make any inquiries until she'd born the king a son.

"Would you?" Mary asked, her eyes lightning.

"On my honor," Jane said the words so matter-of-factly, they garnered no argument. "I've mentioned as much to His Majesty, and he agrees it is time you marry."

"Oh, Jane," Mary gushed, her face taking on an air of naïveté and happiness that did not quite fit her. She always seemed such a serious woman and well beyond her years, but when she truly let herself shine through, you could see the girl beneath the rigid exterior. What a life Mary had led so far, her twenty-one years rife with struggle, pain, and determination. "That would be extremely pleasing."

"I want to see you just as happy as I am," Jane said.

"And are you truly happy?" Beth asked.

It was a question all of us had on our lips. With my being away for the birth of Eddie and then the recent goings-on at court, I hadn't been able to sit down with Jane and have a private talk.

A smile curled her lips. "I am. I've fulfilled part of my duty to His Majesty. Proved I am not barren, that I am ripe and able to carry a babe. Now I just have to finish this one task and birth a prince safely into this world."

*Pray be a prince.*

"The babe has started to kick. Strong little kicks, too. Not at all a fluttering, as I was told to expect. I feel strongly in my heart that it is a boy. He wants me to know he's a prince, so he kicks. God wants me to know, so that I might not fret during the long months ahead, and I can grow the healthiest little baby who will one day be as great a king as his father."

"And he will, Majesty," Mary said, tickling the chin of Eddie.

"What a joy it will be to see it happen," Jane said with a smile before returning to her work.

"What of you, Beth? Think you are ready to remarry?" I asked.

Beth turned to me and smiled. "I am more than ready now, Anne."

I smiled in return. "I have a match in mind for you."

"Who is the lucky gent?" she teased.

"Edward agrees with me the match has potential." I raised my brows at her.

"You have not answered the question. Does this mean he is ugly? Has twelve toes?"

Jane and Mary laughed. Little Eddie let out a squeal of delight.

"Beth, darling, he is extremely handsome," I answered.

"Who then?"

I took a deep breath and let out the name, "Master Gregory Cromwell."

Beth sucked in a breath. Her eyes narrowed at me, and her voice was hushed. "Secretary Cromwell's son?"

"'Tis not so bad. The apple falls far from the tree in that line." I gave a firm nod.

"Hmm... He is handsome. Perhaps his bedroom manner will make up for who his sire is," Beth said.

"Beth!" Jane gasped, exasperated, her embroidery falling onto her lap.

But I only laughed, for if I had been Elizabeth Seymour, I would have been thinking the same thing.

*April 28, 1537*

"My lady, a letter has arrived from your mother." Edward stalked into my solar and handed me the parchment.

I set down my embroidery and stood. Jane, Beth and Mary had all taken to resting this afternoon before the evening meal.

"Did you read it?"

"I thought I would let you do the honors." He slumped into a chair and took a proffered glass of wine from Jenny.

I tore open my mother's seal and read the contents. "She is begging a visit from us."

I motioned for Jenny to bring me some wine.

"You do not sound pleased." Edward glanced toward me, his brows raised.

"You know very well I am not," I huffed.

He stood and came behind me, his hands massaging my shoulders. I rolled against him, enjoying the soothing strength of his hands as he worked away the bunches and tightness in my shoulders.

"Anne…" he drawled.

In that instant, I could tell he was up to something. "Out with it, Edward."

"I have to be away for a sennight or two. Perhaps instead of going to see your mother, you could invite her here to visit."

I whirled around to face Edward. "Have you lost your mind?"

He had the audacity to chuckle and tweak me on the chin. "No need to get your goose up, wife. You have not seen or spoken to your mother in months. As much as you would like to avoid her — and I know you do — it is best to keep some semblance of contact for the sake of our position. We must appear to be gratuitous to all, not just our closest friends."

I frowned so hard a headache started behind my eyes.

"Do not look at me so. I cannot stand to see you unhappy. But you know 'tis for the best. Your stepfather is now sided with Surrey. Who knows what vile things he's said or spread? We need their support. We need to know what Surrey is about. Remember, he is a Howard, and essentially your family is now of the Howard faction. Friends close, enemies closer."

Edward had a point. As much as I abhorred the idea — felt physically sick, in fact — I could not ignore the fact that we not only needed information, but we needed Page and my mother on our side.

"Very well. I shall see if she'd like to come for a visit. I do not doubt she will accept, seeing as how the queen is here."

"Exactly." Edward leaned forward and kissed me fleetingly on the lips before leaving me to write my correspondence.

I did not receive a response back from my mother. Indeed, the woman arrived in the flesh two days later, May Day, to announce her acceptance of my invitation.

I'd had a feeling she would do just that, and so the servants had busily prepared rooms for more guests when the sounds of riders approaching reached me from the rear gardens.

I was wholly unprepared for what greeted me, however. My limbs went cold, and words stopped on my tongue. Brushing my hands down the length of my skirt, I tried to recover myself.

"I must thank you heartily, my lady, for an invitation to visit Wulfhall. I do believe this may be the first time I have ever set foot inside." Henry Howard, Earl of Surrey, bowed low before me.

Instead of curtsying in return, I pressed my lips together to stop a scream and nodded my head.

I turned a glare on my mother that should have melted her to the floor. The woman had the audacity to meet my gaze, although she did step closer to her husband.

"My lady, we thank you for inviting those in residence of Surrey to join you. We hear the queen is visiting?" my stepfather said.

"Indeed, this is her childhood home, and she visits as often as suits her," I said coldly and narrowed my eyes. "Pardon me, Lord Surrey, but I did not issue an invitation to all those who live in Surrey, only those residing in my mother's home. I have not a room prepared for you."

Whatever tricks my mother and Page were up to, they would not win. I simply would not have it, and if Edward were to catch wind of this… Oh, dear Lord, I would not want to see his reaction.

My mother gasped, her hand coming to her mouth. "Daughter, I am confident that in your letter you extended your invitation to his lordship. For certes, the queen would not express pleasure in his departure. Presumably, you've another room the servants can prepare? It would be utterly dreadful for our benefactor to not be able to join us."

Her words shocked me. Why was she doing this to me? Was it to get back at me for not becoming a patron to my half-sister, Lizzie? The little imp took that moment to peer out from behind my mother. Her eyes were wide and filled with confusion and sadness. At once, I knew she was nothing more than a pawn as I had been. I gave her a weak smile and vowed to be nicer to her. Perhaps I could find a way to have her back at court.

"Benefactor?" I queried, tilting my head in question.

"Indeed," Sir Page piped in. "His lordship is renovating our manor home with his own funds and allowing us to stay at his home while the rebuilding takes place."

I swallowed past the ever-increasing lump in my throat. How deeply my mother and Page had entrenched themselves with my own enemy. Living under the same roof, the man paying for their renovations. What had happened to cause such an event?

Again, I looked at Lizzie. There were deep circles underneath her eyes. Her gaze was haunting. At once, I had an idea of what had happened. Anger sliced me anew. Had he compromised my sister?

Before I could lurch at him and gouge his eyes out, Queen Jane glided into the great hall.

"My Lord Surrey, Sir Richard and Lady Page, a pleasure." She leaned to the side and grasped Lizzie's hands. "Miss Elizabeth, I have not seen you in so long. I should like you to visit me. Perhaps we can find a place for you in court."

I turned my gaze on the queen, eyes wide at her words, her invitation. How long had Jane been standing there? How much did Jane know about my past with Surrey? Had she guessed, as I had, that he was abusing my sister?

"Majesty." The trio of people I despised at the moment spoke in unison, dipping low to their queen.

Elizabeth Seymour and Lady Mary approached the crowd with greetings as well. Beth met my gaze with empathy, her lips pressed together. Was everyone at court aware of my past, or had Edward shared it in secret with his sisters? Whatever the case, I was glad to have them with me to strengthen my resolve.

"We are pleased to have new faces here. How long will you be staying?" Jane asked.

My mother opened her mouth to answer, but Page spoke instead, a twitch of his wrist in my mother's direction. "Only a few days. It just so happens we had some time between dealings in Surrey and sought a respite."

"I shall speak with the housekeeper regarding rooms. Lizzie," I said turning toward my half-sister, "you shall share my room."

My mother flinched but quickly recovered herself. Surrey scowled at me and then at my stepfather, who'd turned away to demand ale from a passing servant.

Perhaps Jenny could dig some special herbs out of the cellar to make a sleeping draught, and then our *special* guests could retire early and stay in their rooms for longer.

I dearly regretted listening to Edward about drawing my mother closer, and I was confident if he had known what had happened at his suggestion, he too would have agreed.

On the other hand… Now I knew I must protect young Lizzie, else she become lost in the flurry.

I was a coward.

I'd proved my cowardice tonight as well. I'd curled into a ball inside the window seat of my bedroom and stared out at the moon and a few stars in the sky. Some clouds passed overhead, creating shadows on the darkened lawn below.

I'd nibbled on a bit of chicken that Cook had brought to my rooms. After the unexpected arrival of our guests that afternoon, I had done my duties and prepared a room for Surrey, but then had taken to my room for the remainder of the evening. I had not gone down to dine the evening meal with everyone, although I should have, seeing as how Wulfhall was Edward's home, and I mistress here, but the queen could have played hostess, and if she had not felt well enough to endeavor to the task, Elizabeth Seymour, who'd also grown up at Wulfhall, could have.

I just could not have stomached Surrey. In fact, I was certain that if I had sat to dine with him I would have ended up stabbing him with my dinner knife, or spearing my fork into his eyeballs. While he warranted such a reaction for the things he was guilty of, I could not have created more scandal.

Jenny was to collect my young sister after the meal finished and deposit her in my room. I listened to the sound of the ticking clock, having struck nine times several minutes earlier. The meal and evening entertainments should have been wrapping up, and a girl of her tender age would indeed have been heading to bed any minute.

The servant I sent out to find Edward at one of our surrounding holdings had yet to return. I did not place much hope in that direction in any case. By the time Edward returned to Wulfhall, our guests would most likely have left already.

The lifting of the latch on my door startled me from my reverie and I stood, eyes wide, waiting for Jenny and Lizzie to enter.

"Surrey!" I gasped. He closed the door behind him, leaned on it, with arms crossed.

"My lady." His voice was calm, a smirk on his lips.

"Get out!" I shouted, not caring who heard. "This is most inappropriate. How dare you enter my private chambers."

He shrugged. "You were not at dinner, Lady Beauchamp. And I needed a word with you."

"You will have to wait until morning. Out!" I pointed at the door, my breathing becoming erratic. Panic set in.

He had only come with my mother and Page to Wulfhall to torment me. I could see it in his eyes. He was a sadistic bastard!

"Tsk, tsk. You are not such a gracious hostess."

"You were *not* invited." My fists clenched tight, nails digging into the skin of my palms.

"No matter, I will leave before the sun has risen. I only wanted to deliver a message."

"Be done with it then," I demanded.

He chuckled. "So much fire you have now. If only you'd been so spirited when I had my cock between your thighs."

My face screwed up in disgust, and I wanted desperately to spit in his face. But, instead, I held my head high, steady and gritted my teeth. "You disgust me, Surrey. I care not for whatever message you've to relay. Get out before I call my guards."

Surrey lurched forward and took my chin between his fingers, his nails biting into my flesh. I flailed in his grip, my feet kicking, arms hitting, but he pinned me against the wall, his other arm

240

wrapping around me enough to keep me still. He came within an inch of my face, then pressed his foul lips to mine, even as I struggled.

He spoke harshly against my lips. "Tom and I have become companions, my lady. Close confidantes, if you will. You might keep that in mind."

I knew he lied. The only thing Tom Seymour hated more than being a second son—and myself—was anyone named Howard. But still, he had a loose tongue and who knew what the devil he'd said while under the influence of too much ale. "Go to hell," I bit out. And I truly wished Surrey to go there, the sooner the better.

He laughed aloud and pushed away from me, ducking out of the way as I reached out to slap him.

I had never wanted to kill a man more.

Surrey held true to his promise, and when I awoke the next morning, he was already gone. But the damage had been done. He'd sought to instill fear in me, and while I was intelligent enough to surmise that his threats about Tom and him forming a faction of their own were erroneous, his words still held merit on another account. I shifted my jaw, feeling the bruises from his rough-handedness.

Tom was still a volatile man. Tom still spoke too much when he was inebriated and filled with rancor.

I glided into the great hall to find I was the last one to arrive— bruises covered by a powder Jennie made for me. All stood about the table, waiting for me to arrive so we might go to chapel for morning prayer.

Upon returning to the great hall to break our fast, I was greeted by a sight that both vexed me and filled me with irksome happiness. *Anthony.*

"Sir Anthony, what a pleasant surprise. We did not expect to see you here."

He bowed to us. "Nor I, my lady. But as it happens, I have come with a message for Her Majesty."

Jane stepped forward and took the scroll Anthony held out for her.

"I hope your journey abroad was successful." I openly studied him.

Anthony met my gaze. "My journey was somewhat fruitful. I ran into His Majesty in Calais, on my way...well, doing some business, and he asked me to deliver his letter to his queen."

I narrowed my eyes at his words, itching to know what he was about. But he'd been abroad on business for the crown, searching out the rat Pole, and his doings were of a secretive nature.

Jane gasped, her hand coming to her mouth, and her face lit up while she read. She gently rolled the parchment back, fidgeting with the wax seal. "His Majesty suspects he shall be arriving at Wulfhall in a fortnight. I have missed him so."

"Wonderful news," I murmured, and squeezed her outstretched hand.

"Thank you, Sir Anthony, for bringing such good tidings. We should like to have the pleasure of your company. Will you be staying at Wulfhall or returning to London?" Jane said.

"Majesty, you are too kind. I should like to stay." He turned toward me with a raised brow, his eyes pleading.

Did he seek my forgiveness? Was I ready to give it? Better yet, was he forgiving me?

I detested that with Anthony my emotions were so uncontrollable. Vulnerability was not a feeling I enjoyed having. But I prided myself on my ability to maintain control. And it slipped away every time he was near.

I noticed out of the corner of my eye my mother and Sir Page examining the interaction between myself and Anthony. I could almost feel them calculating their assumptions in their minds. That would not do. As much as I longed to tell him he was forgiven, that I wished to pick up where we had left off, slap him for hurting me, and kiss him all over, I could not. I did the only thing I knew how to do. I lifted my chin, pursed my lips and gave him the courtly Anne that everyone knew and respected.

"I shall have our housekeeper air a room for you." With that much said, I slipped past Anthony, the queen on my arm, and headed for the dais to break our fast.

If disappointment or hurt crossed his features, he did not let on.

After the meal was cleared, Lizzie volunteered to play on her lute, and Beth accompanied her in song. Mary and Jane set about sewing, and my mother joined them. Page and Anthony sat a bit apart to talk about politics.

I attempted to sew but could not concentrate and kept sticking myself with the needle. The fabric was getting more blood on it than stitches. I gazed around at the group, in thought. In another world, this could have been quite a domestic scene. Anthony could have been my husband, having a gentlemanly chat with my stepfather. But instead, he was a man I loved yet despised, who was not my husband, having a chat with the man married to my mother, who I abhorred.

When Beth caught my gaze, her intelligent eyes tried to read into my thoughts. I cast her a genteel smile and returned to my stitches. I could not risk anyone else reading the thoughts doubtlessly written all over my face.

The afternoon passed by quickly, with the men going out to ride and the ladies entertaining the queen with baby talk. I went about my duties as mistress to Wulfhall, and soon it was time for us to have the evening meal.

We all sat about, food was served, wine and ale poured. But I hardly noticed the fare. My eyes landed on Anthony only to see that he'd already been looking my way.

"My humble thanks, my lady, for allowing me to sup with you and your guests."

"Nonsense, Sir Anthony, you *are* one of Anne's guests," my mother interjected.

I glared in her direction for answering for me, and for using my Christian name.

"You are welcome here, Sir Anthony," I added. "How long do you plan to stay?"

If my question came across as rude or out of place, no one seemed to notice, although, to me, with the relationship I had with the man, it had seemed sharp.

He smirked but quickly covered it up, as if feeling the same things I did and trying not to laugh at our situation. "I shall have to leave before dawn, my lady."

"Oh, for shame, sir! Why should you leave so early?" my mother said.

Anthony did not take his eyes off of me when he answered her. "I do not want to overstay my welcome. 'Tis also a fact I am expected elsewhere."

I nodded and took a bite of meat, chewing methodically before swallowing, feeling it land like a lump in my belly. "A pleasant interlude to have you with us, even if for a short time." My voice came out monotone, and I stared at a crack beginning in the plaster of one of the walls. Best have it repaired before it grew any larger.

Again, I caught Beth studying me with a critical eye. Damned if I did and damned if I did not. I could not seem to act normally around Anthony. I tried hard to ignore him and play at being cold, but it only came off as being awkward and strange. Yet, the only other way I could have acted around him would be as if I were melting through the floor, and that simply would have been preposterous.

As soon as the meal was over, Jane bid everyone adieu so she could rest, and I, too, stood to excuse myself. "Sir Anthony, your room is prepared. When you are ready to retire, one of the servants can escort you there."

He bowed to me, as did the others.

"Come, Lizzie," I called to my sister.

I awoke in the night, startled from sleep.
The bed shook slightly, and then a soft moan.
*Lizzie.*

I leaned over toward her, thinking she might be crying. Her cheeks were wet with tears, but she was still asleep. I shook her gently.

"Wake," I whispered.

She jolted awake, her mouth open in a silent scream.

I rubbed her arms and shushed her. "Calm down. 'Twas only a dream."

Slowly, she settled down beside me. I tucked her blankets more tightly against her.

"Anne?" she said so softly I nearly had not heard her.

"Mmm-hmm?"

"Can I tell you something? Will you swear to keep it secret?"

Instantly, I was on alert. "Of course. You can keep me in your confidence."

"You do not esteem Lord Surrey."

How to respond? "He is not my most favorite person, no."

"I share your sentiments."

If I was going to get further with this, and to the bottom of whatever horrors he had enacted on her, now was the time.

"I do believe we are not alone in that. Nearly half of court despises the man. Why is it you've come to such regard of him?"

Lizzie sighed deeply and was silent for nearly a dozen heartbeats. "He has ill-used me, sister."

Just as I had suspected. "Are you hurt?"

I felt her shake her head no. "Only in my mind, and virtue, but otherwise, I fare well."

To me, those were the worst places to be hurt. Bruises and cuts healed, but to have lost your virtue and your mind—those were things you could never get back.

I reached out to her and pulled her in for a hug. "Me, too," I whispered.

Lizzie began to sob, shaking against me, her head tucked against my shoulder, her tears wetting my night rail. I let her cry as long as she needed, until she began to hiccup, and then that, too, subsided.

"What shall I do, Anne?"

Agony dripped from her every word. "Does mother or Sir Richard know of Surrey's treachery?"

"Yes. Surrey told me there was nothing they could do about it."

Rage, pure and sharp, ripped through my rib cage. I wanted to jump from the bed, fling open the door, tear down the door to Mother and Page's bedchamber and beat them both bloody with a chamber pot.

"Hush now, do not worry for it. I shall see that you remain with me, and he can hurt you no longer."

Lizzie soon fell back asleep, but I could not. I rose before dawn so that I could meet Anthony before he left. However, vicious he'd been, I'd been just as cruel.

He had not expected to see me as he came down the main stair to exit Wulfhall. He jumped a little at the sight of me, white in a night rail and robe.

I grasped his arm and pulled him into the shadows.

"Anne, what are you doing up?" he whispered. I wished I could see his eyes, but they were covered in shadows.

"To where do you go?" I asked.

"London. I've a need to make some reports."

I nodded, even if he could not see my gesture. "I've a need for something to be done, Anthony."

There must have been something in my voice, in my words. He reached out, and the warmth of his fingers on my arms as he rubbed up and down soothed me.

"You know you need only ask, and I will do anything in my power to please you," he whispered, as if our past spites had never happened.

I looked around, making certain no one was in sight.

"Yes, I know this." I choked on a sob and then was immediately sickened with myself.

Anthony pulled me close, the flesh of my cheek pressed to his, where I could hear his heartbeat.

"Anne, do you know how much it hurts to see you in agony? As much as I want to despise you, I cannot." He pushed me back, his face coming close to mine. "You hold a piece of me here." He pressed his fist to his breast. "Even when you push me away, stomp

246

on me, I come back to you, ever more enthralled with you, filled with love for you."

I shook my head. "No, Anthony, no! Do not say such things! They are forbidden." But my voice did not hold much authority. I gritted my teeth.

"I know, you cannot abide by my words. Pains me to no end!" He looked away and was silent once more.

Silence passed between us for minutes, and I waited while he got a hold on his emotions. Finally, he turned back to me. "How can I help you, Anne?"

I pulled him close and whispered in his ear.

When he pulled back, even in the shadows I could see his face was dark with anger at what I had revealed.

"I will serve you with pleasure, my lady."

"I will owe you a great deal."

"I've only ever asked you for one thing."

"You've asked me for more than one thing." My heart skipped a beat.

"No, never. You, Anne. You are what I want."

Before I could protest, he pressed his lips to mind. Hard, demanding. He took his kiss from me. Did not wait for me to argue or give in. He crushed his mouth to mine. Arms wound around my waist, he hauled me against him. My legs shook, and I pressed my hands to his chest, feigning to fight him off. But we both knew it was useless. I wanted his lips on mine just as much as he did. How much his kiss differed from Surrey's... from Edward's. Raw passion and emotion.

The scraping of a door from above pulled us apart. Within moments, he was gone, out into the spring dawn and riding hell-bent to London.

With bruised lips, racing thoughts and heart, I glided back to my chambers, knowing all the while that once again, I would have to push Anthony away and crush the love he offered beneath the heel of my slipper.

But what was a broken heart? Had not I lived with the pain of a broken heart and spirit for days? And what of Lizzie? For saint's sake, nearly everyone I knew had a broken heart of some form.

Thinking on this renewed my resolve. I had a husband. A husband who I loved — yet, not in the way I loved Sir Anthony Browne. Was it possible to be in love with two men at once?

I curled my lip in disgust.

A woman of my status did not worry overmuch on such things. I pinched my arm for good measure and walked into my chambers, prepared to begin my day.

What I was not prepared for, was seeing my husband standing in the room and the bed where Lizzie had slept with me empty.

# CHAPTER SIXTEEN

*Other there be whose lives do linger still in pain,*
*Against their will preserved are, that would have died fain (happy).*
*~Henry Howard, Earl of Surrey*

"Edward!"

He narrowed his eyes, sweeping up and down my countenance, no doubt taking in my red-kissed lips and disheveled appearance.

"Where have you been?" he demanded.

I had the good merit to blush at his words and look away. "In the privy... Something did not agree with me last evening." I gestured to the bed. "Where is Lizzie?"

"I had her taken to the nursery, so that I might share the bed with my wife." He continued to gaze at me, his thoughts hidden.

I fidgeted where I stood until I could take it no longer and then went to pour myself some watered wine.

"When did you arrive?"

"I have only just come. I rode through the night as soon as I heard Surrey was here."

"He's gone now."

"I see that. Sir Anthony was here?"

"Yes, he arrived with a message for Jane yestermorning. He plans on leaving this morning, I do believe."

"He's gone now as well."

I nodded nonchalantly and then went to the bed. I pulled back the covers and sank beneath their thickness, glad that some of the warmth was still retained in them. I had grown cold when I saw Edward standing in the middle of the room.

"Come to bed then, you must be exhausted from your journey."

"Yes," was all he said.

I closed my eyes and let sleep take me, for I was too afeared that Edward would have more questions about where I had been, what I had been doing.

*May 12, 1537*

Spring had most certainly arrived. Little buds of flowers broke open in the morning, petals of all colors preening in the sunlight. The air was light and sweet, breezes carrying the scent of new life. The grass even looked softer.

"The king is expected to arrive here this very afternoon," Edward said.

All that had happened when he was away, we'd never discussed. I was not clear on why I kept Lizzie's secret from Edward, only aware that if I'd told him, he would have called Surrey out, and we could not have another scandal as we had with Tom.

"These past several weeks have really flown by," I murmured, startled that in the next few days I would have to prepare to leave Wulfhall, leave Eddie. My gaze went from the gilded looking glass toward the little cradle that sat in my room. I had taken to letting the boy doze in my chambers whenever I could, not wanting to miss a moment of time with him. He was such a good baby, already sleeping through the night, and his wet nurse told me he was a hearty eater.

My mother and Page had left the day after Edward arrived, and I had my suspicions he had forced them out, although with a gentle hand. They had not fussed about Lizzie's staying. Part of me wondered if they'd allowed Surrey to debauch her in order to get me to agree to take her — just like I'd threatened... Was it my fault?

"They have, indeed. But I must confess I am itching to return to court. Are you not?" Edward said.

"I do miss it, but I have found such peace here, and there is Eddie."

"Oh, posh, Anne. The boy has got to learn at some point not to hide behind his mother's skirts. We would not want our son to be the whelp other boys pick on, would we?"

"No, certainly not. You are correct." But inside I laughed, for he was only an infant and certainly not a boy hiding behind his mother's skirts.

Edward smiled and nodded, his face smug with satisfaction that he must know best for his own son.

"Is everything prepared for the king's visit? Have we enough variety to prepare a feast fit for His Majesty?"

"I shall speak to Cook directly."

"Excellent. I received a missive this morning that they landed at Dover yesterday and they rode halfway here before taking shelter for the night. Knowing His Majesty, he rose before the dawn and set out. In fact, he could arrive any minute, really."

"Shoo then." I waved my hands at Edward. "I cannot complete my ablutions with you standing there, and I cannot go about my duties if I have not completed my ablutions."

"Yes, of course, my dear." Edward bowed and then exited the room.

As soon as he was gone, I hurried to complete my toilette, gave directions to Cook and then went in search of Jane, Beth and Mary. The latter two were still lounging in their beds, but Jane was in my solar, embroidering and humming.

"Lo, there you are," I said gaily. "The king should be here very soon." No sooner were the words out of my mouth than a loud commotion of shouts, horns and horses' hoof beats came pounding through the open air of the window.

We stood, rushed to the window and flung it open. The courtyard below held a line of trumpeters facing the front of Wulfhall, behind them guards on foot and more guards on horseback, the ones on the ends holding King Henry's flags. Behind them sat the king by himself, and behind him again were the nobles who served him.

He raised his hand in the air when he spotted Jane in the window. "Jane!"

"Henry, you've returned!" Jane turned from the window and rushed from the room.

How sweet it was that they still burned with a fever for each other.

I followed slowly behind but still within enough time to see Henry dismount, shove aside some of his men and embrace his queen.

"Lady Anne, it appears you do keep your promises. Jane looks ravishing!" He bent down and kissed her again. "Beauchamp."

Edward bowed to his sovereign. "Welcome to our home, Majesty. It is with great pleasure that we welcome you."

"Wulfhall holds many kind memories for me, Beauchamp. For it was one of the first places I became acquainted with Jane."

Edward nodded, as did the rest of the party.

"We are hungry. Shall we dine?" the king asked.

"As it pleases you, Majesty," I said and, with my arm, indicated for him to enter the house first, the rest of us to follow.

By the time the king had entered our great hall, the servants had done a great job of transforming the normally plain room into a grand place for royalty. The way they'd situated the trestle table accentuated the most-prized possession of Wulfhall—the stained glass window of a glorious battle scene.

The prism lights hit the ivory tablecloth just so, making it look like a rainbow. Musicians had been scrounged up from the local village and now played contemporary tunes in the loft above.

Servants stood at the ready with casks of wine and ale. The table was set with goblets, bowls of almonds, fruit, the first sugared flowers of the season and deviled quail eggs—the latter, Queen Jane's favorite.

In addition to the great hall being transformed, Beth, Lizzie and Lady Mary had risen and now waited by the hearth as the king entered. Both rushed to curtsy.

"Mary, my daughter. I trust you are well." The king approached her and took her face in his hands, kissing her gently atop her head.

"Yes, Majesty."

"Father, Mary," he whispered.

"Yes, Father."

"Lady Elizabeth, Mistress Lizzie, a pleasure as always," the king said.

They took turns kissing his offered ring.

The king broke out into a pleased smile and offered Mary his left arm—Jane still occupying his right.

"Come, let us sit together."

The seats of the trestle table upon the dais were soon filled, as were the other two tables that sat perpendicular to us.

"Majesty, I trust your trip abroad was met with great success," Edward said, leaning forward to catch the eye of his master, who sat between Jane and Mary.

"'Twas, Beauchamp. However, let us not discuss it just now. I prefer to have speech that is more jovial, having just returned from a month of political discussion, and I find myself surrounded by beautiful women." Henry shook his head. "So eager you are to please, Edward. Is it not enough that I have come to visit your home? That I have left my queen in your care? There will be plenty of time later to talk of news."

Edward nodded, sufficiently cowed. I hated to see him that way, defeated-looking. And it was not as if his question had been offensive. He'd simply inquired after his master's trip. It had been a question that would have been expected. Just another show of His Majesty's volatile mood swings. "As it pleases you, Majesty," he murmured.

After several goblets of wine and ale had been consumed by all, and mere crumbs remained in the bowls that once held magnificent treats, the servants brought forth roasted meats, poached fish, stewed vegetables, meat pasties and loaves of bread.

I caught the eye of my young sister, Lizzie, who had been staring intently at the king. She snickered and returned to her food. What impudence! She was lucky not to have been caught by His Majesty himself. I turned to see what she'd been so intently watching, only to wish I had not. The king shoveled great gobs of food into his mouth by the handful. Grease dribbled down his chin and onto the front of his doublet. He slurped at his goblet to help rinse the unchewed food down his throat in order so he might shove more food into the never-ending cavern.

My stomach recoiled, and I instead turned my attention to a troupe of players who'd gathered near the front door.

"Majesty, we have prepared a show for your return." I stood and walked toward the players, waving them forward.

The troupe conversed with the musicians, who began to play lively tunes. Henceforth, a satirical play about the Pilgrimage of Grace and the main character of Aske, renamed Ass, took place, leaving the entire great hall in an uproar of laughter.

*"What say you, Mr. Ass,*
*Shall we let you take a pass?*
*For if we do, then surely it poses,*
*A great risk for all men with large noses."*

With that last line, several players came out with abnormally large noses attached to their faces—for it was said Mr. Aske's nose was often so buried up others' behinds as he sought to please them—and began poking the rears of each other, as if to stuff their nasal appendages up the others' behinds.

*"Fellow lovers of the pope,*
*Have you not learned when not to grope?*
*I say, I am not ready now,*
*Come back and receive me on the morrow."*

The play was bawdy, intimating that all the men of the Roman church and followers of the pope practiced buggery. In the end, a player dressed as the king came in to absolve their souls before sending them to their maker.

All in all, the evening went well, and despite the king's miserable mood upon sitting down to the noon meal, by the entertainment's end, he was laughing and merry once more. In fact, he even bestowed kindness upon Edward, tossing him a bag of gold coins and a gift of two new gorgeous and sleek white horses for ensuring the care of his wife was done so properly.

The next morning, King Henry, Queen Jane and Lady Mary set off for Whitehall, as did Edward. Elizabeth Seymour, my sister and I remained behind to see that the house was properly packed of our belongings and instructions left for the nurses who would care for my dear little Eddie while I returned to court.

*May 27, 1537*

The choirboys' voices singing the *Te Deum* rang out loud and like angels on high for the queen. Vast amounts of guests joined the king and queen at Mass today, Trinity Sunday, at St. Paul's Cathedral. A person would have thought they were attending a coronation for all the pomp and squalor that went into today's events. Courtiers, myself included, were dressed in their very best gowns, bejeweled from wrist to neck in the most glorious of gems. And most, if not all of us, offered gifts of money and support to the church — to God. For today was a very special day.

King Henry and Queen Jane had announced her condition to the council members the previous day, and news had spread like a wild forest fire throughout London and even to country manors just outside of the great city. Perhaps even now, those in Northumberland and Wales were hearing the news of Their Majesties' prayers being answered.

The long-awaited babe was due to arrive in less than five months. Lords and bishops crowded the pews, the mayor of London and aldermen of various guilds dressed to the nines in their liveries. All held their hands to the sky, singing and imploring the Lord to bring them a prince.

The pews were filled, stuffed, really, with people. My skirts and the skirts of all the women surrounding me crushed to our legs we stood so close together. Fans waved frantically to stanch the heat, and groomsmen and altar boys lined the sides of the rooms, waving palm fronds at us in an attempt to cool the stifling air.

I shifted my glance around the church, taking in all those in attendance.

Jane looked faint from the heat, and one of her ladies brought a mug to her lips for her to drink every few minutes.

But one person was notably missing—Surrey.

A smug smile curved my lips that I had to quickly swipe free.

All those in attendance praised and sang to the glories of God for the queen's quickening. And I, too, had to offer my prayers, even though I shifted restlessly with the need to find out why Surrey was not at Mass, and if it had anything to do with Anthony and the favor I had begged of him.

Voices rose high to butt against the sopranos of the choir and soon drowned out my thoughts. When the voices died down, Latimer, the Bishop of Worcester, stood and made an oration to the assembly. His whiny, nasally voice echoed in the grand vestibule.

"Praise be to God and to King Henry!"

"Amen," the crowd said in unison.

"The Lord has seen the king's reformation of the corrupt church, has approved of it, and gives good and gracious King Henry a blessing. A blessing in the form of a babe in our own good Queen Jane's belly!" Bishop Latimer called out.

The congregation crossed themselves with Latimer, and while he looked toward the cross of Jesus Christ that hung high behind him, we all bowed our heads and muttered prayers. *I pray to you, Jesu, bring us a prince!* Hundreds of prayers just like that, begging the Lord to give Queen Jane a boy. But as the people murmured and lamented to the good Lord, I looked around, spotting at least one person who prayed something different—Norfolk.

For certain, the man prayed Jane would not birth a boy, but another girl, and we Seymours would be seen in no better light than the Howards. Our queen, another girl-birthing witch, just as their queen had been. A shudder passed through me as Norfolk raised his black, beady eyes, catching my gaze. I could not look away, almost like those eyes held me captive, his vile mind whispering into the depths of my soul. Warning me. Telling me we would not succeed. Or had he rendered me speechless for another reason? Was it that Surrey, at this very moment, was being punished for his misdeeds?

I held his gaze, chin lifted, challenging him. Norfolk might have instilled fear in a lot of people, but he was not going to scare me. Anne Boleyn had stood up to her uncle in the end. If I was truly so like her, so strong-willed and outlandish as Tom claimed I was, then I would not be cowed by this fortune-hunting man.

Latimer's voice rang out again, ending the service, and Norfolk looked away. I took it as a triumph. I had won this round. Five months from now, Jane would need to win us the second.

We filed out, our hearts jumping with hope, and my stomach flipped into my throat. With the number of prayers having just gone up, the Lord had to have heard. A prince would be born!

We walked in a long line back to the castle. Jane was carried in a gilded litter, and the king rode his horse beside her. King Henry wanted to take no risk with Jane and her babe. Her belly had barely popped, but he treated her like the finest of bone china.

I breathed out with irritation, as everyone in front of me seemed content to move at a snail's pace. I wanted to shout for them all to move out of my way, so that I might seek out Anthony in secret to find out where Surrey was.

My sister Lizzie pinched my arm gently, reminding me of my mother. "Anne, what are those people doing?"

I glanced toward where she pointed at the folks of London who stood just outside the gates, arms outstretched. But before I could answer her, the king spoke.

"Light fires across England!" the king shouted. "Let there be a hogshead of wine at every fire. Let no man, woman or child go thirsty on this night, for soon I will be the father of a prince!"

A resounding cheer broke out, so loud the insides of my ears vibrated painfully. "Alms," I murmured to Lizzie.

When we finally made it back to the great hall, where a great feast had been planned for this morning, my nerves were on edge, and I seriously considered going out to the gardens for a bit of air. Lizzie hurried off with a few other maids of honor she'd become close with, and Edward veered toward the other council members.

Jane, occupied with the king, and myself caught in a rare moment of solitude, I sneaked out to the side gardens. The warmth of late spring sun on my face as I lifted it up to the sky was reassuring, pleasant.

I took a deep breath of fresh air, happy to be out of the stifling hall, even if only for a moment. I closed my eyes and sighed in contentment.

Darkness came, the bright light gone from behind my lids. "Anne."

I startled them open at the sound of Edward's voice.

"My lord," I mumbled, suddenly feeling awkward at having him catch me in such a moment.

"You look beautiful today, my lady wife." He smiled, his eyes twinkling. "I confess I watched you, half thinking you might twirl with arms outstretched, but alas, you disappointed me."

I laughed and reached out to pinch his arm. "Do not tease, husband, for the truth is, had you waited a few more moments, I might have done just that."

Edward sighed with exaggeration. "'Tis the truth I am not such a patient man."

"I thought I saw you go off with Suffolk. What brought you out here to me?"

"Is a man not allowed to spend a few moments alone with his wife?"

I narrowed my eyes. "We are alone most nights, my lord."

He smiled, a bit of sadness tingeing the brown depths of his eyes. "'Tis yet another truth you speak, but I find even with the time we have alone, that I miss you greatly."

His words shocked me. Edward was not one for flowery words or romance. We were generally quite reserved with each other unless our bodies were connecting in passion. "Miss me?"

"Aye. We are most of the time engaged in some such political ruse or another. The queen takes up much of your time as the king does mine."

"A part of court life, we both rightly know."

He nodded, that sad smile still filling his features. "Well, no matter, I did not follow you to talk of such things. I came truly to tell you that Surrey has been arrested again."

My heart skipped an excited beat in my chest, and it was all I could do to stop from smiling.

"Let us walk." He offered me his arm, and together we wove our way over the stone path, which sat between blooms of flower beds.

"What has he done this time?" I tried for my voice to be detached, but there was still a hitch at the end that belied my true feelings.

"He has been arrested on suspicion of treason. Talking too much in taverns again. He was overheard whispering how he would see himself and his children on the throne someday."

"He is an arrogant man."

"One who will soon be released. Already, evidence has arrived that Surrey was not even in London when he supposedly made the claims. I suspect that someone has made up the charges in hopes of punishing Surrey. In hopes that this time he will be put to death for certes and no longer a nuisance at court." Edward stopped and turned to me. We stood in the shadows of a few trees, the castle a distance behind us. "I will find him guilty for you, Anne."

My eyes widened, and I swallowed hard. Edward's face was etched with worry lines, and why hadn't I noticed before that a few gray hairs had found their way to sprinkle near his temple? He'd changed before my eyes, and I had barely noticed. Court was a constant strain, and it would begin to take its toll. But I hoped it would not tax Edward too harshly. With his words I realized one thing: His worry over me had brought such distress to him that he was literally willing to kill a man for it. And as the chief justice in this matter, he could do exactly as he said.

This could be the end of Surrey. The end of the pain he'd inflicted on me. "Yes, Edward, yes."

"Oh, Anne," he breathed and pulled me to him in an embrace.

We held tight to each other, my ear pressing to his heart and listening to its wild beating.

"I do not know what has come over me, only that I see the change in you when he is around. I know the things he is capable of, the things he's done. I would be doing the world a bit of good if he were to walk along the scaffold and kiss the ax."

"There will be questions behind your justice. Norfolk is a powerful man, Edward." I pulled away and met his gaze.

Edward nodded. "Likely the king will pardon him, but at least he will know where he stands with me."

"And a new enemy created."

"He was already an enemy, Anne, and we are never without them."

The moment was intense, where he delved into my soul through his gaze, and I was afraid he'd see that I was the one who had had Surrey arrested to begin with. Afraid he'd see my kiss with Anthony.

Instead, he brushed his lips lightly on mine. "I shall punish him for you, Anne. 'Tis the least I can do to ease your suffering."

I hugged him tight, grateful in that moment to have him fighting the demons that haunted me.

The following morning, I penned both a note of thanks and of goodbye to Anthony. He never replied.

# CHAPTER SEVENTEEN

*But now I do perceive that naught it moveth you,*
*My good intent, my gentle heart, nor yet my kind so true.*
*~Henry Howard, Earl of Surrey*

What followed were months of mostly quiet.

Norfolk had convinced the king to pardon his son, though he'd been encouraged to retain his residence in the north instead of at court. 'Twas bittersweet. I'd hoped that we might have seen the bastard axed, but victory was not yet mine.

While the king worked on keeping tabs on the north of England, his territories in France, Wales and Ireland, those of us at court kept vigil over the queen. There was more time spent on interfacing with the Lord our God over those months than I had spent my whole life. My knees had permanent calluses and bruises from the time spent praying on the cold, stone floor. Mass was increased to three times a day, and we all went, got down on our knees and prayed. In between Mass was more prayer, Bible reading, scripture copying into journals sent out into the public for daily prayers, embroidering psalms on shirts and blankets that were given to the poor.

King Henry's church earned more money from its lords and ladies in those five months than it had any other time of year. For we all hoped our gifts would bring forth a prince to the realm. Even had we not offered up our gifts to the Lord, the church's pockets grew thick with coin.

The Reformation was in full swing, the dissolution of monasteries old news, and each day a new one torn down, its money, relics and the like all going to King Henry.

Rumors came from Edward, who spent much of his time traveling with the king — atop one of his new white horses — that the king with all his new coin was itching for another war with France. He did not just want Calais and the surrounding little territories he'd procured. He wanted it all. He wanted to call himself King of England, Wales, Ireland and France, and mean *all* the land when he said it. What's more, he was starting to whisper of trying his hand for Scotland again.

Yet Edward had done well and convinced His Majesty now was not the time. In the gentle way that Edward had, his voice calm, face void of emotion, hands held lightly behind his back, where he could look as though he minded not what your decision was and he'd have been happy with either, he reminded the king of Queen Jane's condition. Would not the king want his wife to worry naught while she carried the future king in her belly? 'Twas said that when a woman who was with child suffered undue anxiety, the baby suffered, too, and sometimes this was why a babe might be born long since gone to its maker — a subtle hint to all the miscarriages Henry and his queens had suffered. A very tactful advance from Edward. I was quite impressed.

According to Edward's missive, the king had thrown an apple at my lord husband's head when he had said this, but also had canceled all of his plans to go to war, not another word spoken henceforth.

Reginald Pole was also keeping himself well hidden. I had received one short and bitterly sweet note from Anthony from abroad, as he'd been sent once again with Sir Francis and Sir Nicholas to rein in the would-be usurper. He had thanked me for the opportunity and dared me to deny I had anything to do with his being chosen to help Sir Nicholas and Sir Francis. I had not even bothered to tell him the truth as I had known he would not have seen it that way in either case. The three men were coming home soon, so that they'd be by His Majesty's side when Jane entered her confinement, but on the understanding that if more news of the traitor Pole arrived, they would leave immediately to see to his capture and subsequent execution.

Annie Bassett has been made most useful to me, and to Jane for that matter, during this time. While His Majesty was in residence, I'd sent her to his chambers, and she had pleased him well. But this time, things were different. I did not know if Mistress Annie had said something to King Henry, or if Jane had spoken, or if perhaps the king had come to some sort of realization himself, but he did not acknowledge Annie Bassett in public, despite the fact that she graced his bed nearly every evening. The king also did not openly seek any other woman's sheath to delve inside. Annie Bassett was all he needed. But one secret the little nymph had told me: He did not call her Annie, but 'Nan instead. He'd confessed he'd never be able to rut another woman and call out *that name* ever again, for fear it would send him straight into the bowels of hell.

My mother and Sir Richard had kept quiet and to themselves after I sent news to them of their overlord being arrested for suspicion of treason and added very cheekily how odd it was that he had been accused on a day that he had been at Wulfhall rather than in London. I had hoped they would understand my hint, and indeed they must have as they'd stayed away from court and had had very little, if any, correspondence with their daughter Lizzie, who had found time to thrive at court. She was quite a fast learner, and I was confident that in a few years I might even be able to establish a suitable marriage for her.

Elizabeth Seymour had approached me again about marriage, and I had promised that as soon as Jane birthed the babe, preparations would be made to procure the betrothal between her and Gregory Cromwell. Hints had already been made prior, and in fact the young man had begun flirting with Beth, even attempting to write her a poem or two.

Thomas Cromwell himself appeared to approve of the match, however much he might have despised aligning himself to our family permanently. With his decline in popularity and the increase in Edward's time spent with the king, he had realized it would be a bold and intelligent move.

Nurse Jacqueline brought my little Eddie to visit me this last month, along with a staff of two dozen of his household. He crawled around my solar and chambers with a vibrancy and exuberance known only to the innocent. He smiled up at me, a grin of two teeth and gums, his tufts of brown hair sticking out at all angles, just before he'd pull things from a shelf. He was a sweet boy, and both Edward and I were very proud.

Alas, Jane called to me. Her back pained her something fierce these days. Her small frame was not managing well with her giant baby belly and all the kneeling. It was time for me to give her spiced cider, press warm compresses to her back while some of the other ladies massaged her feet and legs. With luck, we'd be able to get her to sleep tonight for more than a few hours at a time.

The midwife had warned me, yet I told no one... The babe's head pressed against Jane's spine—breech. With the birth only a fortnight or less away, the child should have turned head down. Yet, this one was stubborn. I would pray extra tonight and offer another pound gold to the church if only God would see fit to make the baby turn.

*October 3, 1537*
*Hampton Court*

Servants ran thither and yon, like a bunch of chickens, heads already chopped off and tossed into the cesspit. We'd only just arrived at Hampton Court—true to His Majesty's word—and preparations were in full swing for Jane's arrival.

Sheets, blankets, linens, basins, oils, herbs, pitchers. They brought every item multiplied by four that the Queen of England might need for her lying in. The windows and mirrors were covered in black velvet as was custom. Candles were lit around the room. The fire blazed so hot the servants and ladies-in-waiting had beads of sweat above their lips and brows and dripping down their spines.

But the room must be perfect, and everything in accordance to His Majesty's wishes. The floors, walls, windows, doors, ceilings, fixtures, furniture had all been scrubbed and disinfected thoroughly. The room smelled clean, fresh. But with the windows covered, the heat of the room and number of bodies coming and going, the fresh clean smell would soon be replaced with a stink worse than that of the great hall on a summer day.

Queen Jane would arrive within the next several hours. Prepared to spend the next month or more in these chambers. She would attend her child's baptism — if the king so wished it — then remain in her rooms until she'd had her churching. I remembered undergoing my own churching, and I did not recall feeling specifically purified, but I did feel spiritually uplifted, freer.

Plans were set in place for the queen to be churched seven days after giving birth, and then she would remain in her rooms for another thirty-three days but would be allowed to receive visitors during that time. Because she was the Queen of England, it was impossible to keep her shut up with only her maids behind closed doors.

I had taken it upon myself to embroider a special churching veil for Jane. It was fringed white, damask, and in the corner I had embroidered her initials and a phoenix. The veil was delicate, feminine. After going through the ordeal of labor, a woman needed to feel feminine again. I had even ordered her some special lavender oils and soaps to smooth her skin and wash away the scents of labor.

I may have been a wolf, but I dearly loved Jane, and she was my lamb.

A tall courtier in the courtyard beyond the window caught the corner of my eyes and thoughts of Anthony flashed in my mind. On closer inspection I saw that it wasn't him, and disappointment sizzled through me. Loneliness filled most of my days, and I regretted having pushed him away just as much as I thanked God I'd had the strength to do it. Thoughts of his kiss that I'd never feel again. Would he be a gentle lover like Edward or full of uninhibited ardor? Anthony held such a passion that ignited and burned. Having such thoughts would only lead to pain, as consummating my relationship with Anthony would be ruination.

I wondered how other women could deal with such emotions. I'd often felt I was a strong woman, indeed had been told by many that I was. Why was it then, that I could be whisked away only to be dropped from the sky into an ocean of hurt?

But 'twas neither here nor there, as I did not plan on letting Anthony enter more fully into my life again. Only Edward and Eddie. All others would get the cold side of me, the political side. No more sharing, tender Anne.

But I had plenty now to keep me occupied.

I would spend the next several weeks with Jane, planning for the arrival of the next heir to the throne, keeping Lady Mary at court, and quelling Sir Anthony's small retaliations toward me since his return to court from abroad—which included taking up a bed with Jane Rochford. This last offense in itself was deplorable and dangerous. Gertrude herself had come to warn me, before I might see them dancing and making merry. Which I had on more occasions than one. Gertrude knew nothing of my past with Anthony, but worried over him sleeping with the enemy.

Jane Rochford had no qualms about tittering gossip, and I had to make use of my various spies to see that she repeated nothing. She was vicious, more so than myself, but the difference was I calculated my moves—an excellent chess player I was, too. Jane Rochford was spontaneous. Her plans often backfired, and when they did, there was no telling what she would concoct to support her story, who would be paid off to corroborate and what damage could be done. Take her poor late husband, George Boleyn... The man had never bedded his own sister...

So when the volatile Anthony and the sniveling Jane Rochford had become bedmates, naturally, I was very horrified.

But, alas, I'd been surprised. Anthony did not bleed a word to her. In fact, it appeared he genuinely enjoyed bedding the wench— which I found completely odd. His own wife, Alice, was quite a beauty, but rumor around court bleated of her prudishness and the tediousness of bedding her. Despite that, she and Anthony managed for her to become with child within the first month of marriage and now had a brood numbering close to a dozen.

Edward was busy running errands for the king and attending council meetings. He and Charles Brandon, the Duke of Suffolk, had become close comrades of sorts, and in so doing, I was spending more time with the Duchess of Suffolk, accompanying Gertrude on many occasions to the duchess' home to dine and while away the day.

Sweet, dear Catherine was a wonderful woman. So friendly and charming. Queen Jane, seeing how close Catherine and I had become, had invited her to court to serve as a lady-in-waiting, but Catherine had declined. For as sweet as she was, the woman had a rigid backbone and declined a life at court. She despised it. "The stench," she called it. But not necessarily an actual smell that bothered her nose. It was more the entire aspect of court. Sniveling, seekers of fortune, gossipmongers, adulterers, the lust and outright licentiousness disgusted her. In truth, when I looked on it with the air of an outside eye, I saw why she thought so. We lived deplorably. Mounds and mounds of delicious food and sugared treats was presented to us, half of it going to waste while those in the city starved, children lay dying of hunger. Indeed, the pox was probably just as prevalent within the castle as it was in the Stewes of London. Prostitutes by the thousand were ready and eager to do any man's bidding and pass along whatever disease and filth covered their woman's parts. 'Twas the influence of dear Lady Suffolk which made me aware, and dare I say it, made me care.

"My lady, all is set and ready."

I turned toward the voice of the servant who'd pulled me from my reverie, a short, squat maid who looked like she'd worked from the time her mother had pushed her out.

"We shall see," I answered.

I went round and inspected every surface, nook and cranny, for King Henry himself would do the same. Ran my fingers along the doorjambs, tops of furniture, to see if any dust came up. The floorboards shone with their newly buffed and waxed surfaces, but they weren't slippery at all. In fact, my slippers felt as though they could grip the surface better now that the floors had been restored.

"Anne." Edward came up beside me, but I did not look up as I examined each bottle of herbs set in an armoire in the queen's bedchamber. "I have a surprise for you."

It was then I caught the smell of that very unique and intoxicating scent—baby. I turned and almost dropped a bottle of chamomile.

"Eddie!" I hadn't seen my baby boy in nearly a month, and already he'd grown so much I barely recognized him.

Soft, light-brown curls fell around his forehead and ruddy cheeks, no longer sticking every which way. His bright blue eyes took me in, and plump red lips curved into a smile, showing six pearly-white teeth.

I grabbed him in my arms and hugged his chubby little body tight. He babbled in my ear and gripped the sapphire and pearl necklace at my throat. He was adorable, and I had not realized until then how much I'd missed him.

I carried him on my hip as I finished checking the rest of the queen's rooms and let him play with my gable hood, yanking at it every so often.

When my inspection was over, I took Eddie with me to my chambers, where his nurses waited. They told me all about his latest moves, that he'd perfected some odd crawl, like a "knight with a bum leg," they called it. I laughed as he demonstrated his skills.

The nurses informed me they'd decided to have the entire manor of Wulfhall cleaned from top to bottom and so had brought Eddie on Edward's order to see me as a surprise. He would not stay long, which saddened me, but then again, I had plenty of work to do anyway.

"Come here, little bird," I crooned, and his squeal and giggles echoed off the stone walls as he half crawled, half dragged his chubby little body toward me.

God, let Jane give birth to such a precious babe. Our futures rode on the queen's ability to push a squalling prince into the world.

*October 10, 1537*

The clock chimed eleven times before it stopped. I lay in bed, unable to close my eyes. Jane had not been feeling entirely well today. She'd eaten little, drunk little, and had barely had the energy to work on the tapestry that would adorn her baby's nursery walls.

I could not help but be worried. Was this a sign she would go into labor soon? Was all well with the child? She had reported that the baby was kicking with full force, which was sweet news to our ears, yet she was not well.

The midwife had been called for. She'd asked Jane several questions and, seeming satisfied, had reported that the queen needed rest, the babe was fine.

My chambers at Hampton Court now were adjacent to the queen's with a connecting door. If anything should go amiss, the servants would come rushing in as I instructed. But, still, I could not sleep, and my nerves were rubbed completely raw. I stood from my bed, slid into my robe and slippers and entered Jane's apartments. A fire was lit to blazing in the hearth. Servants slept around the warmth of its flames, softly snoring.

I tiptoed around them, nodded to two of the guards who were on watch, and then knocked softly on Jane's chamber door.

From inside I could hear what sounded like whimpering and heavy breathing.

"Majesty? It is Anne." I knocked again with the knuckles of my forefinger and middle finger.

"Come," came her weak call through the door.

I entered the room. The fire had died down, and a chill wrapped around my legs. A dim candle was lit on the table beside her, and behind the filmy curtains of her massive oak bed, Jane's frail body was curled into a ball, shaking.

"Oh, Jesu!" I ran forward, knelt on the floor and placed my hand on her forehead. She was sweating but cool. No fever. "Is the baby coming?"

"I do not know! I am fine one minute, and then the next I have much pain in my back," she sobbed.

I rubbed small circles into the small of her back. "Any pain in your belly?"

"No, none."

"Your skin is cool. Can I light the fire?"

"Yes, thank you, Anne. A servant knocked earlier, but I bade them go away."

I nodded and stood to restock the hearth and get the flames burning once again.

"I am so thirsty." Jane's teeth chattered as she spoke, but I suspected it was more from fear than chill.

I handed her a cup of wine, hoping the alcohol would dull her pain somewhat, and her nerves.

"Am I going to die?" Jane's voice was so small and frail.

"No, Majesty." I had to give her hope. Already, she looked ready to bolt from the room, find the nearest window and jump to her death.

"But women die in child birth all the time."

This time a chill of fear shook me. She spoke the truth, and she was so frail already… I shook the thoughts from my mind, refusing to let fear take root.

"The king will see to it you have the best care, Jane. Do not worry about that. You will bring a beautiful baby into the world very soon."

Jane's face paled even further, if that was possible. "What if it is a girl? He will put me aside or have me beheaded." Her tone was shrill. Her hands came up to grip her neck. Small, bony fingers wrapped around her throat.

I pulled her hands away from her neck and held them tight. I looked her straight in the eyes when I spoke. "Jane, do not say such things. I have been at court for a long time, as have you. Never has he loved a woman as much as he loves you. His Majesty would never set you aside or have you sent to your death. If you bear a sweet daughter, then, by the grace of God, you show you can produce children. Sons will follow."

Jane nodded a little too emphatically. I pushed the cup of wine back into her hands, and she gulped heavily.

I sat with her a few more moments. We prayed. I read her a passage in Joshua from the Bible to calm her. "*Have not I commanded thee? Be strong and of a good courage; be not afraid, neither be thou dismayed: for the Lord thy God is with thee whithersoever thou goest.*" By the time I was finished, her eyes had closed in peaceful rest.

I let her sleep and went out to her presence chamber. The midwives assigned to Jane were amongst the servants sleeping. I woke one and told her of Jane's pains. She assured me this was normal with some women and that most likely she would go into labor on the morrow.

With that knowledge, I crept back to my room to try to get some rest. Lord knew, I would need all my wits about me for the coming birth of the king and queen's child.

# CHAPTER EIGHTEEN

*But that your will is such to lure me to the trade,*
*As other some full many years trace by the craft ye made.*
*~Henry Howard, Earl of Surrey*

*October 11, 1537*

Throughout the day, Jane paced about her rooms, hands on the small of her back, as ladies gathered about, fanning her, offering bites to eat, small sips of wine, ale, mead, cider—anything Jane requested. The king came, hugged, kissed her, prayed for safe delivery of their child, and then just as quickly left. His eyes showed as much fear as Jane's, and I suspected he needed to be away from the medical setting—and his wife, who was in obvious pain.

The midwives surmised Jane was, in fact, in real labor, as opposed to pre-labor, which was also confirmed by the king's physician. The baby had turned—thank God!—and was starting to descend somewhat, but little else had happened. The birth canal was still not opening.

"My lady." One of the midwives bowed in front of me.

"What is it? Is everything well with Her Majesty? Is it time?" I was busy instructing the servants on preparations for the impending labor.

"No, my lady. I thought I might inquire of you for some help with this situation."

I pursed my lips. "Yes?"

"I have a hunch that Her Majesty may be impeding the progress of the birthing."

"What do you mean by that?" I started to grow annoyed. I waved the servants away and with another wave bade the midwife come closer so our conversation would not be overheard.

"She is working herself up into a frenzy. Her nerves are frazzled. She is full of fear. When a woman experiences those feelings, she cannot concentrate on the birth and let her body do its duty naturally."

I nodded in agreement. Jane looked more nervous as the minutes passed, and I felt an almost compulsive instinct to ply her with loads of wine and make her drunker than a lord on the day he lost his virginity.

"What do you suggest?"

"Would you speak with her? Perhaps tell her to climb into bed? I think rest is what she needs now or she won't have the energy to endure the pain and rigors of labor."

I nodded and ordered her to give instructions for completing the tasks I had been working on.

Jane stood by her window, rocking from side to side, her hands massaging the small of her back.

"Majesty," I murmured. But for all her reaction I could have shouted. She jumped, her hand coming to her heart, the other hand steadying her balance against the wall.

"Anne, you scared me."

I curtsied deeply, trying to instill some calm into the queen by remaining quiet and respectful. "My apologies, I did not mean to startle you so."

Jane walked toward me or, rather, wobbled. "What says the midwife?"

How had she known the woman had come to talk to me? I smiled at her, a teasing tilt to the corner of my lip, and was surprised and pleased when Jane returned it.

"Come to bed, Jane. Let me put some hot compresses on your back and have the ladies rub your feet. You will feel much better."

"I just do not want to, Anne. 'Tis nothing against the midwife or you. But lying in bed only makes me worry more. At least when I am pacing, I concentrate more on keeping my balance than what is to come."

I understood where Jane was coming from, but I also believed the midwife was correct. Though the pacing was keeping her from worrying, it was putting too much strain on her.

"Ah, look here, your sister has brought you some soup," I said.

Jane licked her lips as Beth came into the room with a steaming bowl.

"Come sit in bed, and I shall be happy to pamper Your Majesty by feeding you." I winked at her.

"Very well, but I shall resume pacing when I have finished."

"Of course, Majesty."

I waved Elizabeth Seymour over to place the tray of soup and extra-strong wine — with a sleeping draught added to help her relax — on the table beside the queen's bed.

I fed Jane slowly, and we talked of dancing and tapestries.

Soon, the bowl was empty, as was the mug, and Jane's eyelids drooped closed.

But the nap only lasted an hour, and she sat straight up, moaning, and clutching her belly.

More strong wine was given, and the mixture seemed to calm Jane somewhat, but the pains were coming stronger and fiercer. Elizabeth brought quail eggs, hoping to entice the queen, but Jane refused the food, and more of the draught was ordered. Her pain was intense, but the baby did not seem to want to descend, nor was her body progressing further. The midwives informed me her birth would be a long, arduous and painful task.

Birthing little Eddie had been painful, a tremendous feat, but nothing compared to Jane's birthing. She was in agony, and all of us suffered along with her, wishing we could make things different.

In the presence chamber of her apartments, messengers, ambassadors and multiple other courtiers stood awaiting the news of a successful birth. Their feet shuffled back and forth. They whispered, yawned, stared into space as they counted the ticking seconds that went by until their eyes crossed. Yet again, I was forced to tell them nothing had happened.

Jane's pains became worse. She screamed, tore the sheets from the force of her grasp.

The midwives turned to Elizabeth Seymour, the Lady Mary and myself, who attended her. "Lay her on her side where we can rub her back and her belly."

Midnight had passed, and all of our ministrations still had done nothing to relieve the queen of her burden. Jane's face was pale, dark-blue circles stained beneath her eyes. Her eyes themselves were glazed, her mouth and brows pinched in pain. Her hair, skin and chemise were drenched in perspiration. I bathed her face with a cool, wet cloth, but it seemed to do little. The air in the room was stifling.

"Your Majesty, you must sit up," the midwives suggested.

But she could barely get into the position herself. Mary, Elizabeth and myself helped our queen to sit. We held her hands, rubbed her with cool cloths. The midwives told her to push with all her might. And push she did. She screamed, she panted, she pushed. But nothing.

After several hours, Jane fell back against the bed, unable to go on. She was limp, drifting in and out of consciousness. What were once strong screams and yells as she worked were now only whimpers.

Dawn was fast approaching.

"Majesty, do not give up!" I urged.

"I cannot continue." Her voice was barely a whisper, more of a breath. "I have failed."

The physician was called for his opinion. He felt her pulse, her forehead, touched her belly. When he'd completed his examination, he turned toward us.

"The queen is weak. She may not make it through this ordeal. Her heartbeat is slow. No fever yet, but if the baby is not born soon, she will take a shock and the fever will come soon after that."

"Do not say such things!" Lady Mary all but shouted, her hands coming to her mouth, which opened in horror.

Elizabeth Seymour rushed to her sister's side and wiped a cool compress along the length of the queen's neck.

The physician started to glare in her direction but quickly remembered himself.

"It may come to it, that we have to decide between the life of the child and the life of the mother."

"No!" Elizabeth and I shouted in unison. Mary stood, her mouth still agape in silent horror.

The midwives nodded solemnly.

I glanced back at Jane, who looked near death. Between her legs, blood seeped onto the bed.

"She is bleeding," I stated, my voice flat.

One of the midwives rushed to Jane to examine her.

"The babe's head is there! I can feel it!"

Everyone rushed back to the queen's side. "Your Majesty, please," we all pleaded. She only turned her head from side to side, murmuring things we could not understand. She was delirious.

"See to the king," I ordered the physician. None of us would be made to make the decision on who lived or died if it came to it. "Pray," I ordered the servants, the midwives, ladies-in-waiting, Elizabeth, Mary and those who loitered in the queen's presence chamber.

We all prayed until the clock chimed five in the morning. The physician returned.

"The king says we save the queen."

I do not think I was the only one taken aback by his statement, for certainly there were times when it was thought that Henry cared only for his future offspring and not the vessels that bore them. My heart quickened at the thought, mayhap this volatile master of the realm had a tender heart after all.

"I am ready," Jane said weakly, surprising us all as she opened her eyes and gazed around. Her pale flesh had taken on some color.

She pushed herself up on her elbows, held out her hands to Elizabeth and I. We slipped our hands into hers, and then she started to push. This time, there was renewed vigor inside her, emanating out.

She pushed, she shouted, she prayed. And within thirty minutes of her new spark, the baby finally slid into the world. I tried to ignore the large gush of blood that came after, but I could not help it. Was there really supposed to be so much blood? I did not remember that much blood when baby Eddie was born...

Jane fell back against her pillow, a smile on her deathly pale face.

"A boy!" came the shout of someone, I cannot remember who, followed by the lusty cry of a babe, which made my heart clench and I yearned for my own little boy.

"Give him to me." The bundle of pink flesh was swaddled and thrust into his mother's waiting arms. Jane nodded. "Beautiful prince." She kissed his forehead and nose. "What day is it?"

"Why, it is the twelfth day of October, Majesty," a midwife answered.

"Edward. We shall call him Edward, for he was born on the eve of St. Edward's day."

She handed the babe to a waiting nurse and fell limply against the pillows, her eyes closing. For a heart-stopping moment, I thought she'd passed, but then I watched the rise and fall of her chest—slow as it was. Relief flooded through me, but along with it an icy sense of foreboding crawled its way up my spine. The midwives fussed furiously with Jane, waiting on the afterbirth, cleaning up the blood that ceased to end its flow. Tittering things I could not hear, their eyebrows scrunched in worry.

But then it hit me, as did the cheers resounding throughout Hampton Court.

The queen had born a son.

Good Lord, hallelujah! A son! A prince! We had succeeded. A Seymour would be crowned king!

*October 13, 1537*

How was it, with so much joy, there could also be so much sadness?

This morning I woke with a start, rushed through my ablutions and morning prayers, skipped breakfast and kissed Edward on the

277

brow in his library before rushing to Jane's apartments. I'd sat with her all through yesterday after her prince was born, and her condition had appeared to only worsen.

I feared the worst... Yet I could not voice those fears. It could not be possible. Jane was what the kingdom needed, especially now that there was a prince!

"Lady Mary, you are here," I said on a breath as I entered. "How is she? Is she awake? Are there any changes?"

The room was lit by a fire and a few scattered candelabras. Still, no sun shone through the windows, as they were closed tight and covered. The air was thick, musty, hot. The scent of blood, sweat, and other bodily odors strong. I lifted the nosegay of dried lavender around my wrist to my nose, inhaling deeply.

"I did not want to disturb them." Mary inclined her head and set down the orange she was piercing with cloves.

"Them?" I peered into the queen's bedchamber and found the king on his knees, his hands clutching Jane's. He was whispering to her fiercely, and she, eyes open, was whispering back. The way his back shook... could it be? Was he crying? My heart lurched, and palms began to sweat.

I came to sit beside Mary, my index finger on my lip as I contemplated all that had happened. The king truly did love his wife. Something I'd never expected.

"How is the little prince this morning?" I asked.

Mary smiled, a wistful look coming over her countenance. "He is perfect."

Poor girl. Most likely she wished the little babe was hers... At the age of one and twenty, she should have had several babes of her own, but still all plans for her had fallen through. And, to be honest, I was doubtful that any would come to fruition in the near future. The king liked to keep himself the strongest, and with so many supporters of Mary, and that the marriage she would contract in would most likely be with a super power, King Henry had a right to be fearful.

Imagine Mary, riding all decked out in silver armor, with her powerful prince by her side as they stormed on London, taking the city, the country, the throne, by force.

But Jane had promised Mary a husband… If she lived…

"What is it?" Mary asked, leaning forward.

I shook my head slightly and patted my knees. "Nothing, my lady, just thinking of the beautiful little prince and our own great queen."

Mary inclined her head. Whether she believed my tale or not, I knew not. But my thoughts on a takeover lingered. *If,* and I discretely crossed myself, *if* the queen were to be taken up by the angels, the Seymours' power would once again be in danger. The Howards would thrust whomever they could under the king's nose for him to wife, and Anne Bassett was only a passing fancy. Cromwell, the slimy bastard, was pushing for a German alliance against France and the Empire. Perhaps then, when things were so completely in chaos, a proposal for the Lady Mary's marriage was due.

As if prompted by my traitorous thoughts, King Henry barreled into the room. We jumped to curtsy before him. With the heat and thick air of the room already, the stench from his leg seemed to reach me stronger than it usually did. I sucked in a deep breath of lavender scent and tried not to gag. I would have to change my nosegay on the morrow to a different flower, for I feared the scent of lavender would now forever more be associated with rotting flesh.

His face was red and puffy, clear confirmation of my earlier guess at his tears.

He nodded to his daughter, and then his red-rimmed blue eyes locked with mine. "Lady Beauchamp, a word?"

I stood with a nod and walked toward him. He held out his arm, and we walked out of the chamber and down the corridor toward his own private suite.

"My wife, the queen… she is not well." His voice was gruff, as if he tried with all his strength not to shed more tears.

His gait was slow, and although he tried to hide it, I was well aware of his limp.

Unsure of how to respond, I simply shook my head. "No, Majesty, but with your great physicians…"

"Nonsense, they will only bleed her, as if the woman hasn't lost enough blood already." His meaty arm beneath my fingers stiffened, and his voice lowered. "I saw them carry the sheets out to be burned."

I nodded. There was no denying it, and he would have only called me out for being false.

"I cannot lose her. She is my phoenix." He stopped and gazed at a beautiful new painting, recently completed by Hans Holbein, that hung in his throne room.

The portrait was of Jane on a white horse, a phoenix taking flight from her hands. Beneath her on the ground knelt a thinner, more fit King Henry, his hands raised up to her. The portrait said it all, and I had been blind to it before. The king idolized his wife, knelt before her.

"She is the mother of my son," he whispered, fingers running along the lines of her painted face. "She is still as pure and white as a summer rose. There is no one in all of England who could match her goodness."

I wished to come up with something clever, something comforting to the king. But all I could say was, "And there never will be."

"Majesty, if it pleases you, might I have a word?" Cromwell slinked from seemingly nowhere, and the king quickly snapped from his despairing mood to kingly strength.

Ordinarily, I would have been quite irritated at the interruption from Cromwell, whom I could never quite figure out. But the change in Henry was tangible, and I surmised the Lord Privy Seal was the perfect distraction for keeping his mind away from his ailing wife.

I excused myself and hurried back to Jane.

*October 14, 1537*

The king was in an outrage.

They had bled her last night.

No one had sought council. The physicians had taken it upon themselves to bleed the queen, even though they had known it was against the king's wishes, for he'd hoped for her to be treated with the latest herbal remedies. As the patron of the Royal College of

Physicians and an avid supporter of herbal treatments, the king was insistent on most of his court using holistic remedies.

Why they would have done such a thing, no one knows, for just after supper Jane had come around, eyes clear and bright, begging an audience with her babe and her king. The king in his merriment had had musicians brought in — all thoughts of churching put out of his mind — and he himself had serenaded his wife.

She had grown tired quickly, and we had ushered everyone from her presence. The king had winked at me as he left. "Keep her well for me, Lady Anne."

I had inclined my head and curtsied.

This morning she was weak, her skin ashen. Even her lips were white. Her body was working so hard to recover from her three days of labor and the bleeding. She lazily opened her eyes to myself, Edward, her sister Elizabeth and brother Thomas, who'd all come to see to her this morning. The latter fairly frothed at the mouth at seeing me, and it was all I could to keep Edward from pummeling his brother into the ground.

The king shouted and raged at the physicians in the rooms down the hall. Every now and then, we heard something crash. Those men might feel the length of the hangman's noose before this day ended. Their only defense was they were certain it would have cured her. Imbeciles.

"Tomorrow my prince will be christened," Jane whispered.

"Thanks be to God," we whispered.

Her limp hand came up to hold Edward's, and the small twitch in her fingers said she had squeezed his hand for comfort.

"I want to be there," Jane said.

"I will see it done." Edward nodded.

"I want the Lady Mary and the Lady Elizabeth there," Jane said, referring to Henry's two other children.

Edward nodded again, flicking his worried gaze toward me.

"Mary will be godmother," Jane whispered.

I tried not to hide the surprise at her choice. Having Mary as the godmother could not have fallen better into my way of thinking if I had told her to do so myself. Mary would be brought even closer to her father and the throne. Sometimes, Jane's astuteness and stubborn streak to see her will done pleasantly surprised. It was also a sign that Catholicism was still in the heart of our precious queen.

*October 15, 1537*

The very next morning as the bells from the king's chapel at Hampton Court chimed loudly, Jane was wrapped in furs and placed in a velvet litter to be carried to the king's chapel. She was not as pale, but deep, purple circles marred the flesh beneath her eyes. The whites of her eyes were sallow and her lips still nearly white. She shivered and shuddered a lot. Licked her lips constantly as if severely dehydrated, but she smiled at everyone. Had a kind word for each person she passed as well. She'd look up and then be drawn back to the bundle of perfection in her arms. Her prince. Her savior. Her glory as a Queen of England.

Behind her were the long line of courtiers in attendance for the christening of Prince Edward. King Henry strode, proud, his chest puffed out, beside his wife, and behind him was the Lady Mary who would be godmother, her arm interlocked with that of Archbishop Cranmer, who would preside over the ceremony as well as serve as the new prince's godfather. Thomas Seymour carried Anne Boleyn's daughter, little Lady Elizabeth, who, for some reason, preferred him. I found it fitting, considering he hated her mother so very much. Behind Tom was Edward, myself and Elizabeth Seymour, followed by the elite members of the king's council and their spouses.

The only other procession to rival this one had been when Jane had entered London in state.

People milled about, begging for alms, and Jane's dainty pale hand came from out of her draped litter to toss gold pieces into the crowds.

Inside the chapel, Jane was taken from her litter to stand beside the king for Mass and the christening. However, she began to wobble at first and then almost swooned. I could not look at the floor, for I had an enormous fear that beneath her feet I would find a puddle of blood.

"Jane!" the king shouted, catching her in his arms. "This is too much for the queen. Get her to the litter. To bed with you, my wife.

Rest, get well. Our son, the prince, needs you. England needs you. I need you."

He kissed her pale cheek, and she was soon away, a retinue of ladies behind her. I started to follow, but Edward held me back.

"We must support our prince, Anne."

There was no doubt that I did not support the prince and future king, but I also supported his mother, the Queen of England. And I wanted to go back to her! Did he not realize how much she meant to me? I had grown to rely on her steadfastness and goodness, and here he was, holding me back. I glowered up at him, but he paid me no heed, for once standing on his own two feet. Rather than cause a scene, I remained where I was and crossed myself, saying a silent prayer for Jane's well-being.

Two thousand shots were fired from the Tower, and even as far away as we were, we could hear their distant cracking. Bells rang throughout the countryside, cheers went up, and bonfires were again lit from the border of Wales and Scotland to the English Channel and North Sea.

Even with all the fanfare, and it was a most joyous occasion indeed, did no one remember the poor ailing mother of the prince?

*October 19, 1537*

Jane shivered. Her body wracked by fever. We covered her in furs, we pressed cool compresses to her head, but none of our ministrations seemed to abate the chills.

"Wine," she called out in her sleep, and we brought it to her lips.

"Stuffed quail!" she shouted, and there laid before her was a meal fit for her—the queen.

"Sugared plums..." She trailed off.

I was amazed at her appetite, and with each delicacy she asked for, she received and ate with gusto, her chills ceasing for a moment or two.

I left Jane's rooms for a short time, ensuring she had enough servants and ladies to see over her. I happened on Cromwell, who spoke with Jane Rochford in the great hall, on my way to see

Edward before he left on progress to his new estate, for yesterday he'd been entitled Earl of Hertford, making myself a countess. To my chagrin, his brother Thomas was knighted and promoted to the king's privy chamber, as were several others. I was very pleased that Elizabeth Seymour's marriage to Cromwell's son Gregory was arranged. If it hadn't been for my ill queen, I would have been overjoyed at the amount of prestige and recognition with which we'd been honored in a matter of one day.

"They call for sweets and rich foods with sauces. That cannot be good for her," Cromwell stated, his eyes sliding to me as he spoke.

Lady Rochford's back was to me as she continued to speak. "Not at all! The physicians are in total disagreement and wish to bleed her, which is by far the better choice. It's all Lady Beau—"

"My Lord Cromwell. Jane," I said, not deigning to give her the proper recognition due her title.

"Countess," Cromwell said, and I watched Lady Rochford's brows rise as she recalled my new elevated status.

"You were saying?" I implored.

"Nothing of concern," Lady Rochford quickly sputtered.

But Cromwell was a bit more solicitous. "I am concerned with the diet which the queen is being served. Having just come from labor and now encumbered with childbed fever, is it not prudent she be eating a diet rich in minerals?"

"That is not for *me* to decide, Cromwell. I am confident you'll agree that what the queen and king want, we are here to provide."

"Ah," was all he said, his eyes roving over me, assessing my position perhaps.

But from then on, I did try to see to it that Jane was served more fruits and vegetables.

*October 21, 1537*

My quest for fresher, mineral-rich meals for the queen lasted less than two days. The queen fell into a delirious fever and then quietly fell into unconsciousness and could not be roused even for a drop of water to be placed on her lips.

Henry had herbalists working on medicines for Jane that he himself concocted. Astrologists were asked to foretell the future of the country. Every man, woman and child was ordered to pray.

I knelt before Jane, my knees already sore, bruised and bleeding from hours of praying. I gripped her frail, hot hand in mine and prayed all the more.

*October 24, 1537*

"Murder!" the king raged, and even went so far as to hit one of the physicians.

The older man fell backward, blood trickling from his lip as the ferocious king lunged forward to take another hit.

Several men of his chamber grabbed onto the savage king, who so very much resembled the lion his first wife had dubbed him. They held him back, settled him, while a few others ushered the shamefaced physicians from the queen's chambers. I heard the groomsmen whisper to them never to return to court, lest the king be reminded of their injury to himself — the death of his wife.

Dead.

The queen was dead.

The clock ticked just before midnight, silencing everyone as the last rattled breath escaped her body. The castle was silent, except for the battle cry that ripped from King Henry's throat when he heard the news.

I collapsed, numb, in a chair by the hearth. Unable to think, unable to move. Edward looked on, stone-faced, as though the death of his sister had little effect on him — or so he tried to hide it. He stood behind me, his warm hand resting on my shoulder. I couldn't bring myself to comfort him. Blaming him partially for Jane's death. He'd wanted so badly for her to become with-child. And so had I. Another death on my head. I shied away from his touch. It was not his comfort I wanted. In fact, in my time of sorrow, I desperately yearned for the touch of another... Anthony. Months since I had seen him or thought of him. And yet, when death was once more upon us, I thought to escape its horror in the throes of delirium. To take away the pain. To release my nightmares on a moan of climax. I shook myself from my demented, disgraceful thoughts and focused on waking life.

Why, of all people, would God see fit to take Jane?

Just barely two weeks had gone by since Prince Edward had been born. Before that, Jane had been alive, well, vibrant. Now she was dead, her body not yet cold, and lying so very still atop her bed.

I took a deep, shuddering breath. Tears had not yet come. Ladies-in-waiting, ambassadors, courtiers and court ladies milled about the queen's presence chamber. Everyone around me appeared just as stunned. We knew she'd been sick with childbed fever, but her case seemed so rare. Never had it been heard before for a woman sick with the fever to awake and demand great meals she would eat with gusto.

Perhaps there was truth to Cromwell's words. If her requests had been denied and instead filled with rich fruits, vegetables, grains, she would have been able to recover her strength, but instead the sweets, sauces and strong wine had weakened her system.

Abruptly I stood, Edward's hand falling from my shoulder.

"Anne," he murmured.

"I must go to my chambers," I mumbled before excusing myself and half walking, half running to my chambers down the hall.

As I broke through the door and rushed toward my bed, the tears began to fall.

I hadn't just lost my queen, I had lost a dear friend. For although Jane had been a means of rising up in the world, she had also been my companion. A sweet innocent foray into the depths of goodness.

I collapsed onto the bed, the tears racking my body. I shook, I sobbed. Unguarded, I let my grief take over.

I had looked forward to our children growing up together, strolling in the parks as the cherubs gathered and presented us with posies. Reveling in the success she'd had in giving the king a prince, a success that two previous wives had not achieved. To celebrate all she'd accomplished in so short a time.

But now she was gone.

One minute there, and the next, rising up into the heavens just as her phoenix motto had done.

Anguish wrenched at my chest. God had swept down and taken her from us. The Lord giveth and the Lord taketh away. The Lord said we must heed his call, we must trust in him, believe what he did was for the best, but I could not help doubting that his taking of our most beloved queen was good. It was *not* good. She was needed here!

Was this not the third queen I had seen die in as many years? *God save the queen's soul!* Or had he already forgotten her?

# CHAPTER NINETEEN

*And thus behold my kinds, how that we differ far;*
*I seek my foes; and you your friends do threaten still with war.*
*~Henry Howard, Earl of Surrey*

*October 25, 1537*

The mood throughout the castle was bleak.

Indeed, the whole of the kingdom was draped in dark melancholy, mourning the passing of a queen who'd promised so many great things, yet was ripped from this world before her time.

The king fared worst of all. While he was holed up in his room, occasional shouts and the shattering of furniture, porcelain and glass could be heard. Three children and no mothers to see about rearing them. He was alone in parentage once again. No wife to comfort him, sew his shirts, listen to him lament on his pillows, or to cry themselves to sleep as he diddled with some other woman.

Edward was frantic trying to pry His Majesty from hysteria while keeping our little nephew in good care. The king could not even see to the making of arrangements for his own son beyond the scrubbing and use of lye soap to make certain all disease was kept well away from the boy. His only thought was to keep the boy alive, but not who actually did it. Just that it was done. The rest fell to

Edward. He hired the remaining staff that Jane had not seen to prior to the birthing.

The little prince was a strong and robust child. A plump, pink baby with a shock of reddish-blond hair atop his crown. He came into the world a true prince and plenty fine with making demands of his nursemaids and various other servants.

I walked numbly through the hallowed halls. When nothing but quiet echoes bounced off the ancient stonework, Jane's voice called to me, or the tinkling of her laughter floated in the somber air.

Even Mother Nature mourned the passing of England's pure and sweet queen. The sky was such a dark gray and filled with angry clouds that even mid-afternoon appeared to be night.

My heels clicked against the polished wood floor as I made my way to the queen's presence chamber. Jane was laid out in state there, already embalmed this morning. She would lay here with three ladies always in attendance of her, the Lady Mary being chief mourner, until the first of November, when Jane would be moved to St. George's Chapel. But I paused before the large wooden double doors. I gazed at them as I'd never gazed at them before. Taking in the reddish brown of the wood. The carvings at the corners, the planks across its middle and the black iron rings of its handles. Even the little iron plates underneath the handles were ornate in a swirling design.

*Pretty.*

What was I doing out here admiring the doors to her chambers? Why not open them and go inside? Pay respects to my Jane?

The reason why curled up inside my belly, making my fingers pull back and my heart clench, my breaths quick and shallow.

Fear, plain and simple. Entering the chamber, seeing Jane's pale and thin body laid out in white linen and silk atop cloth of gold would only have been to admit that she was gone. That the little prince had no mother, England had no queen, and we Seymours were now connected to the throne only by a little baby asleep in his cradle, still so fragile in this world.

Entering would have been to acknowledge that the one innocent and joyful woman in my life was gone forever. I would never get her back, and would never meet another like her. No one was as pure and sweet as Jane had been. I did not know how it had happened, but she truly had been, even after being brought up at court.

"Are you going inside?" Edward's voice startled me, and I jumped. I turned, nearly collapsing against him, but instead somehow pulled myself together enough to stand tall.

"Oh, thank the Lord, it is you."

"Who else would it have been?" He looked around him. There was no one in sight. Most had come by earlier in the day, in the morning after Mass. But I could not. I waited until I could be alone with her. And now I found that I *could not* be alone, did not want to.

"No one. I..." I chewed on my lower lip. "I am having trouble going inside."

"We shall do it together." Edward's voice was soft, filled with pain. How could I have forgotten that Jane was his little sister?

He reached for my hand, and I squeezed his grip into mine. Together we opened the large creaking doors, let the air from inside rush out to greet us, stirring my skirts around my legs. A shiver passed through me, as though the wind rustling my skirts were Jane's spirit welcoming us, berating me for not coming sooner. We walked in.

Her chambers were quiet save for the choirboys in the corner, well hidden, who alternated between themselves so the queen had constant hymns sung for her soul before the king let her funeral take place — yet another reason we needed him calm and out of the fit of insanity that was currently taking over his mind.

It was dark inside, and the stained glass windows did not emit much light, especially with the sun being nearly hidden behind the mournful clouds. Candelabras were lined against the walls with thick white candles on them, the wax dripping down making hard white puddles on the floor.

Our feet shuffled silently to where she lay. Her hair was silky-looking and styled properly for a queen. Her crown rested atop her head, hands folded over her heart. Her eyes were closed... sewn shut, I imagined, to keep them from popping open and scaring holy hell out of anyone who was near. Her mouth was closed in a peaceful smile. She looked so quiet, at peace, almost happy, like she

290

was taking a snooze in a bed of daisies out in a field on a warm summer day.

Was she happy? She was no longer in physical pain, but did she want to be dead? I supposed it was a question not worth answering, since she had passed and I could not ask her.

Edward knelt beside me and began whispering his prayers. I gazed on Jane for a bit longer. This would be one of the last times I saw her, and I wanted to take her all in. Bask in the glory that was her before she was put to ground.

By the time I was ready to kneel and pay respects, Edward had finished.

"Shall I wait for you?" He stood, strong, ready to steady my arm should I need him. But I knew how many other things were in need of his attention, and so I bade him go.

"I shall see you for a private dinner in our chambers then?"

"Yes," I whispered, and then bowed my head.

*October 31, 1537*

The king barreled out of the castle gates as though he were chased by ghosts. To Windsor Castle he went, unable to stay the entire mourning period for his beloved wife. Demons filled him. His face was covered in shadows. Dark, purple bruises stained beneath the haunted eyes of the king. Reddish-gray stubble covered his chin and cheeks. For a man who valued keeping his appearance in check, the king had truly let himself go in his mourning for Jane.

He ate, drank, slept and broke things. He refused to attend to state matters, which were left in the hands of Cromwell, all to the ire of the king's council, who demanded Cromwell hand over any news and decisions to them. A fierce battle was beginning within the council chambers, and Edward was stuck in the middle of it.

Politics of the council were the least of my concern, even if they should have been at the forefront of my thoughts... for Mother, Page and, even the jackanapes, Surrey were now back at court, having felt it necessary to join the mourners.

I arranged for 'Nan Bassett to stick like honey to my sister, Lizzie. They now shared a room and 'Nan was, for better or worse,

291

her constant chaperone. Even though 'Nan was only a few years older than Lizzie, I could not risk anyone else. I trusted 'Nan, and she knew to watch over Lizzie like a hawk, and keep all men away from her—especially Surrey.

Mother and Page requested an audience with me, which I granted, but they sought nothing more than to see how Lizzie's fortunes were faring and how they might benefit from it. I dismissed them and, as soon as they were gone, threw a vase of flowers and stomped the pretty roses to a pulp.

My servants stayed clear the rest of the day, and I cursed my mother for making me lose my temper in such a way.

Why could I not mount my horse and race away? Would that I could go to Wulfhall and hold my own baby. Instead, I took a personal interest in my nephew—the future king.

As soon as my nerves calmed, I put on my black mourning choker and walked with my head held high from my chambers to where the prince was being cared for. Let all who saw me know that that precious baby, the future king, was of my blood.

*November 13, 1537*

The king had not yet returned when it was time for the mourning procession to begin, but we could not tarry. We left Hampton Court yesterday on our way to St. George's Chapel at Windsor Castle. As our procession arranged itself, I proudly carried the tiny, squalling prince to his gilded litter. Every courtier bowed low as we passed. I knew it was for Prince Edward, but, I couldn't help but believe it was also for me.

A journey that could have normally been made on horseback in only a few hours took nearly the entire day. The procession itself was long, appearing like the entire country followed us. Mourners walked, rode in wagons, rode horses. They sang psalms and prayed. We collected more as we went, with each village we passed.

Queen Jane was at the very front of the procession. The deep, cherry wood casket of the queen rode in a gilded chariot led by six white horses. Flowers were strewn atop.

Her three lady mourners of the day were her sister Beth, myself and the Lady Mary as her chief mourner. In the queen's name, we tossed alms to the poor.

When we were only an hour's ride from Windsor, a rumble sounded ahead, and the ground began to shake. It was Henry VIII and a score of his guards thundering toward us. We hauled up our lines and waited for him to reach us. Those of us on horseback bowed our heads, and those on foot knelt before him.

He looked wild, his eyes wide, stubble still on his cheeks, red hair sticking out in odd angles beneath his cap. He was dressed in all black velvet, his mourning clothes. I had the sudden vision of his guilt at having left his beloved to escape his grief, and then the realization hitting him as he left Windsor to find her, just as abruptly as he'd left Hampton Court.

"Good people!" he shouted, his hand up in the air as he greeted us. "I thank you for attending my—*your* queen—on her journey to Windsor and her final resting place. Allow me to now lead the procession beside this woman, this saint, an example of purity we should all strive to follow."

We all nodded and offered murmurings of prayers and condolence. Our ride continued, but this time the singing voices rang out higher, and when I looked, I could even see the king himself, lips moving as he silently sang along.

As we walked, he turned to face me. "Where is the prince?" he asked, his eyebrows drawn together, lips pursed.

It struck me how odd it was that he did not even know the whereabouts of his long-wished-for son.

"Majesty, he travels with us." I pointed to the gilded purple carriage just behind Jane's chariot.

"My son..." he whispered. The king appeared lost. Almost childlike. My heart went out to him. It was an odd transformation from a man who commanded countries. A man who changed the way we prayed, and named himself Supreme Head of the Church. For him to be lost made me feel vulnerable. What was to happen to England if this strong and able ruler came crumbling down?

I would have to see to it that he did not. Our very lives depended on it. Jane would have wished me to make certain the man snapped back.

When we reached St. George's Chapel, the retinue placed Jane at the head of the church, and we all lined up to mourn. There was not a break for food or drink or to relieve ourselves. King Henry made it plain that we were all to do penance today, in hopes that when Jane was buried, some of her goodness would light a spark in our own hearts and minds.

I did not think it would happen, but whatever made His Majesty feel better.

The funeral Mass was more than two hours long, and my knees, which had long since gone numb, would surely have permanent bruises on them.

I thought all this time that while King Henry was at Windsor, he'd locked himself up in his chambers as he'd done at Hampton Court. While the groomsmen who attended him said as much, he had also been at work on preparing his lady's plaque and tomb, which graced the center aisle of the church, so all who passed it from this day forth could look upon their queen.

She was interred, and we all silently and politely ignored the shouts of pain from Henry. Charles Brandon stood by his side, hand on the king's shoulder offering him comfort.

For a moment I could see the human side of the king, the side that hurt. But I had to wonder, with one who suffered such pain, would he not retaliate in some way to make himself feel better?

I turned my eyes from the shaking, sob-riddled shoulders of the king to gaze upon the tomb of Jane.

A great marble sarcophagus had been designed for the queen as her eternal resting place. The stone cutters and painters had been hired to work around the clock to complete it in time. A carving of her likeness graced the top. It was painted richly in color. Robes of state covered the body, a royal crown on her head, scepter and orb in hand, painted fingers covered with jewels. She was given the coronation in death that she never received in life.

The artwork was exquisite, lifelike. She would forever remain young and beautiful, laid here for all to see and worship her. Indeed, like the saint that Henry thought her to be.

Engraved on the sides of the marble tomb, it read:

> *Here a phoenix lieth, whose death*
> *To another phoenix gave breath:*
> *It is to be lamented much,*
> *The world at once ne'er knew two such*

No truer words had I ever seen.

When the service was over, King Henry turned to us all and softly proclaimed, "I will be buried with my one true love, my one true wife, Queen Jane. Whomsoever I take to wife hereafter matters not, for my heart and soul belong to her, and when the time comes for the good Lord above to take me up into the heavens, it shall be by Queen Jane's side that I spend my eternal life."

Heavy words. Strong words.

But the words, nonetheless, jarred me back to reality. He would want a new wife, and I would be damned if I was going to let the Howards get there first. When others would whisper of a new queen, we would encourage the king's grief. Remind him of his love of Jane, of how he had his long sought after prince. And all the while, I'd proudly continue carrying the little prince through the great halls to greet his courtiers—so they could see that I held the future king in my arms.

# CHAPTER TWENTY

*I fawn where I am fled; you slay, that seeks to you;*
*I can devour no yielding prey; you kill where you subdue.*
*My kind is to desire the honor of the field;*
*And you with blood to slake your thirst on such as to you yield.*
*~Henry Howard, Earl of Surrey*

*Mid-August, 1538*

Eight months had passed since Jane died. Her baby was crawling, singing out his praises to those who passed, and admonishing those he detested—namely Cromwell. Smart little prince, he was.

I'd been walking the past ten months in a daze. Missing Jane. Missing Edward. Missing my baby. Missing so many things. Living my life for everyone but myself. Most nights I lay awakr staring at the ceiling and wondering what I was going to do with myself. Then a barrage of berating words flitted through my mind as I reminded myself of all we'd become of who I'd become—aunt to the future king.

Edward had been gone a lot. The king was constantly sending him abroad and across the country to follow through with policies of state, quell rebellions and maintain our foreign relations. He'd been named commander for the English fortifications in Calais. He'd become just as much an asset to the king as Suffolk or Norfolk. But with him gone... with Jane gone... I'd grown lonely. Court was not what it used to be. Some months ago, when Sir Francis and Sir Nicholas had left to hunt Reginald Pole, Anthony had stayed behind. We'd hardly spoken beyond civility.

But he'd started to leave me little notes. They had never been signed, but I had still recognized his handwriting. He'd left me poems. Just a few lines, but the words had told me how he was sorry. How pain and jealousy had made him a crazy, vengeful man.

And this morning was no different. My biscuit and tea sat untouched as I unfolded the crisp paper and his words jumped out at me.

> *The long love that in my heart doth harbor*
> *And in mine heart doth keep his residence,*
> *Into my face presseth with bold pretense,*
> *And there campeth, displaying his banner.*
> *She that me learneth to love and to suffer...*

Tears pooled in my eyes, and I tried to blink them away. I'd not received a letter from Edward save for when he'd arrived in Calais a month before. I pushed away from the table and held the letter to a candle's flame, watching his pretty words disappear from sight, though not from memory — for they were forever ingrained there.

The room was suddenly stifling, and I left for the gardens to walk in the shade of the willows, but as I rounded the corridor, Anthony's tall, lithe figure came into view and my heart sped up, thundering down the stone walls to where he stood. My feet refused to budge as his eyes met mine — longing, deep and raw, resonating. I could hardly move, hardly breathe. Oh, if he'd only just keep going, but he did not. He moved closer, every step he took whisking the breath from my lungs until I was but a quivering shell.

"Anne," he whispered, searching my face, and likely seeing the longing reflected in my eyes.

His spicy male scent overwhelmed me, drawing me closer. A cursory glance showed no one else in the hall. I had grasped

Anthony's hand, squeezing his fingers, and then I whirled around and headed back to my chambers. I turned just enough to see that Anthony followed. Our eyes connected and he stepped into the shadows of an alcove as I opened my chamber door.

"Leave. You may have the rest of the day to yourselves." My servants nodded, not finding it unusual as I often dismissed them to find peace.

As the last of them left, I closed the door, then turned around, breath coming fast as I stared at the door and waited. A few moments later Anthony entered. My breath hitched.

"Close the door, lock it," I said.

Anthony did so without taking his eyes off of me. My heart skipped a beat and I knew a moment of panic. A moment of conscience, where I knew this was undeniably wrong, but I pushed it aside, not caring. My husband had taken his pleasure with countless women. And I'd been mostly good, until now. I'd waited long enough to feel Anthony, to have him hold me. To feel something beyond the darkness I'd fallen into.

We said not a word, our bodies doing the talking as we both rushed toward one another at the same time, mouths clashing in a heated, hungry kiss. 'Twas better than I remember. His mouth a decadent foray into the depths of fantasy and freedom. His hands roved over my back, my ribs, cupping my breasts. I flicked open the buttons of his doublet, yanked up his shirt and splayed my hands on his warm, muscled belly, over his heart, feeling it beat against my fingertips just as erratically as my own.

"Oh, Anne," Anthony murmured. "My sweet, beautiful, Anne."

I sigh of pleasure escaped my lips, their thinned, pinched surface opened and relaxed. I was letting go. I was giving in. Just this once.

Anthony's nimble fingers flicked open every button, hook and tie until I stood nude before him. He sucked in a breath through his teeth and stared at me in awe.

"Good God, you're even more tempting than I'd imagined." He kicked aside my clothes and wrapped his arms around me, his lips on mine, then my neck, until he took a pebbled nipple into his mouth and ecstasy crashed over me.

298

"Anthony," I murmured, pressing my lips hotly to the side of his neck as I worked to remove his clothing.

"I can't wait. Not this time."

I nodded, desperate to have him inside me. We tumbled to the solar floor, my naked back pressed to the Turkish rug, and his partially unclothed, hard body over top of me. A moment later he was plunging deep inside me, my body overjoyed.

We were being reckless, and just plain ignorant. Anyone could walk in—Edward himself could! But neither of us cared. Edward was miles away and the door was locked.

I kept my eyes open, watching as his shoulders moved with the rest of him, droplets of sweat beading his muscled flesh. His gaze locked on mine as he pushed inside me again and again. Nibbled at my lips, my breasts. Passion shook me, making my limbs tingle and sing. Every time I opened my mouth to cry out, Anthony hushed me with a deep and carnal kiss, until we were both shaking, and ecstasy was ours.

Both of us had found release, but neither of us were sated. Anthony carried me back to my chamber and laid me out on the bed before savoring every inch of me with his mouth and making love to me all over again, only he took his time, making every minute stretch out.

When we were too limp to do more than lounge on my rustled sheets, I lay in his arms, breathing in his heady scent, limbs still tingling.

My fingers traced a small scar on Anthony's neck. "What is this from? A battle wound?"

Anthony chuckled. "I have the good and generous King Henry VIII himself to thank for that. We were battling in a tournament with swords, and he had his ire up thinking I may be courting the late Queen Anne Boleyn, prior to their own wedding, when in fact I was not. I do believe it was more of a show for the lady, so she might see his prowess."

I rolled onto my back, and Anthony followed swirled circles around my navel. When he looked up at me, there was such emotion in his eyes, I felt true fear in my gut, for I felt just as attached as he did.

"I love you, Anne," he said, pressing his lips to my heart.

"I love you, too," I whispered. "But 'tis a forbidden love. One we are damned for."

He grinned. "Pray for me then, Anne, for I am damned."

I ran my fingers through his hair, savoring this last selfish moment. If only our pasts had been different. Our coming together was bittersweet.

"I can feel you pushing me away," Anthony said, resting his head on my stomach.

"Not just yet," I said, knowing that when the clock struck the hour, I would indeed push him from my life.

*October 12, 1538 – Prince Edward's first birthday*

Much can happen in a year.

Famines can wipe an entire village off the map. Rulers can change. Religious houses can fall. Children can be born, and war can change the face of the landscape.

Much had happened this past year and yet, so little.

The king still wore black. His once vigor for life and entertainments had dwindled. Court was not the same. But our prince had reached his first birthday!

I'd also gained a new enemy.

Standing in the great hall, holding the little prince for courtiers to gaze on him before he was taken to see his father, Catherine Parr, also known as Lady Latimer, strutted toward me like she was the Queen of England herself, confidence in her every haughty step. I raised my chin, looking down at her as she approached. How I disliked her, and the feeling was entirely mutual.

Her brother William Parr had been knighted around the same time as Tom Seymour, and since then, she'd been prancing like a peacock, waiting for the right time to spread herself wide and proclaim how pretty she was.

"Well, look at this handsome prince," she cooed, tickling Prince Edward's chin. The babe was dressed in ivory robes, adorned with jewels and thread of gold and soft kid-skin slippers. She glared up at me as I tugged the prince a little out of her reach.

"Lady Catherine," I drawled out. "Have you shared your story of triumph with your future king?" I could hardly hide the smirk curving my lips.

She'd been married for two years — to her second husband — and those at court loved to hear her revel in the story of when the traitorous Pilgrimage of Grace rebels held her, her husband and stepchildren hostage. She had become somewhat of a celebrity amongst the courtiers. But I'd grown tired of the story after the first time, let alone the tenth.

Catherine frowned, daggers in her eyes as she prepared for another verbal sparring. "You'd not smirk at me so if — "

"If what?" I said through my teeth, cutting her off.

Despite her being married, Edward's brother Tom followed her like a little puppy. They whispered in dark corners. No doubt they'd consummated their relationship and Tom had told her all sorts of evils about me. Not to mention that Anthony's wife was some sort of distant relation to Catherine's husband. And it'd come to my attention that Anthony's dear Alice was not a fan of mine, either.

"Never mind," she said sweetly. "Just something Tom mentioned."

I laughed, the sound making the little prince laugh too, giving the image he laughed at Catherine with me. "Be warned, Lady Catherine, of the company you keep."

I whirled from her and took the prince to his father, still seething.

An hour or so later, I drummed my nails upon the trestle table in the great hall as I tried with all my concentration to pay attention to what Beth — now Cromwell, since she'd married the young Gregory — was saying. But for the life of me I could not. Catherine Parr was sitting across the room staring at me. Whenever my eyes caught hers, she sneered.

"Anne, are you even listening?" Beth said, annoyance ringing in her voice.

"Yes, yes, my apologies," I said, and turned a smile in her direction.

"You look flushed. Are you feeling at all well?"

301

I stopped drumming my fingers and narrowed my eyes. "Yes, quite in fact." But I was lying, for even though over two months had passed, I couldn't get the image of mine and Anthony's nude forms to vanish from my thoughts. Sweat glistened off our skin, both from the heat and from our passionate lovemaking. The sounds of his gasps, the feel of his fingers pressing into my flesh, his chest rubbing on mine.

Nausea built, and my body threatened to toss up the meager meal I had consumed that morning. I was overwhelmed with shame. I rubbed a hand over my forehead and closed my eyes for a moment. I was so confused. It'd only been the one time four months ago, and yet, thought more of that moment than any of the encounters I'd had with my own husband, and when Anthony and I had been together, I'd not thought of Edward at all, but only the selfish, delicious need that had consumed me.

*Oh, Edward!* Tears stung the backs of my eyes. I was most certainly going to hell, and if he ever found out... He'd send me there all the sooner.

*My way of taking back control. Alas, I am so out of control...*

I could not go on like this. Edward had already been made a cuckold once by his first wife, and though I'd dared not do that to him — I had! And now with the power he wielded... A scorned man could do any number of things if his wrath were great enough — the king being a perfect example.

That idiotic interlude was the last time. Absolutely, unequivocally, the last time. Anthony was now a thing of the past to me. I'd been lucky that soon after our encounter, he had gone abroad. I'd not had to see him, for if I did... My stomach burned all the more. I wasn't sure what I would have done. The intimate moments we'd shared after the bucking of our bodies had subsided... they were more than a fling. The soft-spoken sharing. Confession of love.

Would that I could take every moment back. I'd not had a monthly since... My breasts were tender. My breakfast did not agree with me most mornings. The midwife had confirmed I was with child again.

Edward returned only a sennight after I had bedded Anthony. And we had only made love together one time. Even still, I was not entirely certain who the father of this babe was. For certes, I would rot in hell for allowing such a thing to happen.

My only saving grace was that we both had understood at the time, our making love had been a thing of mercy. Our souls had needed comfort, and only the kind that the bringing of two bodies together could have given. I had run from his charms for years, denied him, kept control, and all it had taken was one painful moment, and I had wilted like a flower near a fire.

"Shall I get you some wine?" Elizabeth said, pinching my arm a little.

"No, thank you. I am tired, 'tis all."

"Mayhap you should go and rest then?"

"Yes, 'tis exactly so."

"Do it soon. 'Nan Bassett has requested of me to arrange a meeting between you and her after this meal."

"'Nan? Whatever for?"

"It appears the king still asks for her, and she has taken a liking to the idea of being queen."

"Really?" It was hard for me to hide my shock at such an idea. Anne Bassett as queen? The girl was dumber than bricks and poorer than a church mouse. "How in all of heaven did she come up with a harebrained idea like that?"

Elizabeth laughed. "I take it you do not like her plan?"

"Not at all. The plan is to put a Seymour on the throne, not some little helpless whelp of a girl who only wants pretty dresses and to dance and fuck the days away."

Elizabeth snorted and choked on her wine. "Have you another in mind?"

"Not yet... But I've heard it from Edward's own lips that the king seeks not a wife as of yet. He still mourns deeply, and with it being the prince's birthday today, and in just a few days' time the anniversary of Jane's death, I am confident we shan't worry on it for some time. Nevertheless, I have begun a thorough search into your cousins." I took a sip of wine that Elizabeth had handed me despite my saying I did not want any, let the contents swirl around on my tongue. "Best not take a nap. Send 'Nan to my rooms. Come, too, if you like."

But I did not make it back to my room to have that talk with Anne Bassett. Instead, a messenger intercepted me in the corridor outside of my chambers.

"My lady," he said breathlessly. "It is the young lord. You must come quick to Wulfhall."

My heart plummeted into my stomach, and my legs shook beneath me. Bile rose in my throat.

"What's wrong?"

"He's got a fever, my lady. His nurses are taking good care of him, and the physician has been called."

"I shall leave at once." I turned to open the door, but remembered I had forgotten to ask him if Edward knew. "Wait!"

The messenger turned and bowed. "My lady?"

"Does Lord Hertford know?"

"Indeed, I told him so myself, and he bid me come find you."

"Did he mention if he would be riding with me?"

"Indeed, no, my lady. I met him in the stables. The king has sent him on an errand."

Disappointment thick and painful filled my gut. I knew in my heart Edward would rather have gone and seen to his son, but the king's business could not be ignored.

When I entered my bedchamber, I found he'd left a short note saying they'd word from informants of traitors planning to raise arms against His Majesty. They'd left with haste and all secrecy, meaning he could not have found me in the great hall to inform me in person.

And so I set out that night on my own, to hold my little babe in my arms and, God willing, nurse him back to health.

*Please, Lord, my God, do not take my little Eddie from me!*

# CHAPTER TWENTY-ONE

*Wherefore I would you know, that for your coyed looks,*
*I am no man that will be trapp'd, nor tangled with such hooks.*
*~Henry Howard, Earl of Surrey*

Although I'd never witnessed a natural disaster myself, word traveled fast from those who had. Volcanoes erupting and hot liquid fire eating the flesh from bones, houses melting into the red, bubbling lava. Avalanches happened in the Highlands of Scotland often enough—entire mountains of snow eating up whole villages. Quicksand beneath a troop of horses' feet just giving way and eating the living whole. What I felt now was like a natural disaster. I was devastated, lost, unprepared and, at times, hysterical.

When I arrived at Wulfhall, little Eddie was worse off than simply the fever the messenger had warned me of. He was pale, so pale, his lips white as snow. I trembled as I took in his tiny frame upon the large four-poster, white linen sheets up to his chest, his little arms on top of the sheets laid out at his sides. Was he breathing?

My heart physically hurt, and my lip bled from how hard I bit into it.

I walked closer and took hold of one of his little hands. His body was hot and his hand limp. His chest rose and fell, but spastically. A cry fell from my lips, and I dropped to my knees and gathered his limp body into my arms. "Please, God. Please, God, have mercy on my baby!"

The fever had sucked most of the life from him and threatened to take the rest as well.

This was my punishment. God was punishing me for breaking my marriage vows and succumbing to lust. *I pray to thee! Never again will I stray! Please, let my baby live! Please!*

I did not care that it was nearing on midnight. I woke the house. The servants would not sleep while their young master lay ill. Fires were stoked throughout the manner. Servants brought fresh pitchers of cool water every thirty minutes. A broth and herbal drought were made, and I sat for three days and nights, personally administering to my baby. He lay so weak, unmoving, not even crying out. I was near delirium checking for a pulse and holding a mirror to his nose to check for breath.

One the fourth morning, his little eyes opened. The whites of his eyes were yellow with sickness, the outsides red-rimmed.

"Mama," he barely whispered.

I squeezed his hand and kissed his little cheek. "Mama is here, Eddie. Mama will make you better."

But he fell back to sleep without saying anything. I waved to the nurse to get the physician, who entered a few moments later.

"He spoke. He said, 'Mama.'" I alternated between wringing my hands and rubbing Eddie's arm. My eyes stung from lack of sleep, and I felt nauseated nearly constantly.

"He is on the mend, my lady. The fever is not quite as hot. You need to rest, else you take ill yourself."

I nodded. If my baby was on the mend, it would not hurt to sleep a few hours myself. I did, after all, have another babe to think about as well. But I did not care so much about the one growing in my belly. I had yet to see it, the spark of life had yet to make the little thing kick, and Eddie had been my baby nigh on two years. His little cherubic face made my world go round.

The physician was correct, though. If I was going to be any good and continue to nurse little Eddie back to health, I needed to get some sleep. I stood on shaky legs and almost collapsed.

The physician pressed the back of his hand to my forehead. "No fever, thank God above. Go and get some rest, my lady. I will have Cook send you some food."

"Yes, I will. You have my gratitude for all you have done." I turned to the nurse who looked just as ragged as myself. "When I return, you may go and get some rest yourself, but if he stirs, come and get me, or if anything else changes, come and get me at once."

"As you say, my lady. God bless you."

"And our little Eddie."

Someone was shaking me.

Hard.

I tried to open my eyes, but they refused. I told the shaker to stop, to let me open my eyes, but they just kept shaking me, kept holding my eyes closed.

"My lady! Wake, you must wake!"

The urgent sound of the woman's voice woke me immediately. My vision was blurred, but at least my lids had obeyed me.

"What in heaven's name are you doing?" I said with authority. How was it this servant thought she could wake me from sleep in such a way? I would need to train these servants better. They'd best not be waking up my own little Ed—

Then I remembered and sat straight up, tossing the covers and jumping to my feet.

"What has happened?" I grabbed the maid by her shoulders, shook her.

Her head flopped back and forth, but she did not speak.

"Answer me!"

"It's Lord Eddie, my lady. His fever's gotten worse."

I threw on my robe not bothering to dress. My feet were bare as I ran from my chambers down the hall to where Eddie's own room was.

When I entered, the physician had a bowl full of blood, and a small incision was on my baby's arm.

"What the hell are you doing?" I bellowed.

The physician looked at me like I was a lunatic. "He needed to be bled, my lady. The humours—"

All I could think of was sweet Jane. And the bowl beside Eddie... there was too much blood there. "You've bled him too much!"

I rushed the physician and pushed him with all my might. He stumbled backward, the blood sloshing from the pan.

"Out! Out! Do not ever lay foot in my home again!"

He sputtered and glared, but I turned away, no longer hearing what things came from his mouth. All I could do was look at my baby. I thought he had been pale before, but now he looked almost transparent, his skin so thin, all the veins showing through its whiteness.

"Summon the priest," I muttered to the nurse who sat beside the boy.

"What, my lady?" Her lips trembled.

"I said summon the priest!"

"Yes, my lady." She rushed from the room.

Eddie looked as sweet as Jane had when laid out in state. So quiet, so at peace. I refused to believe he was going to die. I dropped to my knees and began praying. I offered up penance after penance, if the Lord would just see to it to keep my baby with me.

The priest came in and began to pray and read psalms from his Bible. The servants filed in and prayed. I stayed there on my knees for I did not know how long. The sun was there, then it was gone, and then it was there again. Still nothing changed. I left for only a minute to relieve myself, splash water on my face, but that was it. I refused food, I refused drink. I only wanted to be with my baby boy.

By nightfall, Eddie had not improved. If anything, he grew worse. His once-shallow breaths grew rapid, then slowed again to a rattle. He sounded almost as if he could not get enough air into his chest. He did not wake again. Did not call out, or open his eyes. Did not squeeze my fingers back when I took his hand.

The priest shook his head, prayed and wafted incense around the room. Before I was even aware it would happen, the rattling breaths of my baby stopped. He was breathing normally again!

"Oh, Eddie!" I laid my head on his little chest and hugged him tight.

Something was not right.

No breath blew on my forehead. No little *bump, bump, bump* of his heart against my ear. "Eddie?" I murmured, lifting my head slightly in horror. "No! No! No!" I screamed, and then could not stop.

*October 21, 1538*

Edward arrived the next day, but I barely saw him as he walked into the great hall. I stared unseeing at the hearth, only imagining the once-vibrant life of my baby as he'd toddled around the great hall or the gardens. His infectious laugh. Bright blue eyes. Chubby hands and feet.

"Anne," Edward whispered. He dropped to his knees in front of me and put his head on my lap.

Neither of us spoke, only sat there like that until one of the servants told us our evening meal was ready. Yet, still, neither of us moved.

"I am with child."

Edward looked up, his eyes bloodshot. "When?"

"Spring. May."

"We shall have another Eddie, Anne." Edward reached up and swiped at a stray tear that burned its way from my raw eyes onto my cheek.

"I shall *never* have another Eddie." My voice cracked on a sob, but I refused to let myself cry anymore. And I quickly covered my mouth with my hand, so overwrought I might start sobbing again. What good would it do me? My tears up until now had not saved my little boy.

"Come now, let us have some wine." Edward stood, tears in his eyes, which strangely were also red, as if he too had mourned and cried for our baby. He gripped my hand, gave a little tug, but I did not budge. My grief was too much. It consumed me, ate at me. All my muscles were numb, so even if I did stand as he wished, I was likely to just collapse again.

"I want nothing," I whispered, my lips barely moving, as they too were numb.

"You must eat something." Edward pulled me up somehow and put his arms around me. I sank into the warmth and strength of his body. His voice was filled with pleading, concern, sadness. "Best to take care of the other babe who still needs you. Let Eddie be with God. He is looking down on you now, the little cherub, and wishes his mama to be well."

As though my darling child heard, the candle flames brightened and a little fluttering in my belly made me lightheaded. Was that the babe dancing in my womb? Had Eddie made the candles flicker?

I did not know the answer to either question, and I did not voice them to Edward. My mind could barely grasp the meaning. Instead, I nodded and let him lead me to our chambers for a small, private meal. In the morning, we would bury our baby and life would have to move on.

But even with our Eddie returned to the earth, a part of me would never move on. Part of me would always remain with my baby.


*October 22, 1538*

After seeing the small casket placed into the family crypt, I did not think my life could possibly get any worse.

But it did.

A missive arrived for us later that afternoon, which made Edward's face pale by five shades.

"What is it?"

"Our good friends the Marquess and Marchioness of Exeter have been taken to the Tower." He dropped the letter, his hand falling limp at his side. "So has Lord Montague."

My throat constricted, and my back stiffened. My hand automatically came to my throat to play with the tight choker around my neck. "The Tower? Whatever for?" Oh, God, had they not relayed all they knew about the would-be usurper, Reginald Pole?

Edward just shook his head. I rushed over to where he stood and picked up the letter with trembling hands.

The king's enemy, Reginald Pole, had finally been captured and questioned at length, although he had somehow managed to escape—a clever rescue by the pope's hounds. He'd confessed that his brother Lord Montague and Henry Courtenay, Marquess of Exeter, had supplied him with funds and kept him aware of the King of England's movements. Accusations against our friends of treason against the king.

*Lies!* Pole sought only to burn those who had given their allegiance to King Henry instead of himself.

Did not they know the man would lie? He had nothing to lose! Reginald Pole already knew his brother—Lord Montague—was working against him. He probably knew the pope's men would save him, too. He may have been a man of God, but he was not acting virtuously. The pope sought to put Pole on the English throne—as His Holiness would then be once again in control of England and its inhabitants.

Perhaps Pole and the pope had even orchestrated his capture only to tell of his brother's and the Exeters' treachery—to turn the king against those who betrayed Pole. Murder was what it was! The pope was a clever and devious man. How could one brother turn on another so? How could he throw innocent people under the executioner's ax?

Then again, how could I even ask such a question? Montague had been informing the king of Pole's movements, via Lord Exeter. And brothers were pitted against their brothers all the time—even in biblical times, Cane and Abel had fought one another. It was all quite simple, really. The king was a puppet master, and we all his puppets.

"I must see her." I could not imagine Gertrude stuck in that cold, dank tower. She would starve to death.

311

"Anne, you cannot!" Edward boomed. I startled, eyes wide as I looked up at him. I had never heard him shout at me so.

I stepped back, gritting my teeth. "Why not?" I demanded.

"Shall you be imprisoned as well? Never do you associate with a traitor. Never!"

"But they are not traitors!" They'd been betrayed... My insides revolted, but I swallowed down the bile. How horrid it was that we lived in a place where those who were innocent would be thrown to the dogs for the sake of propriety.

"Perhaps not, but no one knows otherwise. They are in the Tower, Anne. And this is not the first time. Death comes to those who enter the Tower. The king will either see them executed or let them on the streets only to strip them of their titles and banish them from England. Lady Exeter shall share your confidence no more."

I was stunned into silence. Gertrude had been such a means of support and friendship to me. How could I possibly *not* offer her my support and friendship in her hour of need? I had only one other friend... and he, *I* had abandoned. As Anthony's image floated before my eyes, I had a sudden realization that he, too, had been trying to capture Pole. Was he also imprisoned and Edward did not want to tell me? I certainly could not ask him.

"I see the look in your eyes, Anne. I know you well. I forbid you to have contact with her. Did you read further? I am to assist with the investigation and the trial. It is a test from the king to see if I can do it. To see if I am so attached to them that I shan't find them treasonous. Their fate is almost sealed, even if God knows they are innocent."

"Edward, you cannot!" My stomach burned, my knees wobbled. I found a chair but could not sit, instead, clutched the back for support, my fingernails biting into the wood.

"Have I a choice?" Edward's voice was filled with anguish, his arms spread out, questioning.

"Present the truth, show their innocence."

At this, Edward only laughed. "Read the last line of the missive, Anne. It is in His Majesty's own hand."

I flipped to the next page, my mouth dropping wide. *I trust, Edward, that the outcome of this trial will be exactly as it should be, and I put all my faith and trust in such a loyal servant as yourself to see that it is so, and that an example is made of that whosever has challenged my authority and sought to assist those who are already known to be treasonous. If you find the results to be thus, then I shall know you are truly humble and loyal to your sovereign.*

I felt the blood rush from my face. Felt it as it careened through my veins, down my arms to my fingertips — making them tingly and numb. Felt it rush down to my belly and twist it all up in knots. My knees grew weaker, my toes numb. If Edward did not find Exeter and Montague guilty, then he himself would be imprisoned. He had no choice.

The king was a monster! He cared not for justice, only wished to set an example. When had the compassionate and magnificent monarch turned to a vicious and cruel man? Any semblance of humanity I had seen in his eyes on the death of his beloved wife was now gone.

And our friends as good as dead. We'd be next.

*January 9, 1539*

I was still at Wulfhall for my mourning period — my intent to stay through the birth of the next Seymour baby, although I am unconvinced it will be the case. The king was slowly being persuaded by Cromwell, or rather badgered, to take another wife. He still kept 'Nan Bassett as his bed partner, but my sister-by-marriage Elizabeth Cromwell had informed me she heard the king himself gave the senior Cromwell the go-ahead to begin searching abroad for a wife who could form a powerful alliance.

I had yet to converse with 'Nan myself, but through Beth I made my wishes known. The poor girl, 'Nan, wrote me a letter soaked with her own tears, to which I replied that as soon as I returned to court, the hunt for her spouse would begin and, as I had promised her, she would be well-matched.

The days went by slowly, and I slept most of them. My young sister wrote a letter with her condolences for the loss of my babe, as did nearly every female of my acquaintance. Their words meant well, but each letter I crumpled and tossed into the fire. I needed no reminders of my loss.

Edward did his job on finding Henry Courtenay guilty. Came up with a whole new traitorous charge, the Exeter Conspiracy, likened to the Pilgrimage of Grace. I was wholly disgusted with the entire mockery. But, somehow, perhaps because of my arguments with him, he had been able to see Gertrude spared.

Today was the execution day.

Lord Montague and Lord Exeter would be two bodies short of their heads soon. The sun had risen already, and I sat in silence in my solar, gazing out at the horizon. The baby kicked in my womb, but I took little enjoyment in it — indeed none at all.

When the clock chimed eight times, the axes would swing.

The sounds of horses' hooves clopping over the gravel drew my attention. Who would be arriving here so early in the morning?

I stood and smoothed my skirts over my belly, which had just begun to round, and went down the stairs to the great hall.

"Beth!" I gasped as Edward's sister flung open the door and hurried in, the fur of her hood falling back, cloak and thick skirts swinging wildly about her legs.

"Anne." She came forward and grasped my hands in hers. They were cold. A few of her servants filed in behind her and then quietly disappeared, save for one maid.

"What is amiss?" I searched her face, waiting for her reply.

Beth removed her cloak and handed it to her waiting maid. "You must come back to court. I did not sleep all night for need of having a word with you."

I breathed a deep, resigned sigh, my stomach twisting. "What is amiss?" I asked again.

"The king, he has agreed for Cromwell to begin the search for a new wife. He has already begun writing letters to France, Belgium, Spain, and several German duchies."

"Why must I come then? Why is this bad? I received your letter telling me thus. At least we have not a Howard to compete with."

"But 'tis just that. The king is not happy about marrying abroad and for an alliance. He wishes to marry someone light of heart whom he can make merry with. He has been depressed for so long now and misses Jane terribly. He needs someone to take away that pain, not someone to remind him of what he had."

"How do you know of all this?"

"Anne Bassett."

"'Nan?'"

"Aye. She's taken to confiding in me now that you are gone. I confess I have not the heart for it, as you do."

I rolled my eyes and signaled for a servant to bring us refreshments. "Trust me, I have not the heart for it, either."

Beth nodded, her brows drawn together in annoyance. "She is such a drain."

"Indeed." I paused, chewed on my lower lip. "I must confess to you, dear Beth, I am not ready to return to court. I only just buried Eddie a couple of months ago, and my new babe is due to arrive in just over four months. I am more inclined to stay here and let things take their course."

Tears burned the backs of my eyes with just the mention of Eddie. I could not recall the last time his name had left my lips. Still, the pain of his passing was raw, and calling him by name felt as though someone had poured vinegar on my open wounds. The world was still dark and dead to me. No light filtered through. Everything was bleak, and I honestly believed it would never be bright and sunny again.

I pursed my lips just thinking about what my mother had said when she had visited me this past month. *Stop wallowing, Anne. Babies are born, babies die. You'll make another.* So cold. Her words had made me shiver. I'd never asked her before, but now I wanted to know. How many of her babies had died? There was only me and Lizzie. My father had had two sons previously, but by my mother had had only one babe with him, and then only one with Sir Richard.

"What?" Beth looked at me, her mouth open a little, arms stretched out, exasperation written all over her features. "Take their course? This coming from a woman who has worked behind the scenes to change the face of England and its people by the wave of your hand?"

"I would not say all that, Beth." I waved away her words, as if the simple action would truly rid me of them, and glanced at the wall, the crack in the plaster was still there, and had gotten larger. Life was getting away from me.

"You may not, but I am not the only one who has said it. Come back with me." Then Beth played the card she knew would work with me. "Gertrude is in need of your confidence. She has been let out of the Tower, as you must know, and resides in her London house."

Still, I played coy. "She has not written me as of yet."

"She has only just gotten out yesterday, in order she might have a front-row seat at today's proceedings. You do know what today is? Come now. You cannot stay here forever. The Countess of Hertford is good for court, and court is good for her."

Slowly but surely, Beth wore me down.

I would go back to court for a few short months before returning to Wulfhall to deliver of another Seymour child. But I should never let this babe steal my heart as swiftly and solidly as my first babe. That was, if I were even capable of loving another again.

# CHAPTER TWENTY-TWO

*And though some lust to love, where blame full well they might;*
*And to such beasts of current sought, that should have travail bright;*
*I will observe the law that Nature gave to me,*
*To conquer such as will resist, and let the rest go free.*
*~Henry Howard, Earl of Surrey*

*Eleven months later…*
*November 27, 1539*

Anne of Cleves. I smirked as I thought on it. Yet again, *another* Anne. Could not a mother come up with another name for her female child? Anne, Elizabeth, Mary, Katherine and Jane. The most popular female names at court. For those of the male persuasion, Henry, John, Edward and Thomas seemed to have been quite in abundance.

*Hmm.* I supposed I was not one to question seeing as how my second child — thankfully, taking after my likeness so his parentage would never be questioned — was also named Edward, Lord Beauchamp, although we called him Beau. Perhaps the future queen's mother had had an Anne before she'd borne this one.

Furthermore, had my mother?

The future queen was German. Had there ever been a German queen on the English throne?

"Sister!" Michael strode up to me, one of the only men left in my life who could still bring about a real smile. "There you are. I've been looking all over for you."

"Whatever for, Michael?" I slid my arm through his, partly because he'd offered it, and partly because I'd wanted to sink against someone. Michael had been gone from court for nearly a year, traveling to foreign courts for the king. My own Edward was gone constantly now, fighting in the north, fighting overseas. He was the commander of the king's armies along with Norfolk and Suffolk, an instrumental man in the protection and future of our great country and His Majesty. At one time I might have missed him. I might have been saddened by his length of absence, but I no longer had such feelings. I was still numb to the world. A floating shell. My confessor feared I would become embittered toward life forever more if I did not warm outwardly soon. I did not care.

"I have just heard word." He leaned in close to whisper. "Anne of Cleves will be in England before the month is out!"

"How perfectly marvelous for His Majesty," I said dryly. From what I'd heard, the future queen was slow-witted, boring and ugly to boot. However, the king's own personal secretary, Cromwell, and the ambassadors he'd sent to the Duchy of Cleves, swore on their own lives and the blood of their mothers that she was beautiful, intelligent, and loved all sorts of courtly entertainments. I hoped they all rotted for their lies. The king would soon see the error of it. I'd tried to warn him through Edward, but he would not hear of it. The painting Hans Holbein had sent was delicious, he said. Delicious as a forest mouse skewered on a stick, if anyone were to ask me. I pursed my lips and tried not to roll my eyes.

"Why are not you excited? Once he is married, you will have a new queen to serve. More to do at court."

"As I live and breathe, Michael, that is exactly what I was hoping for." My sarcasm was lost on my brother, who was more often than not these days simply enamored of my position as aunt to the prince and heir to the throne.

"How is Shelford? I am sorry I have yet to visit." The king had bestowed Shelford Priory on my brother for his service, and Michael had built a lovely manor home there.

318

"No bother, I am hardly there, although my wife decorated it, and soon we shall see our first child born there."

"That is lovely. Tell me when you return, and I shall endeavor to visit."

"You would be most welcome." He kissed my forehead. "Oh, I forgot to ask, how is the little one doing?"

"Little one?"

"Beau, your babe."

I was stunned silent for a moment, as I tried not to think of how the baby was. As soon as I'd borne him, I'd thrust him away. The little pink swinging arms and legs had threatened to hook my heart again, and I just could not bear it if I lost another one. "He is doing just fine."

"Are you all right? You look a bit pale."

"Perfectly well, Michael. Go along now. I see your wife over there beckoning you."

When Michael turned to see where I'd pointed, I slipped away, only to be stopped by someone gripping my arm.

"Anne."

*Surrey.* I wrenched my arm free. The familiar heart-stopping, gut-wrenching turmoil filled me, as it always did when he was near. Surprisingly, through my numbness, anger burned outward.

"Do not. Speak. To. Me." I managed to get the words out through bared teeth and no growling.

"My lady, please." His voice held a hint of remorse, his eyes pleaded.

I would never show him mercy. "What is the meaning of your imprudence?" I snapped. I had no time for the man, not in this lifetime, no matter how doe-like he made his eyes. He was an evil, vile, disgrace to the human race.

"I wish to dine with you."

I lifted my chin, hands balled into fists at my side, and let out a short bark of laughter. "I have other arrangements. Mayhap you may ask me again... *never.*"

"Anne," he sighed, hands out, imploring.

"I have not given you leave to use my Christian name, *Lord* Surrey."

"If we cannot be civil, then you must at least know it is truly important that I speak with you."

"Civil? Do you recall our past, Surrey?" I leaned closer and glared at him more fiercely. "That of my sister?"

He had the audacity to look confused, then nodded.

"And have you nothing further to say on the matter?"

"I am a changed man."

"Changed? I doubt it. You were cruel to me when we first met and cruel to me still. Cruel to my sister and countless others, I have no doubt. Think you I have forgotten any of the evil things you have sought to do to me?" I tried to keep my voice low, but people were beginning to look our way.

An unusual interest clouded in his eyes, and I could not for the life of me determine what it meant. "You are just as likely to be stubborn, as a horse's ass will still shit in the morning."

I blinked several times, not really quite certain I had completely heard correctly what he'd just said to me. "Are you referring to me as a horse's ass?"

"For the love of God! Just let me inform you!"

Anger burned within me. I wanted to beat this man about the ears with my shoe, like I would to be rid of pestilent vermin. "I would rather eat my dinner from said *horse's ass!*"

"Anne, this is for the good of the Seymour family."

With those words he had me. I could not allow my stubborn pride to get in the way of goodness for the Seymours. Ugh! How it irritated me that I had to concede! My mouth tasted bitter. "Very well, then. But I shan't be seen with you in public. We shall dine in my apartments tomorrow evening."

"I look forward to it."

"I do not. My guards shall surround me."

"I shan't bother with ravaging you, my lady. Do not forget I've already tasted the flower, thorns and all."

Bile rose in my throat, and I wanted so very badly to spit in his face. But I refrained. "Have you? Hmm… Mustn't have been too—" I looked him up and down, "—impressive, for I have thoroughly erased it from my mind."

320

Surrey only smiled cruelly, for he no doubt saw straight through my ruse. "I shall see you on the morrow. Pleasant dreams, Countess."

My lip curled up involuntarily into a snarl. "Try not to die before we meet again." With that said, I whipped around and stalked away, head held high. Lord, how I despised the man!

"You wound me with your words, wolf."

His words faded away behind me.

Before I could escape the great hall, whose walls felt more and more like they were caving in on me, the king's voice rang out above the crowd. "Countess! Lady Anne! Come hither!"

I pasted a smile onto my face, the skin feeling stretched and taut, and walked through the parted crowd to where the king sat upon his throne chair, larger than life, and looking like a fat cat who'd found his rabbit dinner divine. I tried to not to think of my friends whom he had murdered. I tried not to think of how much I detested his very soul. Instead, I thought of Jane, of the young prince, of Edward.

As always he was dressed to impress in a deep-blue velvet doublet with silver threads and pearls sewn into the ornate embroidery. One leg was tossed casually atop the arm of his throne chair.

I heard tell the men of his bedchamber joked that the privy chair he used was also called a throne. How could one man still insist on being levitated so much, even when he took a shit? I suppressed the urge to roll my eyes, and even took a moment to chide myself. I'd become so jaded and bitter over the last year. It was a wonder Edward came home to me at all.

"Majesty." I bowed before him and kissed his offered ring—a large ruby inlaid with gold and diamonds. His fingers had grown even thicker, like fat stubby sausages. When we'd first met so many years ago, they'd been long, strong, slim. Now they just looked fat and short, his jewels digging deep into the skin. Was it possible for him to even remove the rings?

"Do you miss your husband overmuch?" he inquired, which jarred me. The king really could not care less about his subjects' feelings.

I decided to answer him honestly. "I miss him, Majesty. Perhaps not overmuch, but the lack of his presence is somewhat uncomfortable."

He leaned in close, his nostrils flaring as he looked me up and down. A chill of fear skittered over my spine. So far, I had been able to avoid the king's attention. Why did he appear to take an interest now?

"I am also lonely," he drawled. "And in need of...more womanly attentions than what I've been getting."

"Shall we dance then?" I asked, pretending not to understand what he meant. Why was I being accosted by men this eve?

The king laughed, and his head fell back. "Indeed we shall."

He stood and hobbled down the few steps to stand in front of me, his eyes twinkling. "You know what I meant. You are no fool. A clever one you are." He took my arm and placed it on his and began walking me about the room, his limp beside me worse than usual. "I find dancing will be too tiresome. Cards?"

"Yes, Majesty, a pleasure."

We sat at a table, and Henry dealt out the cards.

"Had we never met my second wife, we may have taken a liking to you," he said, placing a card on the table.

I counter placed my own card. "I am flattered, Your Majesty, but I was already married to Edward."

He chuckled. "We would not have had to marry you, although a pleasure it would have been, for certes."

"You are too kind."

"And you are too proper." He sat back in his chair, swallowing hard. His gaze settled on my face, his eyes linking with mine. I was suddenly uncomfortable. The king and I had shared so few tête-à-têtes, I was unclear how to react. "Would you have married us?"

I sat there, blinking. Feeling like a fish out of water, a doe staring at the bow, cocked and ready. "Yes, Majesty."

"A very proper answer." He leaned forward. "But why? Tell me why, Anne? Jane loved me for me. Katharine even loved me for me. Anne loved the crown, and yet before my new betrothal was arranged, I could not find a woman to marry me, and I am the King of England!" The end of his words were bellowed, and I jumped a little in my chair.

"Please, accept my apologies for shouting. My leg pains me overmuch this eve." He dismissed his own formal language of referring to himself as "we" and "us."

"No need to apologize to me, Majesty, as I am forever your servant."

"Escort me to my room?" he asked, tossing all of his cards onto the table.

I nodded solemnly. Perhaps by the time we arrived there, his leg would hurt too much for him to want to do further with me.

As we walked out of the great hall and down the corridor, I could hear the whispers of the people. Even if I did leave his chambers right away, they would all think that the king and I were having an *affaire*. But perhaps, I realized, this was what the king needed. His body was breaking down. He was getting older. He was no longer the lithe, youthful, energetic king of old, but a sallow, fat, moodier version. He had just been rejected by dozens of women across Europe who had not even met him. His self-confidence was now obliterated.

I could have been cruel, but that would only have earned me the blade. I had somehow managed thus far to remain in the king's good countenance, and for God's sake, I was going to remain there.

"Majesty, if I may…"

"You may, Anne."

"Any woman who is worth anything will see that you are a charming, enigmatic man, who feels deeply and is capable of loving greatly. They will see this beyond the crown. They will love you, for you. Just as Jane did. The ones who turned you down were half-wit ninnies. 'Tis why they were still without husbands. You should be lucky none of them will call themselves your wife. You deserve a woman of substance."

"And Anne of Cleves shall be. That is what I've been promised."

"As you say, Majesty."

"Have you heard nothing of her?"

And here was where I lied... "Nothing at all, except what has been relayed to you. She will be quite pleasing for you."

"Contracts have been signed. She bloody hell better be."

We reached the door to his chambers, and he walked through, but I hesitated.

"Goodnight, my lady. Sleep well." He turned away and began bellowing to his groomsmen to assist him with his leg.

I turned away silently and meandered down the corridor to my own chambers as his men surrounded him. A good night's rest was what I needed, for tomorrow's eve, I would do battle with Surrey.

*November 28, 1539*

What had I been thinking?

My legs shook so that I could not sit still, but neither could I stand. My fingers trembled, and from the look of my face in my handheld mirror, I was five shades paler than usual.

Footmen stood every few feet, a dozen in all, around the room. But still, I had not faced Surrey, essentially alone, in several years, and the last time, I had been nearly unconscious when I had.

His knock on the door echoed loudly and slowly through my anxiety-ridden brain. *BANG! BANG! BANG!* Not unlike the sounds of the cannons as they fired from the Tower.

"My lady?" a footman asked, awaiting my direction.

"Bid him enter," I said, my voice chilled and clipped.

I did not stand, for I did not feel that Surrey deserved that from me. Instead, I sat rigid in my seat, face blank of expression, wineglass in hand. He sauntered in as if he owned the place — and considering that his cousin had sat on the throne, however short it had been, he had once been very close to ownership.

"Lady Anne." He turned a leg and bowed low to me.

I refused to bow to him, my stomach already threatening to spill all over his boots. "Surrey. Come have some wine, eat. Tell me your news." I did not waste any time getting to the heart of the matter. The sooner he left, the better.

Lord, how I wished I had the clean air of Wulfhall, the freedom of the grounds to race my horse at breakneck speed. 'Twas what I needed right now, solitude. But I was not to get it, not with the arrogant cad standing in front of me.

"How courteous you are," he said sarcastically.

I ignored his negative response and continued to sip on my wine, waved the servants over to put the food on the table — roasted goose, rosemary potatoes, fresh bread and roasted carrots.

I nibbled on the food as best I could, my stomach filled with what felt like a large rock.

"Will you make me wait until you have stuffed yourself, or did you come here to give me information?" I asked, drumming my fingernails against the polished wood of the table, knowing as though Surrey only wanted to be closer to me because of how close I was to the crown, and because he'd never ridden himself of the bruised ego he thought I'd given him.

Surrey finished chewing, swirled some wine, and his eyes connected with mine. He set down his glass and reached toward me, and I inched back, but he grasped one hand in his, the other able to escape. Three of my footmen stepped forward, but I waved them back.

"Unhand me."

"But I cannot, Anne." His thumb stroked the top of my hand. "Do you realize that every day I see you and you are not mine, a piece of my heart is torn from my chest?"

"I have no time for deceit or mockery, Surrey. If the only reason you came here was to seek some sort of sordid relationship with me, you have come to the wrong place. I have no need to repeat any mistakes I have made in the past, no need to relive them."

"Right you are about mistakes. I was so young, deep in my cups constantly. But I have changed since then. I have grown into a man. And yet you seek to punish me still."

His words only served to anger me further. There were places for a man such as him, bedlam, hell, an oubliette. "There is no excuse for what you did. You are what you are, and I do not recall you being deep in your cups on several occasions."

"Very well, then. I see we are never to be friends." He pouted.

"Not the type of friends you seek. But 'tis beside the point. Did you have nothing else to say to me?"

Surrey looked disappointed. He shook his head slowly.

"Did not you say you had something to inform me of concerning my family?"

He shook his head, his countenance triumphant. "I said such only to get you to accept my invitation and my solicitation of your friendship. I see my tactic worked."

I breathed out a disgusted sigh. "Typical of you, Surrey. There are plenty of women around court for you, including your *wife*. Do not bother me or my sister again. I bid you goodnight."

I stood to leave, but he gripped my arm as I tried to brush by. Again, my footmen stepped forward, but I shook my head for them to let me handle it. "I said, goodnight."

"I heard you, you vicious bitch." His voice was low, threatening. His grip on my arm tightened, and he yanked, pulling me down. "Do not fuck with me." Even as he spoke, the clatter of the footmen's boots on the floors as they rushed forward filled the air. "You and Edward are going down. See, I have a new friend. Tom and I are like this." His fingers hooked together, and then my men were upon him.

One slammed his fist into Surrey's jaw, while the others lifted him, lugged him to the door and literally tossed him out of our apartment.

But he would not go without final words. "I never touched your precious sister, Anne! Deceit runs rampant on wicked tongues!"

His parting words, shouted as the door closed, punched me in the gut, and I sucked in air, unable to breathe.

"Are you all right, my lady? Shall I fetch a physician?"

"I am fine." But I was not. I was shaking. I was terrified. Had I truly been deceived by Lizzie, my mother, and Page? Did the blossom that was my sister belong so truly to the stem? Had the roots of their sordid and twisted minds wrapped their way around her young mind and heart so thoroughly that she could seek to use my weakness against me? What had been their purpose? Or was Surrey lying? I should think he was, but there was something so raw in his tone... It sparked a light of doubt in my mind.

My stomach rebelled, and the food I'd barely tasted came back up with a vengeance. I rushed to my chambers, barely having enough time to slam the door, before the contents spilled into the wash basin.

Keep your alliances close and enemies closer... My family was the enemy. And we had so many.

We were in a bad spot. Who was friend and who was foe?

And Tom, too? Surrey had said as much months and months ago, but I'd brushed aside his tales... But now he'd said it was so, yet again. What to believe?

How many enemies would we make? Our alliance had dwindled so low... Henry Courtenay and Lord Montague both dead...

I cleaned myself up, ignoring the murmurings of my men beyond my bedchamber door, and began penning letters. One to Edward to inform him of the threat, one to the Duchess of Suffolk — my most powerful female friend in our faction. Now was the time to reach out to the new Earl of Shrewsbury, as poor George had passed the year before. His son would be on our side, as his father had been.

After writing my notes, I felt more confident. Tom and Surrey might try to start trouble, but Edward and I had some big hounds on our side, too: the king, Suffolk, Elizabeth Cromwell and her new husband, Gregory Cromwell, the Lady Mary, the church, Anthony and most of the other men of the privy chamber.

Even if you tossed Catherine Parr and her hateful brother into Surrey's ring, we could still stand strong.

A smile crept over my lips as I recalled my conversation with the king yesterday. Cromwell was the instigator in his upcoming marriage to Anne of Cleves. From what I had gathered, and I was almost certain my sources were correct, this marriage could be what toppled Cromwell to the ground — and then into it.

If Surrey could be linked to that...

Then there was my family, who'd used me so cruelly... For them alone, I would have to seek a punishment worthy of their crime, and such an action would take time on my part to plan.

*December 25, 1539*

327

"Sister, I must confess something to you on this most holy day." Lizzie stared up at me from where she sat beside me at the trestle table for the king's great Christmas feast.

"What is it?"

"I fear I have done you wrong. If I could take it all back, I would, I swear it."

I set down my utensils and stared at Lizzie, my countenance void of any reaction. I had an idea of what she was about to confess — and I feared for the hearing of it. Would Surrey's own admission come back to haunt me?

Lizzie glanced around the table. Mother and Page were deep in discussion with several other courtiers.

"Tell me now before they notice we whisper," I urged, a false smile on my lips.

"They made me do it, Anne. They made me pretend that Lord Surrey had ill-used me."

I nodded, squeezed her hand gently. "I had my suspicions, and I thank you for telling me."

"You are not mad?"

I took a long sip of wine, trying to quell the burning rage inside me. Mad did not begin to describe the level of emotion surging through me.

"No, dear Lizzie. You did the right thing in coming to me."

"All right." She pressed a hand to her chest. "The thought of having lied to you has weighed heavily on my soul."

"As it should. Lying is a sin." And I was definitely a sinner.

*January 10, 1540*

"Anne, I've just come from speaking with the king," Edward said, his countenance almost giddy.

"What about?"

"His unhappiness with Anne of Cleves."

I smiled. Poor girl. I hoped she did not end up on the scaffold... but she had been the object of Cromwell's plans and Cromwell had to go. Of late, he'd become more and more cocksure and had even begun to tell the king and his Privy Council what to do. He had his own objectives and sought to rule as king himself—if only behind the scenes. If anyone should do that, it should be my Edward, Uncle to the prince, the future king.

"The girl is rather drab. Not at all as his ambassadors have described her, and the painting Holbein created could be another woman altogether," I said casually.

"Indeed. When I arrived, I asked the king how marriage fared for him. He turned a glare so fierce on me, I actually took a step back. His Majesty was enraged. He started shouting, 'She is nothing so fair as she hath been described to me. I like her not! She reminds me of a Flanders' mare, and her smell is worse! I have been lied to, tricked! Her brother, the Duke of Cleves, seeks to fight against the Empire and expects me to fight as well. And I will not! I want nothing to do with it. Find a way to get rid of her, annul the marriage. I have not seen fit to bed her. My cock forbids it!'"

"Oh, dear me." I could not help but laugh. "So Cromwell, he will bear the brunt of this."

"Oh, aye. But there is some news which shall displease you, Anne."

"Pray continue." I tightened my belly for the blow. I hated bad news. I turned to look out the window, hoping to catch a glimpse of something sweet.

"He has asked to be introduced to another woman."

Oh, Dear Lord in heaven... "Who?"

"Katheryn Howard." His voice was quiet. "Norfolk's niece."

I whipped around to face Edward. "No!"

His lips were pressed together in his own show of disappointment. "Yes, but believe me, we shall work it to our own end." He could not seek her to wife after setting Anne of Cleves aside.

"You are damned right we shall. That girl is low-born and ill-bred!"

"Well put, my love. And who better to point such out than you? His Majesty favors you more than others, tell him what you think of her. And put someone else—a Seymour—under his nose."

I recalled the young silly blonde I'd met whilst visiting the dowager duchess some years before. There'd been nothing to impress me then, besides the beauty of her face. "The silly chit will more than likely get herself into trouble, if she hasn't already."

"Do not worry overmuch. I am seeking to unearth the girl's background. We shall hold a few secrets of our own. The king desires another wife, Anne. We've held him off long enough before Anne of Cleves, he's not likely to follow that road again. There will be too much conflict soon among our foreign allies, and he grows moodier by the day. The rejection seems to him something more of a personal nature rather than the political, as it should be. He needs a woman — a wife — he can fuck whenever he wants and another heir to take the tension away from him. A woman with no interest in politics, which is why, I believe, the Howard girl appeals to him."

"Our own Anne Bassett has been doing just fine with the fucking." I had never been successful in finding anyone in Edward's family more pleasing than 'Nan.

"I asked, even though I know you'd sought to find another. But since he's already sullied her, he does not see fit to marry her. "

"'Tis highly hypocritical." The king once again disgusted me with his egotistical self-righteous attitude.

"I agree, but he is the king. And he had a good point. If he were to marry 'Nan, then he'd be sending another message similar to the one that went out like wildfire when he married Anne Boleyn. He wants his next wife to be virginal when they marry."

"Is the Howard girl?"

"Not hardly, but he has no clue. She will be easily manipulated. Unless we can find someone else quick, she is a good alternative. I'm fairly certain the king has already made up his mind. I'm starting to warm to the idea myself."

And when the king's mind was made up, there was hardly any way to change it. "Edward, this will be dangerous. If they marry and she bears him a son, all we've worked for can quickly come unraveled. Besides that, from what I've heard, she's worse than Anne Boleyn. Just as his marriage to Anne of Cleves is backfiring on Cromwell, his marriage to the Howard girl will backfire on anyone who supported her."

"No, Anne. I've learned much from you, my cynical wife."

"And, do tell, what pray have you learned?" I folded my hands in front of me.

"I shall work to convince him not to marry her, all while pushing him to the altar. When he looks back on it, he shall see only that I told him not to. I have become quite the master at manipulation."

I laughed and crooked my finger at him. "Kiss me, Edward."

"I see you are pleased," he teased.

"Most pleased."

Edward kissed me soundly, leaving me wanting more — but a child in the womb was not something I was even remotely interested in.

"Let us away to the great hall. There is another feast to celebrate this farce of a marriage to Anne of Cleves."

"Let us make merry with the Flanders' mare!"

But I also had another reason for desiring to attend the celebration. You see, revenge was so very sweet, and mine was about to come to fruition. Mother, Page and their little darling would feel the brunt of my wrath, and God willing, I should never have to deal with them for as many days as I had left to breathe on this good earth.

We entered into an unreal world.

The past two years of court life had been so full of dreariness, dank, dark, that my senses were completely assaulted when we entered the great hall. Candles were lit nearly everywhere: sconces, chandeliers, freestanding candelabras, candelabras on tables, candlesticks. It was nearly as bright as if it were a May morning, instead of an evening in the dead of winter.

The music was loud and jovial, echoing off of the stone walls. Flutes, shawms, lutes, drums! The musicians, who normally played out of the way upon the loft overhead, had meandered down to the crowd and weaved their way in and out — almost like a tournament in the great hall.

People shouted and clapped, their voices ringing out as they played at cards. In the center of the room, bordered by a circle of people — dancers! Female dancers, ladies of the court. And King Henry and his new wife, Anne of Cleves, sat upon their thrones. The latter had a peaceful smile on her face, but confusion etched about her eyes. She was not used to such goings-on. The king, however, was what drew my attention. His face was ecstatic, his pallor bright, his eyes twinkling again. I hadn't seen him so happy since he sat upon his chair beside Jane. I followed his gaze to a pretty little blonde, front and center, who danced and swung her hips. She smiled winningly at the king with each twirl — teasing him, inviting him.

So it was true about the Howard girl, for she looked like a Howard, and just like the girl I had met some years before. *Katheryn*. Almond-shaped eyes, creamy skin — she and Mary Boleyn could have been sisters, more so than Mary and Anne. The only difference was Mary's look was more innocent, pure enthusiasm, whereas Katheryn's was Anne's seduction. A perfect combination of them both — no wonder the king was enamored. Would he sleep his way through the Howard family?

"Look Edward, there she is." I nodded my head toward the dancers.

We walked in slowly, inclining our heads in greeting to several courtiers. I followed the crowd, seeking out my relations, and spotted them, the three of them, clustered together and, in fact, having a heated discussion. A cruel smile formed on my lips.

I glanced toward Edward in time to see his gaze fall on Katheryn Howard. "Working her charms already."

"I best make friends with the new queen. She looks lonesome."

"The Lady Mary is with her."

As he spoke it, Mary Tudor walked up beside her new stepmother and placed her hand on her arm. Queen Anne inclined her head and smiled sweetly. Those two would be good friends — they were only a few months apart in age as it was. I was also surprised to see little Elizabeth, the king's second daughter, was in attendance. She sat on the step of the dais by her stepmother's feet, a pretty little red-haired thing, of six years. She toyed with her long red locks, curling them around her finger. From afar she had the look of a Tudor — reminiscent of the king's sisters — but up close, she had her mother's eyes. Dark, sharp, intelligent. She would be a formidable woman one day, unless some man was able to take her in hand.

"Let us go and greet Their Majesties," Edward whispered. "And then you shall make your acquaintance with the young Howard girl."

I nodded as we made our way forward. I spotted Anne Bassett in a corner, where she sulked. It was best I implore King Henry for a match for the girl soon. She'd been thoroughly used up and, thank God, Anthony and myself had both provided her with the information long ago that she needed to keep herself from becoming with child. Then again, she'd held the king's fancy for so long, I might have to let her suffer a bit longer.

"Majesty," Edward said, and I followed suit as he bowed and I made a low curtsy.

"Edward and Anne!" the king exclaimed, his gaze momentarily jolted from the fifteen-year-old Katheryn Howard.

"My Lord Hertford, Countess," Queen Anne said in her thick, German accent. "How good to see you again."

She looked genuinely pleased. If only the king had not had so many complaints about Anne, and there weren't so many political reasons to get rid of her... She was rather sweet, despite her long, dour face.

"Edward, come, I must have speech with you," the king said. He stood and bowed to his queen and daughters and then to me.

Once he'd gone, and I must say I was entirely burning with curiosity for what he had to say to Edward, I turned to curtsy to the queen and bid Lady Mary a good eve.

"Are you enjoying England, Majesty?"

I glanced toward my mother. She and Sir Richard still appeared highly agitated, and the little vixen looked worried. Good.

Anne of Cleves laughed a little, pulling me back to her. "From what I've seen so far, 'tis a beautiful country." She leaned down as if to speak to me in confidence. "I like it much more than I do my own country. They are so, what you say? Stuffy? Yes, stuffy, where I come from."

I could not help but smile at her words. Lady Mary laughed as well.

"Stuffy? How so?" Mary asked.

"For instance, my brother would not allow anyone to see me or my sister, and then only with a veil. We do not play cards at court. We do not dance. There is not much laughter or music. Not like here. Here, 'tis like a celebration every day."

"'Tis because we are so pleased to have you here, Majesty," I said.

Lady Mary nodded. "I think we shall be very close."

"I pray such is the case," Anne of Cleves said. "But—"

She cut herself short, and Mary and I both exchanged a glance.

"What is it, Your Grace?" Mary inquired softly.

"I do not think the king is pleased with me. I am afraid... afraid of what might happen to me," she whispered.

"Why? You are most pleasing, I assure you! Do not even speak of it," Mary said incredulously, her hands coming to her throat. Horror shone in her eyes, and I could almost see her thoughts, her visions of sweet German Anne standing on the scaffold.

Anne of Cleves looked taken aback, nervous. Regret shimmered in her eyes for having whispered the words.

I took her hand in mine and squeezed gently before letting go. It was a bold move to make, but since I fully intended to be as close with her as Mary was, it was the right move—even after she was gone from the throne, she would be a useful ally to have had. Queen Anne squeezed back.

"Majesty, if I may?" I said quietly.

"Yes?"

"Do as the king wishes. For your happiness, and... safety." It was the only piece of advice I could give her, and most likely when the time came, if she followed it, it would save her life, for after speaking with Edward, I could already see this marriage would end one way or another, and I hoped it was with Anne of Cleves walking away alive.

Just then a great commotion filled the center of the great hall— and right in the thick of it was my mother, Page and Lizzie.

"What is this?" the queen mused, worry etching the corners of her eyes.

I looked on, silent.

Mary spoke, "Lady Anne, is that not your mother?"

"Aye, 'tis," was all I offered.

The king's guard filed into the hall and surrounded my family. A twinge of regret filled my chest, but I could not allow such feelings to take root. They had used me cruelly. They had played on my insecurity and, worst of all, their ruse had fooled me utterly.

"Sir Richard Page, you, your wife and your daughter, Lizzie, are hereby arrested in the name of the king!" a guard announced.

Page's eyes, sharp as a hawk, flicked toward mine. I answered with a smile, one that was just as mean-hearted as the ones he'd flashed me often enough. He would know I'd done this to them. He would know that I had not taken kindly to being made a mockery of.

"On what charge?" Page shouted. My mother and young sister wrung their hands together, my sister with tears running over her cheeks.

"Treason."

*Three days later*

At my suggestion, my dear sister had been given over to Lord Surrey, who would now be her guardian, and she would serve as a lady's maid to his wife.

My mother and Page had once again been stripped of their titles, exiled from England and have ceased to exist to me, slinking back into whatever hole they'd curled up into when last they'd been banished from court.

Although absolved of the false charges against them, the king had had much reason to suspect that they would indeed try their hand at their machinations again and thus had thought it best for them to leave the country, or suffer death.

I had been quite careful in preparing the case against them, intercepting letters here and there that were perfectly harmless but could be used against them. Snatching snippets of conversation and paying witnesses of such conversations to say they'd heard them—a simple matter of misconstruing facts, for weren't such misunderstandings the basis for which assumptions were created?

I must say I'd truly hoped Edward would find them guilty, but believing me to be upset by their arrest, he'd found enough to question their guilt, and so the exile. No matter, I had established my place once more and never should the likes of Sir Richard Page or my mother bother me again. And, if I was lucky, placing Elizabeth in Surrey's house, while he might not have defiled her before, he would attempt to, I have no doubt.

# CHAPTER TWENTY-THREE

*And as a falcon free, that soareth in the air,*
*Which never fed on hand nor lure; nor for no stale doth care;*
*~Henry Howard, Earl of Surrey*

*April 17, 1540*

"The bastard was made Earl of Sussex today!" Edward stormed into our presence chamber.

"Who?"

"Cromwell, the leach!"

Now I was interested, not to mention extremely irritated. "What? How is this possible. The king hates him."

"You know how Henry is. Keep thy friends close and thy enemies closer."

I popped the last flower into the vase and put it on the sideboard, unable to finish the design. "But what of Anne of Cleves?"

"The king has still not consummated his marriage to her, at least 'tis what they are both reporting. He has tried. He has lain with her naked. However, he confesses he cannot form an erection with her."

"Anne of Cleves says he only kisses her mouth, her breasts, touches her *there*, but has not yet done the actual deed." I crossed my arms over my chest, tapped my foot, my mind already scheming how to set things to rights.

"Huh," he grunted and flopped into a chair, waving over a footman to give him wine. "I found out something today which shall help in his downfall. Anne of Cleves was previously betrothed to another. Said betrothal was never officially broken. We now have a cause, besides the non-consummation, to formally annul the marriage."

"Perfect. He's still completely infatuated with Katheryn Howard as well. But when he is not looking at her, I still catch his eyes on Anne Bassett. He still desires her, perhaps not for marriage, yet... The girl has asked me several times now to arrange a marriage for her. Her mother is beside herself, she claims. But I say posh! We still need 'Nan."

"You are right, my lady wife. Right now she is the only stock we hold — besides the prince — and we need to keep her clean and clear of a husband, at least until the king no longer desires her."

"Although..." I tapped my chin, deep in thought. "The king often wants what he cannot have. What if we started *talking* of negotiations?"

"Clever woman! We shall talk only, nothing will come of it, but it will satisfy the girl and her mother. The king will naysay it, of course, or perhaps set a date much further into the future."

"I shall go and find the perfect groom." Which, of course, meant someone King Henry would never want her to marry.

*June 10, 1540*

All of our careful plans had fallen into place.

Cromwell had been arrested and the king had disregarded each potential groom brought forth for Anne Bassett.

Edward paced the room in his excitement, even bit his knuckles. "Suffolk, myself and the king's guards stormed into Cromwell's house in London, where he sat penning letters and drinking ale, nipping at biscuits. His sons were there — Gregory, of course, stared at me with hatred, which I suppose will trickle down to my sister, but I shall make it right for her!"

I stood up from the chair I had been sitting at working on my embroidery, something I did more and more for peace and quiet. I poured a cup of wine for myself and offered one to Edward, which he grasped as he continued to pace, sloshing drops over the side onto my new Turkish rug. I frowned and glared at him, but he didn't notice, so embroiled in his retelling was he.

"'What's this about?' Cromwell shouted, fighting as the guards gripped his arms and yanked him up from the table. They brought Suffolk the letters to look over, and I myself was able to walk straight up to his face and say, 'You, Cromwell, are hereby stripped of your title, and stripped of the Privy Seal. You are no longer to refer to yourself as the king's secretary. I hereby place you under arrest for treason, in the name of King Henry VIII.'" Edward took a large gulp of his wine, yet spilling more on my rug. "You should have seen the way his eyes bulged from their sockets. He sputtered and denied it, of course, but even as he did, Suffolk nodded to me and stuffed the letters away for safekeeping."

"And what of the seal, shall you carry it?"

"No," he said bitterly. "You recall Anthony Browne?" He eyed me warily.

My heart lurched. How could I have forgotten him? So much time had passed since… I gritted my teeth. I would never admit how much I missed him.

"Browne's stepbrother, Fitzwilliam—Earl of Southampton—shall carry the seal."

"A poor choice." And indeed it was, but at least the seal would be kept within our own faction, and not by someone who associated themselves with the Howards. My mind wandered at the reminder of my lover. Where was Anthony? What was he doing? Did he miss me?

"For us, yes, but I've fought with the man before, served with him in Calais. He's a good soldier, a good politician."

"Maybe in France, but here in London?"

Edward set down his goblet and turned to me, suspicious eyes on me. "Well, there is nothing we can do about it! I am surprised you were not privy to the information beforehand. Do you not correspond with Sir Anthony?"

I swallowed. Edward had only ever hinted at my relationship with Anthony being *friendlier* than he'd have liked. I had had nothing to do with Anthony since the time I had mistakenly taken him to bed, and possibly conceived a child for it. A child who had eerily changed from my likeness to his with each passing day, for that matter.

"I have not spoken to him in quite some time, Edward."

"No?" Something flashed in Edward's eyes. Disbelief? Mistrust? Maybe hope?

"No."

Then anger flared in Edward's darkened eyes. "Do you deny you fucked him?" The words were barely audible.

There had only been a number of times I had ever seen Edward so angry. My eyes widened. I took a step back. I'd never truly feared him. He was a man of honor, but with the crazed look in his eye, I was no longer confident. What could I say?

And now I had to lie. Had to make him believe my betrayal was not true. "Never." As the word slipped from my mouth it tasted as bitter as Edward probably felt—as bitter as I'd felt every time I watched him saunter off with another woman. But I could never tell him the truth.

Edward blanched as his gaze roved over me for the span of several minutes. Each tick of the clock was like a bell tolling my execution. He'd call the guards and have me arrested for adultery. Toss me in the Tower and preside over my trial himself. Declare me guilty. Watch my head roll.

"I believe you." His voice was strained. He turned around and walked toward the large window in our room. The one I liked to sit at and watch storms in the night.

My relief was so acute my knees threatened to buckle. He believed me? Did he truly, or did he only want to? What had caused him to ask? He must have seen that Beau looked nothing like himself. Most likely, he saw the other man every time he laid eyes on the child.

Then he spoke, his voice cracking slightly. "Do you care that your baby is well? That he reached his first birthday last month with nary a sniffle? He is vibrant with dark, curling hair." *Hair that at birth was golden as a daisy.*

"I've heard." I turned away from Edward, hoping he would just go away. I could not have this conversation. Could not think about my boy. Every time I did, Eddie came to mind and then my heart broke all over again. And every time I looked at him and saw Anthony, I felt sick to my stomach. Had Edward guessed that? Was that why he questioned me now? I took a goblet full of wine and downed it, wishing to be as drunk as Edward.

"Yet you send for him not, nor deign to visit?"

"I cannot," I murmured, and sat down, my wine close, to continue with my embroidery. If I ignored Edward, he'd leave me alone. At least, I prayed he would.

He was not going to leave. Edward came to stand in front of me, one hand on his hip, the other pushing my embroidery aside. "You must."

Tears pooled in my eyes. "I cannot, Edward. Not yet."

Edward threw his hands up in the air, exasperation clear in his countenance. "You lost one boy, Anne. Yet, you gained another. God saw to it to give you back your boy, and you shun His generosity."

"I shun pain," I bit out. Shame filled me, for I knew what was right, but I could not do it. I was too selfish.

"Do you remember little Eddie calling out your name? He knew you. He died. Now you have another Eddie, one *you* call Beau. Does he call you Mama?"

Tears pricked my eyes, and I clamped my jaw shut. How cruel of him to even ask. He knew the answer. Beau did not know me, would not pull my face from memory. He hadn't seen me since he was only a few months old. No matter that I had his portrait sent to me every few months since then. I could not speak. I just stared back at my husband, my voice blank. If I tried to tell him how I felt, my voice might not work.

"I have to go," Edward said, his look of contempt now joined by disgust.

I took a deep sigh. "Where are you going?"

"North."

With that, he walked to the door, opened it and then slammed it behind him. Not so much as a goodbye. He did not even bother to grab his things. Was he really going north? I had long since given up trying to get him to remain faithful to me, and my heart was a block of ice that never seemed to melt. I did not really care where he was going. I walked to the window and looked out. Suddenly, I was overcome with emotion. I did not want to have a heart of ice. I wanted to love and be loved.

I crumpled to the floor and cried. The first time I'd cried in more than a year, since the loss of little Eddie. I cried until the sun fell below the horizon. I cried until there were no more tears left and my face hurt.

I turned away my sister-by-marriage, Beth, when she presented herself, and instead crawled into bed to sleep until the morrow.

For the first time in nearly two years, I longed for Anthony's loving arms around me. But not only Anthony, I longed for the surety and comfort of Edward's embrace. The one he'd given me when we'd first married, and the first year to follow. I craved to hold my babies in my arms, to rock them and sing sweet lullabies.

But what's more, I realized, I *had* longing. I was beginning to *feel* again. And with such a realization came one question: Did I give credence to my longing, or build a steel cage around my ice-filled heart?

*June 24, 1540*

We sat in the queen's chambers, sewing shirts for the poor. Mary was next to the queen, and I on her other side. I had not seen nor heard from Edward. He was still angry at me. But I had found out he'd worked on business and not some other woman's body. And I had yet to give into any of the desires I'd allowed myself to explore.

The quiet solitude of the chamber was suddenly broken by loud banging on the door. The king's guards entered the room, followed by the king himself.

Anne of Cleves dropped her shirt, winced as she stuck herself with the needle, and then quickly stood, her head bowed to Henry.

"Anne of Cleves, do you deny that our marriage has *never* been consummated?"

Her head shot up, as did all of ours. My gut clenched tight.

"No, Majesty." Anne's voice was barely a whisper. The ladies around her stiffened, as did she. I swallowed hard, having known this was coming. Was this what Edward had been doing?

"Will you quietly leave this court and swear to God that we have never been married?"

"But..." Anne's lips parted, her eyes wide and filled with fear. I could see her eyes moving, and she gazed at each of his guards and then back at the king. Mary gripped my fingers. "Say it, woman!" the king bellowed. His fist slammed down on a nearby table, upsetting a vase, which spilled flowers, water and all onto the waxed wooden floor.

Anne of Cleves did not even blanch. "I will swear it."

"Louder," the king demanded.

"I swear it!"

A guard handed the king a document that he unrolled and placed on the table where the vase had been. "Sign this document."

"What does it say?" Anne stepped closer to the table and leaned down to read what was written. I itched to move forward with her to see its contents.

I allowed a brief glimmer of hope to inch its way inside my chest. Could he truly just set her aside? Let her go?

The king's countenance changed suddenly to doting husband. He pressed his hand to the small of her back, leaned into her, smiled. "It is the document which shall annul our marriage, sweetheart, for we have never consummated our union, and you were already legally betrothed to another." Syrupy sweet was his voice, but his words were full of threat. He pressed a quill into her hand. "Come now, rid us both of this farce."

Tears pooled in the queen's eyes. She blinked rapidly, presumably to keep them at bay. "But I do not want to marry another," she choked out. Then the tears did spill, and she raised her hands quickly to wipe them away. "I do not want to return to my brother!"

My mouth fell open. Did she wish to die? To raise her voice to the king? She was becoming hysterical. He'd offered her life! I wanted to shout, *Take it! Take life!*

A chance that three wives before her and countless courtiers had not had. Sweat trickled down my spine, pooling at the base. My throat itched to scream. I couldn't watch another person die.

With the pad of his thumb, Henry swiped away a tear she'd missed. "If you do this," he said solicitously, "you shall never have to marry again. From this day forth, call yourself my sister, and I shall set you up a nice and pretty in a castle all your own, with more money than you could know what to do with."

I wasn't the only one whose mouth fell open. Who was this man that stood before us? For certes he was not the angry, volatile man we knew. Was it possible he actually cared for this uncultured woman—for he was not the only one. Her sweetness had captured us all.

"You will?"

The ladies all sucked in their breath, myself included, mostly shocked we would not have to accompany our queen to the Tower. Would not have to cover her hair or place her in a coffin and mourn her alone.

"I swear it," he said. "We are friends you and I."

A smile curled the queen's lips—one I had never seen before. Was it possible this was her true smile? She looked so... *happy.*

Henry smiled back and pushed the document closer to her. "Sign it, sister."

"Thank you, Majesty!" She scribbled her name on the document and, then shockingly, hugged the king.

He squeezed her back, twirled her around to the shock of everyone in the room.

It was the oddest display I had ever seen. And I'd been at court a long time, where just about anything was bound to happen.

Despite the jovial atmosphere—and abundance of relief—Henry was only paving the way for a new queen. And who would that be?

My heart skipped a beat and I grew faint, for it was almost certainly going to be Katheryn Howard.

*July 9, 1540*

Today was my birthday—I was thirty years old.

Today also marked the day of Anne of Cleves and Henry VIII's official annulment. They were no longer married. Anne of Cleves was now styled the king's beloved sister, given Richmond Palace and Hever Castle, a generous stipend and invited to attend court quite often.

But what's most special about this day—she was alive! There was never any talk of her death. Never any talk of conjuring up suspicions.

She had written me a letter. I'd already read it three times, but I should read it again. I'd never received a letter quite like it. The words had moved me beyond measure.

*My dearest confidante—Lady Hertford,*

*I cannot begin to thank you enough for your friendship and kindness which has meant the very world to me. You have given me my life, and for such I shall be forever grateful to you. You realize that, do not you? You are like my godmother, a guardian angel. For it was when we sat at court, and I so sad and lonely, you gripped my hand, and said to have no fear, only to do as I was asked. I have done that, and now I shall live a great life, with much happiness. But the point is, I shall live, and I owe my good fortune all to you. You are a brilliant woman, and one whom most see as vicious and mean-tempered, but not I. I have never seen such, Anne. I have only ever seen the Angel Anne. My friend.*

*With much friendship and love,*

*Anne – Beloved Sister of Henry VIII*

No one had ever thanked me personally for how I had affected their life. I had never saved anyone's life, either, and while I did not literally save her, I had had much influence on it.

Another chip of ice broke off of my heart, melting its way down my chest. Perhaps this beginning of the thirty-first year of my life would be a good one.

I looked up from the letter as the door to my chamber opened slowly, and Edward walked inside.

"Edward." His name hung on my lips in the silence that stretched out for moments.

He looked wretched. Deep purple marred beneath his eyes. More silver laced in his hair, lines deeply etched around his eyes and mouth. He walked forward and knelt at my feet. He looked up at me imploringly, gripped my hands in his, kissed my fingertips. "I am sorry, Anne. I know how much you loved Eddie. I loved him, too. I was so mad the day he died, I cut the children I had with Catherine out of my will... not that I believe they are mine to begin with."

My heart warmed at his confession and the sincerity in his voice. "You never told me."

"I did not want you to judge me."

"I have never judged you, Edward."

"Let us fight no more. I've suffered miserably while away."

"We shan't." I tilted his head up and kissed him lightly on the lips. Tears streamed down his cheeks, and I kissed those away, too. His hands came up to cup my face, his tongue swiping over my lips.

Our kiss deepened, fingers groped, until finally Edward lifted me in the air and took me to my bedchamber, where we made love for nigh on the rest of the day. The longing I had had ever since his departure slowly melted away. I felt love. I felt the strength of his arms around me.

My heart melted a little bit more.

*July 28, 1540*

An execution just after sunrise and a wedding before the noon meal.

How like the Tudors.

Cromwell was dead, yet we all celebrated King Henry's marriage to the teenage bubblehead of a girl at Oatlands Palace. I would have much rather celebrated the death of a man I despised and what his death represented. For we had nothing to celebrate with a Howard on the throne — save for, God willing, our prince would still be king.

Katheryn Howard was annoying. There was no other way to put it. My eyes could not remain focused for want of rolling into the back of my head whenever she was near, or within earshot. She laughed constantly, and so much so I was reminded of an insane person... cackling was how it sounded. Did she learn it from a jester?

All she desired to do was dance, dance, dance. Dance and sing and play. She wanted to try on dresses, pick out fabrics for new dresses. Style her hair thirty different ways each day.

She was tiresome. I'd begged Edward — on my knees — to not have to serve as lady-in-waiting to the imp, but he'd said I must. It was the only way to get rid of her. Thank God, I was not the only one who could not stand her. Lady Mary was equally disturbed by the young and unintelligent girl. She was no gentle lady, although she played well at it — it was only playing. From the moment the doors closed, she flopped around like a country scullery maid.

We had set our spies in her household, and I'd done myself a favor and made certain Jane Rochford was also a lady-in-waiting. She, in the last few years, while still extremely irritating, had calmed a bit, as well. We simply did not speak to each other. But I did have an agenda, and Jane's big mouth was going to do me a world of good.

I was more than determined to see this marriage ended. The silly chit was not worth a lick, and the Howards could all go to the devil. Unfortunately, Catherine Parr was also a lady-in-waiting, and I found it hard at times not to scratch her eyes out.

For now, I stood in the great hall, sipping on wine and trying to figure out how I could escape this place.

"There you are." Elizabeth Cromwell sidled up next to me. I still felt guilty when I looked at her, that Edward and I played a large part in the demise of her father-by-marriage, but she had not held it against us, despite her husband being severely enraged. "Are you not enjoying our new and... pretty queen?"

"I find her sublime," I said sarcastically. My eyes searched out 'Nan Bassett in the crowded great hall. She was dancing with Katheryn Howard. Whatever jealousy she'd first felt had all dissipated. Perhaps she'd realized the fate of a queen was not how she wanted to end her life, or perhaps the few names I had listed as possible grooms had sought to ease her mind.

Beth laughed. "I hear you went to visit Beau."

I stiffened. "Yes." After Edward had come to me on bended knee, we had gone together to visit Wulfhall and our baby, and in so doing, the ice had melted clear off half of my heart.

"And all is well?" Beth's gaze searched over the crowd. She seemed distracted this evening.

"He is a beautiful boy." And healthy, robust, and oh-so-sweet, and the one whom I would stake my claim, for when I held him in my arms, the distinct vision of him wrapped in royal robes filled my mind's eye. "He took to me right away. It was pleasing."

"I should like to visit with him. I hope to soon provide him with a cousin." She rubbed at her belly and turned to face me.

I gripped her arm, eyes widened, excited at the prospect. "Are you with child, Beth?"

"I believe so!" Her voice was filled with girlish excitement, and I felt myself being caught up.

"I am so very pleased for you! When do you think the babe shall arrive?"

"The midwife says about Christmastime or the first of the new year."

"Marvelous!"

"Mayhap I shall be back at court in time to help the new queen with her own birthing."

"I doubt you'll need to come back so quickly... There were rumors the king and she have been romping like springtime rabbits since the beginning of this year, and she has yet to conceive. With all of the issues he had with Jane, and then not being able to consummate his marriage with Anne of Cleves... No, you shall not worry on it. I have doubts he can become fully erect anyway."

Beth gasped and then laughed. "But does not he dabble with Anne Bassett?"

348

I snickered. "Aye, but she does wicked things no gentle woman would do, and no queen would dare."

"Oh, my! I am most intrigued." She gripped my hands in hers. "Do tell."

"We shall whisper about it on the morrow. Perhaps a walk in the gardens. I've a need to go into the maze and remember better times."

Just then the new queen rushed up to us, a wide toothy smile covering her entire face, laughter bubbling from her lips. "My ladies-in-waiting! Come dance with me!"

She grabbed our hands and yanked us to the center of the great hall, where she proceeded to swirl and twirl, not even remotely in time with the music. She grasped a goblet of wine from a passing footman and downed the contents.

Beth and I exchanged triumphant glances and continued on with the dance.

This queen, poor child that she was, would topple like those before her.

# CHAPTER TWENTY-FOUR

*While that I live and breathe, such shall my custom be,*
*In wildness of the woods to seek my prey, where pleaseth me;*
*~Henry Howard, Earl of Surrey*

*October 25, 1540*

"I suppose you are happy," Jane Rochford sneered. She walked toward me, her gait a little off. She stumbled but quickly righted herself.

"Happy, Lady Rochford?" I stopped in the corridor before my suite, thoroughly exhausted from months and months of feasting, celebrating, dancing and drinking entirely too much wine, yet utterly intrigued by the lady before me.

Jane Rochford tossed her head back and laughed, but it was not a joyous laugh, rather one 'twas bitter, filled with cynicism. "So good at masking your emotions you are, but do not try to pretend you did not know. You of all people know exactly what happens at this court, sometimes even before it occurs."

"Enlighten me, Lady Rochford. You yourself are quite a formidable woman," I purred convincingly. The evidence was clear the woman had had one too many glasses of thick red wine, and judging from the circles under her eyes, she hadn't slept at all since

Katheryn Howard had become queen. It suddenly occurred to me how very much alike these two women were, and yet how very polar opposite, too. Both sought to be away from the real world, to live in a fantasy, because real life was just too painful. Yet, Katheryn was sweet and simple, and Jane was bitter and vindictive. I'd once compared myself to this woman, and the similarities I still saw between us scared me.

She hiccupped and leaned a shoulder on the stone wall. I stepped forward to pull her away from the flame of a sconce from which her hood was only a breath away, but she swayed forward, righted herself, and ended up fixing the problem on her own. "'Tis true, I am! How good of *you* to notice. You are not one to normally dole out niceties and compliments." She eyed me suspiciously.

"No, I am not. But when one is deserved, why should I keep it to myself? Just like you have something of interest to me. Why keep it to yourself?"

"You speak in riddles. It's giving me a headache." She pressed the back of her hand to her forehead.

"Come then, let me take you to your bed, and you can tell me about what I do not know. For, how fortunate you are to be privy to such information." I offered my arm and steered her down the opposite corridor toward her own apartment.

"We cannot all be in the right circles, Lady Anne, or is it Countess?"

"Either is perfectly acceptable to me. We are, after all, close acquaintances, are we not?"

"Close?" She bit out with a short laugh. "I suppose we have shared the same cock..." At this, she broke into a fit of laughter again, doubling over and losing her balance. "I said 'cock' to the formidable Countess Hertford. I shall doubtlessly be flogged!" She looked up at me in surprise, as if she'd thought for a moment she'd been talking to someone else.

Perhaps she was more than just drunk but going mad, too. The notion had merit... I resisted the urge to strike her.

"Very well, I shall tell you," she whispered.

We reached her room, and she opened the door, pulling me inside with her. I helped to strip her out of her gown and into a night rail as she babbled.

"Queen Katheryn lived at Lambeth with the Dowager Duchess of Norfolk — her step-grandmother — before coming to court, so she might gain a proper education. You see, she is from the poor side of the Howard family, nothing more than a scullery maid, really."

*Funny, I had thought as much.*

"When she was just a wee girl, coming into her own, she says, maybe twelve or thirteen summers, her musical teacher began to touch her... What was it she said? Ah, yes, *the secret parts of her body.*" Jane leaned a little too far to the left, and both of us went nearly tumbling to the ground. She laughed and righted herself. "She enjoyed it so much, she allowed him to do it at each lesson, even taking the time to touch his parts, as well." Jane eyed me as she splashed water on her face.

I kept my expression blank, not wanting her to know any of this information was new or even remotely interesting. When she finished splashing more water onto the floor and the front of her night rail than her face, I indicated for her to come sit down so I could plait her hair. "Do go on," I mumbled.

"Well, the duchess did not supervise any person in her household and cared little for her wards. The queen says Henry Manox was diddling half the girls there. A right harem he had going on."

"Henry Manox?"

"The musician."

"Ah." I nodded feigned non-interest and continued to plait her hair.

"Yes, well, that went on for a couple of years, and then she got married!"

"Married?" Shocked at this, I stopped braiding her hair, but I quickly regained my composure.

"Well, not really, but she and this other fellow, Francis Dereham, the secretary to the duchess, would walk around Lambeth calling each other husband and wife. They would go to bed together at night, sometimes with clothes on, and sometimes he would remove his hose." Jane giggled like a young maid of honor hearing about the deeds between males and females for the first time. "You know what that means… But the duchess caught them one time and promptly ended the affair. Katheryn Howard says she did love him, though, and wished they had been married in truth."

"Is that so?" Perhaps my voice was filled with a little too much disdain.

Jane turned in her chair, horror-filled eyes wide. "What have I done?"

"Nothing you have said is something I would not have found out soon enough. Your secret is safe with me…for now." I twisted a ribbon onto the end of the braid of her hair. "Off to bed with you. But you shall continue to report what you know to me… To keep such secrets of the queen is treason."

Jane nodded, her throat bobbing up and down as she swallowed hard. I left her like that and walked quietly from the room.

My plan was falling perfectly into place. Now I just needed to bide my time. The lusty Kitty Howard for certes would want to fill her bed with a lithe young man as she had for years. A fat, stinking, old man—as King Henry had become—was not the type to soothe the appetites of such a girl. I was nearly certain, she would attempt *something*, and soon.

*February 5, 1541*

I only had to wait a little over three months for Kitty Howard to make a mistake.

"Norfolk certainly does have a way with picking queens, does not he?" I walked from my own bedchamber into our solar, where Edward was drinking tea and eating biscuits to break his fast.

He looked up at me, interest flaring in his eyes. "What do you mean?"

I sat down in the chair next to him and took a sip of tea a footman had poured for me. I waved the servants away, who bowed and curtsied and then left.

353

"Girls who themselves are their own undoing. The queen, our lusty, playful little imp, is sleeping with none other than a man of the king's own privy chamber."

"Who?" Edward put down the missives he'd been reading and leaned toward me, eyes filled with light and curiosity.

"Thomas Culpeper."

"Culpeper. Really?" Edward looked confused for a moment. "Now that you mention it, I do recall him eyeing the queen rather peculiarly the past couple of weeks, and he does appear to be eager in stepping forward to deliver messages from the king to her."

"Guess who arranged it?"

"Good Lord, woman, why?" Edward slammed his teacup down, the clatter so loud I thought for certes he'd shattered the delicate porcelain.

"What?"

"If the king finds out you've —"

"Edward, really, you must know me better! It was not I who arranged it." I sat back and pouted for a moment. Edward looked visibly relieved. "Jane Rochford was the imbecile."

A slow smile spread on Edward's lips. "And how fortunate for us she did."

"Exactly. I have had the distinct impression over the last several months that she may actually be going mad."

"Mad, really?" He raised a skeptical brow.

"Mmm...hmm..." I slid my hand up his arm. "She often talks to herself, and George."

"George. Her late husband, George Boleyn?"

"One and the same."

Edward's eyes hooded, gazing at me with sensual interest. "What are you going to do with this information? We have to tell His Majesty."

"Yes, we do need to tell him, but I say let us wait it out. There is more... She has had sexual relationships with at least two men prior to marrying Henry, one of whom she has told Jane Rochford she entered into a pre-contract with. Let these men be found, for when you inform His Majesty of her affair, she can use the fact that she was already pre-contracted to simply annul the marriage as was done with Anne of Cleves. I would not want another death on my hands."

"And what of Jane Rochford?"

"I shall convince her to go to a nunnery. If the two men come forward, we shall have such proof, and then I am confident we shall find another who knows of this affair."

"Good thinking, wife. Very good indeed. Keep your eyes and ears open, and keep me informed. I shall keep the knowledge secret for now. Let us pray Henry does not get wind of it before then."

"You must take care the queen and Culpeper are discreet—more than discreet!" I hissed at Jane Rochford in the privacy of her chamber. "Have I made myself clear?"

"Yes, my lady."

"I will keep your knowledge and involvement, as well as this sordid affair, a secret. But you must swear to me."

Jane fell to the floor in a fit of hysterics. She gripped her neck and then her hair, yanking hard. Tears fell in torrents down her cheeks.

"He will kill me! Without a doubt! This is punishment for the lies I told of my husband! He never bedded his sister Anne. The king had her executed for no reason."

"Get a hold of yourself, woman. Only God can punish you for what you did to George. Now get up!" My fingernails dug into my palms, quelling my trembling at hearing the truth of her deceit.

She stood on shaky legs, kept clutching at her neck, squeezing so hard that red marks appeared.

"Keep yourself together and make certain no one catches wind of this, or sees their naked heaving bodies. People will begin to suspect even if they share a glance in the great hall. School her, Jane. She is nothing but a simpering girl, barely out of the nursery. She has no idea what she's gotten herself into, or who she's dealing with. She did not grow up with Henry VIII in her face, executing and punishing people left and right. It's all a game to her, and she just cannot wait to see what gift he'll give her next."

Jane nodded and swiped away her tears. "What of Catherine Parr?"

A bitter taste swept into my mouth. "What of her?"

"I think she might suspect."

"Tell the queen to ask Lady Latimer to read her a passage from the Bible. Have her do some charity work. No dancing for a day. The woman will cease in her suspicions."

"So easily?"

"Catherine Parr is very easy to manipulate and very easy to see through. She only stares at the queen with eyes like what you have seen because she thinks the young girl is a licentious sinner. Too much dancing, drinking and lusting after the king is what Catherine Parr thinks."

"As you say."

"Yes, as I say."

*August 1, 1541*

Six months of Kitty Howard's wickedness had passed unbeknownst to the king and now look who'd come calling... More rubbish from Lambeth, where the current queen was originally found. Joan Bulmer, a girl who had shared her bedchamber with Katheryn Howard, and subsequently her bed partners, had taken it upon herself to travel to court—unescorted and uninvited.

And she was only the first.

I was not the least surprised when Henry Manox showed up to begin playing his lute in the queen's presence chamber, nor when Francis Dereham was appointed her personal secretary.

What did surprise me was, did they all really wish to die?

Could they have been more stupid? Katheryn Howard was still meeting Culpeper in the night as well, and there were whispers now circulating about court. Dereham was even caught taunting Culpeper that he'd had her first. They were being reckless, flaunting their illicit, treasonous behavior.

Since when had the queen's bedchamber resembled a brothel? Anne Boleyn was accused of sleeping with a number of men, yet much, if not all of it, had been lies created to get her out of the way. This queen, she truly was sleeping with them all.

We had just arrived back from a progress to the north. The whispers of the queen's transgressions were so much so, I was dearly afraid the king would find out before our plans were settled. Before we could coach people on their answers.

I might not be able to save them now. Not with the complete idiocy they were displaying.

Thomas Cranmer, the Archbishop of Canterbury, had traveled with us to the north, and he had expressed his concerns to Edward. He'd said he wanted to investigate the rumors that had passed over his ears. Edward had asked if he would not let him do it instead, that he could be more subtle about it and coax the truth out of people.

I was scared, for the last time Edward had been asked to do something of this nature, albeit by the king, people had died. Death did not have to be the answer.

Thinking on such brought poor Gertrude to mind. How I missed her. She was as of yet unmarried and still shying away from public and court, should the king wish to change his mind regarding her fate and send her to her death as he had her husband. There was still a great hole in my heart from the friends I'd lost touch with over the last year. Even Anthony touched a place in my mind every now and then, even though he was absent from court, having gone abroad to work on the king's alliances in foreign courts.

'Twas too much to hope that I should ever be close to my friends again. At least not in the near future. If I had one.

*November 2, 1541*

"Praise be to God for allowing me to lead this country with such a jewel of womanhood at my side," Henry bellowed to the congregation before allowing Cranmer to take the podium and begin his sermon.

I closed my eyes, my head inclined toward heaven. *Dear God, let the king be merciful.*

Edward had given his report to Cranmer regarding the little *jewel*'s affairs. Here we were at Mass for All Saints' Day. When I opened my eyes, the service was over, and the archbishop stepped down from the podium and approached the king. He handed him a missive. I knew what it contained, and I wanted to reach out with every fiber in my being and snatch it back, because I knew the king would not be merciful. Kitty Howard had taken her behavior too far.

I held my breath, stilled my heart. It was a letter to the king containing charges of the queen's adultery. The congregation was beginning to file out, but Edward and I tarried, actually grabbing the attention of Suffolk and Shrewsbury, who pretended a discussion that was not necessary — for they, too, knew what the missive contained and wanted to see what would happen next.

The king did not open it right away but shared words with Cranmer, looked lovingly at his queen. Cranmer's face was somber. The king took note of his vassal's countenance, dismissed his wife, who had the audacity to pout and look hurt. She was whisked away by Jane Rochford at my nod. Then the king opened the letter.

Three score heartbeats passed... I could scarcely stand it. Then the outburst for which we'd been waiting with bated breath.

"A forgery! This is false! Who would dare lay such claims?" he shouted, his booming voice echoing in the rafters of the chapel.

Cranmer murmured something I could not discern.

Henry crumpled the letter and shoved it into his doublet, then he pressed his finger to Cranmer's chest and said something. Cranmer nodded. They both parted ways, and I quickly averted my eyes, pretending to be vested in the conversation. The king stormed from the chapel, his hand pushed out, warding off anyone who attempted to speak to him.

My heart beat a rapid staccato. This would not end well. The king had been thoroughly humiliated. He would not let Katheryn get away with this. He wouldn't have let anyone get away with it. I swallowed, but my throat was tight.

What had been done could not be undone. And, for certes, many heads would roll. Possibly even mine.

"I have had a visit from the archbishop." Edward slammed his way into our solar.

"And? What did the king say to him?"

"He does not believe the letter. Thinks someone is out to ruin his virginal wife. He ordered Cranmer to come up with glaring evidence, and so it is put on me yet again."

I placed my embroidery down, folded my hands in my lap, ready to listen.

"I do not think I can save them, Anne. I will try my best. I will use your idea of the pre-contract. I will have both the queen and Jane Rochford sent to a nunnery, but 'tis all I can do. They have brought this on themselves. No one can violate the laws and trample on the heart of the king, especially when that king is Henry VIII. Their actions have baffled me from the beginning. Do they wish to die? Is that what this is, a suicide pact?"

"Funny you should say such. I have thought the same thing," I mumbled, a cold block of guilt settling around my heart for all that I'd had a hand in this—for all the wrong that I myself had done. Anthony was never far from my mind.

"I shall have to place her under house arrest until the matter is settled."

I waved my hand in dismissal. My heart was already hardened to the idea. I was not sure why I'd ever conceived of being able to save the young girl queen. Henry was too proud and, when angered, too rash and impulsive. "Do as you must."

"Pray, wife. Pray that Jane Rochford does not share with the king that you knew of the queen's dealings. If such were to pass her lips, we would both walk the scaffold by dawn."

I swallowed hard, for what he said was true. But I had every confidence that Jane would not say a word. Not when she believed I would save her—that I was her champion if she kept her mouth shut.

Good God, but would she shout my guilt if he pushed her across the scaffold?

*November 5, 1541*

"They confessed. The king demanded a sword to thrust through Katheryn Howard's chest himself."

Edward came up beside me in the gardens. All the flowers were dead, but the air was crisp and ripe for a brisk walk.

"What of her ladies of the bedchamber?"

"They named who they thought was guilty, just as everyone else did. All the ladies were released and sent home to their families—except Anne Bassett, who has been allowed to stay at court. Manox, Dereham and Culpeper remain in the Tower. Broken both physically and mentally."

I shuddered to think what had had to be done to get them to confess. I listened to the sound of the gravel as it crunched beneath our feet. I breathed in deeply of the late autumn air. The tall oaks and maples were nearly bare, with only some still holding a few leaves of red, gold and brown.

It was only a matter of time before Katheryn herself would be taken to the Tower. We walked the rest of the way in silence before returning to our rooms.

A loud bang on the door startled us both as we took off our cloaks. Our footman answered, and in came a messenger.

"My Lord Hertford. An urgent message."

Edward stood, took the message and waved the groomsman away.

"Shall I return a message, my lord?" he asked, not heading out as Edward had directed.

Edward raised his head from the parchment he was reading and glared at the young man. "If and when I have a return message, I shall see it delivered myself. Away with you!" His voice ended on a bellow, and the young groomsman bowed and left quietly.

I was surprised at Edward's outburst, but we were both on edge, especially with Jane Rochford unknowingly holding our fate in her mad hands.

Edward returned to me quickly and thrust the parchment into my hands.

*His Grace, Prince Edward is ill with fever.*

Those were the only words I read. My eyes widened with fear. The cherubic face of my own dear Eddie sick with fever blinded my vision. My ears started ringing. My stomach boiled acid.

"I shall ride with the king at once to Hertford Castle. Stay here. Mind our affairs." With that, Edward was gone to the prince's side.

*Written on the seventh day of November, Year of Our Lord, 1541*

*My Dearest Wife and Lady,*
*Our sweet nephew is once again in good health. The Prince of England has proven his blood to be truly royal and slain the dragon called Fever. A more robust boy I've never seen.*
*Your humble servant and husband,*
*Edward, Lord Hertford*

I was grateful that the prince was well once again. I was grateful that our own nephew was the Prince of England. But I was bitter at Edward's words. They only reminded me of my poor baby who had not been so robust. Even worse, I could not know whether his words rang true for Beau, for I'd not seen him since that one time we'd gone together, nor had I bothered to read any of the missives sent by his nursemaids unless they requested money for clothes and other such needs.

I have been a cruel mother.

*November 12, 1541*

"Henry! Henry! Majesty!" The bloodcurdling screams of Katheryn Howard shook the stone walls and rattled the windows. A dozen guards escorted her physically from her chambers. "Let me talk to him! He will hear me speak! He will believe me! Henry! Just let me explain!"

She broke their hold and ran down the hall, people jumping out of the way. The guards chased after her, and I stood, eyes wide, watching the spectacle as if in a dream. For it could not really have been happening. The queen running down the hall like a mad woman? 'Twas impossible… and yet, she was.

"Henry!" she shouted. When she passed me, she gripped my shoulders. Her eyes were wide, bloodshot, her skin mottled. She shook her head back and forth, hysterical. "Lady Anne, help me. Please, *help me*. Tell them. *Tell them* it was nothing. Tell them I love the king. Tell them Henry is my heart."

But all I could do was just shake my head and peel her fingers from my arms. I felt cold inside. Numb. And underneath the cold and numb, my heart raced to clutch her to my breast, for she truly was a naïve child. The guards caught up to her, and she attempted to run again. But this time they took her by the arms and legs. Her head thrashed back and forth as she gnashed her teeth and shouted curses that could sting a whore's ears.

I couldn't move, couldn't take my eyes off the spectacle. Couldn't breathe. Couldn't speak.

Courtiers turned their heads, pretending not to hear, pretending they did not see the queen being carried down the corridor by four guards as she screamed, kicked and punched. Her face was red-blotched now, and her hair streamed in every direction. She was without her hood, which probably had gotten lost in the struggle. Her gown was torn, hardly the attire of a woman who could claim a queenship.

I had almost decided to come forward and ask the guards to let me calm her so she might regain her composure when Suffolk came into view.

"Lady Katheryn, have some dignity, my God!" shouted Suffolk, who'd been summoned to assist the guards.

"I am no longer lady but queen! I am Queen of England!" She gripped her hair and pulled hard. I was horrified by her insanity, for surely that was all it could be.

362

"No, my lady. The king has stripped you of such a title, and you are hereby arrested and to be taken to the Tower for your offenses against His Majesty."

But she was not listening. Just screaming again. And despite that she'd brought her fate upon herself, I sympathized for her. She knew she would die. She knew it was only a matter of time before she saw the fate of her cousin, the first Howard queen married to Henry — Anne Boleyn. And I knew no matter what I tried, I would not be able to help her calm down.

Even Jane Rochford, who'd taken to talking incessantly to ghosts and looking, but not seeing, what was around her, had left with more dignity when she'd been arrested nigh on an hour ago, not a word of my guilt on her lips. Thank God, Kitty had known nothing of my involvement.

The king was nowhere in sight. He ignored her calls for mercy, her calls for an audience, her pleas for her life. He'd heard enough already from those who would testify against her. There was nothing to save her now. I even implored her to admit a pre-contract, and I was not the only one, but she was so stubborn! In her mind she thought if Henry believed there was no pre-contract she would be saved... but that was before.

Now the king was an empty shell. The only contents within were his anger and prejudice toward women. "Why?" he'd pleaded to Edward two days ago. "Why should I be cursed with so many marriages, and none of them have lasted? Five times I've been married... and five times a single man again. I cannot endure it any longer. If I take a wife again, it will be someone to comfort me and be my companion. Send 'Nan to me tonight."

The sound of the queen's screaming reverberated in my ears, ringing there, staying, even though it'd been several minutes since the guards had dragged her away and she had disappeared from earshot. I turned and headed blindly down the quiet corridor to my chambers. I would pack my bags and head to Wulfhall today. I had a need for solitude. Perhaps a need to hug Beau and thank God I was still alive. I would never forget those sounds. I swallowed as I pushed the memory of her voice and pleas slowly away. Whenever I walked down this corridor, her heart-wrenching cries would haunt me.

If I were alive to walk them…

*November 23, 1541*

Had the king become a merciful man?

The monarch who'd been known for fits of violence, war, executing his closest advisors, and who could forget Thomas More, his onetime closest confidante… I crossed myself. He'd burned souls who read from a different book of religion. Torn down houses of God to prove he was the Supreme Head of the Church.

Now he might have grown a soft spot? How many times had I thought such…

Mayhap in his old age, he did not wish for another of his wives' death to be on his head. Lady Katheryn Howard had been stripped of everything and languished at Syon Abbey to wallow in poverty and tears, alone with her conscience and the memories of her various lovers. She wore a simple gown. No jewels, for Thomas Seymour had collected them. Even the ring she had given to Anne of Cleves had been retrieved. In all this mess, he did not bother me so. Surrey's threats about Tom appeared to also have been false as I'd not seen them, nor had my spies seen them, cavorting together. What had been reported, and of which I'd seen with my own eyes, Tom was growing closer and closer to Catherine Parr, which sent chills of dread racing along my limbs.

The late queen was questioned daily for a confession.

After being browbeaten and threatened, she still had not confessed to no more sins than she'd committed before marrying, and nothing thereafter and she refused to admit to a pre-contractual marriage to Francis Dereham. But it didn't matter for she had admitted a friendship with Culpepper and he had admitted her intended to sleep with her and that Jane Rochford had acted as a go-between for their assignations.

Jane Rochford rotted in the Tower. She had gone completely mad, foaming at the mouth, hurling curses at the guards. She urinated on herself and played with rats. She bit her fingers and arms and used the blood to paint hideous pictures on the walls. One rumor was she even used her own excrement to add to her artwork. I would have normally asked how someone could go mad, but I'd known Jane since we were both girls, and I'd watched the slow evolution of her mind as she'd gone from jealous little girl to hateful, vengeful gossipmonger, betrayer of trust and now a demented and broken woman. She would go to hell for the things she'd done.

Which scared me to my very core. Should I go to hell as well? Doomed to walk through purgatory for ten thousand years before descending into the flames? But Cranmer had said just this past Sunday that the Lord had forgiven our sins. And I'd paid double tithes to make it so.

Even still, I reached for the rosary sewn into the sleeve of my gown. I would pray today. I would pray until my knees bled. For I did not want to go to hell. I wanted to rise up to heaven to be with my Eddie and rock him for eternity.

*December 10, 1541*

Edward said he cannot put Jane Rochford on trial. She would most assuredly kill herself before the thing could happen anyway. But the king, he was past his moment of mercy. He wanted her dead. She had been a poison in his court, slithering through the crowds and biting anyone in her path, her venom ruining souls, hearts, and lives. Jane Rochford had confessed she had stood guard as Katheryn and Culpeper had made love in her room. She had spewed in the king's face how once when he'd come to the queen's apartments for the night and found the door barred, she'd kept him distracted while Culpeper escaped down a secret stair. She had sworn to anyone who would listen that it had been her idea, that she had procured the arrangements, she had been the go-between with letters.

I waited anxiously for her to place blame on me, but she did not.

From her actions, 'twould appear she was gloating and wanted to be the only one given credit. I had not the heart to stop her — nor the interest in signing my own death warrant.

Her words had shredded the ego of the king, and if he could have he would have drawn and quartered Jane Rochford himself. His physician had been sent to see her every day, and if for one second she had showed a lucid moment, she would have been ripped from her cell, given a hasty trial and beheaded on the spot.

There were two other people who could not vouch for the king's mercy, for he had shown them none. Dereham and Culpeper.

And here I stood on Tyburn — the grounds where so many were executed publicly.

Dereham was brought out first on a wagon, as he had been drawn, and his wretched limbs no longer worked, he laid in the cart. Blood, sweat and tears dripped from his face onto his stained and torn clothing. His head lolled back and forth. But his eyes were already dead. He did not see anything, and I prayed to God he did not feel anything either. I'd never seen a man so broken before, and I did not make a habit of attending executions. But Edward had said we must to show our support of the king.

The wagon stopped beneath the Tyburn Tree — the gallows in the middle of the square — the noose already prepared. He tried to stand, slipped and began to fall, but before he had completely fallen, the executioner slung the rope around his neck, and then, the carriage horse was kicked forward, the rope tightening around his neck as the wagon disappeared beneath him. He swung there, legs dangling, face purple, tongue thrust out.

I swallowed hard to keep from vomiting. After several moments, they grabbed his lifeless body, drew him away from the Tree and began chopping him to pieces — blood splattering on the cheering spectators. The king had ordered his parts to be dragged by horse to the north, south, east and west, to show those of the kingdom an example — no one slept with his wife and lived to tell about it. His head would be placed on a spike on London Bridge.

Next they brought Culpeper.

He was not so badly broken. He walked on unsteady feet. But even still the long weeks he'd spent in prison had ravaged his body. He was thin, his face gaunt, bruised, his nose crooked from being broken. His once-cocky swagger was not so confident. He stumbled once, but the guards caught him.

They brought him to the scaffold, the block still bloody from some other traitor's severed neck. He stared down at the blood, but there was no recognition there. He whispered something, or at least his lips moved like he might have been speaking, but above the shouts and huzzahs of the crowd, I could not make out the words. Everything started to move very quickly again. He knelt, put his head down, arms out, and the executioner swung his ax.

Culpeper's pretty head was thrust on a spike amid shouts. The executioner held the spike high, and people tossed their rotting garbage at it, hurled obscenities. I had a rabid disgust for these people. Life to them was a game. And this one's turn had expired.

Who next to lay down their cards? To be defeated?

There were not many cards left. It was almost over. What would the king do with Katheryn? Would Jane Rochford show a lucid moment?

I turned from the vulgar disparages of humanity and, with a straight back, headed to mount my horse. It was cold. My teeth were chattering. But I thought they clicked together more from fear than anything else. I was once again reminded how fragile life was, and as much as we tried, none of us were really in control of it.

And, the greatest fear of all—there was still one person alive who knew of my involvement. My encouragement. Lady Rochford. My future, my life, was in the hands of a woman I despised.

# CHAPTER TWENTY-FIVE

*Where many one shall rue, that never made offence:*
*Thus your refuse against my power shall boot them no defense.*
*And for revenge thereof I vow and swear thereto,*
*A thousand spoils I shall commit I never thought to do.*
*~Henry Howard, Earl of Surrey*

*January 21, 1542*

They were going to execute her.

A bill of attainder had been passed that made concealment of past sexual relationships of a queen consort, as well as committing adultery, treason and therefore punishable by death.

"Edward, you have to let me see her." Guilt ate away at my insides. I thrust Beau back into the arms of his nurse and walked to the hearth on the pretext of warming my hands. Wulfhall was so drafty in the dead of winter.

"Why, Anne? 'Twill only sadden you. You were never close with the girl. Why would you wish to see her on death's door? She will be executed in three weeks. 'Tis over, leave it alone."

I turned around to face Edward, who was eating a late dinner after arriving to tell me the news. "But there must be something we can do! I told her to admit to a pre-contract. Why hasn't she done so? If only I'd not encouraged her and Jane Rochford."

"Anne, there is nothing that can be done—even if she were to suddenly admit to a pre-contract. The king is set on having an example made of her. His ego is bruised and he wants revenge. She acted as a harlot. Whether or not you told her to, she was wicked before you ever met her. Was it your idea for her to write a letter to Culpeper stating how her *heart would die* if she could not be with him? I think not."

I shook my head, chewing on my lip, pacing the length of the great hall. I gazed at all the tapestries of great Seymour accomplishments and portraits of Edward's family and ancestors.

"Then you must let me see Jane Rochford."

"Do you wish to join them in death? Do you wish to be buried with your head held in your hands?" He stood abruptly from the table, upsetting his goblet of wine. I watched the dark ruby liquid seep between the slats of the wooden table and onto the floor. The dripping wine, so like blood dripping on the scaffold, only emphasized his words. "Forget about court for now, Anne. Forget about the king, his wives and his children. Forget about our position. Forget about our rank and growing the coffers for our children. Just for one moment. Think about your family, me. We need you. Not them."

He came to stand before me, lifted my chin with his fingers and leaned down to place a kiss on my lips. I closed my eyes and let the warmth of his mouth on mine seep through me. I tried to let the worries of every day slip away. Some of the guilt melted off my shoulders, and I opened my arms to Edward, to the love we'd once shared. How long ago it seemed we'd fallen for each other. How long ago it seemed I'd relied on him for support. I ran my fingers up and down the muscles of his back.

"Let us forget together," he breathed. I nodded, and he took my hand, leading me up to my bedchamber.

He stripped me slowly of my clothes, kissing my shoulders, kneading the tight tension-filled knots until I was loose and languid. My body sang from his touch. I gave in to his supplication, let him take me away, my body humming. Passion ignited, we fell together to the bed, joining together in an embrace that was emotional, powerful. My eyes rolled back into my head as pleasure took over. Edward was slow, purposeful in his mission.

Never had we made love like this. It shook me to my core, to my very soul. I vowed not to scare him again, for that was what I thought had happened. I'd scared him that I had dropped the façade of observer and claimed to be a player in the game of court intrigue. A momentary lapse of what was in sight. I could have truly had my head cropped.

I prayed to never lapse in such a way in the future.

*February 12, 1542*

"Save me, Anne."

Snow fell outside my window at Whitehall Palace. I sipped a warm cup of tea, grateful for the roaring fire that heated the room. The sky was a blanket of white, as was the land as far as you could see. Smoky swirls came out of chimneys on top of the castle roofs, and in the courtyard below, servants trudged to and fro.

"What is it I shall save you from?" I turned from my view of winter wonderment to gaze at the young Anne Bassett, whose use of my name so informally I ignored.

"The king has started to talk of marriage. I cannot marry him."

"Why is that? Is that not what I brought you here for years ago? Is that not what you wished for once?"

"Is it? I thought merely to be a mistress."

"Yes, but you have grown on him. Think on it. You have been the one constant woman in his life for the last four years. He still calls for you. Never has he kept a woman so long who was not his wife. Why not make it official?"

"But I have no desire to die! And I want children!"

"Who says you shall die? And why not children?"

"Five times he's married, four of his wives have died and one is set aside! Only three children alive, the rest dead..."

I stood abruptly and marched toward Anne, who lowered her head, almost cowering in my presence. "Do not speak that way, girl.

'Tis treason, and these walls have ears. Want to die for only speaking?"

"No," she murmured.

"You shall do as requested, but if you'd rather not become his wife, tell me of a woman you want to exact revenge on, and I shall see her married to him."

Anne looked up at me abruptly, her mouth dropping open, and then I realized what I had said. My words had been more treasonous than anything that had come from her mouth.

"Do not worry on it, 'Nan. I shall see you safe. Pack your bags, go and visit your family. When you return, his attentions shall be otherwise engaged."

She nodded, curtsied and left without another word.

The more I thought on it, the more my own words made sense. I could very easily place a name in his ear of a woman I abhorred. I could place my revenge on two such people at once. Two people who had secretly planned to marry once her ailing and aging husband had finally succumbed to death.

Catherine Parr and Thomas Seymour.

Catherine would suffer the king, and Tom would watch painfully as his love was wed to another, and not just any other, but the tyrant himself. Catherine Parr was a pious woman. She would do the king's bidding and never fall from grace. Two aging husbands in her life already, she knew just how to care for an ailing man. Also, she was not a part of the Howard faction, but aligned more to us, with Tom as her lover, despite how much she disliked me.

A perfect plan. Now how to go about it?

The door to the solar opened, and Edward's tall, lithe body came through the frame.

"It appears Lady Katheryn Howard wants to be remembered in a different way than how she left court."

"What do you mean?"

"She's requested the block. She practices on it now."

"The block?"

"The warden tells me she requested the block this morning after her confession, so she might know how to place herself. Her maid reported that after it was delivered, she has been practicing kneeling and then placing her head upon the block, arms out. She is murmuring prayers while doing it, says she does not want to make a mistake."

The vision that came from his words was haunting, eerie. I could imagine the poor, broken girl, just seventeen summers, as she knelt and, with shaking hands, placed her head against the cold wooden block. The very one that she would lay her head on when she was executed the following morning.

"The king has passed another bill."

My head snapped up at that as I tried to push the thoughts of Katheryn and her block from my mind. The foreboding sound in Edward's voice worried me. "What bill?"

"He now has the ability to order a person of unstable mental capacity to be executed."

"Jane Rochford." I pressed my lips together and shook my head. How much the king wanted her gone was clearly evident. He'd had a special bill passed just so he could see it done. Even sadder still that her death was a benefit to me that my part in Katheryn Howard's downfall would never be known. At least I could ease my conscience that what had happened had begun before I had become involved.

"Yes. She will be executed just after Katheryn Howard tomorrow."

I nodded solemnly. So much for the king being merciful. But I should have known. He was violent man, murdering anyone he pleased. Satisfied and solicitous one moment, ordering your head on a platter the next.

*Lord, I pray to thee, do not make me next to be served.*

*February 13, 1542*

The Tower cannons boomed loudly. My walls felt as though they were shaking, and I imagined little pieces of dust and rock shaking loose of the mortar and crumbling down.

Rain pelted the windowpanes, and a little trickle of water came down my wall. Every once in a while chunks of ice pinged against the glass, and I was startled, thinking it would break.

The room was cold despite the roaring fire, and my breath came out in little foggy puffs before dissipating into thin air.

In just a few minutes, Edward would arrive to collect me for Katheryn Howard's execution.

I did not want to go.

I did not want to watch another person die.

Especially not a young and stupid girl who'd been placed in a situation she could never have lived up to. She was a lamb to the sacrifice, paying the ultimate price. But to what end? What had her marriage to the king gained? Nothing... There were no children born of it. The Howards had gained nothing. Norfolk—her uncle—had kept himself well away from the fray, and in so doing, the king still looked on him with respect. Edward had done his job and found out all the secrets of Katheryn Howard, laying them out on display for all to see and fondle.

So a girl was used, abused and now would die for it. Perhaps some of the blame lay at her feet, for was she really so unintelligent to think she could get away with an affair? Had someone, such as Jane Rochford, told her the king would absolutely never know? Had she been so taken up by the love she'd felt for Culpeper, that beyond reason and dignity, she had gone to him time and again? I'd known. I could have warned her but I'd stayed silent. I was just as much to blame.

I had only felt a love once in my life that would have overruled my sensibilities at all costs, and it had been for my Eddie. What I'd felt for Anthony, and sometimes still felt, I was not clear if that was love... and I'd been punished greatly for it. Was God telling us that to love so deeply and unequivocally was wrong?

No, I did not think to love so was wrong, but to take up action that could damage that love—that was wrong. If I'd never been with Anthony, maybe Eddie would still have been alive—although Beau would not. If Katheryn had never consummated her relationship with Culpeper, had not allowed her past to come to her future, then she, too, would have lived and been able to bestow her love freely on others — or would she have been?

Loving Eddie had made me a better person, and out of his existence I took away a piece of that perfect angel and remembered love and sweetness.

Katheryn Howard, she would have died no matter what, so at least she had been able to feel the love and euphoria that came with it, once in her lifetime.

My thoughts were a jumbled mess, and I too confused to sort them.

Edward entered the room quietly and summoned me forward. We made our way to Tower Green with the other courtiers. The king was not here, but I had hardly expected him to be.

Lady Katheryn Howard, seventeen years old and queen for just under two years, was led out. She wore a plain, black velvet gown, dirty, stained. No one had given her a pretty ermine cloak like the one her cousin had worn to her execution. No spicy red petticoats swished from under her gown. No jewels adorned her neck. This girl could have been anyone and yet she represented no one. Her lips were blue from cold or fear or both.

Blazing bonfires were placed throughout the courtyard to warm spectators, but we felt it not. At least the rain had stopped, but the freezing temperatures had left the ground slick with patches of ice. Katheryn Howard slipped, but the one maid who had accompanied her caught her elbow as the guard caught her on the other side.

Suffolk came to stand beside us. His wife, Catherine, came to my side and gripped my hand. Her mouth was turned down in both sadness and distaste, a mirror of my own expression.

The men mumbled to each other, but I could not have cared less what they were saying. I only squeezed Catherine's fingers tight.

"She is such a young thing," Catherine murmured.

"Yes."

"We should all pray forgiveness for her death."

"Why all of us?" Catherine had played no part.

"There are so many points at which this madness could have been avoided." Catherine's voice was a monotone as we watched the former queen being led up the thin and uneven stairs of her hastily made scaffold. When she reached the top, she slipped off the black wool cloak she wore and handed it to her maid. "From the very beginning. The duchess could have watched her further, made certain she grew up properly. When she was sent to court so young and the king eyed her like a fresh strawberry to be plucked from the vines, someone should have said, 'Ah, not that one, too green still.' Or told His Majesty of her upbringing before it was too late. When he married her still, she should have been coached not to take a lover, not to make eyes with another man, not to write of her dying heart."

Guilt consumed me. I could have done more than one of those things. Her death was on my shoulders.

Katheryn Howard, girl queen, knelt to her knees, chin up, head steady. She was no longer the appearance of gaiety as she had been at court. Her hair was thin and dull, cheeks sallow and gaunt.

The executioner mumbled to her.

She gazed out over the top of the crowd, not meeting eyes with anyone. "Pray God have mercy on me! To Jesu, I commend my soul!" Then she did appear to lock eyes with several people. She opened her mouth, but no words came out. Whatever she'd been about to say, she thought better of it. She placed her hands—unshaking—onto the block. Then turning her head to the left, she laid it down. For several moments, she stayed that way. The executioner told her twice to put her arms out, but she held on. When he stepped forward, motioning for the guards to hold her, her arms came out straight at her sides of her own accord, and she closed her eyes.

The executioner's ax sliced through the air and cut off her head with one chop. I did not blink. Could not. My eyes stared intently at the blood spilling from her neck. She was picked up and placed into an unmarked crate, just as her cousin before her. The maid covered Katheryn with her cloak and followed the groomsmen who carried the body away. Her death over just as swiftly as her life.

"Where will Katheryn be buried, Edward?" I asked.

"Buried in an unmarked grave at St. Peter ad Vincula, same as her cousin, the first Howard queen."

Before I had time to react to his words, Jane Rochford appeared, walked out by two guards who eyed her warily. But for once in the last months she appeared completely calm and lucid.

She walked up the stairs, not a break in her stride, and stood before the crowd. Her eyes met mine for a brief moment, and her lips twitched, almost in a smile. She mumbled her prayers so quietly, I could not hear from where I stood. Guilt washed over me anyway for having wished her downfall. 'Twas one of the reasons I hated to attend the executions. Invariably, I was guilt ridden, because at some point during their lives I had wished them gone. And now here I stood, watching as the life was struck from their bodies — and I not only wished this time, but had had a play in it.

After the queen's execution, King Henry went into a state of melancholy. There had been no feasting, no music, no laughing. His mood was bleaker than it had been when Jane Seymour had died.

His health was fading, and his ego had taken a beating. But true to form, the king bounced back and this time ordered a party of twenty-nine ladies to come and dine with him so he might charm them and make merry with them.

I had every intention of declining my invitation, but Edward forbade it. And so after a long-awaited lengthy visit with my dear friend Gertrude, who languished in her own type of misery — one that came from poverty and widowhood, which I tried to improve on by giving her coin and gifts — I returned to Hampton Court, where Henry planned to have his harem for the evening.

Every room in the castle was drafty except this one. The king had seen to it that the room was comfortable for the ladies who would attend him this evening. The windows were shuttered and covered with lavish tapestries. A roaring fire was constantly monitored by two groomsmen. Cloth of gold draped from the ceiling, and velvet curtains were hung on the walls between the tapestries. The floor was covered in a rush woven mat, sprinkled with herbs and spices, large wool and fur carpets placed atop.

Candles lit up the room, so even though the sun had not shone for hours, inside this room it was bright, cheerful. Minstrels strolled, playing songs and singing sweet ballads. Wine flowed from casks, and delicious fruits, candied nuts, and tasty tarts were only an arm's length away.

The king sat upon his throne, already surrounded by women who fawned on him.

"Lady Anne," he breathed, taking me in. I had the distinct feeling of being weighed, measured and indeed found acceptable. "Come and sit here." He shooed away a couple of women and patted the seat beside him.

"How long have we known each other, Countess?"

"Seems like a lifetime, Majesty."

He laughed. "And for some it may have been." I ignored the fact that I had known him for as long as his last wife had lived. He tapped his chin, now grown full of a reddish-gray beard. "I like you still."

"I am fond of you also, Majesty." The lie left my lips with ease.

"I have languished too long in misery, and I am glad you've come to celebrate my escape from melancholy."

"As it pleases, Majesty."

"So formal you are, my lady. A constant, that is what you are. Everyone knows what to expect from you. You shall surprise us all one day."

I smiled and inclined my head, ready to leave the room, for its warmth was now making me uncomfortably hot.

"Where have you sent my little 'Nan?" he asked.

At this, my ears prickled. "She has gone home to the country for a time. She wishes to marry."

"As it happens, I am in need of a wife," he said with a sly grin.

I smiled indulgently. "Might I suggest one then?"

"Is it not the one whom I have just been speaking of?"

"Another, Majesty. She will please you infinitely more, I should think."

He leaned closer, intrigued with what I had to say. "Who?"

"Lady Catherine Parr." Her name left my lips in a bitter, guilt-riddled, rush.

At this, the king sat back and scanned the room until his eyes alighted on her. "Yes..." he drawled. "She is beautiful and mature, a woman I could have a conversation with."

"Indeed, Majesty."

"Albeit, she is married to Lord Latimer."

"Yes, but he is ailing. I do not wish ill or death on the man, but I am only suggesting... Should Your Majesty feel inclined, she is a prize worth waiting for."

"Indeed, my lady, you are correct. It is settled then." He smiled as he watched his future bride. Another lamb to be brought forth. "I shall begin courting her."

"It may take some wooing, Majesty, but she will be amendable to it."

"Who would not want to marry the king?" His voice was filled with confidence, much changed from the man I had sat and talked with months ago who'd sounded so dejected after a number of women had in fact *not wanted* to marry him.

"There is not a woman I know who would not—and not just because you are king, either."

"You flatter m—" The king lurched forward, his hands pressed to his leg. His eyes bulged, and a gurgling sound came from the back of his throat.

"The king!" I leapt from my chair and grabbed a goblet of wine, offering it up to his lips.

Groomsmen rushed forth, managing to pick up the hefty load of a man and carry him from the room. I rushed along with them but did not immediately follow. Instead, I ran to Edward's study to summon him.

When we reached the king's chambers, Edward was allowed to enter. The people in the presence chamber whispered of the king's ulcerous leg. The physicians were summoned, and they drained the leg, made poultices and brews. In just a short time, the king had begun to rage with fever.

*Dear Lord our God, save the king!*

# CHAPTER TWENTY-SIX

*And if to light on you my luck so good shall be,*
*I shall be glad to feed on that, that would have fed on me.*
*~Henry Howard, Earl of Surrey*

*January 5, 1543*

The king took months to recover. Nearly a year had gone by and even still his health was failing. The leg had to be drained nearly twice a week, and the sore never healed. He had a poultice applied daily, and he now walked with a cane.

To make up for his misery he had taken to gluttony. Lavish feasts, of which he ate everything offered. He'd grown to massive proportions.

I was a mother yet again, having found out I was with child just after the king's harem party. My precious daughter had been born on Christmas morning, and just as I had sworn I would never do, I had named her Anne. Yet, another Anne at court. But I could not *not* have named her such. She was the spitting image of me. Edward had laughed when he'd seen her, and she'd frowned at him, eyebrows drawn together in such a way, he'd said it mimicked my stern glance like no other he'd ever seen.

Edward placed the baby back in my arms. "Tom came to my office roaring mad before I departed Whitehall."

I rolled my eyes, preferring to languish in the bright blue gaze of baby Annie. "Whatever for?"

"Seems the king has set his sights on a new bride."

"So soon?" I asked innocently.

"You are a coy and devious woman."

"Edward, you flatter me."

"So you know of what I speak."

"I may."

"He intends to court Catherine Parr," he stated accusingly.

'Twas about time. I ignored his irritation and smiled winningly. "How did Tom find out?"

"He went to the king asking for permission to court her with the intent to marry—even though her husband still lives. Apparently the old sod is so ill he no longer speaks, and they expect him to pass at any moment." Edward paused and studied me as if he waited for me to say something. I did not, and so he continued. "He was turned down. King Henry told him he'd taken a liking to the woman himself, and Tom's dear sister-by-marriage had in fact recommended the great lady."

I smirked. "How lovely of the king to confess it."

"Tom and Catherine will try to ruin you, Anne."

"They won't be the first, Edward." I smoothed a blonde curl on baby Annie's forehead.

"But this is my brother and the future queen." His arms were outstretched, imploring.

"Yes, it is, and since when have you ever been afraid of your simpering, foolish brother? He and I have been at odds for years. Yes, everything might be at stake should the king marry her, but we are stronger than they are. We are aunt and uncle to the future king. Who is Catherine Parr? The king favors us over Tom, and do not worry. We shall come to the field with an arsenal should battle ensue."

"I trust you will make good on your promise."

"I shall, Edward. When have I ever failed you?"

Edward eyed me warily, and I had the distinct impression he was thinking of two times in particular: my affair with Anthony and the loss of our baby. I swallowed hard, tears stinging my eyes.

Finally, he whispered intently, "Never. You have never failed me."

But I knew better.

*February 25, 1543*

Even though we were miles from court, Wulfhall bustled as if the king had laid down his house here.

Messengers came every few hours, and the servants were busy with daily chores, meal preparations and the caring of my two children.

Not only did Edward keep a steady stream of news and updates coming my way, but I was in receipt of letters from the Duchess of Suffolk, Elizabeth Cromwell, and the Lady Mary. All had eyes open to the goings-on at court and were keeping me privy, even seeking my advice as to their own course of actions. Gertrude sent me correspondence that was light of heart, and she'd embarked on an affair that seemed to be keeping her in pleasant countenance.

Soon, I would travel back to the viper's den, immerse myself within it, and wait for Catherine Parr's fangs to sink into my flesh, whereby she would next send me into the waiting and violent embrace of her thrust-aside lover, Thomas Seymour.

But I had news for them. Best they kept to themselves, or perhaps a rumor of their own lusty escapades would whip rampantly on wagging tongues.

I walked out of the great hall and toward the stables. The grass was crisp underfoot, little tiny icicles popping beneath my feet from the evening's dew freezing upon the blades. My breath came out in a fog. The temperature was slowly rising, and spring would soon be here. But this was my favorite time of year, when the weather was still cool and crisp from winter and trying desperately to grasp the dawn of a new season, new life.

Amid the turmoil of court and family demands, I must find some escape, and having been confined to the interior of Wulfhall for months, I needed to break away! Feel the wind fly through my hair. I was looking for just a moment of peace and abandon before returning to court.

No groom was in sight as I walked through to find my mare. Tizzy was lazily gnawing on some hay when I found her. I rubbed her muzzle, and she lipped my palm, looking for sugar.

"You are up early, my lady." The voice of Francis Newdegate, our steward, startled me, and I jumped, which in turn caused Tizzy to startle and whinny.

"Did not mean to frighten you both. Shall I take her out and saddle her up for you?"

"Yes, please."

"I was going to take a ride myself. Would you like some company, my lady?"

I eyed him warily, not really wanting any company, but he was a pleasant man and perhaps simple conversation would take my mind away from things. "Yes, that would be nice."

I was both surprised and disappointed when Francis did not speak on our ride. I had wanted to chat with someone, but then again, just the common peace and tranquility we found as we rode were comforting. I liked this man. He seemed to know what I needed without me having to tell him and without me really knowing myself. I suppose that was his job.

Whatever the reason, I hoped the next time I was at Wulfhall, we could go for a ride around the grounds again. My heart warmed at the idea. A spark of something tried to ignite inside me, but I quickly extinguished it. I was a grown woman who'd learned quite well the rights and wrongs of life.

*July 12, 1543*

They were to marry today. With Lady Latimer's husband dead and buried nearly four months ago, she was free to marry again.

Catherine Parr and King Henry.

The rumor of my matchmaking had become rampant, and Catherine had no qualms about glaring blazing daggers in my direction. However, Henry himself was pleased of my idea, and so I had no need to worry on that respect.

Although, I did worry greatly of a repeat of past events... Catherine and Tom were so heartbroken over the turn of events, I could almost see him breaking into her bedchamber at night to ravish her before running down the back stairs as the king came to claim his marital rights from his bride.

As much as I abhorred the both of them, I disliked *more* someone else dying — even if only remotely by my hands. But, sadly, I was the only one with such feelings. Others would have had things another way. The Howards, Norfolk and Surrey mostly, had gone into hiding after the latest queen debacle, but now they were inching from the woodwork again. They were a family of non-quitters, just like Edward and I — and even Tom.

But thank God for small favors. There was no denying we held a powerful position at court — or rather, Edward did, over the Howards and over Tom. Edward had gained my respect immensely over the years and had become quite a man of his own word. While he still took my advice, it was not as often. He made his own choices, which were sometimes reckless.

I still had the recurring dream. The one I once believed Jane Seymour had shared with me. The scaffold. The wood was splintered now, and large, jagged pieces of it stabbed into my bare feet as I marched up the precariously thin steps to the top. But when I got there, it was not my execution.

It was Edward's, and I'd come to collect his body. His head was in a bloody straw basket, and I picked it up as if I were shopping on market day. His limp body lay on the floor of the scaffold, blood seeping from the stump that used to hold his head. His bloody neck.

Then I'd wake, drenched in sweat, rapid-beating heart, breaths coming so fast they nearly choked me.

I was afraid. For he was increasingly taking on more duties, playing with power, playing with the king. The king's new bride despised us. Catherine had taken up arms with Tom, and Tom would see Edward dead for both revenge on losing the only woman he wished to marry and to gain a title, lands, wealth.

I shook the vision from my limbs and began preparing for the day with Jenny's help. A gown of silver silk, pearls and diamonds encrusted on the bodice, hem and cuffs. My hair in a perfect coiffure, matching hood. Dainty slippers on, and my toilette was complete.

"You look beautiful."

Edward stood in the doorway, a winning smile on his face. I could not help but appreciate the man. He stood tall, well-muscled and handsome. The strain of court living had done nothing to mar his features, only distinguish him. Little crinkles had formed at the sides of his eyes, and a few strands of gray lightened his dark hair and beard, but other than that, he was still the image of the young man I had married.

"Thank you." I curtsied and smiled, before placing a kiss on his lips. "Shall we go and show the people what a handsome and formidable pair we are?"

"Indeed. For there are many who have wished, and still wish, to see us put asunder."

The wedding ceremony was brief and yet, while regale, not as full of splendor as those ceremonies in the past—a true testament to what Henry now wanted. Companionship.

The king ambled slowly down the candlelit aisle and took his place, dressed in cloth of gold and silk. You could almost see the shadow of the man he'd once been.

On my left stood Edward, and to my horror, Sir Anthony took his place on my right, his own wife just on the other side of him. Years it had been since I'd laid eyes on him, and I'd thought my feelings for him long since banked, but they rushed to the surface again. My stomach plummeted. Fire flashed in Edward's eyes as he leaned forward and nodded a greeting to Anthony. I looked straight ahead, suddenly very interested in the depiction of Jesus on the cross hanging above the altar. And then the future queen entered the chapel. Our gazes followed her as she walked slowly down the aisle, and her longing look in Tom's direction did not go unnoticed by anyone, save the king himself, who believed Catherine fancied him above all others.

Archbishop Cranmer began the sermon, and Anthony began to whisper in my ear.

"How is our child?"

Shock registered in my gut, and my heart stopped beating for half a second. I ignored him.

"I know Beau is mine, Anne." His words tickled against my ear, sending pleasurable memories careening along my flesh, and fear that what he had said was true.

Still, I did not speak for fear of Edward becoming privy to our conversation.

Anthony continued, even though I tried desperately to ignore him. "Just turned four this spring, he did. A handsome little fellow."

I sucked in my breath. How had he seen my boy?

"I stopped by Wulfhall on my way back to court from visiting my own estate. He was a most gracious host and Lord strike me now if he is not the spitting image of me."

I swallowed hard. Would he blackmail me? Use me in some ill fashion to keep the truth secret?

"Have no fear of me, Anne. I would never do anything to harm a child, especially not one of my own, and despite how angry it makes me, I realize he is better off with Edward's name than mine. But I would ask a boon of you."

My fingernails curled into my palms at my sides.

"When he is seven, let him come to my estate for his fostering. Let me at least have that part of his life."

The idea had merit, and Anthony's home would be just as good a place as any when Beau was ready to be fostered out for his education. Imperceptibly, I nodded — despite the fact that Edward would certainly never allow it. I felt Anthony's fingers curl around my own and squeeze for just a few brief moments, but then they were quickly gone.

I was overcome with sadness, the emotion washing over me in waves, tears pooling in my eyes. I blinked them away and pretended to be totally engrossed in what Cranmer was saying, listening to the songs of the choirboys and then as King Henry gave his new queen a light kiss on the lips. If only things had been different. If I had never met Surrey and never had to rely on Edward as my savior, if I had been allowed to dance, flirt and be merry at court as any other court lady, it was entirely possible I could have fell for Anthony first, lived out my life with passion.

But those were the stupid and foolish notions of a girl. I never would have risen up as far as I had if I had not suffered first. The greater the climb, the harder I'd work to get there. That was me. In my soul, in my blood, I could not settle for less.

The king and queen walked down the aisle with the archbishop and his attendants following.

"Hell." The word fell off of Catherine Parr's lips in a whisper as she passed by me, a fierce rage in her light-blue eyes.

"That woman needs some manners," I murmured to Edward.

He chuckled. "I shall petition the king at once."

"For what?"

"You have yet to be called forth as one of her ladies-in-waiting. What better way to teach her than that?"

I crinkled my brow as we followed the crowd from out of the chapel and to the gardens, where a great feast and tournament-style fighting had been arranged in celebration of the king's wedding.

"If it has to be that way, then I shall be glad of the position and the chance to teach her a lesson."

The gardens were filled with entertainers, jongleurs, musicians, bards, and on a nearby field, a list had been set up. Knights mounted horses and raced toward each other with lances held high until they crashed into one another. King Henry had ambled his way over to a throne arranged right in the midst of everything.

"Are you happy, Hell?"

The sound of Tom's whispered voice grated on every nerve in my body.

I slowly turned toward him and gave him an annoyed look. "Cannot come up with your own vile nicknames but must hide behind the skirts of your woman? Oh, pardon me, *the king's* wife," I bit out.

"Leave off, Tom. The match is good. Find a woman who can bear you children. Neither of us wants to see you dead for loving the queen too much," Edward chided, as if Tom were still a boy in leading strings.

Tom's face blanched white, but he did not leave right away.

"You know why she calls you Hell, Anne?"

"I said leave off," Edward threatened. A few guests had turned their attention toward us, the king and queen included.

"Because there is a special place in Hell waiting for you. A special place where only women of your vicious caliber reside. You hide in shadows, my lady, spewing your venomous control and willpower into the wind and those lesser beings, those unable to get away from the spray, do your bidding. Those willing to die for you so you might get ahead. How many of your friends have died? How many of your enemies?"

"What's this?" The king raised his voice, obviously annoyed that a family squabble was taking the attention away from him and his new bride.

"Yes, what is this, Tom?" I raised a brow in challenge. "You want Hell, you'll get it," I threatened under my breath.

"Nothing more than a family dispute, Majesty. My apologies." Tom bowed low to the king, as we all did, like little children fighting over a sweet treat.

"I say, Edward and Thomas, to the lists with you! We shall all watch you ride out your differences using horses and lances." The king raised his goblet and downed the contents.

Queen Catherine looked stricken, as did Tom, but Edward smiled with cocky assurance. He would win this fight.

The two men went down to the fields, armored up, mounted their horses and readied to ram each other. The king himself dropped the flag, and the two brothers took off toward one another. Wood splintered in a hundred different directions. Thomas fell backward, and Edward kept his seat, the lance in his hand minimized to only a stick in his fist. The victor!

"It appears Edward is the winner on this day!" the king bellowed.

Catherine turned toward me with a fierce glare, but I only smiled smugly and shook my head at her. If she wanted to play games, she had better play harder than she was. For Edward and I would be the winners on more than just this day.

# CHAPTER TWENTY-SEVEN

*And thus farewell, Unkind, to whom I bent and bow;*
*I would you know, the ship is safe that bare his sails so low.*
*Since that a Lion's heart is for a Wolf no prey.*
*With bloody mouth go slake your thirst on simple sheep, I say*
*With more despite and ire than I can now express,*
*Which to my pain, though I refrain, the cause you may well guess.*
*As for because myself was author of the game,*
*It boots me not that for my wrath I should disturb the same.*
*~Henry Howard, Earl of Surrey*

More than three years later... A letter dated September 12, 1546

My Dearest Gertrude,

How I miss you, my darling friend! It has been difficult to get away from court over the last couple of years since King Henry married Catherine Parr. But I have arranged with Edward to go on a progress to Sussex, where our eldest boy, Beau, shall be fostering in Sir Anthony Browne's household. His own boy, Anthony, who will be celebrating his eighteenth year next month, shall be working personally with our son. I know such news must shock you, but dear Edward has struck a bargain which he has not allowed me to be privy to.

*I shall be bringing gifts with me from the Lady Mary, which I know you were so pleased to hear she was back in the line of succession, although still deemed illegitimate.*

*I thank you ever so much for sending the lovely gifts for my twin babes, Margaret and Henry, last year, and the lovely necklaces to my little Jane and my eldest girl, Anne. Beau was also pleased with his new doublet, which made him feel so like a grown man, despite him being only seven summers.*

*We shall be leaving on progress in the next sennight. I cannot wait to behold you, as we have so many things to catch up on.*

*With the greatest friendship,*
*Anne, Countess of Hertford*

*October 2, 1546*

Gertrude's face was stricken, and she raised her eyes to mine. We stood in the center of her solar. A silent message passed between us, and I was glad Edward had gone to see to the horses after we'd arrived at the former marchioness's home.

"He looks like…" Her voice trailed off.

"His father, does he not?" I continued, speaking of Beau.

"Yes," she said, and then being the gracious woman she was, continued, "Where are the others?"

"They are all at home with their nurses. Beau is going on to Sussex so he can train to be knight and the next Earl of Hertford."

He puffed out his chest and lifted his handsome face to the sky. He was truly a Beau at heart.

"I must tell you, Anne, you look beautiful. I've never known a woman to bounce back to her figure as you have after having children. Exquisite you are!"

My face heated from her praise. I was quite proud of having been able to remain in my figure, but I thought part of it was mostly due to many missed meals and much brisk walking around the grounds and within the walls of the castle.

We gathered inside and took our rest before coming down to supper in Gertrude's great hall. She had gone to a great deal of trouble to prepare the meal for us. Edward chatted with Gertrude's only son, Edward Courtenay. He had the look of his father, tall, handsome, and just turned nineteen years of age.

"You must tell me all the news of court. We do not hear much out here, and my own Edward has just returned to me from fostering. He seeks a spot in King Henry's court, but I have doubts they will give it to him."

"He could always come with us, Gertrude. You know that. Edward would be happy for another squire to earn his spurs."

"The Duchess of Suffolk said the same thing. You are both so very kind. But enough about us. Tell me, how is the new queen? I have a vague recollection of her."

I took a long swallow of wine. "She is a quandary to me. On the one hand, she hates me to her very core, even took to calling me 'Hell' for a little while, until the king made it clear he holds myself and Edward in high esteem, and of course I reminded her of the treason she'd be committing by continuing to flaunt her love of Tom."

"Yes, I thought I had heard such."

My eyes widened at that. "Really? So far from court?"

Gertrude tapped at her chin. "Scandal always travels faster than anything else."

"How right you are," I murmured, realizing I needed to come north every once in a while to see how much they knew and how twisted tales became so far from anyone who could set them to rights.

"Do they continue to love one another?"

"She and Tom? Not that I am aware, and I've been very careful and keen to it—the one reason Edward wants me near the queen, and I suspect the king, as well. The king knows how volatile our relationship with Tom is and that he can trust us to ferret out any indiscretion."

"What about her gives you pause?" Gertrude refilled her goblet with wine.

"She is a great believer in the Reform and has gone to great lengths to embrace Mary—one of the reasons Mary and Elizabeth were put back into the succession was Queen Catherine's influence. Of course their positions don't hurt Prince Edward and it is unlikely she'll conceive. So why, I wonder, does she push me away? Together, we could be a formidable force."

"That is odd. I suspect most of it is for her separation from Thomas."

I inclined my head and nodded. "Yes, but even before then, she hated me so."

"Perhaps it stems from some unknown jealousy. All you can do is attempt to gain her friendship."

I fingered my skirts and the flowers embroidered there by my own hand. "Perhaps her anger also stems from being friends with Frances de Vere, Surrey's wife, who has always held a vicious grudge against me. Who knows what wagging tongues will say when dripping with vinegar? No matter, Queen Catherine has calmed toward me somewhat in the last few years. I think part of it originated from Edward's support of her when she ruled as regent while King Henry was on campaign in France two years ago and then again with the plot against her earlier this year."

"A plot against her that was not your own?" Gertrude laughed.

"Odd, is it not? I had nothing to do with it. In fact, I believe I may have helped to save her, and still she holds me at arm's length, although I am glad to not be called 'Hell' anymore."

"But such an endearing name!" Gertrude sipped her wine. "Who was behind the plot, do you think?"

"Most definitely the Howards. Surrey, if you ask me personally, put the bug in Wriothesley, Lord Chancellor's ear. They conjured up all sorts of charges for heresy, saying the queen and her intimate ladies held and read with great enthusiasm banned religious books. They had so much fake evidence that they drew up an arrest warrant for her. One of the guards, whom Edward and I have employed as our eyes and ears, dropped the warrant and allowed me to pick it up and read it. As soon as I saw what was contained within, I ran to Edward and then straight to the queen."

Gertrude gasped. "How fortunate you were able to do that."

"I agree. Edward coached Catherine on how to reply to the king when he came to chastise her. Her words of only seeking his instruction on such great matters smoothed the king's ire like sweets to a tantruming child. I do not know how she does it. She is nothing like our Queen Jane, but she handles the king well, even had special chairs made for him, so his groomsmen can take him about the castle and outdoors. His health, the leg, his size have all declined so much, the man cannot walk on his own." I tapped my finger against my glass in tune to the chime of the clock. "But I do fear with all the opposition against her, we have only just begun our journey to defend her." A shock to myself indeed, since I'd suggested her to the king out of revenge. But she was actually good at caring for the king.

"Do you think Thomas will try to gain her favor... intimately?"

"He is still hopelessly in love with her, but he has tried to move on. The king wanted to arrange a marriage between Tom and Mary Howard—Richmond's widow and Norfolk's daughter—but her brother, Surrey, was opposed to it. After the latest Howard tragedy, Norfolk was resigned to align our two families. Even Edward was open to it. As the king has always said, keep your friends close and your enemies closer. But Surrey was so outspoken about the matter that we laid our ideas to rest." I leaned in to whisper, "I do believe Surrey is much like his father was. I heard some of the queen's ladies whispering that Surrey told his sister, Mary Howard, to not accept the betrothal and instead assert her feminine wiles on the king."

"But she was married to the king's bastard son, for God's sake!"

I rolled my eyes and nodded. "Surrey is a beast, and he has become increasingly cocky, argumentative and taken to drink in excess—more than before. I won't be surprised if the king soon tires of his disturbances and bans him from court. Albeit, the king has always loved him for his enthusiasm in the past, in his old age he is starting to find it cumbersome. There are any number of increasing arguments and rifts between the courtiers, and Surrey's hatred of Edward has grown beyond measure. At times I think he might actually be losing touch with reality."

"'Tis sad in a way, but the man has always had a side to him that rubbed in the wrong way."

I nodded but said nothing. Personally, I believed that whatever was coming for Surrey he fully deserved. He'd tormented me. 'Twas God's will, and I fully trusted in God.

*December 12, 1546*

Tension at court was rising. It was palpable, and I think everyone could feel it just as strongly as I could. When I walked through the great hall, through the king's and queen's presence chambers, the air was thick, the people strung like violin strings pulled too tight. Without a moment's notice someone would break and the whole of court would erupt into chaos.

Beside me walked the fair prince, slight for his nine years, and just as red in hair as his father, and also just as extreme.

"Highness, my lady, a pleasure to find you both here." Francois van der Delft, the replacement for Ambassador Chapuys, who'd retired the previous year, walked up beside us as we entered the great hall. The prince had taken a liking to walking with me, perhaps he saw me as somewhat of a replacement to the mother he'd lost—unlike the three stepmothers he'd now had.

"Ambassador, you are looking well," I said.

Prince Edward eyed the man wearily, as if already weighing how much the man would try him when he became king.

"I feel just as young as I was when I first arrived at this marvelous court," he said with a laugh. "And you know how hard that can be to maintain."

"I wish I could say the same." I wished for Chapuys, a man who at one time had annoyed me greatly but who had become somewhat more than an acquaintance, although we'd never been too close on a personal level. He had been a man I could trust, and one who had been complete in his support of Lady Mary. Van der Delft was a younger man, newer to court and most eager to please His Majesty.

"You are still very beautiful, if you will allow me to bestow such a compliment on you."

I glanced sideways at the prince, who feigned boredom, though his gaze was riveted on the two of us.

"I thank you kindly." The ambassador was stalling.

"My lady, if I may, I need to have speech with you...regarding something of an important nature."

"By all means, Ambassador. Your Highness, if you would excuse me." I glanced about and saw that the Duke of Suffolk stood

393

on the opposite side of the room. "There is Charles, go with him now to see your father." I curtsied to my nephew, who loved to follow the rules of etiquette. Once he'd gone in the direction of his father's dear friend, the ambassador and I walked to a corner of the room where our conversation would be less likely overheard.

"While at Oatlands Palace, the king fell ill with fever a few days ago."

"Yes, I heard this. I am glad he recovered soon." And he'd arrived back at court just that morning.

"Yes, but his health is failing, and very fast. I feel I must inform you Surrey has begun making whispers that he should be placed as protector of the prince. It is even said he has redesigned his new coat of arms, replacing the coronet with a crown and the initials H. R."

I gasped at this last bit of news, H. R. being a specific signature for Royal Highness, and wondered why the ambassador was coming to me with such warnings, as we had not had so many dealings previously. "You cannot be serious."

"If only I were joking, my lady. I think it best you and Lord Hertford begin an investigation into these allegations, as I am afraid should the man be allowed to continue down this path, there will be much heartache."

"He has created quite a bit of it already," I muttered.

"Exactly. Faction pitted against faction. Arguments are not only not unheard of, they have become the norm during the afternoons of courtiers meeting, greeting and discussing politics."

Yes, the factions… There were the Howards and the Seymours. The ring leader of the Howards was Surrey, and on his side was, unfortunately, Wriothesley. The Seymours were headed by none other than Edward—and Tom was not even always on our side. For finally the truth had come out, and he had joined with Surrey who, for one, thought he himself should have been named Lord Protector over the prince. In the event that he was not chosen, he backed Tom. But we had gained favor with John Dudley, Lord Lisle, as well as many other powerful nobles at court.

For Tom it would have been the perfect fit—as he saw it. He would have been Lord Protector of the young king, and most likely married to the dowager queen. In essence, he would have been king himself, and by doing so rising above and beyond his brother as he seemed fit to do.

"What's more, Henry's health deteriorates with each passing day, and sometimes within those days, by the hour. And then just as suddenly, the next day, he could be in good spirits and ask to be taken outside, hoisted onto a horse and go riding. I've heard from many at court they are worried he will not last much longer, but no one is willing to tell him."

"No, the king does not deal well with the imminence of his own death. If he could have found a potion, a fountain of youth and remained immortal, he would have."

"*Si*. He is young at heart, and his aging body does not agree with his mind. 'Tis why he often seems depressed. Be certain to speak with Lord Hertford soon, for from the looks of it, His Majesty will not rally much longer."

"Why do you tell me these things?" I could not help but ask. My curiosity burned to know.

"Lady Hertford, I am the ambassador to Spain, and as such I have the confidence of the Princess Mary. She esteems you greatly. I first approached her with this news, and she saw fit for me to inform you directly."

"Thank you, Ambassador. I shall seek out Edward promptly."

"Good day to you, my lady." Van der Delft crooked a leg and bowed low before turning to find some other courtier to talk with.

Was it just luck Edward that tended to the prince, the queen and our most gracious sovereign, Henry VIII? Or had he planned for such all along? He'd fought wars, argued his way through the council, and dug out traitors, including two of Henry's wives. He had always been a ruthless man of Henry's court, doing what needed to be done. And now, it appeared Edward had adapted to yet again what Henry needed, a nurturer, a man of quiet compliance, yet still just as fearsome. At times if someone confronted him or attacked his principles, he would engage in an argument, but for the most part, he was massaging our future, and the king thanked him for it.

Ever since the plot against Catherine Parr was hatched, she had become a most pious woman and tended to her husband, and his children equally. Although it was said she and the king had engaged in connubial visits, there had never been cause to think she was with child. And having been married two times previously without issue, it was hard to say this was for no other reason than her being barren.

I searched above the crowd of various-colored caps with feathers stuck in the sides for Edward finding him with a few courtiers. After catching his eyes, he excused himself and made for my direction. I relayed the news to him from the ambassador, and then we both parted ways to once again speak with our allies in the room.

Not an hour later, a loud commotion came from the front of the hall.

"Henry Howard, Earl of Surrey! Show yourself!" It was Suffolk, and beside him stood Edward, and the prince not in sight.

A moment of panic seized me until I realized the young heir was most likely still with his father, perhaps even observing this disturbance from a secret place cut in the wall.

"Surrey!" Edward's voice boomed above the din of courtiers, who all slowly turned, their mouths closed in silence, the sounds of fabric swishing, the clicking of heels on the stone floor and chink of swords swaying in scabbards.

Surrey swaggered into the middle of the hall, where courtiers stepped aside, so he was in the middle of a wide-open space.

"What the devil do you two want?" he spat out.

I swallowed hard, forcing my smile down. A dozen of the king's guards entered the hall behind Edward and Suffolk.

Suffolk opened a scroll, unrolled it and began reading.

"By order of the king, you, Henry Howard, Earl of Surrey, are hereby arrested for treason against His Majesty, King Henry VIII." Suffolk actually smiled, as he'd always found Surrey to be a pain in his arse.

I turned grateful eyes on Edward, who also seemed pleased, albeit more reserved than Suffolk. He gave me a curt nod—all the reassurance I needed that he'd finally been able to get rid of Surrey for me.

"Preposterous!" Surrey slurred with a drunken tongue.

"There are witnesses who state otherwise," Suffolk said dryly.

"My father—"

"Is already making a new home out of his cell in the Tower," Edward replied.

At this latest news, gasps and hushed whispers went up all over the great hall.

"Let us not make any more of a scene. Come willingly, or I shall have the guards force you," Suffolk said cheerily.

Surrey turned hate-filled eyes on the crowd, scanning the people, searching, briefly flicking over me. When he did not find what or whom he was looking for, he turned his rage on Edward.

"This is your fault! You seek to take what is mine! You always have!" His words were a punch in my gut, as he'd always considered that Edward had stolen me away from him.

"All that is mine was rightfully earned and humbly accepted," Edward said patiently, as if talking to a child.

Surrey began to draw his sword, but before it was halfway out of its scabbard, Lord Lisle, out of nowhere, punched him in the jaw. The crack resounded in the stone-walled room. Surrey stumbled to the left, and the guards swarmed on him, carrying him from the great hall.

It was all bittersweet. For many years, I had wished for such a fate for Surrey, and here it was happening, and I was not satisfied. From the looks of it, Suffolk and Edward would find him guilty beyond a reasonable doubt, and this time he would climb to the top of the scaffold and meet Monsieur le Ax. Perhaps I felt this way because I did not get to ball my fist and punch him in the jaw. Whatever the reason, it most definitely fell flat of any plans I may have made to torture him myself.

*December 21, 1546*

The king's health continued to decline. In fact he'd ceased all feasting, and musicians had been turned away so that he might take solitude, as he called it, with only a handful of people allowed to attend him, and even fewer with whom he was granting an audience.

397

Edward had moved the Privy Council meeting to our London house. He had moved me there as well, as the queen had not been in need of so many attendants since she had been by Henry's side each and every day or at the chapel attending Mass and staying even longer to pray.

Today was to be the meeting, and a private chamber had been composed to accommodate the lords. However, to make the meeting seem much less formal, and not to jar the council members too much with the statement this move had made, Edward had prepared a feast, which I was overseeing. I walked up and down the length of the trestle table, counting the chairs, the dishes and goblets, assuring there were exactly enough.

"My lady, so filled with concentration." Anthony came up beside me and eyed the table. "Is it to your liking?"

How was it he was so easily able to be congenial with me? Perhaps he had perfected the art of manipulation.

"Sir Anthony. How is Beau?"

"Are you not glad to see me?" His eyes teased, and I was nearly struck off balance. A flash of what we used to be came to mind, but I shoved it aside. Another life, perhaps, but not now.

I turned away from him and began counting linen napkins.

"Ah, I see, we cannot be friendly with one another. So hard and cruel you are to me. Did we not once share a heart? Have we not a child—"

"Shh! Do not say such things in my house!" I hissed.

His hand came up over his heart. "I shan't do it again. But, honestly, Anne, can we not be friends?"

"'Tis not possible." And I left off the reason why…because to be friends with Anthony was inconceivable, because all I wanted was to be his lover, his companion, his midnight dalliance, and his heart. Not to mention Edward forbade it.

"Why ever not? We were once."

"We were never only friends, and you well know it. Now hush before Edward comes in here. Tell me about *my* son."

Anthony pursed his lips in disappointment. The twinkle in his eyes faded. How many times would he come at me with an olive branch that I might thrust it away? My gut twisted at the thought that this could be the last time, for I longed to accept it. To rush into his arms, even if only for one last embrace.

"The boy is well and taking to his lessons quite like a sponge. He shall grow up to be intelligent, articulate and a good soldier."

"Ah, you speak of our Beau do you?" Edward chose that moment to enter, eyeing us warily and, taking in my disinterested accounting of the linens, remained in good spirits. But his suspicious nature was not lost on me and, in fact, only reinforced my ideas of pushing Anthony away.

"Lord Hertford, the man of the hour. Yes, indeed, your boy is quite a fine pupil. My son is truly enjoying his tutelage of young Beau."

I soon tuned out their conversation, rechecked the servants' work and left the feasting hall. Elizabeth Cromwell was in my solar since her husband would attend the meeting as well, and I was in dire need of female companionship.

*January 17, 1547*

"I think the king just might rally once more," Edward said, after his men left the second council meeting held at our London house.

"Why do you say that?" I had mixed feelings on the topic. On the one hand, I had no desire for the king to die. But, at the same time, if he did, Edward and I could move on with our lives, begin the next phase — even closer to the crown.

"He gave audience to both the French and Spanish ambassadors today. Van der Delft came by my office just prior to the meeting to let me know the king had been lucid, jovial even, and discussed much regarding political affairs, military campaigns, and that he was planning the investiture of Prince Edward as Prince of Wales."

"Did he mention Surrey and Norfolk?" My stomach had been tied into knots with that situation yet to be resolved. The two men still languished away in the Tower.

"The ambassador did not, but Paget did during the meeting. We passed a bill of attainder against the father and son. Their lands and possessions shall be forfeited, and they both shall be executed. Paget is taking it to the king on the morrow to have him sign it." But Edward only frowned, not really showing true joy at the outcome.

"That is good news. Why do you not appear to be pleased?"

"How can one be pleased at planning the death of another? I am never happy when it comes to that, Anne. I wish Surrey to rot in a hole, but Norfolk, although bad as he was to our ideals, he was making an attempt to come around at least. He has done so much for the king, given his very life to see to the king's pleasure, and he is thanked for it with the ax of an executioner." Edward swallowed hard and loosened his doublet ties around his neck. "I, too, have given my life to the crown, and I fear one day I shall see my life's end met with the steel of a blade."

I frowned at his words, even though I had thought them many times myself and still had that recurring nightmare. "Only on the battlefield like any noble knight."

"If only I could be so lucky."

I came forward and placed my hand on his arm, squeezing. "Luck has nothing to do with it, Edward, and you of all people should know. Indeed, the only thing we can count on is ourselves and what we make happen. No luck, only the success of carefully laid plans."

At this, Edward laughed. "You would have made a good soldier, Anne, had you been born a man."

"Give me a blade and shield, and I shall show you how accomplished a soldier I am as a woman."

Was I truly the hellish viper they called me?

*January 21, 1547*

Today saw the end of a long chapter in my life.

This morning the warden had walked in on the Earl of Surrey as he had scooped stone and rubble with his bare hands from his privy hole, trying desperately to escape his fate.

But he had been caught.

Snowflakes fell slowly, tranquilly, blanketing the ground in powdery-white. Despite the thick ermine within my cloak, I was chilled to the bone. I feared even if my body were covered in flames, I would have felt icy all the way to my bones.

When Surrey arrived at Tower Hill, with me standing not five feet from the scaffold, he was covered in offal. Streaks of brown marred the light sprinkling of snow on the cobbles where he walked. Regret shone in his eyes as he stood on the wooden platform, his gaze directed on mine and mine alone. My stomach twisted, my head seared with pain, threatening to make me close my eyes, but I held steady. Held his gaze as and he knelt and mumbled his prayers. Held his gaze until the executioner pushed his head down on the block and all that was within my view was the top of his head.

With Surrey's arms stretched out, his offer of forgiveness to his executioner, the ax was raised and came crashing down on his neck.

I stiffened as the crunch of bone and slosh of blood echoed in the morning. Beside me, Edward wrapped his arm around me, offering comfort I wished to take but somehow couldn't grasp.

Surrey was dead. He could no longer torment me, and yet there was no rush of peace. No elation at being free of him. Only a sick feeling deep in the hollows of my heart.

Funny how the death of one person who had tormented me so much in this life did not make those feelings of anguish go away. I could still feel his hands violently gripping my body, tearing my flesh. I could still hear the sinister tone of his voice as he'd berated me, or the threatening tones he'd used only to put me on edge.

Instead of rejoicing in his execution, I found myself wondering if he had been cold while he'd knelt on the scaffold. Had the small snowflakes falling hit his skin and melted right away or had they lingered? Had the regret in his eyes been for me, or for himself?

I wondered why I even cared.

But the truth was this… If it hadn't been for Surrey, I would not have been where I was today.

So, regrettably, despite him being an awful and despicable man, I must also, in some odd and twisted realm of fate, thank him for it.

And with that realization, my knees buckled.

*January 28, 1547*

Someone was shaking me. I opened my eyes to the dim light coming from the fire in the hearth.

"Anne, you must wake."

"Edward, what is it?"

I heard the sound of the flint, and then a candle flared to life on the table beside my bed. Edward's clothes were rumpled. Dark circles smudged beneath his eyes.

"Tonight the king's breaths became labored, his lungs rasping, his lips turning white. Archbishop Cranmer was called to his side, and Henry made his confession and received a blessing." Edward recanted the tale in a monotone voice.

I sat straight up in bed. "Did he…"

Edward nodded, tears in his eyes, and sat down beside me. "After Cranmer gave his blessing, Henry lost his ability to speak. He called out once, for Jane, then his lungs rattled, his body shook, and everything was very still. He died before our very eyes."

I embraced him, and he sagged against me. "Does the queen know?"

Edward shook his head. "Not yet. No one knows except the few members of the Privy Council who attended him tonight."

"When shall you tell her?" I was curious how long she would wait before marrying Thomas, as he remained an unmarried man — mostly likely waiting for his time to be with her.

"We must get affairs in order first. I think it will take two days. But I have done something, I must confess."

At this, my eyes widened in fear. "What?"

"I changed the Will of the king."

"How did you do that?" Whatever blurriness had been left in my eyes dissipated, and I felt my throat swell.

"Paget holds the chest which protects the Will, but I hold the key. The king wanted a council regency and no Lord Protector. I changed it to add a Lord Protector to reside over the council."

My mouth dropped open. "But what about witnesses? The king had witnesses sign the original."

Edward nodded. "Yes, but I was able to convince Paget to sign as a witness giving the regency over to me — a council of regency

402

would only create problems. You saw what rifts just the mention of the lord protectorship brought at court. Paget agrees with me."

"Yes, but what of the king's signature?"

"We forged it." He took a deep breath, and I had the feeling he was about to confess another great sin. "I also had Tom sign it."

"What?" My voice was raised to a near shout. Tom had only confessed to us some months prior to being on the side of Surrey, and with the death of Surrey, he'd tried to regain Edward's love. But it was all a ruse. I believed none of it.

"He was blackmailing me, Anne. I had him added as a privy councilor." His head fell into his hands, and he obviously was scared.

I could see the black cloud descending. We'd made it so far, and now we should fall. "This will be your downfall, Edward."

Edward's head shot up, and he glared at me through bloodshot eyes. "Do not say that, Anne. Remember, we make our own fates, you said it yourself. I have promised him my approval in the name of King Edward VI, in his request to marry the queen dowager."

My mouth went dry. All I could do was stare at him. For all his work, I envisioned he would see his fate at the end of a blade.

"You must retain a tight leash on your brother, Edward. He is a rabid dog, more dangerous than even Surrey."

Edward nodded, opened his mouth to say something else and then closed it. He took a deep breath. "The king has pardoned Norfolk."

"I am actually glad of that fact."

"Why?"

"It shows he had mercy at the end and gave reprieve to a man who'd devoted his life to him. I hope the new king will see that in you and give mercy should it ever be requested. Let his father have set a good example."

Two days later, the king's body still lay in his bed the same way it had when he'd passed into heaven.

Edward had ridden at breakneck speed to Hertford Castle so he might be the first to bring the news to Prince Edward, now the new king. And then he would bring the boy to the Tower, where he would be proclaimed king on the morrow.

Paget would open the chest containing the fake Will, and I would have to take a deep breath and pray we did not feel the executioner's blade when Edward was proclaimed Lord Protector.

Although the king had been ill for so long, his health fading over time, his girth growing so large, and the ulcer in his leg constantly paining him, I still found that I was shocked by his death. King Henry had been an important part of my life for twenty-five years. Longer than most. While I wouldn't miss his volatile moods and would always be angry at the swift and unjustly punishments he'd placed on some, I would miss the charming, convivial man he'd been when I'd first come to court.

Everything would change now. We were rising! Filled with power! The Seymours — Edward and I — we were victorious.

When King Edward arrived at the Tower, he was accompanied, to my surprise, by Sir Anthony Browne. And sitting so tall next to him was my little Beau.

"Mother," he said, so grown up since he'd been away.

"Beau, darling, come and give me a hug."

"I came to pay homage to the new king. I shall be a member of his household. I shall serve him well, Mother."

"Yes, you shall." A broad smile curled my lips. My son would grow up beside the king, guiding him in his rule.

God had blessed us for certain. We'd survived King Henry VIII with our necks intact, and now, we all but owned the realm!

Shouts rang out. "The king is dead! Long live the king!"

*February 16, 1547*

Today, Edward was named Duke of Somerset, making me a duchess. I'd reached the pinnacle of my career as a court lady, and I would not let that fall for anything.

I now knew how Edward had struck his bargain with Anthony — as the knight would be one of the seven council members who would sign letters of patent granting Edward office as the Lord Protector.

My son had already risen beyond the nursery and his foster house and would grow up with the king. One day he would become a member of the Privy Council, as his father had been for the king's father.

Several days after the king's death, fear truly mounted for those left in charge when those in the north began grumbling for the yet unwed, Princess Mary, to take the throne. Mary herself came to me with tears in her eyes, for fear that Edward would imprison her. But, lucky for Mary, we were her friends, we knew her and knew that she wished for her brother, Edward, to take his place and rule as he should. And we convinced our nephew of Mary's good will. He was a smart young prince — now a king.

All the uprisings had been laid to rest, as had Henry, according to his wishes, beside his loving and true wife, Jane.

It had taken sixteen strong members of the king's guard to carry his coffin into St. George's Chapel and then lower it into the vault. I hoped and prayed that now he could be at peace, spending eternity with the one woman who'd given him pause to see the better side of life, the virtue and purity one soul could have.

For Edward, myself and our children, everything had fallen into place.

Tom would marry Catherine Parr. They were both so overcome with joy, they did not have time to glower in our direction. Although, Catherine did take the time to mention that, as queen dowager, she would still be above me in station. I'd ignored her.

My husband, Lord Protector for King Edward VI, was the ruler *de facto* of England, and I, as his wife, was the most powerful woman at court. Until King Edward took a bride, I would be queen in all but name. Not Anne Boleyn. Not my dear Jane. Not Catherine Parr. I had survived and triumphed to preside over England. They might call me hell, they might call me viper, and they would never call me queen. But they all knew, it was just what I had become.

# THE END

# AUTHOR'S NOTE

A note on historical research, detail and accuracy... While extensive research was done to write this book in the most historically accurate fashion as possible, I did take liberties as a creative artist and a writer of fiction. Most of the characters within are real figures in history, and major events are true and accurate to the best of my knowledge. I am no historian by profession, only a history lover and a great fan of the Tudor dynasty and court. Things that are not factual have been tweaked or created in the recesses of my imagination to fit this story.

The life of Anne Seymour (nee Stanhope) is intriguing, to say the least! Not much is written about her other than to give a few facts and report she was a vicious woman. A romantic at heart, I do believe that we are products of our environment, and Lady Anne was no different. Judging from how Anne led her life and the events that it entailed, I was able to come up with a story that is not only intriguing in itself, but parts of which could have possibly happened in her time.

There is some discrepancy on Anne's birth date. Some have her as being born in 1497, and others in 1510. I do believe the latter is the appropriate date. She married Edward Seymour in 1533/34, and then proceeded to have about ten children. If she had been born in 1497, that would mean she was thirty-seven when she married. Her last child was born in about 1552, which would have made her fifty-five years old. This would have just been a miracle at court. Additional support of my belief in her birth date comes from the fact that Anne was the product of her father's second marriage to Elizabeth Bourchier. The children from his first marriage are recorded as having been born around 1502, which would negate that any children from a second marriage could have been born beforehand. One more thing: If she had been born in 1497, then she would have died at the age of ninety. Therefore, I have put her at being born roughly thirteen years later, in 1510.

There is no evidence that Henry Howard, Earl of Surrey, and Anne had any sort of sexual relationship. I conjectured that she must have had some sort of past personal relationship or encounter with Lord Surrey for him to have penned the poem that graces the beginning of each chapter and even some places within the manuscript. Poems are passionate pieces of art that bare your soul to the world. Thus, Lord Surrey must have felt passionately about Lady Anne—whether as a scorned lover, or not.

There is also no evidence that Anne had a relationship with Anthony Browne—or that she had a child with him. However, they were linked at court. Additionally, after Anthony passed away, his titles of Lieutenant and Keeper of the chase and other parks for the realm was awarded to Anne's brother, Michael Stanhope.

Anne's brother Richard, died before the story takes place—and the cause of his death was not documented that I could find. For a little intrigue, I kept him alive a few years longer.

According to sources, when Jane Seymour's labor continued to be difficult and they were speculating on whether or not Jane would live, Henry was asked what his choice should be if it came to that, and he did supposedly choose the child. I chose to change that—give him a little bit of humanity.

As for the burial of Queen Jane... Her opulent tomb was never constructed as Henry requested. I added it to the book, so that even though in "real life," it didn't happen, at least in the world of *My Lady Viper,* Jane received what she'd deserved. King Henry and Jane both are now buried in the center aisle of the church, beneath a plaque, together forever.

Little Eddie (I took creative liberty with the nickname) actually died in 1539. The exact date or cause of death I was unable to find. However, for the purposes of the story, I moved his death to October 1538.

Henry VIII really did have a great interest in natural medicine and was a patron of the Royal College of Physicians. He was also an advocate of herbalists and at some point contributed the Herbalists Charter of Henry VIII.

The poem that Anthony sends to Anne was written by Thomas Wyatt—The Long Love that in my Heart Doth Harbor.

Anne Bassett was a mistress of the king, and for a brief time, considered for the place of his fifth wife.

There was a lot a speculation as to the Will of Henry VIII and his desires for a regency council and the Lord Protectorship. What I've written is pure fiction, and I cannot say what actually happened, only that there was some foul play and trickery at hand, according to the facts.

The majority of conflicts and drama that happen within this book are based in fact—including Lord Lisle punching Surrey in the jaw! The Tudor court was rife with drama, making it one of the most fun eras to research and re-create.

## MORE TALES FROM THE TUDOR COURT!

The next book in the Tudor Court Tales will release mid-2014!

Don't miss PRISONER OF THE QUEEN!

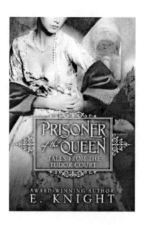

*I have served three queens in my life.*
*One was my sister, one was my savior, and one my bitterest enemy.*

Knowing she was seen as a threat to the Queen she served, Lady Katherine Grey, legitimate heir to the throne, longs only for the comfort of a loving marriage and a quiet life far from the intrigue of the Tudor court. After seeing her sister become the pawn of their parents and others seeking royal power and then lose their lives for it, she is determined to avoid the vicious struggles over power and religion that dominate Queen Elizabeth's court. Until she finds love — then Kat is willing to risk it all, even life in prison.

# ABOUT THE AUTHOR

E. Knight is a member of the Historical Novel Society, Romance Writers of America and several RWA affiliate writing chapters: Hearts Through History, Celtic Hearts, Maryland Romance Writers and Washington Romance Writers. Growing up playing in castle ruins and traipsing the halls of Versailles when visiting her grandparents during the summer, instilled in a love of history and royals at an early age. Feeding her love of history, she created the popular historical blog, History Undressed (www.historyundressed.com).

Under the pseudonym Eliza Knight, she is a bestselling, award-winning, multi-published author of historical and erotic romance. She is avid in social media and readers can find her at:

Website: www.elizaknight.com
Facebook: www.facebook.com/elizaknightauthor
Twitter: @ElizaKnight

CPSIA information can be obtained at www.ICGtesting.com
Printed in the USA
LVOW10s1503040914

402458LV00025B/1820/P